The yellowbacks... classics of popular fiction

The yellowjackets or yellowbacks were a great series of bestselling adventure and crime thrillers that had its origins in the mid to late 19th century following on from the 'penny dreadfuls'. They virtually began the mass market revolution of the early 20th century with a clear standard format and imprint/series livery (what would today be called branding). Hodder & Stoughton published the yellowjackets in two main series with series run dates of: 1923-1939 and later 1949-1957.

As the tagline ('where thrillers really began') on the back cover implies, the imprint and series focused on thrillers that were the bestsellers of their time. This current reissue or retro revival if you will, brings back many of these masterpieces, now classics in their own way and extends it further by including key titles from that period that were either great crime or thriller or even general commercial fiction (including sub-genres of noir, horror, gothic, romance, westerns, etc.) influences of their time. There are some perennial favourites and many rarities either lost or not easily available being revived in the current series. Writers and characters ranged from adventure heroes like Bulldog Drummond, Allan Quatermain, Richard Hannay or the Saint through thriller grandmasters Edgar Wallace and E. Phillips Oppenheim, crime and mystery maestros like Patricia Wentworth, GK Chesterton, Agatha Christie and the Detection club, to western and swashbucklers like Zane Grey, Max Brand, Captain Blood and even romance or general fiction classics like Hermina Black, Denise Robins, Marie Corelli or Stella Morton. These were books that had storytelling at their heart and always entertained.

The yellowbacks had both hardback (with varying design elements) and paperback (which built the series look) versions with the latter still carrying the imprint 'yellowjacket'. The current reissues pay tribute to both and use an amalgam of elements from both editions while retaining the complete yellow (or 'mustard-plaster') livery with the author's name in blue beveled type with a 'simulated emboss' effect and a white outer 'outline', and the book title in black. These reissues retain the distinctive size of the original mass market paperback and follow the three main category variations—the thrillers (crime, westerns, mystery, adventure) had blue lettering for the author's name, while Romance and softer general fiction had red; and other categories like humour had green.

For more detail and a full list of titles visit https://www.hachetteindia.com/home/yellowbacks

THE CASEBOOK OF SOLAR PONS

THE CASEBOOK OF SOLAR PONS

August William Derleth (February 24, 1909 – July 4, 1971) was an American writer and anthologist. Though best remembered as the first book publisher of the writings of H. P. Lovecraft, and for his own contributions to the Cthulhu Mythos and the cosmic horror genre, as well as his founding of the publisher Arkham House (which did much to bring supernatural fiction into print in hardcover in the US that had only been readily available in the UK), Derleth was a leading American regional writer of his day, as well as prolific in several other genres, including historical fiction, poetry, detective fiction, science fiction, and biography. Derleth wrote more than 150 short stories and more than 100 books during his lifetime.

THE CASEBOOK OF SOLAR PONS

August Derleth

Hodder and Stoughton Yellow Jacket

hachette INDIA

The Casebook of Solar Pons

First published in book form in 1965 by Mycroft & Moran

This Yellowback edition published in 2023
as authorized by the August Derleth Estate and reprinted under licence and with permission from Belanger Books USA for the Indian subcontinent.

An Hachette UK Company www.hachetteindia.com

1

The texts in these editions in most cases have been reprinted as is, with minimal editorial changes and by and large no bowdlerizing for political correctness; though in some editions, a few words and phrases considered archaic, or those considered offensive now, along with archaic punctuation may have been modified in places to make the text more accessible to today's readers. The narratives, language, beliefs, social mores and/or cultural depictions, in these volumes are a reflection of their times and must be viewed as such. They may also contain certain cultural, racial and gender prejudices and stereotypes that may be outdated or clearly wrong then and wrong today; but their removal would be tantamount to claiming these prejudices never existed. The Publisher does not endorse or support those depictions or stereotypes; and these books have been made available for a discerning audience that will read it for entertainment value and a chronicle/record of popular fiction of past times.

Cover design by Priya Singh adapted from the original classic yellowjacket by Hodder & Stoughton.

Cover illustration by Ishan Trivedi.

Series note: Some of the books in the series (unless otherwise credited) may have cover or inside illustrations from the original yellowbacks or early editions, and while full restoration has been attempted, some images may be grainy or faded due to the condition of the original material. The end notes or bonus material or blurb details may have been sourced from the public domain or free use publications such as Wikipedia and attribution is hereby made also allowing similar free use reproduction from here. Sources requiring further specific attribution may write in and further detailing and/or corrections shall be made in subsequent printings/editions.

Reprint specifications may be subject to change including but not limited to finishes, paper, colour sections.

ISBN: 978-93-5731-186-1

Hachette Book Publishing India Pvt. Ltd.
4th & 5th Floors, Corporate Centre,
Plot No. 94, Sector 44, Gurugram - 122 003, India

Typeset in Electra LT STD 10/12.5 pt by Manipal Technologies Limited

Printed and bound in India by Manipal Technologies Limited

MIX
Paper from responsible sources
FSC™ C043100
FSC www.fsc.org

CONTENTS

Foreword

The Casebook of Solar Pons

AUGUST DERLETH
the Casebook of Solar Pons
foreword by VINCENT STARRETT

Foreword

PONS AT HIS FINEST
BY DAVID MARCUM

With the publication of *The Casebook of Solar Pons* in 1965, Derleth had matched the five original volumes of short stories from the Sherlock Holmes Canon, title-for-title. By this point in his life, he was a well-respected author at the top of his game in several genres – historical novels exploring the area around his beloved Sauk City, Wisconsin, and his efforts to preserve and expand H.P. Lovecraft's Cthulhu Mythos. But he was also continuing steadily to add to the Pontine Canon, and slowly but surely the legion of Pons admirers was growing.

Throughout these years, some of the Pons stories occasionally appeared in mystery magazines before being collected into the "official" volumes – sometimes with years in between the first magazine publication and the book appearance. Derleth was patient. He later wrote that in his early days he would sometimes write several Pons stories in a day, but in later years, he apparently did just a few per year, often writing them based on an intriguing title, rather than first composing the story and then picking the best name for it.

I've often wondered about just how well Pons was known in those days. Surely there were fans who enjoyed picking up the latest *Alfred Hitchcock's Mystery Magazine* and seeing a new adventure with this Holmes-like detective, but then what did they do? The original Pons books from Mycroft and Moran, Derleth's own publishing house, were printed in limited runs. (Notes in the back of the original Mycroft and Moran editions of the first four books, *In Re: Sherlock Holmes, The Memoirs, The Return,* and *The Reminiscences,* indicate that only two-thousand copies of each were printed. In the back of *The Casebook,* a more optimistic three-thousand copies were produced.)

I don't know but I suspect that in 1965, the year that *The Casebook* was published (and that I was born), the Pons books weren't stocked in bookstores across the land. Rather, one had to know about them, and then to seek them out. There were no paperback editions yet, and the books had by that point been published across a span of twenty years. Tracking down the initial volume, *In Re: Sherlock Holmes* (1945) in those pre-internet 1960's days might have been a task worthy of Pons himself.

And yet, Pons was gathering devoted admirers. They certainly knew of him within the Sherlockian world. Famous names like Ellery Queen, Edgar Smith, Vincent Starrett, and Michael Harrison supported him and spread the word. And like so many who were inspired to study The Sherlockian Canon, there arose a group of Pons Scholars as well.

A year after *The Casebook* was published, Pontine legend Luther Norris founded *The Praed Street Irregulars*. In February 1967, the first of a number of irregular newsletters, *The Pontine Dossier,* was published by the "Pontifical Council of the PSI". Reading those old amateurly produced journals is a lot of fun from half-a-century later. And unlike Dr. Watson's First Literary Agent, Sir Arthur Conan Doyle, who came to resent Sherlock Holmes and who most unforgivably called Watson "stupid", Derleth enjoyed this interest. In fact, he participated in *The Pontine Dossier* with contributions, including providing additional narratives from Dr. Parker in the form of Notebook entries (which are included in the final volume of this reissued series, *The Apocrypha of Solar Pons.*)

Additionally, some Pontine scholarship was even included in *The Casebook*, such as a biography of Parker by Michael Harrison, and an endpaper map featuring locations of Pons's cases, as drawn by PSI founder Luther Norris.

No doubt Derleth was having a blast, and throughout the late 1960's, after the publication of *The Casebook*, he continued to write additional Pons stories. Sadly, he would pass away in 1971, but there would be enough for several more volumes, including the Pons novel, *Mr. Fairlie's Final Journey* (1968) and the posthumous collection *The Chronicles of Solar Pons* (1973). It was also during this time that he published an associational book, *A Praed Street Dossier* (1968), with essays and extra stories.

But for now, it's time to enjoy the book in hand – *The Casebook*. This contains some very interesting Pons adventures, including "The Sussex Archers", which Derleth explained...

> *... grew out of a dream. I dreamed one night that I was secreted somewhere in a copse or grove in the dusk, and from this hiding-place saw a man, surrounded by six mastiffs, running through the twilight without a sound other than that made by their steps; within hours of waking from that dream, I had evolved* "The Adventure of the Sussex Archers"*, into which I incorporated the events of the dream.*

And then there's "The Haunted Library", one of my favorites, when Pons takes a case that has been turned down by a well-known supernatural investigator, Carnacki.

These adventures, crafted by Derleth at the prime of life, show Pons at his finest.

For those meeting him for the first time, Pons is very much like Holmes. He solves crimes by using ratiocination and deduction. He plays the violin, smokes pipes, and lounges around his rooms in dressing gowns, as well as occasionally conducting chemical experiments there. His brother, Bancroft Pons, is an important fixture in the British Government, rather like Sherlock Holmes's brother, Mycroft. His landlady is Mrs. Johnson, and his closest contact at Scotland Yard is Inspector Jamison. And his friend and biographer, in the mold of Dr. John H. Watson, is Dr. Lyndon Parker.

While most of Holmes's Canonically-recorded adventures stretch from the 1870's until his retirement to Sussex in 1903, Pons operates in the post-World War I era, with his cases extending from when he and Dr. Parker meet in 1919, after Parker has returned to England following his war service, to 1939, just before the beginning of World War II. Pons had also served in the War, in cryptography, and when the two meet, Parker is disillusioned at the England to which he has returned. However, this is quickly subsumed as the doctor's interest in his new flat-mate and friend grows when he joins Pons on a series of cases that he later records.

For too long, the Solar Pons adventures have been too difficult to obtain. Fortunately, these new editions will change that. Here's how that came about.

In the late 1970's, I had been a Sherlockian for just a few years, having found Mr. Holmes in 1975. Those were the early days of the Sherlockian Golden Age that began with the publication of Nicholas Meyer's *The Seven-Per-Cent Solution* in 1974, and has continued to the present. Meyer reminded people that there were *other* manuscripts by Dr. Watson out there, still waiting to be found – hidden in attics, filed away in libraries, or suppressed by paranoid individuals for a plethora of reasons. These began to be discovered, one by one. Meyer himself subsequently published the amazing *The West End Horror* (1976), along with an explanation as to how the appearance of the first book had led to the second. Other Sherlockian adventures continued to surface – *Hellbirds* by Austin Mitchelson and Nicholas Utechin (1976), *Sherlock Holmes and the Golden Bird* by Frank Thomas (1979), and *Enter the Lion* by Sean Hodel and Michael Wright (1979), to name just a very few. The Great Sherlockian Tapestry, after consisting of mainly just sixty main fibers for so long, was about to get much heavier.

And around that time, someone with great wisdom realized that Solar Pons should be a part of that.

Pinnacle Books began reprinting the Pons adventures in late 1974, just months after the July publication date of *The Seven-Per-Cent Solution*. In the world of book publication, at least in those days when things took forever, Pinnacle certainly didn't jump on the bandwagon at the last minute to get the books immediately into print, after seeing how popular both *The Seven-Per-Cent Solution* and Sherlock Holmes were. Rather, the re-publication of the Pons books must have been planned for quite a while, and it was just their great good luck that their Pons editions appeared right around the same time as Meyer's *The Seven-Per-Cent Solution*. Planning and setup would have required a great deal of planning and effort, as would designing the distinctive "Solar Pons" logo that they would use on both their Pons books, and later on Sherlock Holmes books by Frank Thomas. And most of all, they would have needed time to solicit the wonderful cover paintings of Solar Pons and Dr. Parker.

It was these paintings that drew me into the World of Solar Pons.

Living in a small town in eastern Tennessee, finding things related to Sherlock Holmes in the latter 1970's was difficult. My hometown had both a new and used bookstore, and I regularly scoured them looking for new titles. Strangely, several of my most treasured Sherlockian books from these years were found – not in the bookstores – but on rotating paperback racks at a local drugstore. However, it was at the new bookstore, a few weeks before my fourteenth birthday, that I happened to notice seven books lined up in a row, all featuring a man wearing an Inverness and a deerstalker.

I grabbed them, thinking I'd found a Holmesian motherlode. Instead, I saw that they were about... *Solar Pons?*

I had a limited amount of Sherlockian research material then, and I don't recall if I found anything about Mr. Pons to explain why he dressed like Sherlock Holmes. (I had quite forgotten then, although it came back to me later, that I'd first read a Pons story back in 1973 – before I'd ever truly encountered Sherlock Holmes. That story, "The Grice-Paterson Curse", was contained in an Alfred Hitchcock children's mystery anthology, and I credit how much I enjoyed it then with shaping my brain to be so appreciative when I first read about Holmes a couple of years later, in 1975. That one is still my favorite Pons story to this day.)

Those seven books haunted me, and I somehow managed to hint strongly enough to my parents about it that they ended up being birthday gifts a few weeks later – along with some other cool Holmes books. And so I started reading the Pontine Canon, as it's called – the first of countless times that I've been through it. (It's strange what the brain records. I vividly remember reading and re-reading those books frequently in an Algebra class throughout that year – particularly one story on one certain day, "The Man With the Broken Face". I was lost and behind for a lot of that year in that class, and instead of trying to catch up, I'd pull out a Pons book, which felt much more comfortable. The teacher, who later went on to be beloved and award-winning for some reason that escapes me, knew what I was doing and did nothing to pull me back. Pfui on her! But I did like reading about Pons.)

As time went on, I discovered additional Pinnacle paperbacks, featuring new Pons stories by British horror author Basil Copper. It was great to have more Pons adventures, but his weren't quite the same. Around the time I started college, I discovered that Copper had edited a complete *Omnibus* of the original Pons stories, and it was the first grown-up purchase that I made with my first real paycheck. (Many thanks to Otto Penzler and The Mysterious Bookshop!) I was thrilled to see that the stories had been arranged in chronological order, which appealed to me. (That kind of thing still does.) Little did I realize then that Copper's editing had been so controversial within the Pons community.

For it turned out that Copper had taken it upon himself to make a number of unjustified changes. For instance, he altered a lot of Derleth's spellings in the *Omnibus* edition from American to British, causing some people to become rather upset. I wasn't too vexed by that, however, as I was there for the stories.

Copper continued to write new Pons stories of his own, published in various editions. I snapped those up, too, very happy to have new visits to 7B Praed Street. Over the years, I noted with some curiosity that Copper's books came to take on a certain implied and vague aspect – just a whiff, just a tinge – that Pons was *his* and not Derleth's.

Meanwhile, the Battered Silicon Dispatch Box published several "lost" Pons items, and also a new and massive set of the complete stories, *The Original Text Solar Pons* (2000), restoring Derleth's original intentions. It was in this book that I read Peter Ruber's extensive essay explaining Copper's changes in greater depth, and the reaction to them within the Ponsian community. However, Ruber didn't mention what I found to be Copper's even more egregious sin. But first a little background...

Over the years, there have been various editions of the Pons books – the originals published by Derleth's Mycroft & Moran imprint, the Pinnacle paperbacks, the Copper *Omnibus*, and the Battered Silicon Dispatch Box *Original Text Omnibus*. (There has also been an incomplete set of a few titles from British publisher Robson Books, Ltd.) Only a few thousand of the original Mycroft & Moran books were ever printed, and for decades, Pons was only known to a loyal group of Sherlockian enthusiasts by way of these very limited volumes. The Pinnacle books made Pons available to a whole generation of 1970's Sherlockians – such as me – that would have never had a chance to meet him otherwise if he'd only remained in the hard-to-find original editions.

As time has passed, however, even these Pinnacle books have become rare and quite expensive. For modern readers who have heard of Pons and are interested in learning more about him, or for those of us who are Pons enthusiasts who wish to introduce him to the larger world, it's been quite difficult, as all editions of his adventures are now quite rare and expensive, unless one is stumbled upon by accident. The Mycroft & Moran books can be purchased online, usually for a substantial investment of money, and the Copper and Battered Silicon Dispatch Box *Omnibi* were always expensive and hard to come by, and now it's only worse. Finally, with these new publications, the Solar Pons books will be available for everyone in easily found and affordable editions. With this, it's hoped that a new wave of Pons interest will spread, particularly within the Sherlockian community which will so appreciate him.

In 2014, my friend and Pons Scholar Bob Byrne floated the idea of having an issue of his online journal, *The Solar Pons Gazette*, contain new Pons stories. Having already written some Sherlock Holmes adventures, I was intrigued, and sat down and wrote a Pons tale – possibly almost as fast as Derleth had written his first Pons story in 1928. It was so much fun that I quickly wrote two more. After that, I pestered Bob for a while, saying that he should explore having the stories published in a real book. (I choose real books every time – none of those ephemeral e-blip books that can disappear in a blink for me!) When that didn't happen, I became more ambitious. Bob put me in touch with Tracy Heron of The August Derleth Society, and he in turn told me how to reach Danielle Hackett, August Derleth's granddaughter. I made my case to be allowed to write a new collection of Pons stories, as authorized by the Estate, and amazingly, I received permission. I introduced Danielle (in this modern email way of meeting people) to Derick Belanger of Belanger Books, and then set about writing some more stories, enough to make a whole book. Amazingly, the first new authorized Pons book in decades, *The Papers of Solar Pons*, was published in 2017.

But that started me thinking...

Realizing that this new books had the possibility to reawaken interest in Pons, or spread the word to those who didn't know about him, I wondered if the original volumes could be reprinted. After all, interest in Sherlock Holmes around the world is at an all-time high, getting the word out by way of the internet has never been easier, and shifts in the publishing paradigm mean that the old ways of grinding through the process for several years before a book appears no longer apply.

The Derleth Estate was very happy with the plan. Now came the hard part.

Being fully aware of the controversy surrounding Copper's *Omnibus* edition, it was evident that that new editions had to be from Derleth's original Mycroft & Moran volumes – for after all, he had edited and approved of those himself. Thankfully, modern technology allows for these books to be converted to modern electronic files with only a moderate amount of pain and toil.

I had several friends, upon hearing of this project, who very graciously offered to help me to "re-type" the original books. I can assure you that, if these books had needed to be re-typed from scratch, there would have been no new editions – at least not as provided by me. Instead, I took a copy of each of the original Mycroft & Moran Pons books, of which I am a very happy and proud owner, and scanned them, converting them all into electronic files. So far so good – that only took several hours of standing at a copy machine, flipping the pages of the books one at a time, and hitting the green button. (And sometimes re-doing it if a scanned page had a gremlin or two.)

After that, I used a text conversion software to turn the scans into a Word document. That raw text then had to be converted into another, more easily fixed, Word document. Then came the actual fixing. Early on, it was decided to try and make the new editions look as much like the originals as possible. Therefore, many inconsistent things that niggled me as an editor-type remain in the finished product, because they were that way in the originals. For instance, Derleth's punctuation improved quite a bit from his early books to the latter – but it was very tempting to start fixing his punctuation in the earlier books. If you see something that looks not-quite-right, chances are it was that way in the original books.

There were times that a letter or a note, as quoted in a story, would be indented, while on other occasions it would simply be a part of the paragraph. I wanted to set up all of those letters and notes in a unified way throughout the various books, but instead I kept them as they had appeared in the original editions, no matter how much the style varied from story to story. Finally, some of the racial stereotyping from those stories would not be written that way today. However, these are historical documents of sorts, and as such, they are presented as written, with the understanding that times have changed, and hopefully we have a greater awareness now than before.

Since the early 1980's, whenever I've re-read the Pons stories – and I've done so many times – it's been by way of the Copper *Omnibus* editions. I enjoyed having them all in one place in two matching handsome and heavy books, and I was very pleased that they were rearranged for reading in chronological order. The fixing of British-versus-American spelling didn't bother me a bit. This time, as part of the process to fix up the converted-to-text files, I was reading the stories as they had originally appeared, in the order that they had been published in the original volumes. I hadn't done it that way for years. The conversion process captures everything, and that means some items do have to be corrected. For instance, when setting up for printing, original books from the old days often *split* words at the end of a line with hyphens, whereas modern computer programs *wrap* the text, allowing for hyphens to be ignored. When converting the text of the original books, the program picked up every one of those end-of-line hyphens and split words, and they all had to be found and removed. Likewise, the text-conversion program ignores words that are italicized in the original, and these each have to be relocated and re-italicized. (However, in some cases, Derleth himself was inconsistent, italicizing a word, such as a book title or the name of a ship, at one point in a story, and not at a later point. That had to be verified too.)

I have long been a chronologicist, organizing all of the thousands of traditional Sherlock Holmes stories that I've collected and read into a massive Holmes Chronology, breaking various adventures (book, story, chapter, and paragraph) down into year, month, day, and even hour to form a *complete* life of Holmes, from birth to death, covering both the Holmes Canon and traditional pastiches. It was inevitable that I would do the same with Pons. For several decades, I've had a satisfying Pons Chronology as well, based on research by various individuals, and largely on Copper's arrangement of the stories within his

Omnibus – with a few disagreements. By re-reading the original stories in their original form, for the first time in years, I realized that, in addition to changing spelling, Copper had committed – as referred to earlier – a far bigger sin.

I discovered as I re-read the original stories for this project that a number of them weren't matching up with my long-established Pons Chronology, based a great deal upon Copper's arrangement in his *Omnibus*. Some of the stories from the originals would give a specific date that would be a whole decade different from where I had placed the story in my own chronology. A quick check against Copper's *Omnibus* revealed that he had actually changed these dates in his revisions, sometimes shifting from the 1920's to the 1930's, a whole decade, in order to place the story where he thought that it ought to go. Worse, he sometimes eliminated a whole sentence from an original story if it contradicted his placement of that story within his *Omnibus*.

As a chronologist, I was horrified and sickened. This affront wasn't mentioned in Ruber's 2000 essay explaining why Ponsians were irritated with Copper. I can't believe that this wasn't noticed before.

There has always been ample material for the chronologist with the Pons books, even without these changes. Granted, the original versions, as written, open up a lot of problems and contradictions about when various stories occur that Copper smoothed out – apparently without anyone noticing. For this reason, and many others, I'm very glad and proud that the original Solar Pons adventures, as originally published by Derleth, are being presented here in these new volumes for a new generation.

David Marcum
"The Obrisset Snuffbox", PSI
(excerpted from the Belanger edition reissues)

CURIOUS HAPPENINGS

> *"Who is Mr. Carnacki?" I asked.*
>
> *"A self-styled psychic investigator. He lives in Chelsea, and has had some considerable success, I am told."*
>
> *"A charlatan!"*
>
> *"If he were, he would hardly have turned down our client."*

This conversation between Parker and Pons occurs in the beginning of "The Adventure of the Haunted Library", the second story in this collection. What is most striking about it is that Parker is the one dismissive of a psychic investigator, and Pons comes to the mystical detective's defense. He actually goes so far as to imply that Mr. Carnacki is legitimate. In the world of Pons, ghosts may apply.

We are now fully in the realm of Solar Pons, a world unlike that of other pulp fiction from this period. While the Sherlock Holmes influence is still strong, there is no doubt that Pons is his own man, with his own collection of nemeses and interesting side characters, dabbling in genres outside of straightforward detective fiction.

Take for example, "The Adventure of the Whispering Knights", where Pons must solve the ritualistic killing of a man dressed in paganistic garb. The murder takes place at the site of a megalithic burial chamber, complete with druidic stone circles. Add in a mention of Aleister Crowley, and one can see how this story could almost fit into Derleth's Lovecraftian work. Though no monsters show their hand in the story, it feels as though they may be lurking at the threshold.

In a nod to ghoulish death traps set by sinister villains, we also have quite possibly the only mystery where a character is murdered by deadly binoculars. This is more fitting in an adventure of The Shadow more than that of Sherlock Holmes.

That isn't to say that the blood of the Great Detective isn't flowing through the veins of his Praed Street successor. Perhaps the best story in this collection is "The Adventure of the Ascot Scandal", a wonderful traditional pastiche with two vibrant characters as clients. This one has humor worthy of Wodehouse and is phenomenal for the witty dialog alone. It may remind one of some of Holmes's more humorous clients, such as Jabez Wilson in "The Adventure of the Red-Headed League".

Other excellent traditional tales include "The Adventure of the Innkeeper's Clerk", which has a conclusion reminiscent of *A Study in Scarlet*, and "The Adventure of the Missing Huntsman", which begins as a missing person case but quickly becomes an investigation into supposedly accidental deaths. These cases have Holmes's prints all over them.

While Holmes purists may scoff at a few of these tales, I think everyone can agree that Derleth's writing is top notch, the mysteries difficult to solve, and involving wonderful twists and turns. This collection is one of the finest in the Pontine canon, and like Dr. Parker, we may scratch our heads or form baseless theories, but we can enjoy the remarkable observations and conclusions of the great Solar Pons. The game's afoot!

Sincerely,
Derrick Belanger
July 2018

The Casebook of Solar Pons

FOREWORD

BY VINCENT STARRETT

(From the 1965 Mycroft & Moran Edition)

Years ago I met a very sweet old lady, all lavender and lace, who had been an avid reader of fiction all her sweet old life. She had read everything, and was still reading everything that came into the house. It occurred to me that her opinion would be interesting, so I asked her what kind of stories she liked best. She replied instantly: "I like stories of illicit relations between the sexes."

There was a twinkle in her eye as she spoke, but I think she meant it. After a moment, she added: "And I must confess I like mystery stories."

With reservations that do me credit, I am in both camps myself. But, on the whole, the kind of stories I like best are the kind I have been trying to write acceptably for about half a century. I like the kind of stories in which things happen, and *keep on happening*. In my opinion, a writer's *first* duty is to entertain. Not his whole duty, but his first duty. And where better can one find relaxing entertainment than in a good detective story?

August Derleth has been writing and publishing such stories since 1928, when his first Solar Pons "adventure" appeared in print, and admirers of Sherlock Holmes fell upon it with enthusiasm and asked for more. It was my pleasure to write an introduction for the first collection of Pons stories in hard covers, as sparkling a galaxy of Sherlockian pastiches as we have had since the canonical entertainments came to an end.

It is clear that he is following the sequence of titles inaugurated by grand old A. Conan Watson with the *Adventures* of you-know-who, and has now reached the *Casebook* stage of his happy project. But there is no time limit on sequels, and there are still a score and more of Watson's "untold tales" that require elucidation. Already August Derleth has communicated a few of them in earlier Solar Pons volumes. One hopes there will be others.

What sort of murder do you particularly fancy? I mean, of course, in a book. What is your secret relish in the way of fictive corpses? A nameless body with a jeweled dagger still quivering in the warm flesh? A bullet-slain card expert clutching the jack of spades in his lifeless fingers? A hideous gargoyle swaying beneath a blackened rafter? Or do you like a still, cold form about whose pale lips the transcendent fathomer detects the familiar odor of bitter almonds?

And, in the matter of fathomers, what will you have? A hulking bully from Headquarters with a gob of tobacco in his cheek? A lean scientist with high-domed brow, speaking a jargon of the higher mathematics? A dull inspector from the Yard, pursuing his investigations in the stodgy precincts of an English village? A cheeky amateur of unbelievable intuition, with a passion for tea and sausages? Or an amiable dilettante with mismatched eyes? Or a blind polyglot, retired? Or a grave professor from the universities? Or Father Brown?

Thank you! I will myself take Mr. Sherlock Holmes of Baker Street. I will take him, if need be, to a desert island and do without the Bible, the *Iliad*, and Shakespeare. Failing him, I will take Mr. Solar Pons of Praed Street, the best of all his pupils.

But to get back to the little old lady. What a satisfying admission was hers! "I must confess I like mystery stories." Don't we all!

Darkness is setting in, a storm is rising, and there is potential danger in every creak and whisper of the locked-up house. But it is only a short stroll to the bookcase – a short *dash*. One passes the windows going and returning. *So!* I am back in the big chair now, and all is well; all save that queer bulge in the curtain, and that recurrent sound on the stair.

In safe surroundings people like to be frightened. Sometimes I wonder if writers *write* the kind of stories they like best. I'll wager August Derleth does!

Vincent Starrett
27 September, 1964
Chicago, Illinois

(CUTHBERT) LYNDON PARKER

BY MICHAEL HARRISON

(From the 1965 Mycroft & Moran Edition)

Motivated by the conviction that the reader of the Pontine tales might like to know something of the origins and background of the man who made these tales possible – Dr. Parker, I have spent some agreeable hours in the British Museum library, at Somerset House, with the Headmaster of Dover College, with the Academic Registrar of University College – and so on – digging up the facts concerning Dr. Parker, facts which, I am bound to say, Dr. Parker's agent has been strangely reluctant to set forth.

Parker is a notable name in what we may call the "second pressing" of our vintage fame. Apart from the most famous Parker of them all – the redoubtable and immortal Nosey – we may think on Archbishop Parker, a notably supple man in a profession where all are supple; on Charles Parker, an Englishman with the most improbable appointment of history: Commander-in-Chief of the Pope's Navy. This Commander Parker, HRN – *i.e.*, Holy Roman Navy – has other claims to fame than the mere fact that he flew his flag on a Papal warship: the Commander's daughter married Charles Vernet, the French painter – and (thus I know that this is the first time that the fact has ever been recorded in print) Commander Parker became a maternal ancestor of the next most famous detective in history: the late Mr. Sherlock Holmes. The architect, Charles Parker, is not now regarded highly in his native country; a few days ago, I passed along Stamford Street, and saw that 'They' were preparing to pull down a fine Doric chapel that Parker built in about 1820. But the Hoare's Bank building that Parker designed for Fleet Street is still standing; Mammon can always hope to be one up on God any day in Britain. But – to get back to the point – Parker is a notable name in British history; and of all the Parkers, Dr. Lyndon is one of the best known, and yet the least well particularized. I leapt, I may say, at the opportunity to correct this fault in the record; I trust that I have collected all the worthwhile facts about Solar Pons's Achates.

My contribution represents no one single extract from a work of reference such as *The Medical Registrar*, but is a compound of many extracts, to which I have added some facts unearthed by my own industry. All the same, I have thought it best to adopt the biographical style – terse to the point of starkness – that the first editor of *Who's Who* adopted many years ago. Where might I find a more worthy model?...

Parker, (Cuthbert) Lyndon. b. Ramsgate, Kent. 3rd s. Charles Knightley Chetwode Parker, C.B., civil engineer, and Florence Mary Agatha Ramsden, e.d. Rev. Dorance Simgrove Ramsden, D.D., M.A., Minor Canon of Rochester Cathedral, and Perpetual Vicar of Shapcote Monachorum, Kent.

Educ. Dover College; University College, London; Heidelberg University; Medical School, Columbia University, New York. M.R.C.P., London, 1897; M.R.C.S., London, 1898; B. Ch., London, 1899; M.D., Columbia, 1901.

Principal Medical Officer, The Allegheny Sheet & Tube Corporation, 1901-3 (the most savage era of American heavy industry; it took a tough man to stick the harsh conditions); Principal Resident Physician, Diseases of the Ear, Nose & Throat, Harrison's Hospital, Madison, Wisconsin, 1903-8; Medical Superintendent, Jefferson Institute for the Treatment of Paraplegia and Epilepsy, Auburn, New York, and Consulting Honorary Surgeon, Auburn Penitentiary, 1908-1910.

Brief return to England on death of Mother, 1908. Visited Franco-British Exhibition, Earl's Court, 1908. There met General Shevket Gamal Ali Pasha, *chef du cabinet militaire* to His Highness the Khedive. The resultant friendship between Gen. Ali and Dr. Parker led to an invitation to Dr. Parker to take charge of the proposed new hospital to be erected at Mansura, principally for the treatment of Egypt's endemic scourge, ophthalmia, amongst the *fellahin*. The invitation was prompted by Dr. Parker's series of six articles, in *The American Journal of Ophthalmology* (November 1906-April 1907), reprinted in *The Lancet* (October 1908-March 1909), under the title: *Considerations of an Alternative Treatment for Ophthalmia to the Recognized Treatment by Silver Nitrate.*

Dr. Parker agreed to take up the appointment, but returned to New York to complete his contract with the Auburn Hospital. On his return to the United States, he married Miss Louisa Skelton, a schoolteacher of British descent, whose family had been settled in New York State since before the Revolution. Mrs. Parker, an accomplished amateur pianist and vocalist, accompanied her husband when he resigned his appointment with the Jefferson Institute, Auburn, and took up his appointment at Mansura, in November, 1910.

The great tragedy of Dr. Parker's life came in 1912, when Mrs. Parker, on a return visit to her parents, perished in the sinking of S. S. *Titanic* on her maiden voyage. There were no children. Dr. Parker, who had already been decorated by the Khedivial Government with the Order of Osmanieh (3rd class) and the Order of Medjidieh (2nd class), now threw himself into his salutary work with redoubled dedication, raising money by his own appeals to build a new wing on to the Mansura Royal Ophthalmic Hospital. His Highness the Khedive (Abbas Hilmi) graciously ordered that the new wing be named, in perpetuity, the Louisa Parker Wing, and the Wing being opened, with considerable pomp, by the Khedive himself. His Highness was always well disposed to Dr. Parker, and shewed himself at all times a valuable support against the jealousy of certain Egyptian medical men. When on the outbreak of the first World War, and the alignment of the Sultan of Turkey with the Central Powers, Great Britain declared a protectorate over Egypt, the resultant deposition of Abbas Hilmi by the British distressed Dr. Parker greatly.

The British Government commissioned Dr. Parker to continue his work at Mansura, where all the hospitals had now been taken over by the British military authorities. Dr. Parker, gazetted 2nd lieutenant in the Royal Army Medical Corps, 18th January, 1915, served in many theatres of war, chiefly in the Middle East, ending his temporary war-time service as Brevet Colonel, R.A.M.C. In the collapse which followed the end of the war in Europe, Colonel Parker served on several relief commissions in Serbia (awarded Order of St. Sava, 1st class), Roumania (Order of the Crown, 2nd class), Poland (Order of Polonia Restituta, 3rd class; Order of the White Eagle, 4th class), and Austria (offered Order of Liberation by the Provisional Republic, but refused permission to accept by the Inter-Allied War Commission).

After resigning from the Allied Relief Commission in Vienna, Dr. Parker, whose friend, Abbas Hilmi, had been replaced by Hussein Kamel, and by Achmed Fuad, on Hussein Kamel's death in 1917, declined to take up the offer of his old appointment at Mansura. Dr. Parker's father, the well-known civil engineer, had been killed while working on an under-river tunnel in California.

Dr. Parker's twenty years' absence from London – whence he went to New York – accounts for the obvious Americanisms in Dr. Parker's speech. In Egypt, though Dr. Parker mixed with the British colony, his associates at the Hospital were either

Egyptian, Greek, French or American. The speech-habits learned at Columbia University, and thereafter as physician and surgeon at Madison and Auburn, were to be given every chance to impress themselves ineradicably on Dr. Parker's behavior.

He was writing to refuse a last-minute call from St. Mary's Hospital, in nearby Praed Street, when he encountered Solar Pons in the buffet on Paddington Station – or a pub not far from it (not improbably, the Norfolk Arms, in Spring Street, a large, rambling place, with plenty of room for writers of letters). It was an encounter destined to rank with that of Boswell's meeting Johnson in Mr. Davies's shop – Solar Pons needed a biographer; he found the best of all in Lyndon Parker, who took up residence in the inquiry agent's quarters at 7B Praed Street in the summer of 1919.

There is evidence to show that Dr. Parker began to take notes on his companion's habits and adventures within two months of beginning his residence at 7B, though the first chronicled adventure did not appear until late in 1928 (*The Adventure of the Black Narcissus*). Dr. Parker established separate medical offices during the winter of 1931-2, but continued to reside at 7B Praed Street until early in 1933, when he married Constance Dorrington, only daughter of Amos T. Dorrington, son of Alexander Dorrington, discoverer and part owner of the Premier Diamond Mine, Kimberly, and owner of the Maracot Diamond. Thereafter he and his wife lived in South Norwood.

What appeals most about Parker's biographical method is that he is no soulless reporter. He writes down the "spirit" of events – not their precise character. He knows, for instance, that no British journalist would write *Unidentified Woman Found Slain in Thames*. The word "slain" has not even yet become a part of the journalist's vocabulary in Britain. But Parker does not care. That is what the newspaper meant – in Dr. Parker's idiom – and down he puts the headline, rewritten by him. It would be easy enough to fault Dr. Parker – it must be enough to say, not that he is careless or unobservant (surely, one might ask, he *knows* that *The News of the World* has never appeared save on Sundays?), as that he cannot be brought to believe that the unimportant can possibly be given importance. If you pointed out to him that he had made *The News of the World* appear on a weekday, he would probably mutter: "Well, it must have been some other paper – probably the *Telegraph* or the *Standard.* The indisputable fact is that it was definitely mentioned in the papers. You may take my word for that."

And take his word we may. But note one important thing: it is always *Parker* who appears to be slightly at fault; it is never Pons, even though we have to rely on Parker's memory for the record. And, yes, this is important. Though Parker, through his Americanization, uses American idiom where he will – he calls it a "stoop" when a British-educated-and-brought-up-Briton would call it a "porch" – he uses titles with the easy correctness of the educated Englishman. This is the test. Parker, we are proud to point out, is definitely One of Us! He may say, "on Victoria Street," when the Englishman would say "*in* Victoria Street"; but when it comes to knowing how to handle the handles of British names, Parker and I are at one: we *both* say "Sir Alexander" – and what more could even Sir Alexander ask?

Michael Harrison
Carlisle Mansions
London, England
17 August, 1964

I

THE ADVENTURE OF THE SUSSEX ARCHERS

On a balmy summer evening late in the 1920's I returned to our quarters at No. 7B Praed Street to find my friend Solar Pons slouched in his armchair deep in contemplation of an unfolded piece of ruled paper.

"Ah, Parker," he said, without looking up, "you are just in time for what promises to be a diversion to brighten a few summer days."

So saying, he handed to me the paper he had been studying.

It appeared to be cheap tablet paper, of a kind readily obtainable in any stationer's shop. On it had been pasted, in letters cut from a newspaper, PREPARE FOR YOUR PUNISHMENT!

In addition, there had been pasted to the paper a printed drawing of an arrow.

My alarm must have betrayed itself in my face, for Pons smiled and said, "No, no, Parker – it was not intended for me. It was directed to Joshua Colvin of Lurgashall, Sussex, and reached me by messenger from Claridge's late this afternoon. This letter came with it."

He fished the letter out of the pocket of his lilac dressing-gown and gave it to me.

"Dear Mr. Pons,

"If it is convenient for you, I hope to call on you at eight this evening in regard to a problem about which my father will do nothing in spite of the fact that one such warning has already been followed by death. I enclose the warning he has received. Since I believe you are fully aware of current crimes and mysteries in England, may I call your attention to the death of Andrew Jefferds of Petworth, ten days ago? Should it be inconvenient for me to call, a wire to me at Claridge's will put me off. I am, sir, respectfully, yours.

Hewitt Colvin."

"I see by the newspapers beside your chair you've looked up the death of Jefferds," I said.

"The development of your deductive processes always gives me pleasure," said Pons. "Indeed I have. I found it a delightful little puzzle. Jeffreds, a man with no known enemies – we read nothing of those unknown – was done to death at twilight ten days ago in his garden at the edge of the village by means of an arrow in his back. The police are baffled, but the investigation is continuing."

"Surely that is an unusual weapon," I cried.

"Is it not! But a profoundly significant one, for it occurs also on the warning, and would then no doubt have some significance to Mr. Colvin which so far escapes us." He raised his head briefly and listened. "But that is a motor slowing outside, and I suspect it is our client. We need speculate no more until we hear his story."

In a few moments Mrs. Johnson showed Hewitt Colvin into our quarters. He was a man in his thirties, with a ruddy face and keen grey eyes. He wore a moustache and sideburns, and looked the picture of the country squire in his tweed suit.

"Mr. Pons," he said without preamble, "I hope you will forgive the abruptness of my letter. I appreciate your willingness to listen to my problem, which, believe me, sir, is urgent. Six men have received a copy of the warning I dispatched to you earlier – one is already dead."

"Ah," said Pons, "the significance of the arrow! The warnings were identical?" He waved our client to a seat, but Colvin was too agitated to take it, for he strode back and forth.

"Yes, Mr. Pons."

"What have these six men in common?"

"All belonged to the Sussex Archers."

"Active?"

"No, sir. That is the background of my problem. They have been disbanded ever since the death of Henry Pope twenty years ago. Pope was the seventh member of the Archers. He died, Mr. Pons, like Mr. Jefferds – with an arrow in his back, an arrow belonging to the Sussex Archers. The inquest brought about a verdict of death by accident, and I have always understood that this was a true verdict. I am no longer so certain."

"Let us begin at the beginning, Mr. Colvin," suggested Pons.

"It may be that is the beginning, Mr. Pons – back in 1907. As for now, well, sir, I suppose it begins with the return of Trevor Pope – brother of that Henry Pope who died twenty years ago. He had been in Canada, came back to England, opened the old house near Lurgashall, and went into a reclusive existence there.

"I shall not forget my first sight of him! The country around Blackdown is, as you may know, great hiking country. I was out one evening in the dusk when I heard someone running toward me. I made for some undergrowth and had just effected my concealment when there burst out of the woods across a little opening from where I was hidden a short, dark, burly man surrounded by six great mastiffs, all running in absolute silence save for the sound of his footfalls. He looked, sir, inconceivably menacing!

"That was in May. Two weeks later I saw him again. This time I did not hear him; he burst suddenly upon me, pedaling furiously on a bicycle, with his mastiffs running alongside – three on each side of him, and though he saw me clearly he said not a word – simply went past as fast as he could. Nor did the dogs bark. Mr. Pons, it was uncanny. In the interval I had learned his identity, but at the time it meant nothing to me – I was but twelve when Henry Pope died, and was off at school at the time.

"Then, late in June, the messages arrived."

"To all six members of the onetime Sussex Archers?" interrupted Pons.

"Yes, Mr. Pons. Of course, I didn't know this at the time. It has come out only since Jefferds' death. Father made inquiry."

"All six of the Archers still live in the vicinity of Lurgashall? Petworth, I believe, is but three miles or so away."

"All but one. George Trewethen moved to Arundel ten years ago."

"What was your father's response to the warning?"

"He dismissed it as the work of a crank."

"Until Jefferds' death?"

"Until then, yes, Mr. Pons. Then he wrote or telephoned to the other members and learned for the first time that all of them had received identical warnings. It put the wind up him for a bit, but not for long. He's very obstinate. When he goes out now he carries his gun – but a gun's small defense against an arrow in the back; so my brother and I take turns following him and keeping him in sight whenever he goes out."

"You are here with his consent?"

"Yes, Mr. Pons. He would not be averse to a private enquiry, but seems determined to keep the police out of it."

"But are the police not already in it?" asked Pons. "They will surely have discovered the warning Jefferds received."

"Mr. Pons, no one knows of it except my father. He would not have known, had Mr. Jefferds not come to visit him some time ago and mentioned having received and destroying it. So the police do not know."

"I see," said Pons thoughtfully.

"Mr. Pons, I am driving back to our home on the lower slopes of Blackdown tomorrow morning. Dare I hope that you and Dr. Parker will accompany me?"

"What precisely do you expect us to do, Mr. Colvin?"

"I hope, frankly, that you will devise some way in which to trap Trevor Pope before an attempt is made on my father's life."

"That will surely not be readily accomplished, Mr. Colvin. Six mastiffs, I think you said. And the man either runs or pedals as fast as possible." Pons flashed a glance at me. "What do you say, Parker?"

"Let us go by all means. I am curious to see this fellow and his dogs."

"Thank heaven, Mr. Pons! It is little more than an hour from London. I will call for you tomorrow morning at – but you name the hour, Mr. Pons."

"Seven o'clock, Mr. Colvin. We are early risers."

"I will be here. Good night, gentlemen."

After our client's departure, Pons sat for a few moments staring thoughtfully into the dark fireplace. Presently he turned in my direction and asked, "What do you make of it, Parker?"

"Well, it's plain as a pikestaff that Colvin senior doesn't want the police nosing about that twenty-year-old accident," I said. "And that suggests it may have been more than accident. From that conclusion it is but a step to the theory that Mr. Trevor Pope has come back from Canada at last to avenge the murder of his brother."

"Capital!" cried Pons. "That is surely exemplary deduction, Parker. I am troubled by only one or two little aspects of the matter which no doubt you will be able to clear up when the time comes. We have as yet no evidence to connect Trevor Pope with the warning letters."

"It is surely not just coincidence that Pope's appearance in the neighborhood is followed by the arrival of warning letters," I cried. "Their very wording points to him!"

"Does it not!" agreed Pons. "The intended victims are not told to prepare for death, but for 'punishment.' That is surely ambiguous! 'Punishment' for what?"

"Why, for the murder of Henry Pope, what else?"

"The coroner's inquest determined that Henry Pope came to an accidental death."

"Inquests are not infallible, Pons; none knows this better than you."

"True, true," murmured Pons. "Yet I find this disturbingly simple, and I incline a little to distrust of the obvious."

"It all hangs together," I protested. "What other significance could the printed arrow on the warnings have but a reminder of the Sussex Archers – and, specifically, of the occasion of their disbanding?"

"I think the reference cannot be disputed," agreed Pons. "What troubles me is simply this – why warn these gentlemen at all?"

"It is elementary psychology that avengers have a pathological wish to let their victims know *why* they are being punished. These warnings, with their printed arrows, seem to have achieved their purpose, now that the first one of the surviving six members of the Sussex Archers has been slain."

"They do, indeed – but not yet to the extent of sending any one of them for the police. What coy reluctance to act!"

"If any proof were needed that Henry Pope's death was not all it seems, that is certainly it."

"Is it? I wonder. These waters, I fear, are darker than we may at this moment believe. We shall see. Just let me have that Sussex Guide not far beyond your elbow, will you? There's a good fellow!"

Thereafter Pons retreated for the remainder of the evening behind the book I handed to him.

An hour after our client stopped for us next morning, we were driving through the quaint Wealden village which is Lurgashall – a small, quiet hamlet, composed of a green surrounded by several picturesque cottages – and climbing the height of Blackdown, the highest hill in Sussex. Not far up the slope stood our client's home, a rambling house of stone set behind stone gate piers and a yew hedge, with outbuildings down slope from it at one side. Its tall casement windows were shaded at this hour, and, indeed, the house and grounds were almost lost in the surrounding woods.

Our client had wired his father of our impending arrival; as a result, Joshua Colvin awaited us in the breakfast room. He was a sturdy, middle-aged man wearing a fierce, straggly moustache, and a dogged look in his dark blue eyes.

He acknowledged his son's introductions in a gruff, self-confident manner. "You'll join me at breakfast, Mr. Pons – Dr. Parker?" he asked.

"A cup of tea, sir," said Pons. "We have breakfasted. Besides, I like to keep my mind clear for these little problems."

Colvin favored him with an even, measuring glance. "Sit down, Gentlemen," he said. "I take coffee and brandy for breakfast – always have done, in addition to muffins, jam, and a bit of bacon. You'll not mind my eating? I waited on your coming."

"By no means, Mr. Colvin."

We sat at the breakfast table, and would have been readily at ease had it not been for an almost immediate interruption.

A young man, obviously just out of bed, burst into the room, his sensitive face flushed and upset.

"Father – I saw Pearson about again last night..." he said, and, catching sight of us, stopped. "I beg your pardon."

"Come in, come in – you're late again," said Colvin. Turning to us, he added, "My son, Alasdair – Mr. Solar Pons, Dr. Parker. Now, then – Pearson. You're quite sure?"

"Certain, sir. Skulking outside the gate-posts. I got in about midnight."

"Pearson," put in our client, "is a beater my father discharged over two months ago. Been hanging around ever since."

"Man's dotty," said Colvin senior, snorting. "Ought to be off getting himself another place."

"May I ask why he was discharged?" inquired Pons.

"He was party to a poaching ring," said Colvin shortly. "Sort of thing I won't tolerate."

Alasdair Colvin, meanwhile, had swallowed only a cup of coffee. Then he got to his feet again, made his excuses, and left the room.

"The boy has an editorial position of some kind," growled Colvin. "Softening job. Let's him sleep late. These people in publishing are like bankers – they get to the office any time between ten and twelve. Disgraceful, I call it."

Our host had now devoured three slices of bacon, a muffin covered with bramble-berry jam, and two cups of coffee in the time it took Pons to drink half a cup of tea. I saw that Pons' eyes were not only upon the senior Colvin, but were also flickering about the gracious room, taking in its appointments.

Joshua Colvin pushed back from the table, arms akimbo, hands gripping the arms of the captain's chair in which he sat.

"Well, sir," he said to Pons, "now that you're here at my son's invitation, we may as well get on with it."

"Tell me something about the Sussex Archers, Mr. Colvin," said Pons quietly.

"Little to tell, sir. Organized 1901. Disbanded 1907. Accidental killing of one of our number, Henry Pope. Never had more than seven members. Pope, Jefferds, myself. George Trewethen, Abel Howard, Will Ockley, and David Wise. That's the lot of us. All devoted to archery. We got together to practise archery. That's the long of it and the short of it. All congenial chaps, very. Liked a nip or two, now and then. No harm in that. Had our own special arrows. That sort of thing. Competed now and then in contests with other clubs. Henry's death took the stuffing out of us and put an end to the Sussex Archers."

"The death of Mr. Pope," said Pons musingly, "would seem to warrant a few trifling questions."

"Twenty years ago, Mr. Pons," said Colvin with a mounting air of defense. "He's all dust and bone by this time. The coroner's inquest said accident."

"You insist on that, Mr. Colvin?" pressed Pons.

Beads of perspiration appeared suddenly on our host's temples. He gripped his chair arms harder.

"Damn it, sir! That was the coroner's decision, the decision of the jury."

"Not yours, Mr. Colvin."

"Not mine!"

"I submit, sir, you accepted it with reservations."

"Since you're not the police, Mr. Pons, I may say that I did."

"Not an accident, then, Mr. Colvin."

"Murder!" Our host growled the word and almost spat it out. Once having said it, he relaxed; his hands slipped back along the arms of the chair and he himself sank back. He took a deep breath, and the words came out in a rush. "I don't see how he could have been killed by accident, Mr. Pons. I don't see why he should have been murdered. We were all experienced archers, sir – *experienced*! Not given to accidents. We were all friends – close friends. Certainly I don't pretend to know what waters run between my fellowmen, but there never was an uncongenial word among us. Besides, none of us had anything to gain by Henry's death. We had it to lose. We lost the one thing we prized among us – our archery. I've not touched my bow and arrows since the day."

"How was he killed, Mr. Colvin?"

"We were on the Weald, Mr. Pons. Woods all around us. We were somewhat separated, taking positions for distance in loosing our arrows. After we had discharged arrows we pushed forward to mark our distances and see who had shot his arrow the farthest. We found Henry with an arrow in his back, dying. It was one of our arrows – we had special arrows, Mr. Pons – but unmarked."

"Unmarked?"

"Since we were trying for distance that day, we had marked our arrows individually. When we found our arrows we found that Henry had had time to discharge his – ironically, he had made the greatest distance." He paused, licked his lips, and continued. "All our arrows were marked that day, Mr. Pons – but the arrow that killed Henry wasn't marked. This wasn't brought out at the inquest, I need hardly say. It seemed to mean that whoever had killed Henry had brought along an unmarked arrow for that purpose."

"Was the Archers' schedule widely known?"

"Set up annually sir," replied our host. "Anybody could have known it, if he were interested. Not many were."

"Is Mr. Pope's family still in the vicinity?" asked Pons then.

"Henry was unmarried, sir. A quiet man, retired early in life. Quite wealthy, too. His younger brother, Trevor, was his only heir. I remember what a time we had trying to reach Trevor – we didn't, in fact, get in touch with him until after Henry was buried. He was on a walking tour of the Scottish Highlands. He came back only long enough to take care of Henry's affairs, closed the Pope house on the other side of Lurgashall, and went to Canada. He came back last May."

"And this, Mr. Colvin?"

Pons spread the warning our host had received on the table before him.

"Monstrous!" Colvin gave Pons a hard look. "I could be punished for many things, sir – but the death of Henry Pope is not one of them."

"About the arrow that killed Mr. Jefferds?" asked Pons. "Was it one of those belonging to the Sussex Archers?"

"It was. I took occasion to look hard at it at the inquest. No question about it. Fair put the wind up me."

"I should not be surprised," said Pons. "Let me return for a moment to your former beater, Pearson. How long had he been with you?"

"Ten years."

"You, too, have seen him skulking around?"

"Not I. Alasdair chiefly. Hewitt saw him on two occasions."

"Only recently, Mr. Pons. He seemed to be waiting for Father to come outside," put in our client.

"Man knows my habits," growled Colvin senior. "He could find me outside any time he wanted to."

"I take it you've been married more than once, Mr. Colvin."

"Ah, you saw that Alasdair's no whit like him," our host said, jerking his head toward our client. "True. Married twice. Twice a widower. Alasdair was my second wife's son; I adopted him. A good, quiet boy, a little scatter-brained. Perhaps that goes with publishing."

Pons sat for a few moments in silent contemplation, his eyes closed. Colvin flashed an impatient glance from Pons to our client, who only smiled in answer.

"And Mr. Jefferds' murder," said Pons presently " – does it occur to you that the same man whose arrow killed Henry Pope might also have been responsible for Jefferd's death?"

"Wouldn't it occur to you?" answered our host a little wildly. "But I tell you, sir, I'm at a complete loss as to who might have done it, and why it should be done! I know every member of our Sussex Archers like an open book."

"Each reader brings his own interpretation to every book," said Pons dryly.

"True, sir. – But no, I don't believe it."

"You have not been to the police," said Pons.

"Damn it, sir! – we've suppressed evidence. We don't want it out now. What good would it do? An arrow used by the Sussex Archers is the only thing that ties the two murders together. The *only* thing. Mr. Pons, I know! Henry Pope was an inoffensive man; so was Andy Jefferds. Who stood to gain by their deaths? Trevor Pope, who was miles away when his brother died! Ailing Mrs. Jefferds, who needed him alive far more than anything she might inherit! Such crimes are senseless, sir – the work of a madman."

"Or a diabolically clever one."

"But this is your game, not mine, sir," said our host, pushing back his chair and rising. "I leave you to my son."

So saying, he stalked out of the room.

"I must apologize for my father," said our client uneasily.

"Pray do not do so," said Pons. "He is a badly troubled man – a simple, straightforward gentleman to whom the complexities of crime are a cloud of darkness." Pons, too, got to his feet. "About Pearson, Mr. Colvin – when was the first time you saw him skulking around?"

"Why, I believe it was the night after Mr. Jefferds' was killed."

"But he *had* been about before?"

"Well, yes, Alasdair saw him – though he didn't mention it until I told Father I'd seen him. Then he came out with it – said he hadn't wanted to say it before and excite Father."

Pons stood for a moment deep in thought. Then a little smile touched his lips, and I knew he was off on a new line which pleased him. "Now, then," he said to our client, "we shall want to move about the neighborhood. Pray do not wait upon us for luncheon or dinner. Can you spare a pony cart?"

"Come with me, Mr. Pons."

Late that afternoon we drew up at a pub on the Lurgashall side of Petworth. We had spent the day calling on the other three resident members of the disbanded Sussex Archers – Will Ockley, a semi-invalid – David Wise, who was now a clergyman – and Abel Howard, a taciturn man of late middle-age who was still engaged in stock farming experiments – from all of whom I could not determine that Pons had elicited any more information than he already had.

In the pub we made our way to the bar and sat down. Pons ordered a gin and bitters, and I my customary ale. Since it was still early evening – indeed, the sun had not yet set – there was little patronage in the pub, and the proprietor, a chubby fellow with sparkling eyes and a thatch of white hair, was not loath to talk.

"Strangers hereabout?" he asked.

"On our way to see Joshua Colvin on a matter of business," said Pons. "Know him?"

"Aye. Know him well."

"What sort is he?"

The proprietor shrugged. "There's some that likes him and some that don't. Has a gruff manner and a bit of a way of telling the truth. Makes people uncomfortable."

"And his sons?"

The proprietor brightened. "Cut from different cloth altogether. Alasdair, now – he's a real sport. Comes in for the darts." He shook his head. "A bit of a loser though – he's no hand for it. Still owes me five quid." He chuckled. "But Hewitt – well, sir, in business he's all business, and he don't come here much. But don't ye be fooled by that, sir – he's an uncommon eye for the ladies. There's them could tell ye a tale or two about Hewitt and the ladies! But I ain't one for gossip, never was. Live and let live, I say."

"Does not a Mr. Pope live nearby?" asked Pons then. The proprietor sobered at once. "The likes of him don't come here," he said darkly. "He don't talk to no one. And there's them that say they know why."

"And Mr. David Wise?"

"Aye – as close to a saint as ye can find these days." But abruptly he stopped talking; his eyes narrowed. He flattened his hands on the bar and leaned closer to Pons, staring at him searchingly. "Ye're asking about the Archers. Aye! I know ye sir, damne if I don't. We've met."

"I don't recall it," said Pons.

"Ye're Mr. Solar Pons, the detective," he said, flinging himself away from us.

Thereafter he would say no more.

We took our leave shortly after, Pons no whit displeased by the proprietor's refusal to speak.

"We have one more stop to make," he said. "Little more than two miles hence."

"Trevor Pope," I said.

"Precisely. Let us have a look at him."

"He may be dangerous," I said.

"I suspect he is. Are not all men, under the right provocation?"

"We have not had what I should call a profitable day," I said.

"Ah? Every little grain of sand contributes to the making of a road," replied Pons enigmatically. He said no more until, following the directions our client had given us, we drove down a lane into a hollow in the Weald and came to a semi-Tudor house behind a low, vinegrown stone wall. It wore a deserted appearance.

Pons halted the trap at the gate, got out, and walked to the door, where he plied the knocker.

There was a long wait before the door opened. An old servant stood there.

"Mr. Trevor Pope?" asked Pons.

"Mr. Pope doesn't wish to see anyone," said the servant. "He's going out, sir."

"I am on a matter of some urgence," said Pons.

"Mr. Pope will see no one," said the servant and closed the door.

Pons came back to the trap, got in, and drove back up the lane to the road, where he turned off into a coppice, got out once more, beckoning me to follow, and tied our steed to a sapling.

"Let us make our way back, Parker. If Mr. Trevor Pope is going out, it must be for his constitutional. He seems to go nowhere else."

We circled toward the rear of the house, taking advantage of every tree, and had scarcely come into good view of it before there burst from the direction of the kennels half a dozen great mastiffs, and in their midst, running at dead heat, a short, dark man wearing a turtle-neck sweater, tight-fitting trousers, and rubber-soled canvas shoes. They bore toward a woodland path which would take them around Lurgashall in the direction of Blackdown. The dogs made scarcely any sound; all that fell to ear was the footfalls made by Trevor Pope, and all that held to the mind's eye was the tense straining expression on his dark face, and the clenched fists at his sides.

"What madness drives him to this?" I whispered, after they had vanished in the Weald.

"What, indeed! There must be an easier exercise. You cannot deny, however, that it is an impressive performance. Small wonder it startled our client."

"What do we do now?"

"It is sundown. Surely he will not be gone too long. Let us just go to meet him."

"But the dogs!" I protested.

"We shall have to chance them," answered Pons imperturbably.

He strode forward. I followed.

The course Trevor Pope had taken led in an arc away from the house; we were soon out of sight of it on a Wealden path that would take us well around Lurgashall toward Blackdown.

Pons paused suddenly at the edge of an open glade, where the path led down a slope in the direction of the village. There he relaxed.

"I fancy this will do as well as any place," he said. "Let us wait here."

"Pons, I don't like this," I said.

"A pity. I have an appetite for it. You may return to the cart, if you like."

"And leave you alone?"

"We are all alone, Parker. Never lose sight of that. And none of us, I fancy, is more alone than Mr. Trevor Pope." The sun was gone, the afterglow began to fade, half an hour passed. Then came the sound of running footsteps.

"Ah, he is coming," said Pons.

Almost instantly the mastiffs and their master swept around a grove of young trees and bushes at the bottom of the slope within sight of Pons.

"Mr. Trevor Pope!" Pons called out in a loud voice and began to advance toward him.

Pope came to a stop and heeled his dogs with a savage cry.

He turned a furious face toward us, flung up his arm to point at Pons, and shouted, "Stand where you are! What in hell do you want?"

"To see you."

"You see me."

"To ask you some questions."

"I answer no questions."

"One, then, Mr. Pope!" Pons' voice echoed in the glade.

"Who are you?"

"Only a curious Londoner. You may have heard my name. It is Solar Pons."

There was an audible gasp from Pope. Then, "So they've sent for you!"

"One question, Mr. Pope!"

"Go to hell, sir!"

"Can you furnish me with an itinerary of your walking tour in the Scottish Highlands in 1907?"

There was a moment of pregnant silence. Then a fierce cry of rage, a curse, and Pope's furious words, "Get out – get out! – before I turn the dogs on you. You meddling nosy parker!"

"You may not have seen the last of me, Mr. Pope."

"*You* have seen the last of *me*, sir!"

Pons turned and we went back the way we had come. There was no immediate movement behind us. When last I saw him, glancing over my shoulder as we were descending the slope toward the house and the cart beyond, Trevor Pope was standing motionless in the circle of his mastiffs, a dark figure literally bursting with rage and hatred in the deepening dusk.

Once back in the trap, I could not help observing, "A violent man, Pons."

"Indeed," agreed Pons.

We rode in thoughtful silence until, just before reaching the stone gate piers of our client's home, Pons caught sight of someone slipping behind a cedar tree at the roadside.

He halted the trap at once, flung the reins to me, and leapt to the road. He darted around the cedar.

I heard his voice. "Mr. Pearson, I presume?"

"That's my name," answered a rough voice gruffly.

"What's your game, Pearson?"

"I got m' rights. I'm doin' no harm. This here's a public road."

"Quite right. Over two months ago you came to see Mr. Colvin."

"No sir. Two weeks is more like it."

"You carry a gun, Mr. Pearson?"

"I ain't got a bow an' arrer!"

His inference was unmistakable. Pons abruptly bade him good-evening, and came back to the cart. He said not a word as we drove on in the deepening dark.

Our client waited for us in the hall. He was too correct to inquire how Pons had been engaged during the afternoon, though he must have been able to draw some conclusions.

"Can I get you anything to eat, Gentlemen?" he asked.

"Perhaps a sandwich of cold beef and some dry wine. Chablis, or Moselle," said Pons.

"And you, Dr. Parker?"

"The same, if you please."

"I should like to talk to your father once more," said Pons.

"Before or after your sandwich, Mr. Pons?"

"Now, sir. Just take our sandwiches to our room, will you?"

"Very well, Mr. Pons. Father's in his study. We just got back from his usual walk. It was my turn to guard him tonight." He sighed. "Father makes it very difficult; it angers him to catch sight of us behind him. Just in there, Mr. Pons."

The senior Colvin sat before his stamp collection. His glance was rather more calculating than friendly.

"I am sorry to trouble you, Mr. Colvin – but may I see your bow and arrows?"

Colvin leaned back, a baffled expression on his ace. "Ha!" he exclaimed. "I wish I knew where they were. Put them away when Henry was killed, and then later put them somewhere else. Hanged if I know where they are now. That was twenty years ago, sir. Why d'you want to see 'em?"

"I have a fancy to see the weapon that killed Mr. Pope and Mr. Jefferds – and may some day kill you unless I am able to prevent it."

"You speak bluntly, sir," said Colvin, his face flushing a little. "The bow I can't show you – but you'll find one of the arrows up there."

He pointed to the wall above the fireplace. He got up. "I'll get it down for you."

"No need, sir," said Pons. "I'll just take this hassock over and look at it."

He did so. He stood for a while before the arrow, which I thought an uncommonly long one, with a very sharp tip.

"I observe this arrow is sharp and lethal, Mr. Colvin. Is this usual?"

"Not at all, Mr. Pons. Average archery club wouldn't think of using tipped arrows. That was what made the Sussex Archers unique. Ours were all tipped. I told you, sir – we were experienced archers. Took pride in that. Took pride in the danger of tipping our arrows."

"Until Mr. Pope died."

Colvin grunted. "Until then," he said.

Pons retired from the hassock, restored it to its position, and bade our host good night. Our client waited at the threshold to conduct us to our room, where our brief repast was ready for us.

"Is there anything more, Mr. Pons?" asked our client at our threshold.

"One thing. Does your father take his walk every evening?"

"At about sundown, regularly, rain or shine. Only a severe storm keeps him in. He's rugged, Mr. Pons – very rugged."

"Does he usually follow the same route?"

"Roughly, yes."

"Is his route generally known in the neighborhood?"

"I should imagine so."

"Can you take time to show me tomorrow morning where he walked tonight?"

"Certainly, sir. My office in Petworth can easily do without me for an extra hour or two."

"Thank you. Good night, sir."

Pons ate in contemplative silence, sat for a while cradling his wine, then got up and began to pace the floor in that attitude I knew so well – head sunk on his chest, hands clasped behind him. Back and forth he went, his brow furrowed, his eyes far away, smoke from his pipe of shag making a blue cloud about his head. I knew better than to interrupt his train of thought.

After almost two hours of this he stopped before me.

"Now, Parker, what have you to say of it all?"

"Little more than I said before. Trevor Pope flees through the dusk like a man trying to escape his guilt."

"Indeed he does!" said Pons agreeably. "I have no question but that Mr. Pope is the agent upon whose actions the entire puzzle turns."

"As I pointed out before we left Praed Street," I could not help saying.

"I recall it," continued Pons. "It does not seem to you significant that Pearson, who has been trying to see Joshua Colvin, has not yet been able to do so, though he knows his routine and could find him outside the house any time he wishes?"

"The fellow is clearly playing some game intended to put the wind up his former employer."

"That is surely one way of looking at it. But let me put another question – did it suggest nothing to you that each of the onetime Sussex Archers we questioned today held exactly the same views as our host? None would speak a word against any other, yet each was convinced that Henry Pope's death was not an accident."

"Theirs seems to be the only tenable view, the inquest notwithstanding," I said, not without some smug satisfaction.

"I fear you are only too content to find support for your views," said Pons with equanimity. "I would find it more challenging another way."

"If we doctors failed to face up to the obvious, I'm afraid our patients would soon be in peril of their lives."

"Yet medicine is, comparatively speaking, no more an exact science than that of ratiocination," said Pons, with a twinkle in his eyes. "The chemistry of each individual differs from that of every other, however infinitesimally. But to go on – I submit it is an interesting coincidence that Jefferds should have been killed at twilight, the precise hour Trevor Pope is about with his mastiffs."

"Would you have it otherwise?" I cried. "That was the hour for him to commit the crime!"

"One would have thought he would be less bold about it and given himself some kind of alibi."

"Ah, well," I could not help saying, "how was he to know that Solar Pons might be called in!"

"*Touché*!" cried Pons, laughing.

"I suppose," I went on, "you have constructed a perfect case about Pearson?"

"Ah, Parker, you continually surprise me. Pearson is certainly in the matter – up to his eyes, shall we say? – or I am dead wrong. Let me see," he went on, looking at his watch, "it is now after eleven o'clock. Inspector Jamison will certainly be at home by this time. Now if I can manage to reach the telephone without arousing the household, I will just have a little talk with him."

So saying, he slipped out of our room to place a trunk call. When he came back, he vouchsafed no information.

Next morning Pons deliberately dawdled about the house until the trunk call he was expecting came at ten o'clock. He took it, listened, said less than ten words, thanked Inspector Jamison, and rang off.

All this time our client had been standing by, waiting to be of service to us.

"One more thing, Mr. Colvin," said Pons. "As I mentioned last night, I have a mind to follow the course your father customarily takes on his evening walks. Can it be done?"

"Certainly, sir. Come along."

Hewitt Colvin led the way out of the house and struck off into the surrounding woods. We followed him, Pons commenting now and then on nothing more profound than the chaffinches or thrushes put up at our passing.

Our course led down the slope of Blackdown toward the Weald, away from Lurgashall. Pons' eyes darted here and there. Occasionally he commented on the view to be had from openings in the trees, and once he asked about the proximity of Trevor Pope's course.

"The courses intersect at that copse just ahead, Mr. Pons," said our client. "That's where I saw Pope and his mastiffs." We passed through the copse, which consisted of one very large old chestnut, surrounded by fifty or more younger trees. We had not gone far beyond it, when Pons suddenly excused himself, and ran back into it, bidding us wait for him. "Odd chap," said our client dryly.

"There are others who think so," I said.

In a few moments Pons rejoined us, his eyes dancing. "I believe we have seen enough, Mr. Colvin," he said. "I wanted especially to make sure that there was a point of intersection between your father's course and Trevor Pope's. It seems to serve the purpose for which it is intended."

"I am glad you think so, Mr. Pons."

Pons looked at his watch. "And now, if you will forgive me, we seem to have accomplished for the time being everything we can, and if you will drive us into Petworth, we can catch the 12:45 to London."

"I can drive you to London, Mr. Pons."

"I would not dream of putting you to the trouble, sir. Pray pay my respects to your father, and say to him that I have every hope of laying hands upon the murderer of Mr. Jefferds within forty-eight hours."

"You've laid a trap for Trevor Pope!" cried our client.

"We shall have to take the murderer in the act," said Pons. "Pope is desperate. I rattled him severely last evening. Tell your brother to take exceptional care when he follows your father tonight."

We walked back to the house, and within a few minutes we were in our client's car on our way to Petworth, where we were deposited at the station.

"Surely, Mr. Pons," said Hewitt Colvin from his driver's seat, "you will permit me to take you to London. Your train is still half an hour away; we could be half way there by that time."

"I have a fancy to look about this charming old village, Mr. Colvin. I prefer to do so now. You will hear from me soon."

With this, our client had to be content. He drove away, I knew, filled with misgivings, but surely with no more than troubled me.

"Now, then," said Pons the moment he was out of sight, "let us cloak our bags and spend a little time wandering about Petworth. We might take a bit of luncheon."

"We'll miss our train, Pons!"

Pons favored me with an amused smile. "We're not taking the train, Parker. We have an engagement with a murderer this evening. I expect to keep it. For the nonce, we'll look about Petworth – visit Old Petworth Church, just a hundred years old this year, and Petworth House adjacent to it – about them the entire village revolves, as spokes about the hub of a wheel. Petworth House is eminently worth your attention, the deprecations of Ruskin's followers notwithstanding. And the village's narrow, wandering streets with their kinship to the contours of this land have a charm quite their own."

I gazed at him, I fear, with open-mouthed astonishment. "And afterward, I almost hesitate to tell you, we have at least a three mile walk into the Weald – closer to four, I make it."

"Pons!" I cried at last – "You're mad!"

"It becomes me," said he.

Just before sundown we made our way into that copse of trees where Joshua Colvin's course crossed that of Trevor Pope. Pons had an objective clearly in view – it was the old chestnut tree with a hollow at shoulder height and down one side of the tree – a low-branched tree which dominated the copse, and, indeed, much of the surrounding landscape.

"This is our rendezvous," said Pons. "If I am not in error, this is Joshua Colvin's night of peril. I hope to prevent his death and take his would-be murderer in the act. Now, his death into the tree, Parker. Well up."

Within a few moments we were out of sight up along the trunk of the old chestnut, Pons taking care to be along the far side, away from the direction from which Pope might come, but a place from which he might freely drop to the ground.

"But the dogs, Pons," I cried. "What of them?"

"We shall deal with them if the need arises," he answered. "Now, then, the sun is setting – we may expect Joshua Colvin to set out soon on his round. It will take him half an hour to reach here."

"And Pope, running from a greater distance, as long," I mused. "How it all works out!"

"How indeed! Now let us be silent and wait upon events. Whatever you see, Parker – make no sound!"

The sun went down, the sky paled, changing from aquamarine to a band of magenta and saffron with mother-of-pearl clouds moving toward the zenith. The vespers of the birds fell sweetly to ear – the songs of skylarks, cuckoos, wrens, wheatears and curlews – and bats began to flitter noiselessly about. Then, promptly on schedule, Joshua Colvin entered the wood, his gun held carelessly in the crook of one arm, and passed within sight of the tree.

He had hardly gone before Alasdair Colvin sauntered within sight. And then there occurred one of those strangely terrifying scenes which the mind is always unwilling at first to accept. The younger Colvin came straight to the chestnut tree and set his gun down against the old bole. He took from his pockets a pair of skin-tight gloves, into which he hastily slipped his hands. Then he reached down into the opening in the chestnut tree and drew forth a bow and arrow! At this moment Pons hurtled down upon him.

Startled at last from my almost paralyzed shock, I scrambled clown the trunk and dropped after Pons.

Alasdair Colvin fought like a beast, with a burst of strength surprising in one so slight of body, but Pons and I managed to subdue him just as the elder Colvin came running upon the scene, drawn back by the sound of the struggle. Seeing the bow and arrow lying nearby, Joshua Colvin understood the meaning of the scene at once. He raised his gun and fired twice to bring help.

"Serpent!" he grated. "Ungrateful serpent!" Then, spurning the prostrate young man, he turned to Pons. "But why? Why?"

"You will find that your son was heavily in debt, Mr. Colvin. I suspect also that he was being blackmailed by Pearson. Your son killed Andrew Jefferds and planned your death in an attempt to recreate an old crime and pin it upon an old murderer."

"An old crime?"

"Henry Pope's murder. It was almost certainly his brother who slew him. Your paths crossed here, within minutes, though tonight, unaccountably, he is evidently not coming – which would have served Alasdair grievously had he succeeded in his diabolical plan."

From the direction of the house came the sound of running footsteps.

In our compartment bound for London at last, Pons yielded to my inquiries.

"It seemed to me at the outset that, while not impossible, it was highly improbable that anyone would exact vengeance twenty years after the event to be avenged," he said. "And it would certainly have been the greatest folly to announce 'punishment' to those suspected of having committed the murder of Henry Pope, for this would surely focus attention upon Trevor Pope, the one man who might conceivably want to avenge his brother's death. It seemed therefore elementary that these messages were intended explicitly to do just that.

"Proceeding from this conclusion, I had only to look around for motive. Who would benefit at Joshua Colvin's death but his sons? Hewitt Colvin would hardly have enlisted my help had he been involved in any plan against his father's life. That left only Alasdair. But what motive could he have? Curiously enough, it was the proprietor of the pub in Petworth who furnished a motive when he mentioned that Alasdair still owed him so trifling a sum as five quid – a motive which was strengthened when Jamison informed me this morning, in response to my request for an inquiry into the matter, that Alasdair Colvin was deeply in debt at the track and in various gaming houses – a matter of over five thousand pounds.

"The plan was conceived with wonderful cleverness. A pity Andrew Jefferds had to die – a sacrifice to Alasdair Colvin's vanity. Everyone knew the elder Colvin's routine – and Alasdair knew that Trevor Pope would not be able to supply himself with an alibi at that hour of the day. Moreover, the arrows and the bow Alasdair had taken from his father's storage and hidden in the tree could as readily have belonged to the late Henry Pope. Trevor Pope alone knew that there was no reason for vengeance against the Sussex Archers – for he unquestionably killed his brother; he alone had motive and opportunity – that vague walking tour of the Highlands enabled him to slip back, commit the crime – the schedule of the Archers was set up annually, according to Colvin senior – and return to the Highlands to be 'located' after well planned difficulties.

"Unhappily for Alasdair, two little events he had not counted upon took place. The beater, Pearson, came upon him the night of Jefferds' murder, – which also occurred at twilight, when Trevor Pope was out with his mastiffs – and very probably saw him with the bow in hand before he had the chance to conceal it. Though Pearson may have come originally to see the elder Colvin, he came thereafter to see Alasdair for the purpose of blackmailing him. You will recall the discrepancy between Alasdair's statement that he had seen Pearson months ago, and Pearson's own claim, corroborated by Hewitt's failure to see him, that it was 'more like two weeks' than two months. So Pearson suspected, and was thus in it up to his eyes!

"The other event, of course, was Hewitt's application at 7B. A neat little problem, Parker. Tomorrow, I fancy, I shall have a go at Trevor Pope's Highlands itinerary – difficult as that will be."

But the solution of the secondary mystery was not to be Pons', for the morning papers announced the suicide by hanging of Trevor Pope, who, though he left no message behind, evidently saw in Pons' presence on the scene of his own dastardly crime the working of a belated nemesis.

II

THE ADVENTURE OF THE HAUNTED LIBRARY

When I opened the door of our lodgings one summer day during the third year of our joint tenancy of No. 7B, Praed Street, I found my friend Solar Pons standing with one arm on the mantel, waiting with a thin edge of impatience either upon my arrival, or that of someone else, and ready to go out, for his deerstalker lay close by.

"You're just in time, Parker," he said, " – if the inclination moves you – to join me in another of my little inquiries. This time, evidently into the supernatural."

"The supernatural!" I exclaimed, depositing my bag.

"So it would seem." He pointed to a letter thrown carelessly upon the table.

I picked it up and was immediately aware of the fine quality of the paper and the embossed name: Mrs. Margaret Ashcroft. Her communication was brief.

"Dear Mr. Pons,

"I should be extremely obliged if you could see your way clear to call upon me some time later today or tomorrow, at your convenience, to investigate a troublesome matter which hardly seems to be within the jurisdiction of the Metropolitan

Police. I do believe the library is haunted. Mr. Carnacki says it is not, but I can hardly doubt the evidence of my own senses."

Her signature was followed by a Sydenham address.

"I've sent for a cab," said Pons.

"Who is Mr. Carnacki?" I asked.

"A self-styled psychic investigator. He lives in Chelsea, and has had some considerable success, I am told."

"A charlatan!"

"If he were, he would hardly have turned down our client. What do you make of it, Parker? You know my methods."

I studied the letter which I still held, while Pons waited to hear how much I had learned from his spontaneous and frequent lectures in ratiocination. "If the quality of the paper is any indication, the lady is not without means," I said.

"Capital!"

"Unless she is an heiress, she is probably of middle age or over."

"Go on," urged Pons, smiling.

"She is upset because, though she begins well, she rapidly becomes very unclear."

"And provocative," said Pons. "Who could resist a ghost in a library, eh?"

"But what do you make of it?" I pressed him.

"Well, much the same as you," he said generously. "But I rather think the lady is not a young heiress. She would hardly be living in Sydenham, if she were. No, I think we shall find that she recently acquired a house there and has not been in residence very long. Something is wrong with the library."

"Pons, you don't seriously think it's haunted?"

"Do you believe in ghosts, Parker?"

"Certainly not!"

"Do I detect the slightest hesitation in your answer?" He chuckled. "Ought we not to say, rather, we believe there are certain phenomena which science as yet has not correctly explained or interpreted?" He raised his head suddenly, listening. "I believe that is our cab drawing to the kerb."

A moment later, the sound of a horn from below verified Pons' deduction.

Pons clapped his deerstalker to his head and we were off.

Our client's house was built of brick, two and a half storeys in height, with dormers on the gable floor. It was large and spreading, and built on a knoll, partly into the slope of the earth, though it seemed at first glance to crown the rise there. It was plainly of late Victorian construction, and, while it was not shabby, it just escaped looking quite genteel. Adjacent houses were not quite far enough away from it to give the lawn and garden the kind of spaciousness required to set the house off to its best advantage in a neighborhood which was slowly declining from its former status.

Our client received us in the library. Mrs. Ashcroft was a slender, diminutive woman with flashing blue eyes and whitening hair. She wore an air of fixed determination which her smile at sight of Pons did not diminish.

"Mr. Pons, I was confident that you would come," she greeted us.

She acknowledged Pons' introduction of me courteously, and went on, "This is the haunted room."

"Let us just hear your account of what has happened from the beginning, Mrs. Ashcroft," suggested Pons.

"Very well." She sat for a moment trying to decide where to begin her narrative. "I suppose, Mr. Pons, it began about a month ago. Mrs. Jenkins, a housekeeper I had hired, was cleaning late in the library when she heard someone singing. It seemed to come, she said, 'from the books'. Something about a 'dead man'. It faded away. Two nights later she woke after a dream and went downstairs to get a sedative from the medicine cabinet. She heard something in the library. She thought perhaps I was indisposed and went to the library. But the library, of course, was dark. However, there was a shaft of moonlight in the room – it was bright outside, and therefore a kind of illumination was in the library, too – and in that shaft, Mr. Pons, Mrs. Jenkins believed she saw the bearded face of an old man that seemed to glare fiercely at her. It was only for a moment. Then Mrs. Jenkins found the switch and turned up the light. Of course, there was no one in the library but she. It was enough for her; she was so sure that she had seen a ghost, that next morning, after all the windows and doors were found locked and bolted, she gave notice. I was not entirely sorry to see them go – her husband worked as caretaker of the grounds – because I suspected Jenkins of taking food from the cellars and the refrigerator for their married daughter. That is not an uncommon problem with servants in England, I am told."

"I should have thought you a native, Mrs. Ashcroft," said Pons. "You've been in the Colonies?"

"Kenya, yes. But I was born here. It was for reasons of sentiment that I took this house. I should have taken a better location. But I was little more than a street waif in Sydenham as a child, and somehow the houses here represented the epitome of splendor. When the agent notified me that this one was to be sold, I couldn't resist taking it. But the tables turned – the houses have come down in the world and I have come up, and there are so many things I miss – the hawkers and the carts, for which cars are no substitute, the rumble of the trains since the Nunhead-Crystal Palace Line has been discontinued, and all in all, I fear my sentiments have led me to make an ill-advised choice. The ghost, of course, is only the crowning touch."

"You believe in him then, Mrs. Ashcroft?"

"I've seen him, Mr. Pons." She spoke as matter-of-factly as if she were speaking of some casual natural phenomenon. "It was a week ago. I wasn't entirely satisfied that Mrs. Jenkins had not seen something. It could have been an hallucination. If she had started awake from a dream and fancied she saw something in their room why, yes, I could easily have believed it a transitory hallucination, which might occur commonly enough after a dream. But Mrs. Jenkins had been awake enough to walk downstairs, take a sedative, and start back up when she heard something in the library. So the dream had had time enough in which to wear off. I am myself not easily frightened. My late husband and I lived in Kenya, and some of the Kikuyu are unfriendly.

"Mr. Pons, I examined the library carefully. As you see, shelving covers most of the walls. I had very few personal books to add – the rest were here. I bought the house fully furnished, as the former owner had died and there were no near heirs. That is, there was a brother, I understand, but he was in Rhodesia, and had no intention of returning to England. He put the house up for sale, and my agents, Messrs. Harwell and Chamberlin, in Lordship Lane, secured it for me. The books are therefore the property of the former owner, a Mr. Howard Brensham, who appears to have been very widely read, for there are collections ranging from early British poetry to crime and detective fiction. But that is hardly pertinent. My own books occupy scarcely two shelves over there – all but a few are jacketed, as you see, Mr. Pons. Well, my examination of the library indicated that the position of these books as I had placed them had been altered. It seemed to me that they had been handled, perhaps even read. They are not of any great consequence – recent novels, some work by Proust and Mauriac in French editions, an account of life in Kenya, and the like. It was possible that one of the servants had become interested in them; I did not inquire. Nevertheless, I became very sensitive and alert about the library. One night last week – Thursday, I believe – while I lay reading late, in my room, I distinctly heard a book or some such object fall in this room.

"I got out of bed, took my torch, and crept down the stairs in the dark. Mr. Pons, I sensed someone's or something's moving about below. I could feel the disturbance of the air at the foot of the stairs where something had passed. I went directly to the library and from the threshold of that door over there I turned my torch into the room and put on its light. Mr. Pons, I saw a horrifying thing. I saw the face of an old man, matted with beard, with wild unkempt hair raying outward from his head; it glared fiercely, menacingly at me. I admit that I faltered and fell back; the torch almost fell from my hands. Nevertheless, I summoned enough courage to snap on the overhead light. Mr. Pons – there was no one in the room beside myself. I stood in the doorway. No one had passed me. Yet, I swear it, I had seen precisely the same apparition that Mrs. Jenkins had described! It was there for one second – in the next it was gone – as if the very books had swallowed it up.

"Mr. Pons, I am not an imaginative woman, and I am not given to hallucinations. I saw what I had seen; there was no question of that. I went around at once to make certain that the windows and doors were locked; all were; nothing had been tampered with. I had seen something, and everything about it suggested a supernatural apparition. I applied to Mr. Harwell. He told me that Mr. Brensham had never made any reference to anything out of the ordinary about the house. He had personally known Mr. Brensham's old uncle, Captain Jason Brensham, from whom he had inherited the house, and the Captain had never once complained of the house. He admitted that it did not seem to be a matter for the regular police, and mentioned Mr. Carnacki as well as yourself. I'm sure you know Mr. Carnacki, whose forte is psychic investigation. He came – and as nearly as I can describe it, he *felt* the library, and assured me that there were no supernatural forces at work here. So I applied to you, Mr. Pons, and I do hope you will lay the ghost for me."

Pons smiled almost benignly, which lent his handsome, feral face a briefly gargoylesque expression. "My modest powers,

I fear, do not permit me to feel the presence of the supernatural, but I must admit to some interest in your little problem," he said thoughtfully. "Let me ask you, on the occasion on which you saw the apparition – last Thursday – were you aware of anyone's breathing?"

"No, Mr. Pons. I don't believe ghosts are held to breathe."

"Ah, Mrs. Ashcroft, in such matters I must defer to your judgment – you appear to have seen a ghost; I have not seen one." His eyes danced. "Let us concentrate for a moment on its disappearance. Was it accompanied by any sound?"

Our client sat for a long moment in deep thought. "I believe it was, Mr. Pons," she said at last. "Now that I think of it."

"Can you describe it?"

"As best I can recall, it was something like the sound a book dropped on the carpet might make."

"But there was no book on the floor when you turned the light on?"

"I do not remember that there was."

"Will you show me approximately where the spectre was when you saw it?"

She got up with alacrity, crossed to her right, and stood next to the shelving there. She was in a position almost directly across from the entrance to the library from the adjacent room; a light flashed on from the threshold would almost certainly strike the shelving there.

"You see, Mr. Pons – there isn't even a window in this wall through which someone could have escaped if it were unlocked."

"Yes, yes," said Pons with an absent air. "Some ghosts vanish without sound, we are told, and some in a thunderclap. And this one with the sound of a book dropped upon the carpet!" He sat for a few moments, eyes closed, his long, tapering fingers tented before him, touching his chin occasionally. He opened his eyes again and asked, "Has anything in the house – other than your books – been disturbed, Mrs. Ashcroft?"

"If you mean my jewelry or the silver – no, Mr. Pons."

"A ghost with a taste for literature! There are indeed all things under the sun. The library has of course been cleaned since the visitation?"

"Every Saturday, Mr. Pons."

"Today is Thursday – a week since your experience. Has anything taken place since then, Mrs. Ashcroft?"

"Nothing, Mr. Pons."

"If you will excuse me," he said, coming to his feet, "I would like to examine the room."

Thereupon he began that process of intensive examination which never ceased to amaze and amuse me. He took the position that our client had just left to return to her chair, and stood, I guessed, fixing directions. He gazed at the high windows along the south wall; I concluded that he was estimating the angle of a shaft of moonlight and deducing that the ghost, as seen by Mrs. Jenkins, had been standing at or near the same place when it was observed. Having satisfied himself, he gave his attention to the floor, first squatting there, then coming to his knees and crawling about. Now and then he picked something off the carpet and put it into one of the tiny envelopes he habitually carried. He crept all along the east wall, went around the north and circled the room in this fashion, while our client watched him with singular interest, saying nothing and making no attempt to conceal her astonishment. He finished at last, and got to his feet once more, rubbing his hands together.

"Pray tell me, Mrs. Ashcroft, can you supply a length of thread of a kind that is not too tensile, that will break readily?"

"What color, Mr. Pons?"

"Trust a lady to think of that!" he said, smiling. "Color is of no object, but if you offer a choice, I prefer black."

"I believe so. Wait here."

Our client rose and left the library.

"Are you expecting to catch a ghost with thread, Pons?" I asked.

"Say rather I expect to test a phenomenon."

"That is one of the simplest devices I have ever known you to use."

"Is it not?" he agreed, nodding. "I submit, however, that the simple is always preferable to the complex."

Mrs. Ashcroft returned, holding out a reel of black thread. "Will this do, Mr. Pons?"

Pons took it, unwound a little of the thread, and pulled it apart readily. "Capital!" he answered. "This is adequately soft."

He walked swiftly over to the north wall, took a book off the third shelf, which was at slightly over two feet from the floor, and tied the thread around it. Then he restored the book to its place, and walked away, unwinding the reel, until he reached the south wall, where he tautened the thread and tied the end around a book there. He now had an almost invisible thread that reached from north to south across the library at a distance of about six feet from the east wall, and within the line of the windows.

He returned the reel of thread to our client. "Now, then, can we be assured that no one will enter the library for a day or two? Perhaps the Saturday cleaning can be dispensed with?"

"Of course it can, Mr. Pons," said Mrs. Ashcroft, clearly mystified.

"Very well, Mrs. Ashcroft. I trust you will notify me at once if the thread is broken – or if any other untoward event occurs. In the meantime, there are a few little inquiries I want to make."

Our client bade us farewell with considerably more perplexity than she had displayed in her recital of the curious events which had befallen her.

Once outside, Pons looked at his watch. "I fancy we may just have time to catch Mr. Harwell at his office, which is not far down Sydenham Hill and so within walking distance." He gazed at me, his eyes twinkling. "Coming, Parker?"

I fell into step at his side, and for a few moments we walked in silence, Pons striding along with his long arms swinging loosely at his sides, his keen eyes darting here and there, as if in perpetual and merciless search of facts with which to substantiate his deductions.

I broke the silence between us. "Pons, you surely don't believe in Mrs. Ashcroft's ghost?"

"What is a ghost?" he replied. "Something seen. Not necessarily supernatural. Agreed?"

"Agreed," I said. "It may be hallucination, illusion, some natural phenomenon misinterpreted."

"So the question is not about the reality of ghosts, but, did our client see a ghost or did she not? She believes she did. We are willing to believe that she saw something. Now, it was either a ghost or it was not a ghost."

"Pure logic."

"Let us fall back upon it. Ghost or no ghost, what is its motivation?"

"I thought that plain as a pikestaff," I said dryly. "The purpose is to frighten Mrs. Ashcroft away from the house."

"I submit few such matters are plain as a pikestaff. Why?"

"Someone wishes to gain possession of the house."

"Anyone wishing to do so could surely have bought it from the agents before Mrs. Ashcroft did. But, let us for the moment assume that you are correct. How then did he get in?"

"That remains to be determined."

"Quite right. And we shall determine it. But one other little matter perplexes me in relation to your theory. That is this – if someone were bent upon frightening Mrs. Ashcroft from the house, does it not seem to you singular that we have no evidence that he initiated any of those little scenes where he was observed?"

"I should say it was deuced clever of him."

"It does not seem strange to you that if someone intended to frighten our client from the house, he should permit himself to be seen only by accident? And that after but the briefest of appearances, he should vanish before the full effectiveness of the apparition could be felt?"

"When you put it that way, of course, it is a little far-fetched."

"I fear we must abandon your theory, Parker, sound as it is in every other respect."

He stopped suddenly. "I believe this is the address we want. Ah, yes – here we are. 'Harwell & Chamberlin, 210'."

We mounted the stairs of the ancient but durable building and found ourselves presently in late-nineteenth century quarters. A clerk came forward at our entrance.

"Good day, gentlemen. Can we be of service?"

"I am interested in seeing Mr. Roderic Harwell," said Pons.

"I'm sorry, sir, but Mr. Harwell has just left the office for the rest of the day. Would you care to make an appointment?"

"No, thank you. My business is of some considerable urgency, and I shall have to follow him home."

The clerk hesitated momentarily, then said, "I should not think that necessary, sir. You could find him down and around the corner at the Green Horse. He likes to spend an hour or so at the pub with an old friend or two before going home. Look for a short, ruddy gentleman, with bushy white sideboards."

Pons thanked him again, and we made our way back down the stairs and out to the street. In only a few minutes we were entering the Green Horse. Despite the crowd in the pub, Pons' quick eyes immediately found the object of our search, sitting at a round table near one wall, in desultory conversation with another gentleman of similar age, close to sixty, wearing, unless I were sadly mistaken, the air of my own profession.

We made our way to the table.

"Mr. Roderic Harwell?" asked Pons.

"That infernal clerk has given me away again!" cried Harwell, but with such a jovial smile that it was clear he did not mind. "What can I do for you?"

"Sir, you were kind enough to recommend me to Mrs. Margaret Ashcroft."

"Ah, it's Solar Pons, is it? I thought you looked familiar. Sit down, sit down."

His companion hastily rose and excused himself.

"Pray do not leave, Doctor," said Pons. "This matter is not of such a nature that you need to disturb your meeting."

Harwell introduced us all around. His companion was Dr. Horace Weston, an old friend he was in the habit of meeting at the Green Horse at the end of the day. We sat between them.

"Now, then," said Harwell when we had made ourselves comfortable. "What'll you have to drink? Some ale? Bitter?"

"Nothing at all, if you please," said Pons.

"As you like. You've been to see Mrs. Ashcroft and heard her story?"

"We have just come from there."

"Well, Mr. Pons, I never knew of anything wrong with the house," said Harwell. "We sold some land in the country for Captain Brensham when he began selling off his property so that he could live as he was accustomed to live. He was a bibliophile of a sort – books about the sea were his specialty – and he lived well. But a recluse in his last years. He timed his life right – died just about the time his funds ran out."

"And Howard Brensham?" asked Pons.

"Different sort of fellow altogether. Quiet, too, but you'd find him in the pubs, and at the cinema, sometimes watching a stage show. He gambled a little, but carefully. I gather he surprised his uncle by turning out well. He had done a turn in Borstal as a boy. And I suppose he was just as surprised when his uncle asked him to live with him his last years and left everything to him, including the generous insurance he carried."

"I wasn't sure, from what Mrs. Ashcroft said, when Howard Brensham died."

Harwell flashed a glance at his companion. "About seven weeks ago or so, eh?" To Pons, he added, "Dr. Weston was called."

"He had a cerebral thrombosis on the street, Mr. Pons," explained Dr. Weston. "Died in three hours. Very fast. Only forty-seven, and no previous history. But then, Captain Brensham died of a heart attack."

"Ah, you attended the Captain, too?"

"Well, not exactly. I had attended him for some bronchial ailments. He took good care of his voice. He liked to sing. But when he had his heart attack and died I was in France on holiday. I had a young locum in and he was called."

"Mrs. Ashcroft's ghost sang," said Harwell thoughtfully. "Something about a 'dead man'."

"I would not be surprised if it were an old sea chantey," said Pons.

"You don't mean you think it may actually be the Captain's ghost, Mr. Pons?"

"Say, rather, we may be meant to think it is," answered Pons. "How old was he when he died?"

"Sixty-eight or sixty-seven – something like that," said Dr. Weston.

"How long ago?"

"Oh, only two years."

"His nephew hadn't lived with him very long, then, before the old man died?"

"No. Only a year or so," said Harwell. His sudden grin gave him a Dickensian look. "But it was long enough to give him at least one of his uncle's enthusiasms – the sea. He's kept up all the Captain's newspapers and magazines, and was still buying books about the sea when he died. Like his uncle, he read very little else. I suppose a turn he had done as a seaman bent him that way. But they were a seafaring family. The Captain's father had been a seaman, too, and Richard – the brother in Rhodesia who inherited the property and sold it through us to Mrs. Ashcroft – had served six years in the India trade."

Pons sat for a few minutes in thoughtful silence. Then he said, "I take it that the property has little value."

Harwell looked suddenly unhappy. "Mr. Pons, we tried to dissuade Mrs. Ashcroft. But these Colonials have sentimental impulses no one can curb. Home to Mrs. Ashcroft meant not London, not England, but Sydenham. What could we do? The house was the best we could obtain for her in Sydenham. But it's in a declining neighborhood, and no matter how she refurbishes it, its value is bound to go down."

Pons came abruptly to his feet. "Thank you, Mr. Harwell. And you, Dr. Weston."

We bade them goodbye and went out to find a cab.

Back in our quarters, Pons ignored the supper Mrs. Johnson had laid for us, and went directly to the corner where he kept his chemical apparatus. There he emptied his pockets of the envelopes he had filled in Mrs. Ashcroft's library, tossed his deerstalker to the top of the bookcase nearby, and began to subject his findings to chemical analysis. I ate supper by myself, knowing that it would be fruitless to urge Pons to join me. After supper I had a patient to look in on. I doubt that Pons heard me leave the room.

On my return in mid-evening, Pons was just finishing.

"Ah, Parker," he greeted me, "I see by the sour expression you're wearing you've been out calling on your crochety Mr. Barnes."

"While you, I suppose, have been tracking down the identity of Mrs. Ashcroft's ghost?"

"I have turned up indisputable evidence that her visitant is from the nethermost regions," he said triumphantly, and laid before me a tiny fragment of cinder. "Do you suppose we dare conclude that coal is burned in Hell?"

I gazed at him in open-mouthed astonishment. His eyes were dancing merrily. He was expecting an outburst of protest from me. I choked it back deliberately; I was becoming familiar indeed with all the little games he played.

"Have you determined," I said without a smile, "whether he comes from the Catholic Hell or the Protestant Hell?"

"*Touché*!" he cried, and laughed heartily.

"More to the point," I went on. "Have you determined his identity and his motive?"

"Oh, there's not much mystery in that," he said almost contemptuously. "It's the background in which I am interested."

"Not much mystery in it!" I cried.

"No, no," he answered testily. "The trappings may be a trifle bizarre, but don't let them blind you to the facts, all essentials of which have been laid before us."

I sat down, determined to expose his trickery. "Pons, it is either a ghost or it is not a ghost."

"I can see no way of disputing that position."

"Then it is not a ghost."

"On what grounds do you say so?"

"Because there is no such thing as a ghost."

"Proof?"

"Proof to the contrary?"

"The premise is yours, not mine. But let us accept it for the nonce. Pray go on."

"Therefore it is a sentient being."

"Ah, that is certainly being cagey," he said, smiling provocatively. "Have you decided what his motive might be?"

"To frighten Mrs. Ashcroft from the house."

"Why? We've been told it's not worth much and will decline in value with every year to come."

"Very well, then. To get his hands on something valuable concealed in the house. Mrs. Ashcroft took it furnished – as it was, you'll remember."

"I remember it very well. I am also aware that the house stood empty for some weeks and anyone who wanted to lay hands on something in it would have had far more opportunity to do so then than he would after tenancy was resumed."

I threw up my hands. "I give it up."

"Come, come, Parker. You are looking too deep. Think on it soberly for a while and the facts will rearrange themselves so as to make for but one correct solution."

So saying, he turned to the telephone and rang up Inspector Jamison at his home to request him to make a discreet application for exhumation of the remains of Captain Jason Brensham and the examination of those remains by Bernard Spilsbury.

"Would you mind telling me what all that has to do with our client?" I asked, when he had finished.

"I submit it is too fine a coincidence to dismiss that a heavily insured old man should conveniently die after he has made a will leaving everything to the nephew he has asked to come live with him," said Pons. "There we have a concrete motive, with nothing ephemeral about it."

"But what's to be gained by an exhumation now? If what you suspect is true, the murderer is already dead."

Pons smiled enigmatically. "Ah, Parker, I am not so much a seeker after punishment as a seeker after truth. I want the facts. I mean to have them. I shall be spending considerable time tomorrow at the British Museum in search of them."

"Well, you'll find ghosts of another kind there," I said dryly.

"Old maps and newspapers abound with them," he answered agreeably, but said no word in that annoyingly typical fashion of his about what he sought.

I would not ask, only to be told again, "Facts!"

When I walked into our quarters early in the evening of the following Monday, I found Pons standing at the windows, his face aglow with eager anticipation.

"I was afraid you might not get here in time to help lay Mrs. Ashcroft's ghost," he said, without turning.

"But you weren't watching for me," I said, "or you wouldn't still be standing there."

"Ah, I am delighted to note such growth in your deductive faculty," he replied. "I'm waiting for Jamison and Constable Mecker. We may need their help tonight if we are to trap this elusive apparition. Mrs. Ashcroft has sent word that the string across the library was broken last night. – Ah, here they come now."

He turned. "You've had supper, Parker?"

"I dined at the Diogenes Club."

"Come then. The game's afoot."

He led the way down the stairs and out into Praed Street, where a police car had just drawn up to the kerb. The door of the car sprang open at our approach, and Constable Mecker got out. He was a fresh-faced young man whose work Pons had come to regard as very promising, and he greeted us with anticipatory pleasure, stepping aside so that we could enter the car. Inspector Seymour Jamison – a bluff, square-faced man wearing a clipped moustache – occupied the far corner of the seat.

Inspector Jamison spared no words in formal greeting.

"How the devil did you get on to Captain Brensham's poisoning?" he asked gruffly.

"Spilsbury found poison, then?"

"Arsenic. A massive dose. Brensham couldn't have lived much over twelve hours after taking it. How did you know?"

"I had only a very strong assumption," said Pons.

The car was rolling forward now through streets hazed with a light mist and beginning to glow with the yellow lights of the shops, blunting the harsh realities of daylight and lending to London a kind of enchantment I loved. Mecker was at the wheel, which he handled with great skill in the often crowded streets.

Inspector Jamison was persistent. "I hope you haven't got us out on a wild goose chase," he went on. "I have some doubts about following your lead in such matters, Pons."

"When I've misled you, they'll be justified. Not until then. Now, another matter – if related. You'll recall a disappearance in Dulwich two years ago? Elderly man named Ian Narth?"

Jamison sat for a few moments in silence. Then he said. "Man of seventy. Retired seaman. Indigent. No family. Last seen on a train near the Crystal Palace. Vanished without trace. Presumed drowned in the Thames and carried out to sea."

"I believe I can find him for you, Jamison."

Jamison snorted. "Now, then, Pons – give it to me short. What's all this about?"

Pons summed up the story of our client's haunted library, while Jamison sat in thoughtful silence.

"Laying ghosts is hardly in my line," he said when Pons had finished.

"Can you find your way to the Lordship Lane entrance of the abandoned old Nunhead-Crystal Palace High Level Railway Line?" asked Pons.

"Of course."

"If not, I have a map with me. Two, in fact. If you and Mecker will conceal yourself near that entrance, ready to arrest anyone coming out of it, we'll meet you there in from two to three hours' time."

"I hope you know what you're doing, Pons," growled Jamison.

"I share that hope, Jamison." He turned to Mecker and gave him Mrs. Ashcroft's address. "Parker and I will leave you there, Jamison. You'll have plenty of time to reach the tunnel entrance before we begin our exploration at the other end."

"It's murder then, Pons?"

"I should hardly think that anyone would willingly take so much arsenic unless he meant to commit suicide. No such intention was manifest in Captain Brensham's life – indeed, quite the contrary. He loved the life he led, and would not willingly have given it up."

"You're postulating that Ian Narth knew Captain Brensham and his nephew?"

"I am convinced enquiry will prove that to be the case."

Mecker left us out of the police car before Mrs. Ashcroft's house, which loomed with an almost forbiddingly sinister air in the gathering darkness. Light shone wanly from but one window; curtains were drawn over the rest of them at the front of the house, and the entire dwelling seemed to be waiting upon its foredoomed decay.

Mrs. Ashcroft herself answered our ring.

"Oh, Mr. Pons!" she cried at the sight of us. "You *did* get my message."

"Indeed, I did, Mrs. Ashcroft. Dr. Parker and I have now come to make an attempt at least to lay your ghost."

Mrs. Ashcroft paled a little and stepped back to permit us entrance.

"You'll want to see the broken thread, Mr. Pons," she said after she had closed the door.

"If you please."

She swept past us and led us to the library, where she turned up all the lights. The black thread could be seen lying on the carpet, away from the east wall, broken through about midway.

"Nothing has been disturbed, Mrs. Ashcroft?"

"Nothing. No one has come into this room but I – at my strict order. Except – of course – whoever broke the thread."

She shuddered. "It appears to have been broken by something coming out of the wall!"

"Does it not?" agreed Pons.

"No ghost could break that thread," I said.

"There are such phenomena as *poltergeists* which are said to make all kinds of mischief, including the breaking of dishes," said Pons dryly. "If we had that to deal with, the mere breaking of a thread would offer it no problem. You heard nothing, Mrs. Ashcroft?"

"Nothing."

"No rattling of chains, no hollow groans?"

"Nothing, Mr. Pons."

"And not even the sound of a book falling?"

"Such a sound an old house might make at any time, I suppose, Mr. Pons."

He cocked his head suddenly; a glint came into his eyes. "And not, I suppose, a sound like that? Do you hear it?"

"Oh, Mr. Pons," cried Mrs. Ashcroft in a low voice. "That is the sound Mrs. Jenkins heard."

It was the sound of someone singing – singing boisterously. It seemed to come as from a great distance, out of the very books on the walls.

"*Fifteen men on a dead man's chest*," murmured Pons. "I can barely make out the words. Captain Brensham's collection of sea lore is shelved along this wall, too! A coincidence."

"Mr. Pons! What is it?" asked our client.

"Pray do not disturb yourself, Mrs. Ashcroft. That is hardly a voice from the other side. It has too much body. But we are delaying unnecessarily. Allow me."

So saying, he crossed to the book shelves, at the approximate place where she had reported seeing the apparition that haunted the library. He lifted a dozen books off a shelf and put them to one side. Then he knocked upon the wall behind. It gave back a muffled, hollow sound. He nodded in satisfaction, and then gave the entire section of shelving the closest scrutiny.

Presently he found what he sought – after having removed half the books from the shelving there – a small lever concealed behind a row of books. He depressed it. Instantly there was a soft thud – like the sound a book might make when it struck the carpet – and the section sagged forward, opening into the room like a door ajar. Mrs. Ashcroft gasped sharply. "A sound like that, Mrs. Ashcroft," said Pons.

"What on earth is that, Mr. Pons?"

"Unless I am very much mistaken, it is a passage to the abandoned right-of-way of the Nunhead-Crystal Palace Line – and the temporary refuge of your library ghost."

He pulled the shelving further into the room, exposing a gaping aperture which led into the high bank behind that wall of the house, and down into the earth beneath. Out of the aperture came a voice which was certainly that of an inebriated man, raucously singing. The voice echoed and reverberated as in a cavern below.

"Pray excuse us, Mrs. Ashcroft," said Pons. "Come, Parker."

Pons took a torch from his pocket and, crouching, crept into the tunnel. I followed him. The earth was shored up for a little way beyond the opening; then the walls were bare, and here and there I found them narrow for me, though Pons, being slender, managed to slip through with less difficulty.

The aperture was not high enough for some distance to enable one to do more than crawl, and it was a descending passage almost from the opening in Mrs. Ashcroft's library. Ahead of us, the singing had stopped suddenly.

"Hist!" warned Pons abruptly.

There was a sound of hurried scuttering movement up ahead.

"I fear he has heard us," Pons whispered.

He moved forward again, and abruptly stood up. I crowded out to join him. We stood on the right-of-way of the abandoned Nunhead-Crystal Palace Line. The rails were still in place, and the railbed was clearly the source of the cinder Pons had produced for my edification. Far ahead of us on the line someone was running.

"No matter," said Pons. "There is only one way for him to go. He could hardly risk going out to where the nearby Victoria line passes. He must go out by way of the Lordship Lane entrance."

We pressed forward, and soon the light revealed a niche hollowed out of the wall. It contained bedding, a half eaten loaf of bread, candles, a lantern, books. Outside the opening were dozens of empty wine bottles, and several that had contained brandy.

Pons bent to examine the bedding.

"Just as I thought," he said, straightening up. "This has not been here very long – certainly not longer than two months."

"The time since the younger Brensham's death," I cried.

"You advance, Parker, you advance, indeed!"

"Then he and Narth were in it together!"

"Of necessity," said Pons. "Come."

He ran rapidly down the line, I after him.

Up ahead there was a sudden burst of shouting. "Aha!" cried Pons. "They have him!"

In ten minutes of hard running, we burst out of the tunnel at the entrance where Inspector Jamison and Constable Mecker waited – the constable manacled to a wild-looking old man, whose fierce glare was indeed alarming. Greying hair stood out from his head, and his unkempt beard completed a frame of hair around a grimy face out of which blazed two eyes fiery with rage.

"He gave us quite a struggle, Pons," said Jamison, still breathing heavily.

"Capital! Capital!" cried Pons, rubbing his hands together delightedly. "Gentlemen, let me introduce you to as wily an old scoundrel as we've had the pleasure of meeting in a long time. Captain Jason Brensham, swindler of insurance companies and, I regret to say, murderer."

"Narth!" exclaimed Jamison.

"Ah, Jamison, you had your hands on him. But I fear you lost him when you gave him to Spilsbury."

"The problem was elementary enough," said Pons, as he filled his pipe with the abominable shag he habitually smoked and leaned up against the mantel in our quarters later that night. "Mrs. Ashcroft told us everything essential to its solution, and Harwell only confirmed it. The unsolved question was the identity of the victim, and the files of the metropolitan papers gave me a presumptive answer to that in the disappearance of Ian Narth, a man of similar build and age to Captain Brensham.

"Of course, it was manifest at the outset that this motiveless spectre was chancing discovery for survival. It was not Jenkins but the Captain who was raiding the food and liquor stocks at his house. The cave, of course, was never intended as a permanent hiding place, but only as a refuge to seek when strangers came to the house, or whenever his nephew had some of his friends in. He lived in the house; he had always been reclusive, and he changed his way of life but little. His nephew, you will recall Harwell's telling us, continued to subscribe to his magazines and buy the books he wanted, apparently for himself, but obviously for his uncle. The bedding and supplies were obviously moved into the tunnel after the younger Brensham's death.

"The manner and place of the ghost's appearance suggested the opening in the wall. The cinder in the carpet cried aloud of the abandoned Nunhead-Crystal Palace Line which the maps I studied in the British Museum confirmed ran almost under the house. The Captain actually had more freedom than most dead men, for he could wander out along the line by night, if he wished.

"Harwell clearly set forth the motive. The Captain had sold off everything he had to enable him to continue his way of living. He needed money. His insurance policies promised to supply it. He and his nephew together hatched up the plot. Narth was picked as victim, probably out of a circle of acquaintances because, as newspaper descriptions made clear, he had a certain resemblance to the Captain and was, like him, a retired seaman with somewhat parallel tastes.

"They waited until the auspicious occasion when Dr. Weston, who knew the Captain too well to be taken in, was off on a prolonged holiday, lured Narth to the house, killed him with a lethal dose of arsenic, after which they cleaned up the place to eliminate all external trace of poison and its effects, and called in Dr. Weston's *locum* to witness the dying man's last minutes. The Captain was by this time in his cave, and the young doctor took Howard Brensham's word for the symptoms and signed the death certificate, after which the Brenshams had ample funds on which to live as the Captain liked."

"And how close they came to getting away with it!" I cried.

"Indeed! Howard Brensham's unforeseen death – ironically, of a genuine heart attack – was the little detail they had never dreamed of. On similar turns of fate empires have fallen!"

III

THE ADVENTURE OF THE FATAL GLANCE

"Surely that was a shout," said Solar Pons, coming to a pause and turning.

We stood on the moor road at Askrigg Town Head and, looking back down the precipitous descent toward houses rising on both sides of the street against the hillside, we saw a cyclist coming toward us.

"Isn't that Constable Lambert?" said Pons. "We had a game of darts last night at the Crown."

"I hope you'll remember you came to Askrigg for a holiday," I said, pointedly.

"We've had three days without a single thought but of resting in this Yorkshire country," said Pons. "Very trying days, if I may say so. I'm never certain why I let you talk me into these holidays from time to time. But here he is."

Constable Lambert came up and slid off his bicycle. He was a young man, whose plain, freckled face customarily wore an expression of almost apologetic honesty. This morning there was trouble in his eyes.

"I wondered when I caught sight of you, Mr. Pons, whether I could persuade you to come along," he said, and added – "It looks like my first murder, sir."

"Ah," said Pons sharply, his eyes lighting up. "Let us hear about it."

"I don't know much, and that's a fact," replied the Constable. "But we can talk while we walk. It's just up ahead, at Thornhill Hall."

He started forward as he spoke, wheeling his bicycle beside him; we fell into step. The road curved and dipped here between walled pastures and meadows on its way toward the moor above Askrigg, passing the last few isolated houses on the edge of the village, a group of larches, and one or two groves of bushes and small trees. Our destination was visibly the country house set back from the moor road among trees perhaps half a mile out of Askrigg.

"It's the Squire, Mr. Pons," resumed Constable Lambert. "Dr. Scarr telephoned me – says he's been murdered."

"You've not seen him, then?" asked Pons.

The Constable shook his head. "I've only just now had the call. Hawgood found him lying dead in the study – Hawgood's the Squire's man. Miss Emily called the doctor. Dr. Scarr saw right off it was a case for the police."

"Did he say how the Squire was killed?"

"Well, he did, sir – but I don't quite understand it. Doesn't seem to have been shot – or anything, as you might say, simple. As nearly as I could follow Dr. Scarr, the Squire was killed by a pair of binoculars."

"Capital! Capital!" murmured Pons. "Something new under England's sun. Who would have had motive?"

"Mr. Thornhill wasn't a popular man," said the Constable dryly. "Who *wouldn't* have motive would be easier to say. There's one man likes him – that's Hawgood; he swears by him, for all that the Squire got young Hawgood sent up six months for pilfering. They do say even his own daughter can't stand him, and village talk has it that his late wife died to be free of him. There's Fred Mason, a gardener he sacked without reference –

and Arthur Robson – the Squire knocked him down a week ago or thereabouts – oh, there's plenty with motive, Mr. Pons. The Squire was a hard man, and not one to cross."

We reached the gate opening on to the flagstone walk that led to Thornhill Hall. Constable Lambert pushed it ajar and stood aside for Pons to walk through.

Our approach had been observed, and the door was opened to us by a square-jawed man with the expressionless face of a long-time servant. Though he had been expecting only Constable Lambert, nothing but the flickering of his glance toward us betrayed his surprise at facing three men instead of one.

"Good morning, Hawgood."

He closed the door behind us, then came around to lead us.

"Right this way, if you please, gentlemen."

From the broad hall, Hawgood led us to the right, through a small sitting-room into what was manifestly the study. There Dr. Scarr waited – a burly, ruddy-faced man in his middle years, standing like a sentinel on guard beside the cloaked mound which was the body of Squire Thornhill.

"Most shocking thing I've ever seen," he said, after introductions had been exchanged. "Man cut down like this in his prime! I've survived the war, gentlemen – never saw anything like it."

He bent and flicked the cloak aside, disclosing the body.

It was that of a robust man of middle age clad in riding clothes. He lay partly on one side, with his head at an abnormal angle. Save for the awkwardness of his position, the Squire might have been sleeping. It was only at second glance that I saw the lines of blood from the mutilated eyes. Not far from the body lay the instrument of death – a pair of binoculars, from the eye-pieces of which projected needles of at least four inches in length.

"Will you examine him, Doctor?" asked Dr. Scarr.

I dropped to my knees for a closer look. But there was nothing more to be seen than had already been disclosed, and it was perfectly evident that the dead man had come to his death by means of the lethal binoculars. Since the body lay just before open French doors, it was logical to assume that the Squire had taken up the binoculars for a glance outside, and that, very probably at his manipulation of the focussing wheel, while the glasses were at his eyes, the mechanism within had released the fatal needles which had plunged into his brain through his eyes. I said as much.

"Horrible," muttered the Constable.

Pons came forward now and in turn examined the body and the binoculars. He looked toward Hawgood.

"Have you seen these before, Hawgood?" he asked.

"No, sir."

"They were not Mr. Thornhill's?"

"No, sir."

Pons moved away from the body, his keen eyes darting here and there. He made a quick circuit of the room, pausing to pick up a little rectangle of paper on the carpet near the fireplace, and stopping finally at the hearth, where he crouched to look at the remains of a fire.

"Paper was burned here this morning," he said, flashing a glance at Hawgood.

"I burned nothing, sir," said Hawgood at once.

Pons came back to where we waited. "You found the body, Hawgood?"

"Yes, sir. I came into the room and saw him."

"Mr. Thornhill could hardly have died without sound. You heard nothing?"

Hawgood paused uncertainly, biting at his lower lip. "Come, come, man – what did you hear?"

"I couldn't say, sir – but I thought – *after* I found him – that I had heard him cry out. Just once."

"I see." From his pocket Pons took the rectangle of paper he had picked up. "Have you see this before, Hawgood?"

The rectangle was a piece of stout linen card on which had been written: *From an admirer.*

"No, sir."

"Does it not seem likely that it came with the binoculars?"

"I don't know, Mr. Pons."

"Did you receive the post this morning?"

"No, sir. Mr. Thornhill did."

Pons took another turn around the room, while Constable Lambert watched curiously.

"What do you make of it, Lambert?" he asked, as he came back to stand before the constable.

"Mr. Pons, it looks as if somebody made Mr. Thornhill a present of these binoculars. They were intended to kill him, and when he took a glance through the binoculars, he was killed as he tried to focus them. They could have been sent or brought by anyone."

"Do you think so?" asked Pons dryly. "Surely only a man with some skill in mechanics could have devised this fatal instrument."

"He could have been hired to do so," said the constable.

"Capital!" cried Pons. "Just so." He turned abruptly again to Hawgood. "Let us return for a moment to the cry you fancied you heard. Did you respond to it?"

"No, Mr. Pons. It was too indefinite. It might have been a dog somewhere."

"I see. So that some time elapsed before you found Mr. Thornhill?"

"Yes, sir. I'd guess it was half an hour after he might have cried out. I was at work below stairs."

Pons regarded him thoughtfully for a moment before he spoke again. "In that case, Hawgood, you must have heard him fall."

"Sir," said Hawgood stiffly, "I was under the left wing. The Squire was in the right. If I had heard anything I'd lay it to his stomping around or turning something over – he'd do that if he were upset or angry."

"You are not only then the Squire's butler?"

"No, sir. I do whatever's needing to be done. I was just at the foot of the stairs when I heard the postman's ring this morning. I heard the Squire stomping around to get the post. Then I went on into the left wing belowstairs and didn't hear much of anything else. I suppose the Squire went back to the study to open the mail, as he usually did. I knew his habits. I've been his man ever since the war."

"You were his batman in service?"

"Yes, sir."

"And general factotum ever since?"

"Yes, sir."

"Were you fond of him, Hawgood?"

"Sir, I was used to him," answered Hawgood stiffly.

"Mr. Thornhill was always kind and considerate?"

"I would not say so."

"Oh. What would you say, Hawgood?"

"The Squire was a rough man. He had certain principles and he lived up to them. Rough as he was, he meant well."

"Autocratic, would you say, Hawgood?"

"Quite, sir."

"Accustomed to obedience, and outraged at any defection. Self-righteous. Perhaps a martinet?"

"I suppose he was all that, sir," said Hawgood cautiously.

At that point, Dr. Scarr interposed. "If you'll forgive me, gentlemen – are you finished here? Mr. Thornhill's body should be removed."

"By all means, Doctor," said Constable Lambert. "Will you attend to it? In the meantime, I'd like a word with Miss Thornhill – if you'll lead the way, Hawgood."

Dr. Scan left the room, followed by Hawgood and Constable Lambert.

Pons flashed me a quick, quizzical look. "A morbid little puzzle, eh, Parker?"

"Horrible," I said.

"I noticed your concentrated silence. What conclusions have you drawn?"

"Only that someone must have hated this man with singular passion," I said.

"You do not think it odd that this should be so?"

"I don't follow," I said.

"Forgive me. I failed to make myself clear. I submit that this is a curious method of seeking revenge on a man like the Squire. The Squire was given to abrupt, disagreeable reactions – the kind which would inspire equally quick anger and, if vengeance at all, sudden violent action – a blow with a poker, seized on the place, a shot from a handy gun, or stabbing with a convenient weapon. Such premeditation as is implied in the use of this weapon indicates something more than sudden blind rage."

"Perhaps that's true for most occasions when the Squire had an outburst of rage," I said. "But not all. Consider young Hawgood, for instance, who had six months in quod to brood about his father's employer."

"Remote – but a possibility," conceded Pons.

"Moreover," I pressed my point with some assurance, "it took premeditation to work out such a diabolical plan for murder as this."

Pons smiled. "I believe I made the same point for a different effect," he said. "What we shall have to have, I fear, is some sort of record of the Squire's outbursts."

"Perhaps I can help you, Mr. Pons," said a feminine voice from the threshold of the study.

"Miss Emily Thornhill," said Constable Lambert at her heels.

The attractive young woman advancing toward us, her dark eyes flashing, continued, "I learned you were on the premises, Mr. Pons. I do not propose to be interrogated twice. Please come to the drawing-room, gentlemen."

"As you wish, Miss Thornhill," said Pons.

Our hostess led the way with an almost feline grace. She was striking too, in a curiously feline way – with high cheek bones, a narrow face, and a kind of petulant, sensuous mouth. The drawing-room was in the wing opposite the study. Once there, Miss Thornhill asked us to be seated, making a sweeping motion with her right arm.

"Mr. Lambert, if you please," she said.

"I wanted to ask whether you knew who might wish to see your father dead, Miss Thornhill."

"At least a score of people – and I think I am being conservative."

"Could you be specific?"

"Let me get my diary."

She excused herself and went out.

"Miss Thornhill strikes me as considerably more her father's daughter than she may think," said Pons dryly.

Constable Lambert raised his eyebrows and nodded.

"Capable," Pons went on, "of anything the eternal feminine is capable of doing."

"You open up limitless possibilities, Mr. Pons," said the constable.

"I have somewhat more skill at this than at darts, Lambert."

We fell silent, and in a few moments Miss Thornhill returned, carrying a hasped, leatherbound, book. Her manner was coldly business-like, as if she were determined to get this unpleasantness over with as soon as possible.

"Ever since my mother died, I have kept a record of Father's rages," she said with an almost chilling matter-of-factness. "Where would you like me to begin?"

The Constable glanced at Pons.

"A fortnight ago," said Pons.

She gave him a calculating glance, then opened her book.

"Twelfth," she said. "Nothing pertinent.

"Thirteenth. Father sacked Fred today – that's Fred Mason, who was our gardener. He would not give him reference. Fred left in a towering fury.

"Fourteenth. Father struck John this morning. John Blakiston was Fred's assistant. John quit.

"Fifteenth. Nothing.

"Sixteenth. Father quarrelled with the postman."

"Mr. Quigg?" interrupted the Constable.

"Yes, Mr. Lambert. Father expected a letter he didn't receive in the mail that morning. Characteristically, he blamed the postman for it. One word led to another. They all but came to blows."

"Go on, Miss Thornhill, please."

"Seventeenth. Father dressed down poor Keith today for presuming to have fallen in love with me. It was especially hard on him after what I had told him."

"What had you told your father?" asked Constable Lambert

"Not Father – Keith Hallis. That was my fault, really. Keith is our head trainer, Mr. Pons. I suppose he thought himself in love with me – and perhaps I did encourage him a bit." She smiled. "I fear that's the nature of a woman. That morning Keith asked me to go to Doncaster with him. I always go, of course – but it was quite impossible to do as he asked. I'm afraid I found it necessary to be quite unforgivably brutal. It was afterward that Father had words with him. He wanted to discharge him, but of course, that was absurd – he's our best trainer, so good with the horses, and such a handyman."

"I see. Pray continue," said the Constable.

"Eighteenth. Father and Arthur Robson quarrelled. Father knocked him down.

"Nineteenth. Nothing.

"Twentieth. Father humiliated Hawgood by ragging him about Alan. That's Hawgood's son. Father had him in gaol six months for stealing some trifle from the study."

"Did Hawgood ever protest this action?" interposed Pons.

"He pleaded with Father, of course – but I'm sure Hawgood knew it was of no use to do so. He offered to pay many times what the thing was worth, but Father said the law must take its course."

"What was the object stolen?" asked Pons.

"An inlaid dagger, Mr. Pons."

She went on. "Twenty-first. Nothing.

"Twenty-second. Father and I had words today. He referred to me with his usual endearments."

She paused, leafed over three pages, and finished with, "That seems to be all, gentlemen."

"If I may ask, Miss Thornhill – what were those 'usual little endearments'?"

"If you must know, Mr. Pons, my father was quite often in the habit of referring to me as 'My little bitch' or 'My damned slut.'"

"Thank you."

"Is there anything more?"

"I think not," said Pons before the Constable could speak.

"Then, if you'll excuse me, I'll return to my room. Good day, gentlemen."

We came to our feet and stood while she left the drawing-room. Then Constable Lambert turned to Pons.

"You'll want to speak with some of these men, I suspect, Mr. Pons. Hallis and young Hawgood are on the grounds. We can begin with them."

"If you don't mind, Constable – I have a fancy to begin with Mr. Quigg. Do you know where we might find him at this hour?"

After he had recovered from his astonishment, Constable Lambert took out his watch and consulted it. "He should be in the vicinity of West End House," he said, "at the far end of Askrigg."

"Let us just see whether we can intercept him on his way back from there to the Post Office. I take it that is his course, Constable?"

"Yes, Mr. Pons."

"Let us not forget to impound those lethal binoculars," said Pons.

"I have no intention of forgetting them."

"And, before I forget, Constable," continued Pons, "you should have this. Its script may prove of singular importance."

He gave to Constable Lambert the little rectangle of linen paper he had picked up from the carpet in the study.

"Thank you, Mr. Pons."

Within a few minutes we left the house, Squire Thornhill's body having preceded us on its way to the undertaker's. Constable Lambert wheeled his bicycle for a way down the road in silence. But his curiosity finally got the better of him. "If you don't mind my asking, Mr. Pons – despite my knowing something of your methods – but why Mr. Quigg before anyone else?"

"Ah, that is elementary, Constable. I am looking for the most direct path to the identity of the murderer. Let us first by then fix upon the source of the binoculars. Did they come by hand or by post? I should think it highly unlikely that they came by hand, in the circumstances. That leaves us the post."

"I see, Mr. Pons." But it was perfectly evident on Constable Lambert's honest features that he did not see any more than I.

We walked in silence, save for the cries of birds, the occasional barking of a dog from behind a hedge, and the rising sound of traffic from the street before us. Constable Lambert walked in manifest perplexity, and Pons went along, his grey eyes dancing, an annoyingly suggestive smile touching his thin lips, as if he cradled some knowledge which had escaped us.

We descended into the village, crossed the High Bridge over Askrigg Beck, passed the Crown Inn, passed Robinson's Gateways and the Post Office, and then, as we were approaching the Conservative Club, saw the postman bearing us from the opposite direction.

"There's Quigg," said the Constable.

"Capital!" cried Pons, quickening his steps.

"Quigg!" called the Constable, and, having succeeded in getting his attention, he added, "We'd like a word with you." The red-haired young man waited upon us.

"Mr. Quigg," said the Constable, as we came up, "this is Mr. Solar Pons. He'd like to know about that quarrel you had with the Squire."

Quigg's faced colored hotly. "Go ask him!" he said, in manifest irritation.

"Squire's dead," said the Constable bluntly.

"Dead!" cried the postman.

"Murdered," said the Constable.

"I'm not surprised," said Quigg tartly.

"Forgive me," said Pons. "Constable Lambert mistook my intention. I have no interest in any words you had with Mr. Thornhill."

"Yes, sir. What then?" Quigg waited.

"This morning you delivered at Thornhill Hall a package addressed to Miss Emily Thornhill, did you not?"

"Yes, Mr. Pons."

"Did you happen to notice where it was posted?"

"London, E. C. 4. Didn't see any return address."

"Thank you, Mr. Quigg. Be on your round."

"Miss Emily!" cried Constable Lambert, as the postman walked away.

"The binoculars were intended for her, Constable. Keith Hallis is your man. She struck his vanity a cruel blow. Her father, characteristically, accepted the package, tore it open, burned the wrappings, and was slain as he focussed the glass while taking a glance out the windows.

"I thought it extremely unlikely that an anonymous gift would be sent to the Squire or any other man with a card inscribed in a masculine hand: *From an admirer.* You should have no difficulty gathering the evidence to convict Hallis – turning up the manufacturer of the glasses, tracing Hallis's movements on his last visit to London, sampling his script. I commend the patient task to you."

For a long minute Constable Lambert goggled at Pons, but at last he said, "Mr. Pons, I don't know how to thank you."

"Say nothing, Constable. The deduction is easy, if logical. The task of assembling the evidence to convict is rather more difficult."

"I would never have thought it, Mr. Pons!"

"Come, come – it would inevitably have occurred to you, Lambert." Pons turned to me. "I think, Parker, we have ample time in which to complete our little jaunt."

IV

THE ADVENTURE OF THE INTARSIA BOX

Solar Pons and I were at breakfast one fair morning only a week after our return from the country and the curious affair of the Whispering Knights, when the door below was thrown violently open, and there was a rush of feet on the stairs that stopped short of our threshold. Pons looked up, his grey eyes intent, his whole lean figure taut with waiting.

"A young woman, agitated," he said, nodding. He flashed a glance at the clock. "Scarcely seven. It is surely a matter of some urgency to her. The hour has only now occurred to her. She hesitates. No, she is coming on."

The sound of footsteps was now scarcely audible, but they came on up the stairs. In a moment there was a faint, timorous tapping on the door to our quarters, and an equally timorous voice, asking beyond the door, "Mr. Pons? Mr. Solar Pons?"

"Pray play the gentleman, Parker," said Pons.

I sprang up and threw open the door.

A sandy-haired young woman not much over her middle-twenties stood there, a package wrapped in a shawl pressed to her breast. She looked from one to the other of us out of candid blue eyes, her full lower lip trembling uncertainly, a slow flush mounting her cheeks toward the scattering of freckles that bridged her nose and swept under her eyes. Then, with that unerring intuition that women especially seem to have, she fixed upon Pons.

"Mr. Pons! I hope I'm not intruding. I had to come. I had to do something. Uncle will do nothing – just wait for whatever is to happen. Oh, it's dreadful, Mr. Pons, dreadful!"

"Do come in, Miss... ?"

"I am Flora Morland of Morland Park, Mr. Pons. You may have heard of my uncle – Colonel Burton Morland?"

"Retired resident at Malacca," said Pons promptly. "But do compose yourself, Miss Morland. Let me take that box you're holding."

"No, not" she cried, and pressed it momentarily closer to her body. Then she bit her lip and smiled weakly. "But that is why I came. Forgive me, Mr. Pons. You shall see for yourself – now."

Thereupon she threw back the shawl and revealed a box, scarcely as large as a cigar box made of *kamuning* wood. It was beautifully carved on the top and around on all sides, with curious figures, like a bas-relief. It seemed obviously Oriental in design.

"Open it, Mr. Pons, do!" She shuddered a little. "Oh, I don't know how I could bear to have carried it all this way. I can't look again!"

Pons took the box gently from her. He pushed the breakfast dishes to one side and set the box on the table. He stood a moment admiring its workmanship, while Miss Morland waited with an apprehensive tautness that was almost tangible in the room. Then he threw it open.

I fear I gasped. I do not know what area expected to see – a priceless jewel, perhaps? – a bibliophile's treasure? – something fitting to the exquisite box containing it. Certainly it was nothing I could have dreamed in my wildest imaginings! In the box laid a mummified human hand, severed at the wrist, affixed to the bottom of the box by two bands of white silk.

Pons' emotion showed only in his eyes, which lit up with quick interest. He touched the dried skin with the fingertips of one hand, while caressing the carved box with the other.

"Intarsia," murmured Pons. "An Italian art, Miss Morland. But this box would appear to be of Oriental origin; the subjects of the ornamentation are all Oriental. Would you care now to tell us how you came by it?"

He closed the box almost with regret, and, Miss Morland having taken the stuffed chair near the fireplace, came to stand against the mantel, filling his pipe with the detestable shag he smoked.

Miss Morland clasped her hands together. "I hardly know how to begin, Mr. Pons," she said.

"Let us start with this fascinating object you have brought us," suggested Pons.

"It was delivered to my uncle three days ago, Mr. Pons. I myself took it from the postman. It was mailed first-class from Kuala Lumpur. My uncle was in his study that morning, and I took it in to him. I recall that his face darkened when he saw the package, but I supposed that it was only in wonder as to who might have sent it. It was ten years ago that he left Malaya. He looked for some clue as to its origin; there was no return address on the package. He began to take off its wrappings. I had turned away from him to put some books back on the shelves, when suddenly I heard him make a kind of explosive sound, and on the instant he slipped from his chair to the floor. He had swooned dead away. I ran over to him of course, Mr. Pons – and that's how I came to see what was in the box. There was a little card, too – linen paper, I thought, Mr. Pons – I believe such details are important to you. On it was written in a flowing hand a single sentence: *I will come for you.*"

"The card is not now in the box," said Pons.

"I suppose my uncle removed it. I closed the box, Mr. Pons – I couldn't bear to look at what was in it. Then I brought my uncle around. I expected him to tell me what was in the box and what it all meant, but he said nothing – never a word. Seeing that the box was closed, he assumed that he had closed it before or as he fainted, and that I didn't know what was in it. Mr. Pons, I was deeply shocked by what was in the box, but I was even more profoundly disturbed by my uncle's failure to say anything at all of it to me. Since the day he received it, furthermore, he has been very busy – and everything he has done is in the way of putting his affairs in order."

"Did your uncle notify the police?"

"If so, I don't know of it, Mr. Pons."

Pons puffed reflectively on his pipe for a moment before he asked, "I take it you are an orphan and have been living with your uncle. For how long?"

"Five years," she replied. "My mother died when I was very young, and my father five years after Uncle Burton returned from Malaya. He has been very kind to me. He has treated me as his own child."

"Your uncle is not married?"

"Uncle Burton was married at one time. I believe there was some cloud over the marriage. My father occasionally talked about my aunt in deprecatory terms – called her 'the Eurasian woman'. My cousin Nicholas, who spent the last five years of Uncle Burton's tenure with him in Malacca, also married a Eurasian woman. My aunt died before my uncle's return to England."

"Your cousin?"

"He returned with Uncle Burton. He's a barrister with offices in the City. His wife is the proprietress of a small – but I believe thriving – importing business in the Strand."

"Your cousin – Nicholas Morland, is it?"

"There were three brothers, Mr. Pons – my father, Nick's father, and Uncle Burton."

"Your cousin, I take it, was your uncle's assistant in Malacca?"

"Yes, Mr. Pons."

"How old is your uncle, Miss Morland?"

"Seventy."

"How long had he been the resident in Malacca?"

"Fifteen years. He went out there when he was forty. I never really knew him, Mr. Pons, until his return. I hadn't been born when he was sent out. But Uncle Burton seemed to be very fond of me from the moment he saw me, and it seemed only natural that he would invite me to live with him when Father died. Uncle Burton is very wealthy, he has many servants, and, though he is regarded by some of them as a martinet, they do stay – most of them. And he has a large and secluded home in Chipping Barnet. It seemed the most natural thing to do – to live with him. He sent me to school, and through a small private college. For my part, I am expected to play hostess whenever he has one of his small parties, which are attended chiefly by my cousin and his wife and some other ex-Colonials and their wives. I rather like that now – I didn't at first. But my uncle is the soul of rectitude; he will tolerate no deviation from proper conduct – so there are never any social problems for me to deal with."

"Your uncle's heirs – who are they?"

Our client looked momentarily startled. "Why, I suppose Nick and I are his only heirs," she said. "I know nothing of his affairs, Mr. Pons. But there is no one else. All our relatives of my uncle's generation are dead, and Nick and I are the only ones of our generation. Nick has no children – so there is no coming generation, either." She took a deep breath and asked impulsively, "Mr. Pons – can you get to the bottom of this mystery? It troubles me very much to see Uncle Burton – well, preparing for death – that's what he's doing, Mr. Pons – it really is."

"Your uncle has no knowledge of your coming here, Miss Morland?"

"None. I left at dawn. He seldom rises before eight."

"Then you've not had breakfast, Miss Morland."

"No, Mr. Pons."

"Allow me!" Pons strode to the door, opened it, stuck his head out and called. "Mrs. Johnson, if you please!" He turned back to our client. "Pray give me a few minutes to ponder your problem, Miss Morland. In the meantime, Mrs. Johnson will be happy to prepare breakfast for you in her quarters. Will you not, Mrs. Johnson?" he asked of our long-suffering landlady as she appeared on the threshold.

"That I will, to be sure, Mr. Pons. If you'll come with me, Miss?"

Miss Morland, too surprised to protest, allowed herself to be led from the room by Mrs. Johnson.

The door had hardly closed behind them before Pons was once again at the box, opening it. I was drawn to his side.

"Is this not an unique warning indeed, Parker?" he asked.

"I have seldom seen anything as gruesome."

"It was intended to be. I submit that this severed hand must have a deep significance for our client's uncle. What do you make of it?"

I bent and peered closely at it, examining it as well as I could without disturbing it or removing it from the box. "A man's right hand," I said. "Of probably about forty, not much older, certainly. It is brown-skinned, not only from age. Eurasian?"

"Native. See how beautifully kept the nails are! This man did little work. There are no observable callouses. The hand is smooth even to the fingertips. How long would you say this hand has been severed?"

"Without more scientific apparatus, I should think it impossible to say."

"Could it be as old as, say, Colonel Morland's tenure in Malacca?"

"I should think so. But what could it mean to Morland?"

"Ah, Parker, when we can answer that question we will know why it was sent to him." He smiled grimly. "I fancy it concerns some dark episode of his past. He retired at fifty-five. Is that not early?"

"His health, perhaps, demanded his retirement."

"Or his conduct."

"Miss Morland speaks of him as a model of rectitude."

"And as something of a martinet. Conduct in search of rectitude may be as reprehensible as its opposite." He touched the silk bands. "What do you make of these, Parker?"

"If I may venture a guess – white is the color of mourning in the Orient," I said.

"The bands are new," observed Pons.

"That is certainly elementary," I could not help saying. "I can think of several reasons why they should be. What puzzles me is the reason for being of the hand in the first place."

"I submit its owner kept it as long as he lived."

"Well, that's reasonable," I agreed. "It has been properly mummified. Are we to take it that the owner is still alive?"

"If he were sufficiently attached to this appendage while he lived, would he so readily have sent it off?"

"Hardly."

"Unless it had a message to convey or an errand to perform."

"Absurd!"

"Yet it did convey a message to Colonel Morland. It may be gruesome, but surely not so much so as to cause a normal and healthy man to swoon at sight of it. It reminds me of that horrible little trifle of wizard lore known as the glory hand – the bewitched, animated hand of a dead man sent to perform its owner's wishes, even to murder."

"Superstitious claptrap!"

"Colonel Morland, at least, is convinced that his life is in danger, and that the threat to it emanates from Malaya. Let us just have a look at the ship's registry, before our client returns, to determine the number of ships that have docked from Malaya in the past few days."

We had time to search back five days before our client returned from Mrs. Johnson's quarters; during those five days no ship from Malaya had docked at England's ports, though a freighter, the *Alor Star*, was listed as due within twenty-four hours. At Miss Morland's entrance, Pons thrust the papers aside.

"Thank you, indeed, Mrs. Johnson," said Pons as our landlady turned at the threshold. "And now, Miss Morland, two or three questions occur to me. Pray be seated."

Our client, now somewhat more composed and less uncertain in her manner, took her former seat and waited expectantly.

"Miss Morland, when your uncle came around, did he say or do anything significant?" asked Pons.

"He didn't say a word," she answered. "He was very pale. He looked for the box and seemed relieved to find it closed. He picked it up at once. I asked him, 'Are you all right, Uncle?' He said, 'Just a trifle dizzy. You run along.' I left him, but, of course, I did watch to be sure he would be all right. He hurried straight to his bedroom – with this box. He hid it there, for when he came out again in a few moments, he no longer carried it. He then locked himself in his study, and within two hours his solicitor came; he could only have sent for him, because Mr. Harris would certainly not otherwise have come to call at that hour."

"You evidently found the intarsia box, Miss Morland."

"My uncle has in his bedroom only a cabinet, a bureau, and an old sea-chest which he fancied and which had accompanied him on his journeys. He served a short term in the Royal Navy as a young man, before entering the foreign service. He acquired the chest at that time. I knew that the box had to be in one of those three places, and I found it carefully covered up in the chest while my uncle was closeted with Mr. Harris. Last night, about eleven o'clock, after he went to sleep, I slipped in and took the box so that I might be ready to come to you without the risk of waking Uncle Burton by taking the box this morning."

"Did your uncle mention the box to anyone?"

"I don't know, Mr. Pons. But I should think that if he had spoken of it to Mr. Harris, he would have shown it to him. Yet Uncle Burton never left the study while Mr. Harris was in the house; so he could not have done so."

"I see. I think, then, Miss Morland, our only recourse is to ask your uncle the questions you cannot answer."

Our client's hand flew to her lips; an expression of dismay appeared in her eyes. "Oh, Mr. Pons," she cried, "I'm afraid of what Uncle Burton might say."

"Miss Morland, I believe your uncle's life to be in great jeopardy. This belief he evidently shares. He can do no more than refuse to see us, and he can certainly not take umbrage at your attempt to be of service to him."

Her hand fell back to her lap. "Well, that's true," she decided.

Pons looked at the clock. "It is now nine. We can take the Underground at Baker Street and be at Watford Junction within the hour. Let us leave the box, if you please."

Our client sat for but a moment, undecided. Then, pressing her lips determinedly together, she got to her feet. "Very well, Mr. Pons. My uncle can do no worse than give me the back of his tongue!"

As we drew near to the home of Colonel Morland in the cab we had taken at Watford Junction, Pons' face grew more grim. "I fear we are too late, Miss Morland," he said presently.

"Oh, Mr. Pons! Why do you say so?" cried our client.

"No less than four police vehicles have passed us – two returning, two going our way," he answered. "I should be very much surprised not to find the police at Morland Park."

Miss Morland pressed a handkerchief to her lips.

Nor was Pons in error. Two police cars stood before the tall hedge that separated the park-like grounds which our client indicated as her uncle's home, and a constable stood on guard at the gate in the hedge.

"Young Mecker," murmured Pons at sight of him.

As the cab pulled up, Mecker stepped forward to wave it away, then, his arm upraised, recognized Pons getting out. His arm dropped.

"Mr. Pons!" he cried. "How could you have learned?" Then he caught sight of our client. "Could this be Miss Flora Morland?"

"It could be," said our client. "Please! Tell me what has happened?"

"Inspector Jamison has been looking for you, Miss Morland. Please come with me."

"Never mind, Mecker," interposed Pons. "We'll take her in."

"Very well, sir. Thank you, sir." He, shook his head, frowning. "Dreadful business, sir, dreadful."

Our client stood for a moment, one hand on Pons' arm, trembling.

"I am afraid, Miss Morland," said Pons with unaccustomed gentleness, "that what your uncle feared has come to pass."

We went up a closely hedged walk arbored over with trees to a classically Georgian country house of two and a half storeys. The front door was open to the warm summer morning; just inside it stood the portly figure of Inspector Seymour Jamison of Scotland Yard, talking with another constable. He turned abruptly at our entrance, frowning.

"Mr. Solar Pons, the private enquiry agent," he said heavily. "Do you smell these matters, Pons?" Then his eyes fell upon our client. "Aha! Miss Flora Morland. We've been looking for you, Miss Morland."

"Please! What has happened?" she beseeched him.

"You don't know?"

"I do not."

"Colonel Morland was found murdered in his bed this morning," said Jamison coldly. "The house was locked, no window had been forced, and you were missing. I must ask you, Miss Morland, to come into the study with me."

"I should like to look into the bedroom, Jamison," said Pons.

"By all means. The photographer is there now, but he should be finished soon. Just down the hall, the third door on the left. Around the stairs."

Our client shot Pons a beseeching glance; he smiled reassuringly. Then she turned and went submissively with Inspector Jamison into the study, which was evidently on the right.

Pons pushed past the police photographer into the late Colonel Morland's bedroom. Before us lay a frightful scene. Colonel Morland – a tall, broad-chested man – lay outspread on his back on his bed, a wavy Malay *kris* driven almost to the hilt into his heart. Most shocking of all – his right hand had been severed at the wrist and lay where it had fallen in a pool of blood on the carpet beside the bed. Gouts of blood had spattered the bed; a froth of blood had welled from the dead man's lips to colour his thick moustache; and the wide staring eyes seemed still to wear an expression of the utmost horror.

The room all around was a shambles. Whoever had slain our client's uncle had torn it apart in search of something. The colonel's sea chest lay open, its contents strewn about; the drawers of the bureau – save for the very smallest at the top – had been pulled open and emptied; and the contents of the tall wardrobe-cabinet, even to the uppermost shelves, were banked about the hassock that stood before it. The sight was almost enough to unnerve a stronger man than I, and I marveled at Pons' cool, keen detachment as he looked searchingly upon the scene.

The photographer, having finished, departed.

"How long would you say he has been dead, Parker?" asked Pons.

I stepped around gingerly and made a cursory examination. "At least eight hours," I said, presently. "I should put it at between midnight and two o'clock – not before, and not very long after."

"Before our client left the house," murmured Pons.

He stood for a moment where he was. Then he stepped gingerly over to the bed and looked down at Colonel Morland's body.

"The *kris* does not appear to have been disturbed," he said, "which suggests that the murderer carried a second weapon solely for the purpose of severing his victim's hand."

"A ritual weapon!" I cried. "And carried away with him."

Pons smiled lightly. "Cut with a single sweeping stroke, very cleanly," he observed.

He stepped away from the bed and began to move carefully among the objects strewn about, disturbing nothing. He went straight to the bureau, the top of which had evidently not been disturbed, for what I assumed to be the dead man's watch and wallet lay there. The wallet was the first object of Pons' attention; he picked it up and examined its contents. "Twenty-seven pound notes," he murmured.

"So the object of this search could hardly have been money," I said.

Pons shook his head impatiently. "No, no, Parker – the murderer was looking for the intarsia box. The top of the bureau was not disturbed because had it been there, the box would have been instantly apparent; nor have the top drawers been opened because they are not deep enough to hold the box."

He moved cautiously to the side of the bed, avoiding the pool of blood which had gushed from Colonel Morland's cleanly severed wrist. "The murderer must have stood just here," he said, and dropped to his knees to scrutinize the carpet intently. He was somewhat hampered by the presence of bloodstains, but I could see by the glint in his eyes that had seen something of significance, however invisible it was to me, for he gave a small sound of satisfaction as he picked something from the carpet just back from the edge of the great bed and put it into two of the little envelopes he always carried.

Just as he rose from his position, Inspector Jamison came into the room, wearing a patent glow of confidence.

"Nasty little job here, Pons," he said almost cheerfully. "You'll be sorry to learn I've sent Miss Morland off to the Yard to be put through it."

"Indeed," said Pons. "What admirable – and needlessly precipitate dispatch! You have reason to think her involved?"

"My dear fellow," said Jamison patronizingly. "Consider. Every window and door of this house was locked. Only four people had keys – Colonel Morland, whose key is on his ring; his valet – who was his batboy in Malacca and who discovered his body; the housekeeper, and Miss Morland. All their keys are in their possession. Nothing has been forced. Miss Morland, I am told by Mr. Harris, the Colonel's counsel, stands to inherit sixty percent of a considerable estate – considerable even after the Crown duties."

"It does not seem to you significant that on so warm a night this house should have been locked up so tightly?" asked Pons.

"You're not having me on that, Pons," retorted Jamison, grinning. "We know all about that intarsia box. Morland was in fear for his life."

"You are suggesting then that Miss Morland slipped into the room, stabbed her uncle, cut off his right hand, searched the room until she turned up the box, and then made her way to Number 7B to enlist my services?"

"Hardly that. She is hardly strong enough to have driven that *kris* into him with such force."

"Hardly," agreed Pons dryly.

"But there is nothing to prevent her having hired an accomplice."

"And what motive could she possibly have had for cutting off her uncle's hand?" pressed Pons.

"What better way could be devised to confuse the investigation into the motive for so gruesome a crime."

"And Miss Morland seems to you, after your conversation with her, the kind of young lady who could lend herself to such a crime?"

"Come, come, Pons. You have a softness for a pretty face," said Jamison.

"I submit that this would have been a most fantastic rigmarole to go through simply to inherit the wealth of a man who, by all the evidence, granted her every whim. No, Jamison, it won't wash."

"That intarsia box – she tells me it is in your possession. We shall have to have it."

"Send 'round to 7B for it. But give me at least today with it, will you?"

"I'll send for it tomorrow."

"Tell me – you've questioned the servants, I suppose? Did anyone hear anything in the night?"

"Not a sound. And I may say that the dog, which habitually sleeps at the front door of the house, outside, never once was heard to bark. I need hardly tell you the significance of that."

"It suggests that the murderer entered..."

"Or was let in."

"By the back door."

Jamison's face reddened. He raised his voice. "It means that since the dog did nothing in the nighttime the murderer was known to him."

Pons clucked sympathetically. "You ought to stay away from Sir Arthur's stories, my dear chap. They have a tendency to vitiate your style."

"I suppose you will be telling us to look for a giant of a man who can charm dogs," said Jamison with heavy sarcasm.

"Quite the contrary. Look for a short, lithe man who, in this case at least, probably went barefooted." He turned and pointed to the scarcely visible hassock. "Only a man shorter than average would have had to use that hassock to look at the top shelves of the cabinet. The indentations in the carpet indicate that the hassock's usual position is over against the wall beside the cabinet."

Jamison's glance flashed to the hassock, and returned, frowning, to Pons.

"If you don't mind, Jamison, I'll just have a look around out in back. Then perhaps you could send us back to Watford Junction in one of the police cars."

"Certainly, Pons. Come along."

Jamison led the way out and around the stairs to a small areaway from which doors opened to the kitchen on the right, and a small store room on the left, and into the backyard. A maid and an elderly woman, manifestly the housekeeper, sat red-eyed at a table in the kitchen; Jamison hesitated, evidently of the opinion that Pons wished to speak with them, but Pons' interest was in the back door, where he crouched to look at the lock.

"We've been all through that, Pons," said Jamison with an edge of impatience in his voice.

Pons ignored him. He opened the door, crouched to examine the sill, then dropped to his knees and, on all fours, crawled out to the recently reset flagstone walk beyond it.

From one place he took up a pinch of soil and dropped it into one of his envelopes. At another he pointed wordlessly, beckoning to Inspector Jamison, who came and saw the unmistakable print of human toes.

Then he sprang up and went back into the house, Jamison and myself at his heels. He found a telephone directory, consulted it briefly, and announced that he was ready to leave, if Jamison would be kind enough to lend us a police car and driver.

Once again on the Underground, I asked Pons, "We're not going back to 7B?"

"No, Parker. I am delighted to observe how well you read me. I daresay we ought to lose no time discovering the secret of the intarsia box. Since Colonel Moreland is dead; we shall have to ask Nicholas Morland whether he can explain it. You'll recall that he spent the last five years of his uncle's residency with him. He has an office in the Temple. I took the trouble to look him up in the directory before we left Morland Park."

"I followed the matter of the murderer's height readily enough," I said, "but how did you arrive at his being barefooted?"

"There were in the carpet beside the bed, just where a man might have stood to deliver the death blow, three tiny files of soil particles, in such a position as to suggest the imprint of toes. The soil was quite probably picked up among the flagstones."

"And, you know, Pons – Jamison has a point about the dog."

Pons smiled enigmatically. "The dog did nothing. Very well. Either he knew the murderer – or he didn't hear him, which is quite as likely. A barefooted man could travel with singular noiselessness. And Morland Park is a paradise for prowlers!" He looked at me, his eyes dancing. "Consider the severed hand. Since you are so busy making deductions, perhaps you have accounted for it."

"Now you press me," I admitted, "that seems to me the most elementary detail of all. I suggest that an indignity the late

Colonel Morland committed in the past has now been visited upon him."

"Capital! Capital!" cried Pons. "You have only to keep this up, my dear fellow, and I can begin to think of retiring."

"You are making sport of me!" I protested.

"On the contrary. I could not agree with you more. There are one or two little points about the matter that trouble me, but I have no doubt these will be resolved in due time."

For the rest of the journey Pons rode in silent contemplation, his eyes closed, the thumb and forefinger of his right hand ceaselessly caressing the lobe of his ear. He did not open his eyes again until we came into Temple Station.

Nicholas Morland proved to be a somewhat frosty man in his early forties. He was dressed conservatively, but in clothes befitting his station. Save for the difference in years, he was not unlike his late uncle in appearance – with the same kind of moustache, the same outward thrust of the lips, the same bushy brows. His frosty mien was superficial, for it collapsed as he listened to Pons' concise summary of events, and little beads of perspiration appeared at his temples.

"We must rely upon you, Mr. Morland," concluded Pons, "to explain the significance of the intarsia box and its contents.

Morland came shakily to his feet and walked back and forth across his office, biting his lip. "It is something I had hoped never to have to speak about" he said at last. "Is it really necessary, Mr. Pons?"

"I assure you it is. Scotland Yard will expect to hear about it before the day is out. I am here in advance of their coming because I am acting in the interests of your cousin."

"Of course. I quite understand."

He took another turn or two about his office, and then sat down again, dabbing at his forehead with a handkerchief.

"Well, Mr. Pons, it is a matter that does not reflect at all well upon my late uncle," he began. "As Flora may perhaps have told you, Uncle Burton married an Eurasian woman – a very fine, very beautiful woman some ten years his junior – perhaps as much as fifteen, I cannot be sure, though I suspect my wife would know. I am sure you are aware that matters of moral conduct among the ethnically mixed peoples of the Federated States of Malaya are considered lax by British standards, and perhaps it was true that my aunt engaged in improper conduct with Bendarloh Ali – an uncle of my wife's, one of the better native families in Malacca. My uncle thought he would lose face, and he set about to prevent it. My aunt died – there is some reason to believe that it was by poison at my uncle's hands. Her lover was arrested – some valuable items belonging to my uncle were found in his home – he was accused of having stolen them, on no stronger evidence than their presence in his home – and he suffered the indignity of having his right hand cut off at the wrist. That is the sum total of the matter, sir."

"How long ago did this happen, Mr. Morland?"

"Only a month or two before he was sent home. The Sultan of Malacca was outraged – though he had approved the punishment, he was later led to repudiate it – and demanded the recall of the resident. The Governor really had no alternative but to relieve my uncle of his post."

"Over fifteen years, then. Does it seem likely that he would wait so long to take vengeance?"

"Not he, Mr. Pons, My uncle's victim died three months ago. I think it not inconsistent of the Malay character that his son might believe it incumbent upon him to avenge the honor of his house and the indignity done his father."

"I submit it would be an unnatural son who would separate his father's right hand from his remains," said Pons.

Morland shook his head thoughtfully. "Mr. Pons, I would tend to agree. There is this point to consider – the hand sent my uncle may not have been Bendarloh Ali's. Even if it were, I suppose the family represents that ethnic mixture so common in Malacca that no standard of conduct consistent with ancient Malay customs could be ascribed to it."

Pons sat for a few moments in contemplative silence. Then he said, "You are very probably aware that you and your cousin will share your uncle's estate."

"Oh, yes. There is no one else. We are a small family, and unless Flora marries, we will very likely die out entirely. Oh, there are distant cousins – but we have not been in touch for many years." He shrugged. "But it's a matter of indifference to me. My practice is quite sufficient for our needs – though I suppose my wife can find a use for what Uncle Burton may leave us, what with the constant innovations at her shop."

The telephone rang suddenly at Morland's elbow. He lifted it to his ear, said, "Morland here," and listened. When he put it down after but a brief period, he said, "Gentlemen, the police are on the way."

Pons got to his feet with alacrity. "One more question, Mr. Morland. Your relations with your uncle – were they friendly, tolerant, distant?"

"The three of us had dinner at Morland Park once a month, Mr. Pons," said Morland a little stiffly.

"Three?"

"My wife's cousin lives with us. Uncle Burton naturally would not exclude him."

"Thank you, sir."

We took our leave.

Outside, Pons strode purposefully along, some destination in mind, his eyes fixed upon an inner landscape. Within a few minutes we were once more on the Underground, and rode in silence unbroken by any word from Pons, until we reached Trafalgar Station and emerged to walk in the Strand.

"Pons," I cried finally, exasperated at his silence. "It's noon. What are we doing here?"

"Ah, patience, Parker, patience. The Strand is one of the most fascinating areas in the world. I mean to idle a bit and shop."

Within half an hour, Pons had exchanged his deerstalker for a conservative summer hat, leaving his deerstalker to be dispatched to our quarters by post; he had bought a light summer coat, which he carried loosely on his arm; and he had added a walking stick to his ensemble – all to my open-mouthed astonishment. He presented quite a different picture from that to which I had become accustomed in the years I had shared his quarters, and he offered no explanation of his purchases.

We continued in the Strand until we came to a small shop modestly proclaiming that antiques and imports were to be had.

"Ah, here we are," said Pons. "I beg you, Parker, keep your face frozen. You have an unhappy tendency to show your reactions on it."

So saying, he went into the shop.

A bell, tinkling in a back room, brought out a dapper, brown-skinned man of indeterminate age; he came up to us and bowed. He looked little older than a boy, but he was not a boy. He smiled, flashing his white teeth, and said, "If it please you, gentlemen – I am here to serve you."

"Are you the proprietor?" asked Pons abruptly.

"No, sir. I am Ahmad. I work for Mrs. Morland."

"I am looking," said Pons, "for an intarsia box."

"Ah. Of any precise size?"

"Oh, so – and so," said Pons, describing the size of the intarsia box Miss Morland had brought to our quarters.

"Just so. One moment, if you please."

He vanished into the room to the rear, but came out in a very few moments carrying an intarsia box, which he offered to Pons.

"Seventeenth century Italian, sir. Genuine. I trust this is the box you would like."

"It is certainly exquisite work," said Pons. "But, no, it is not quite what I would like. The size is right. But I would like something with Oriental ornamentation."

"Sir, there are no antique intarsia boxes of Oriental manufacture," said Ahmad. "I am sorry."

"I'm not looking for an antique," said Pons. "I am, of course, aware that intarsia boxes were not made in the Orient before the eighteenth century."

Ahmad's pleasant face brightened. "Ah, in that case, sir, I may have something for you."

He vanished once more into the quarters to the rear of the shop.

When he came out this time he carried another intarsia box. With a triumphant smile, he gave it to Pons. Then he stood back to wait upon Pons' verdict.

Pons turned it over, examining it critically. He opened it, smelled it, caressed it with his fingers, and smiled. "Excellent!" he cried. "This will do very well, young man. What is its price?"

"Ten pounds, sir."

Pons paid for it without hesitation. "Pray wrap it with care. I should not like any of that beautifully wrought carving to be damaged – even scratched."

Ahmad beamed. "Sir, you like the intarsia?"

"Young man, I have some knowledge of these things," said Pons almost pontifically. "This is among the finest work of its kind I have seen."

Ahmad backed away from Pons, bowing, his face glowing. He retired once again into the back room, from which presently came the sounds of rustling paper. In just under five minutes Ahmad reappeared and placed the carefully wrapped intarsia box in Pons' hands. He was still glowing with pleasure. Moreover, he had the air of bursting with something he wanted to say, which only decorum prevented his giving voice. Pons strolled leisurely from the shop and away down the street. But, once out of sight of the shop, he moved with alacrity to hail a cab and gave the driver our Praed Street address. "Did you not have the feeling that Ahmad wished to tell us something?" I asked when we were on our way.

"Ah, he told us everything," said Pons, his eyes glinting with good humor. "Ahmad is an artist in intarsia. I trust you observed the costly antiques offered in Mrs. Morland's shop?"

"I did indeed."

"It suggested nothing to you?"

"That her business is thriving, as Miss Morland told us."

I reached over and tapped the package Pons held. "Did it not seem to you that this box is very much like Miss Morland's?"

Pons smiled. "Once the first box is turned out, the pattern is made. The rest come with comparative ease. They are probably identical, not only with each other, but with a score or more of others."

Back in our quarters, Pons carefully unwrapped the intarsia box he had bought and placed it beside our client's. Except for the fact that there was some difference in age between them, they were virtually identical. Pons examined the boxes with singular attention to detail, finding each smallest variation between them.

"Are they identical or not?" I asked finally.

"Not precisely. The box Miss Morland brought us is at least seventy-five years old; it may be a hundred. It is made of the same beautiful *kamuning* wood out of which the Malays fashion the hilts of their weapons – I trust you observed that the handle of the *kris* which killed Colonel Morland was of this same wood. It has been polished many times and waxed; there is actually some other visible wearing away the wood. The other is a copy of a box like this, made by a skilled artist. I suppose there is a demand for objects of this kind and I have no doubt they are to be had in all the shops which have imported pieces from the Orient for sale. Chinese boxes like this are most frequently in metal or ceramic; wood is more commonly in use from Japan down the coast throughout the Polynesians and Melanesians in the south Pacific." He dismissed the intarsia boxes with a gesture. "But now, let us see what we have from the late Colonel Morland's bedroom."

He crossed to the corner where he kept his chemistry apparatus and settled himself to examine the contents of the envelopes he had used at Morland Park. There were but three of them, and it was unlikely that they would occupy him for long. Since I had a professional call to make at two o'clock, I excused myself.

When I returned within the hour, I found Pons waiting expectantly.

"Ah, Parker," he cried, "I trust you are free for the remainder of the afternoon. I am expecting Jamison and together we may be able to put an end to Scotland Yard's harassing of our client."

"Did you learn anything at the slides?" I asked.

"Only confirmation of what I suspected. The particles of soil I found on the carpet beside the bed were identical with the soil around the flagstones, even to grains of limestone, of which the flagstones are made. There seems to be no doubt but that the soil was carried into the house by the bare toes of the murderer. Other than that, there was also just under the edge of the bed a tiny shaving of camphor wood – which is also commonly used by the Malays who work the jungle produce of that country."

"We are still tied to Colonel Morland's past," I said.

"We have never strayed from it," said Pons shortly. "But thus far in the course of the inquiry – unless Scotland Yard has turned up fingerprints on the handle of the *kris* – we have only presumptive, not convicting evidence. It is all very well to know the identity of the murderer; the trick is to convict him. Ah, I hear a motor slowing down – that will be Jamison."

Within a few moments a car door slammed below, and Jamison's heavy tread on the stairs fell to ear.

The Inspector came into our quarters gingerly carrying a small package, which he surrendered to Pons with some relief. "Here it is, Pons," he said. "I had a little trouble getting the loan of it."

"Capital!" cried Pons. He took the package and carried it to the intarsia box he had bought in the shop on the Strand. "I don't suppose you're armed, Jamison?"

"The tradition of the Yard," began Jamison ponderously.

"Yes, yes, I know," said Pons. "Parker, get my revolver."

I went into the bedroom and found Pons' weapon where he had last carelessly laid it down – on the bureau.

"Give it to Jamison, will you?"

"I don't know what you're up to Pons," said Jamison, with some obvious misgiving on his ruddy face. "P'raps that young woman's turned your head."

The contents of the Inspector's package had vanished into the intarsia box, which Pons now took up, having resumed the garb he had bought in the Strand shops.

"Let us be off. I want to try an experiment, Jamison – frankly, it is no more than that. It may succeed. It may not. We shall see."

Our destination was the antique and imports shop in the Strand, and all the way there Pons said nothing, only listened with a sardonic smile on his hawk-like features to Jamison's weighty discourse on the damning circumstances which made our client seem guilty of arranging her uncle's death.

As the police car approached the shop, Pons spoke for the first time to Constable Mecker, who was at the wheel. "Either stop short of the shop or drive past it, Mecker."

Mecker obediently stopped beyond the shop.

"Now, Jamison," said Pons brusquely, as we got out of the car, "hand on gun, and pray be ready. Try to look a little less like a policeman, that's a good fellow."

Pons led the way into the shop, carrying the carefully wrapped intarsia box he had bought only a few hours previously. An extraordinarily handsome Eurasian woman came forward to wait upon him. She was of indeterminate age; she could have been anywhere between twenty and forty, but certainly did not seem over thirty.

"What can I do for you, gentlemen?"

"The young man who waited on me this noon," said Pons, unwrapping the intarsia box as he spoke. "Is he here?"

She nodded, raised her voice to call, "Ahmad!" and stepped back.

Ahmad came out, a look of polite inquiry on his face. He recognized Pons as his noon-hour customer; his eyes fell to the box.

"Sir! You are disappointed?"

"In the beauty of the box, no," said Pons. "But the interior!"

Ahmad stepped lightly forward and took the box, discarding the wrappings. "We shall see," he said, bowing almost obsequiously.

Then he opened the intarsia box.

Instantly, a dramatic and frightening metamorphosis took place. Ahmad's smiling face altered grotesquely; its mask of politeness washed away to reveal dark murderous features, suffused with sudden rage and fear. He dropped the intarsia box – and from it rolled the severed hand of Colonel Burton Morland! Simultaneously, he leaped backward with a feline movement, tore down from the wall behind him a scimitar-like chenangka, and turned threateningly upon Pons.

For scarcely a moment the scene held. Then Mrs. Morland began to waver, and I sprang forward to catch her as she fainted. At the same moment, Inspector Jamison reacted and drew his gun upon Ahmad.

"My compliments, Inspector," said Pons. "You've just taken the murderer of Colonel Morland. I think," he added blandly, "if I were you I should take Mrs. Nicholas Morland along and question her about the profit motive in the death of her husband's uncle. I believe it almost certain that hers was the brain in which this devilish crime was conceived. – Is the lady coming around, Parker?"

"In a few moments," I said.

"Call Mecker," said Jamison, finding his voice.

Pons stepped into the street and shouted for the constable.

"It was not alone the fact that no ship had docked recently from Malaya that made an avenger from the Orient unlikely," said Pons as we rode back to Praed Street on the Underground, "but the same aspect of the matter that so impressed Jamison – the murderer clearly had prior knowledge of Morland Park, something no newly arrived foreigner could have had, and he must have been someone who had ample opportunity to take an impression of the back door key, since he would prefer to enter by that door not guarded by the dog. Nothing in that house was disturbed, save Colonel Morland's room; not a sound aroused anyone throughout the entry into the house and the commission of the crime.

"Yet it was evident that the murderer also had knowledge of the indignity done to Bendarloh Ali. Miss Morland had no such knowledge. Her cousin Nicholas had. Presumably, since his wife was of Bendarloh Ali's family, and had been in Malacca at the time Ali was so brutally punished, she knew as much as her husband. It is not too much to conclude that her cousin – who was therefore also of Bendarloh Ali's family – knew the circumstances as well. Ahmad, of course, is that cousin. Ahmad had been as frequent a visitor at Morland Park as his employer; he knew the grounds and the house. The shaving of camphor wood – as much a product of Malaya as *kamuning* wood – places Ahmad indisputably in the late Colonel Morland's bedroom.

"Manifestly, the preparations were made with great care. Mrs. Morland directed her relatives to send the hand of Benderloh Ali to Colonel Morland in the intarsia box which she forwarded to Malaya for that purpose. That the box had served as a model for Ahmad's carefully-wrought imitations did not seem to her important, since Ahmad had been instructed to bring the box back from Morland Park. Ahmad undoubtedly killed Colonel Morland to avenge the family honor after Bendarloh Ali died – but I think it inescapable that his desire for vengeance was planted and carefully nourished by Mrs. Nicholas Morland, whose real motive was not vengeance, but the control of the unlimited funds which would be at her disposal when her husband came into his share of his uncle's estate.

"One of our most sanguinary cases, Parker. And though have taken the murderer, I suspect that the real criminal will go free to enjoy the expansion of her shop according to her plan. It is one of life's little ironies."

V

THE ADVENTURE OF THE SPURIOUS *TAMERLANE*

"A summer idyl," was what my friend Solar Pons called the curious adventure which began one July afternoon with the appearance on the threshold of our quarters in Praed Street of a street gamin bearing a somewhat begrimed folded note. Under touseled blonde hair, his blue eyes looked up at me out of a freckled face.

"Mr. Pons?" he asked. "Mr. Solar Pons?"

It was a rare occasion on which a visitor did not immediately identify Pons, who stood behind me in the living-room, and I hesitated a moment before replying.

"'E said as it was 7B," said the boy urgently.

"And it is, my lad," said Pons, coming up behind me and reaching for the paper clutched in our visitor's fingers, while with the other hand he tossed him a bob.

The boy caught his tip and was off like a flash, clattering down the steps in marked contrast to the careful manner in which he had mounted to our floor.

Pons stepped over to the window, unfolding the note as he walked. He read it without expression, but his eyes were twinkling when he handed me the paper. It was rough to the touch, and had a torn edge characteristic of the valley of a book. Its message had been hastily scrawled with a pencil on the first piece of paper to come to hand.

"Mr. Pons, dear sir," it read, "I would be obliged to you if you could step around to my barrow. I have something of a problem that may interest you. I am, sir, your respectful servant, Joshua Bryant."

"What do you make of that, Parker?" asked Pons.

I was sure of my ground and answered confidently. "This note is written on the endpaper of a book – an old book, and no doubt secondhand," I said. "Mr. Bryant is very probably a dealer in secondhand books."

Pons burst into approving laughter, clapped me heartily on the back and cried, "At any time now I can retire to Sussex and keep bees! Is it not remarkable what a little exposure to ordinary ratiocination will do for one!"

"You know him, then?"

"He has a book barrow in Farringdon Road. I have on occasion paused to look over his wares."

"You're going then?"

"I never scorn the possibility of a little adventure to vary the prosaic routine," he said. "Let us just step around and pay Mr. Bryant a call."

The Farringdon Road Book Market consisted of a row of barrows – some on wheels, some on wooden supports which held only boards on which books were displayed – set along the kerb. The wheeled barrows were supplied with canvas covering which could be rolled back on sunny days, and unrolled to cover books and browsers on days of rain and weather. The market was not far from the Farringdon Station in one direction and the Great Northern Railway Depot in the other, and the spire of St. Paul's rose on the horizon behind the row of barrows. A score of people browsed among the books at the kerb, most of them men.

Joshua Bryant was a short, rotund man with a florid face which made a strong contrast to his thatch of white hair. His eyes were bright and alert, and bespoke more than ordinary intelligence. He acknowledged his introduction to me with a friendly nod, but his face told us nothing.

"I appreciate your coming, Mr. Pons," he said, without preamble. "Have a look at that."

So saying, he took from the side pocket of his jacket a slender, tea-colored, paperbound booklet and laid it before Pons, deftly turning back the cover to the title page, which could be read at a glance. "*Tamerlane and Other Poems. By a Bostonian.*" A quotation from Cowper followed, though somewhat badly printed: "Young bards are giddy, and young hearts are warm, / And make mistakes for manhood to reform." Then came the name of the publisher: "Boston: Calvin F. S. Thomas... Printer." and the date: "1827".

I glanced at Pons and saw his eyes lit with interest. He in turn looked inquiringly at Bryant.

"Mr. Pons," he said earnestly, "that book was not in my barrow when I came here this morning. It doesn't belong to me. I neither bought it nor took it in in trade. Yet I found it among the books about two hours ago." His eyes challenged Pons. "Do you know its value?"

"It is one of the rarest of American books," said Pons. "Worth perhaps five thousand pounds."

Bryant nodded. "It's worth more than I am," he said wryly. "I said to myself right away, There's a smell of fish about so I sent off that note to you."

Pons picked up the booklet. "May I borrow it?"

"Do, Mr Pons."

"But first, a question or two. What of your clientele this morning?"

"Oh, the usual. I have the regulars, Mr. Pons, the same as anyone else. Then there are those who come and go."

"Ah, but anyone unusual?"

Bryant looked thoughtful. "A lady," he, said presently. "She bought a book of poems. Rupert Brooke."

"Describe her."

"Young, well-dressed, married. Not the sort I'd have expected to see here, but then, Mr. Pons, books draw from all of life."

"Dark or light?"

"Oh, on the dark side. Chestnut brown."

"The color of her eyes?"

"She wore tinted glasses."

"I see. Anyone else?"

"A young barrister, I took him to be. He bought a *Raffles*. Then there was the elderly gentleman in morning clothes. Got out of a Daimler, driven by a chauffeur. The barrister was perhaps thirty-five, the elderly gentleman certainly thirty years older. They lingered a bit, whereas the lady more or less drifted by."

"What did the elderly gentleman buy?"

"Nothing, Mr. Pons. I thought he'd take a book on chess he looked at for a while, but he put it back."

"Did any of these people go to any other barrow, if you noticed?"

"The barrister stopped at them all. The lady just walked away, and the elderly gentleman returned to his car and was driven off."

"Can you describe him?"

"Grey-haired, but not as white as I am, Mr. Pons. He wore a Masonic ring. His hands were well groomed. There was a moustache on his upper lip, but his chin was clean-shaven. He had blue eyes, and a squarish face."

"Anyone further?"

Bryant shook his head.

"Very well. You'll hear from me, Mr. Bryant."

Pons said not a word all the way back to 7B, and, once there, he retired at once to the corner of the room by the window where he kept his scientific laboratory, such as it was. There I left him to attend to three calls I had to make.

When I returned to our quarters in time for dinner, I found Pons sitting deep in thought in his favorite chair, his eyes closed and his fingers tented before him. He had evidently only just finished a pipeful of the odoriferous shag he smoked, for our quarters reeked of it.

"I suppose you've solved the mystery of Mr. Bryant's valuable book," I ventured.

"No, no," he said almost irritably, "it is more of a mystery than ever. And the book is not valuable. It is spurious – a very clever copy, but a forgery."

He came to his feet and strode to the table where the *Tamerlane* lay.

"Look here, Parker. The date of publication is 1827. Less than a dozen copies of this book are known to exist, though a considerably larger edition was printed. Poe wrote that the book was 'suppressed for private reasons' – this accounts for its scarcity. But this copy could not have been printed in 1827, for an analysis of the paper on which it has been printed shows that the paper is made of chemically treated wood pulp. Chemical treatment for wood pulp was not, however, until after 1880. Further, paper contains esparto grass, which was not used until 1861. And most obvious of all, the type has no kerns, and alphabets without kerns were not introduced anywhere in the world until the early 1880's. This book therefore has no value except as a literary curiosity."

"Then no one, after all, has lost or misplaced a valuable book," I said.

"Ah, that is the nub of the problem. I submit that the reason for being of this spurious *Tamerlane* is likely to be of more interest than its discovery in Bryant's barrow. One of his customers this morning left it there."

"But which?"

"I submit it was the lady. I detected lint from her white gloves on the book, but even so, it is quite the sort of thing a lady would be more likely to do than a man. The book is a skilled, professional job. How came it into being? Was it done with the intention of deceiving someone into buying it? If so, how came it into Bryant's barrow?"

"It was certainly done with the intention of deceiving someone," I said. "What other purpose would a spurious copy of anything have?"

"Elementary," agreed Pons. "But I submit that the precise purpose of the deception is not nearly so clear. Presumptive evidence suggests that the copy was not made to be sold."

"What then, was it made for?"

"That seems to be the problem. Had it been made to be sold, we could hardly expect to discover it 'lost' in a barrow in Farringdon Road. But its only other purpose must have been to deceive a collector for some reason."

"You infer then that it served its purpose?"

"Precisely."

"Then why not simply destroy it?"

"A man would logically have done so. But women are not as logical. I put it to you that the lady could not bear to destroy something in the creation of which so much effort was expended."

"Where do you go from here, then?" I asked.

"I hoped you might be able to tell me," he said gently. "Does no course of action suggest itself to you?"

I threw up my hands. "To find a woman on so slight a description as that supplied by Bryant seems to me next to impossible. There must be a hundred thousand women who fit that description in greater London."

"More," agreed Pons.

"But perhaps there is a genuine *Tamerlane* in London."

"Capital!" cried Pons. "My dear fellow, I congratulate you. It so happens that there is such a book. It is in the possession of the well-known bibliophile, Lord Heltsham. My brother knows him reasonably well. While you were on your rounds I took the opportunity of sending around to Bancroft asking him to dispatch a note by messenger to His Lordship asking that I be permitted to examine his genuine *Tamerlane* for a few minutes directly after noon tomorrow."

"Heltsham is hardly likely to be home at that hour," I pointed out.

"Oh, it isn't His Lordship I wish to see. I count on seeing his wife. He would hardly be likely to trust a servant to show me such a treasure."

"Lady Heltsham!"

"I fancy Her Ladyship knows considerably more about the spurious *Tamerlane* than Lord Heltsham does. I am eager to add her knowledge to my own," said Pons with an enigmatic smile. "I chose tomorrow, because I saw in this morning's *Times* that His Lordship has a committee meeting in the Lords at noon."

Promptly at one o'clock next day we presented ourselves at the front door of Lord Heltsham's town house in Bedford Square. The butler admitted us, showed us into the drawing-room, and retired. Presently Lady Heltsham swept into the room – a young, attractive and vivacious woman, considerably her husband's junior. Her pleasant brown eyes looked from one to the other of us, and without hesitation fixed upon Pons.

"Mr. Pons? I have the pleasure of your brother's acquaintance."

"I presume upon it, Your Ladyship," said Pons, and introduced me.

"You are reclusive, sir," said Lary Heltsham. "While your brother moves about socially, I see nothing of you."

"Ah, Your Ladyship, we move in different circles. Bancroft would not be seen in mine, and I do not derive much profit in his."

"You are a collector of books?" she asked then.

"Say, rather, of circumstances, events, and curious happenings," said Pons. "My interest is in the human comedy."

A little nonplussed, Her Ladyship came to the point of our visit. "My husband tells me you wish to examine his copy of *Tamerlane*."

"If I could impose upon you for a few minutes," said Pons.

"This way, please."

Lady Heltsham led the way into her husband's study, a room lined with books behind locked glass doors almost from floor to ceiling to such an extent that the room was unnaturally dark. Lady Heltsham moved directly to the mahogany table in the center of the room and turned on the strong light there.

"I will bring it to you, Mr. Pons," she said.

She crossed to one of the cases, unlocked it, and took from it a slender slipcase. This she brought to the table, and from it removed what seemed at first glance to be the duplicate of the book Joshua Bryant had laid before Pons the previous day.

Pons, however, was peering not at the *Tamerlane*, but at the wall behind Lady Heltsham. "Forgive me," he said, "but surely that is not a set of Dickens in first editions?"

She turned.

Instantly Pons exchanged for the genuine *Tamerlane* on the table the spurious copy he had carried along from our quarters.

"I believe it is, Mr. Pons," said Lady Heltsham, amused. "It hasn't the value, of course, of this little book – hardly more than a chapbook, as you see."

Pons turned back the cover with a reverent air.

"What could have been the 'private reasons' which caused Poe to suppress it?" he murmured.

"I suppose we will never know, Mr. Pons."

"That is surely a challenge for some biographer," Pons went on, turning to the first page of text.

He bent to peer closely at the page, then turned from this position to look strangely at Lady Heltsham.

"What is it, Mr. Pons?"

"Surely His Lordship is aware that this is not a genuine *Tamerlane*?" he asked quietly.

Lady Heltsham bent instantly at his side, her face quickening with alarm.

"The absence of kerns, you see," began Pons.

But he did not go on. Lady Heltsham's simultaneous reaction was so violent that Pons' words were stopped in his throat. She uttered a great cry of anguish, and without a moment's hesitation rushed headlong from the room.

Pons immediately exchanged books once more, returned the genuine *Tamerlane* to its slipcase, and the encased book to its place on the shelf. He turned the key in the lock and brought the little ring of keys to which it was attached to the table to leave it in place of the book.

The motor of a car roared into life somewhere outside the house.

"Her Ladyship is now on her way to Farringdon Road," said Pons.

"That was a cruel trick, Pons," I said hotly.

"Was it not!" he agreed. "I rather think, however, that Lady Heltsham would never have admitted to any part in the matter of the spurious *Tamerlane* if I had not tricked her so. I regret the shock to her."

Pons sat in silence in the cab on the way back to our quarters until I broke into his meditation.

"I fail to understand Lord Heltsham's role," I said.

"If I am not mistaken, the spurious *Tamerlane* was used to occupy the slipcase during the absence of the genuine one," said Pons.

"Then Lord Heltsham never saw it!"

"In all likelihood he did not. I submit that the forgery was intended to deceive him should he have occasion to glance into the slipcase, though a close examination would have revealed the deception. The forged copy having served its purpose, it was dropped into Bryant's barrow. The gambit I took was intended to make Lady Heltsham believe that, in spite of her certainty to the contrary, she had inadvertently dropped the real *Tamerlane* in Farringdon Road. She has gone there to see. Bryant, who has no reason to dissemble, will tell her what has happened to the copy she left there, and in all probability Her Ladyship will then arrive at the correct explanation of the little scene in which she played such an impetuous role. She will return to her husband's study and discover the real *Tamerlane* in its slipcase; she will then know that I deliberately tricked her."

"And she will call on you," I put in.

"I doubt it. Lady Heltsham will wait upon me to make the next move."

"Pons, you cannot go back to the house."

"At the moment I have no intention of doing so. If I read Her Ladyship aright, she will tell us nothing. I shall have to use other means to learn why she found it necessary to remove her husband's valuable *Tamerlane* for some time from its slipcase and substitute a spurious copy."

"Could it not have been used to make a potential buyer of the spurious copy believe he was buying the genuine *Tamerlane*?" I asked.

"If that were the explanation," said Pons a trifle impatiently, "surely I would not now be in possession of the forgery."

"Of course not," I agreed.

"You imply further that Lady Heltsham might have been guilty of such criminal deception. Far from it. I submit that the lady acted out of desperation."

"I find this matter more baffling every moment," I said.

"Tut, tut! If we accept the premise that the spurious copy was meant only for the casual deception I have postulated, an interesting use for the real *Tamerlane* then suggests itself. Indeed, at the moment, unlikely as it seems, it remains as the only tenable one. You will remember my credo – when all the impossible explanations have been eliminated, then whatever remains, improbable as it may be, must be the truth."

"And that?"

"Surely so valuable an object as the rare *Tamerlane* would make excellent collateral!"

"Of course."

"And if Her Ladyship needed money urgently and could not ask her husband for it, she might persuade herself to borrow the *Tamerlane*. I myself would lend her up to three thousand pounds on such security – providing I had it to lend. I submit that any bank in London would do the same."

"Then you need only apply to the banks."

"Ah, that is information no reputable bank would divulge. Yet, in the interests of Lady Heltsham, we shall have to examine into this matter from another quarter. Unless I am badly mistaken, she may yet have further need for the spurious *Tamerlane* she had made for her desperate purpose."

"I daresay you are hardly the person Lady Heltsham would care to see at this point."

"I do not doubt it," agreed Pons. "She will not see me."

"Lord Heltsham then?"

"The very last person to whom to make application." He shook his head. "No, Parker – these waters run a little deeper than you may think. We shall have to proceed with caution lest we precipitate the very tragedy Lady Heltsham seems to fear."

Thereafter he said no more, and we rode the rest of the way in silence, Pons leaning back with his eyes closed so that the passing scene might not distract him from his train of thought.

Pons was up and away before I rose next morning, and without touching the breakfast Mrs. Johnson had brought up. I went out on my rounds soon after, pausing only briefly at our quarters in passing at mid-day, only to find Pons still absent. He did not return until the dinner hour, following me in by thirty minutes, and wearing a sober, preoccupied air. "I have been inquiring into that little matter of the spurious *Tamerlane*," he said as he took up a position at the mantel and began to fill his pipe with shag.

"Ah, you have solved it," I cried.

He shook his head impatiently. "Come, come, Parker, it is not a matter of solving, as you put it, but of knowing just where to take hold of it to bring about its resolution. How did Lady Heltsham strike you? A woman of character?"

"I thought so."

"And I."

"And under considerable stress."

"Elementary."

"But controlled – apart, that is, from exposure to sudden shocks prepared by Mr. Solar Pons."

Pons bowed his acknowledgment. "Would you not conclude, then, that if such a woman needed money, she would attempt to raise it through her own possessions before she borrowed her husband's?"

"I would, indeed."

"I have been making the rounds of the pawnshops for the better part of the day," said Pons then. "A description of the lady, with tinted glasses added and, no doubt, an assumed name, has led me to conclude that Lady Heltsham has borrowed money against all but her most essential jewels, two autographed books of some rarity belonging to her, some valuable furs – and, at last, the *Tamerlane*, which alone has been redeemed because Lady Heltsham was fortunate enough to come into a small inheritance from an uncle. Indeed, announcement of it appears only in the afternoon papers, though the inheritance was obviously paid some days ago – two thousand pounds, all of which, I venture to guess, went to redeem her husband's *Tamerlane*."

"You've not confronted her with these facts?"

"Certainly not. I shall not. This need for money has been of comparatively short duration. Scarcely a year. Would it surprise you to learn that within that time Lady Heltsham has also begun to bet on horses and to invest in the stock market?"

"Ah, it is that vice!"

"Gently, gently, Parker. That is surely not a vice so rapidly acquired."

"But it is one in which she could hardly expect her husband to foot the bill," I put in.

"It does not strike you as curiously coincidental that Lady Heltsham who had previously shunned the races and the market, should suddenly begin to wager money and to invest it – somewhat incautiously?"

"Which came first?" I asked. "The pawning of her valuables or the wagering?"

"The pawnings."

I shrugged. "And with that money she gambled!"

"You have a tidy mind, Parker, and you are always singularly direct. It does not seem to you unlikely that Lord Heltsham is too penurious to deny his wife a little money for a pleasure which has always commanded the allegiance of the upper classes?"

"I haven't the noble Lord's acquaintance, so I can hardly speak for him," I said, "but it is not improbable."

Pons nodded, his lips pursed, his eyes intent upon some point in space beyond the walls of our quarters. "There is one little aspect of the matter that puts an added light on it," said Pons then. "Her wagers and her investments have been far from matching the money she has borrowed – and I can say nothing of such securities as she may have taken to the banks."

"Did she in fact borrow against securities as well?" I asked.

"I think it highly likely that she did. There is everything to show that in her need to raise considerable sums of money, she explored every avenue before turning to securities that were not her own."

"Like Lord Heltsham's *Tamerlane*."

Pons nodded.

"But there is plenty of precedent for sudden changes in living patterns," I said. "Lady Heltsham is not the first woman who has suddenly altered her way of life; she will not be the last."

"In these matters I must defer to your judgment, Parker," said Pons dryly.

"What do you propose to do?" I asked. "After all, you've solved the matter as far as Bryant is concerned."

"True, true. But I have not satisfied myself. And at this point I have gone as far as I can go alone."

"If there is anything I can do," I began.

"I count on your loyalty always, Parker, but in this case, I need expert help. I have called upon Bancroft and commanded the power that is only the Foreign Office's. I have had to inform him in the strictest secrecy that I have reason to believe Lady Heltsham is the victim of a conspiracy that may involve espionage."

I studied his face to see whether he jested, but the grimness of his features gave me no alternative but to believe him. Nevertheless, I could not but express my amazement. "Surely not Lady Heltsham! Perhaps her husband."

"Lord Heltsham is on the Munitions Committee," said Pons significantly.

"But what can Bancroft do?"

"He has done what I asked, and discreetly. Lady Heltsham's mail will be opened and her telephone tapped. I need to know who communicates with her. Unless I am very much mistaken, she will receive a communication of some importance within twenty-four hours. I am prepared to act upon it."

"You astound me," I cried.

"It is surely not the first time," said Pons, his eyes twinkling.

Early the next evening, Pons received from his brother the first batch of photostats of the mail delivered to Lady Heltsham during the day. He pounced upon it eagerly. There were nine letters in all; I could not see that Pons read most of them, only beginning each of them, and tossing it aside. But at last, when he came to the seventh one, he paused, read it at a glance, and smiled.

"I fancy this is what we want, Parker," he said, handing it to me.

It was but the briefest of notes.

"Dear Lady,

"I count on your joining me tomorrow at two for a cocktail at Sardi's.

"Victor."

I looked up. "You cannot know the sender?"

"I fancy I do. He is Victor Affandi, a man about town. He is hardly more than an international gigolo, but highly popular with the ladies. He is of Egyptian descent, and lives at The Larches in Laburnum Crescent."

"You think him guilty of espionage?"

"I should not be surprised if he were. He is an ingenious man, one who has managed to live conspicuously well without visible means of support other than a small allowance left him many years ago. If you are not averse to an adventure in larceny, we shall pay his quarters a visit tomorrow afternoon."

I looked at Pons askance. "As your friend Bryant puts it, 'There's a smell of fish about this'," I said. "What can you hope to find at Affandi's place?"

Pons smiled. "We shall see."

However much I may have been inclined to hold back, I was at Pons' side next afternoon when his skeleton keys let him into the sumptuously furnished apartment occupied by Victor Affandi. Once the door was closed behind us, Pons stood quietly in the middle of the living-room examining our surroundings. His keen eyes darted from one to another of the framed pictures on the walls – some patently original watercolors and oils – until he came to one only a trifle out of line. He strode across the room and lifted the picture enough to disclose a wall safe.

He stood for a moment contemplating it, then gently lowered the picture. "Affandi could hardly be so obvious," he murmured.

He resumed his scrutiny of the room. He contemplated the furniture, but discarded this, too. He went around the rug, raising it for any evidence of a receptacle in the floor. He passed on into the spare kitchen, the bathroom, and the bedroom, examining each in turn before he came back into the living-room.

"We don't have much time," he said. "I daresay Affandi's cocktail engagement will be a cruelly short one."

Apart from the costliness of its appointments, the living-room was simply furnished. Pons examined the furniture, but only desultorily; clearly he did not believe that what he sought was hidden in it any more than he believed the wall safe to be its place of concealment.

Finally, his eyes fixed upon a recessed shelf of books. He crossed to it, and I followed. The volumes Victor Affandi had collected were almost depressingly prosaic – a Forsyte novel by Galsworthy, a Proust novel in French, books by Dickens, George Meredith, Thomas Hardy, the poems of Byron, and, somewhat incongruously, two oversized leatherbound volumes containing the Old and the New Testament. It was this two-volume edition of the Bible which had caught Pons' attention.

His eyes quickened as he drew one of them from the shelf and opened it.

"An uncommonly light book for one of its size," he said. "I fancy this is what we are looking for, Parker."

He turned back the pages until he came at last to a page that would not turn – and the rest of the pages were solid. The book was a dummy.

Pons sought and found the tiny lever that unlatched the cover of the dummy portion, and the lid flew back. There lay disclosed papers, documents, packets of letters, and newspaper clippings.

Without a moment's hesitation, Pons dipped into Affandi's treasure and proceeded methodically to stuff the contents of the book into his pockets.

"Pons, what are you doing?" I protested.

"Robbing Affandi of his treasures," said Pons blandly. "How many of his visitors would think of looking into a Bible!" he added, chuckling.

He locked the book, closed it, and returned it to its place on the shelf.

Then he took down the other book, which was also a dummy, and emptied this in similar fashion.

"Now, quickly, Parker, out of the place," he said.

In short order, we found ourselves back at our quarters. There Pons lost no time in sending a note to Lady Heltsham, inviting her to call at 7B at her convenience, and promising that she would learn something to her advantage. To all my questions, he turned a deaf ear, or worse, a scornful retort.

"It is as plain as a pikestaff, Parker. You disappoint me. You began so well in this matter, and you have been misled so easily."

He spent the next two hours, spurning supper, making an inventory of the contents of Victor Affandi's Bible. Some of the papers and letters he slipped into manila envelopes and addressed them for mailing; some he put aside for further examination.

Lady Heltsham presented herself promptly at eight o'clock.

She entered our rooms with understandable reserve, and as she threw back the veil which covered her features it was patent that she was under tension not untouched by indignation. "Ah, my dear Lady Heltsham," said Pons, "I owe you an apology for that little substitution I played upon you. Nevertheless, it has led to a result I am sure you will agree is a happy one for you. I believe these belong to you."

So saying, he handed her a packet of letters from Victor Affandi's collection.

For a few moments she gazed wide-eyed at the letters Pons held out to her. Then she seized hold of them with trembling hands, and her liquidly beautiful eyes stared uncomprehendingly at Pons.

"Pray make sure they are all there," urged Pons.

She untied them eagerly and went through the packet. She nodded as if she did not trust herself to speak.

Pons turned and indicated the fire on the hearth. "I assure Your Ladyship I have not read them, but surely their nature is such that it would be dangerous for you even to carry them home."

She crossed to the fire and threw the letters into the flames.

Then she turned and fell back against the mantel with a great sobbing sigh of relief.

"Oh, Mr. Pons!" she cried. "I cannot thank you enough. I cannot pay you. I cannot tell you how much this has meant to me. If my husband had learned of them – as he threatened..."

"Pray say no more, Lady Heltsham. If I may retain that spurious *Tamerlane*, I shall feel amply repaid."

"Please do!" she said earnestly. "Thank you, sir. I am happy to learn there are still gentlemen left in England!"

She bade us good night and slipped away.

"A woman of rare discretion," said Pons. "You will note she asked no questions, but accepted gratefully what fate had been kind enough to offer her."

"So it was blackmail," I said, chagrined. "Why then all this talk of espionage?"

"My brother would hardly have responded to anything other," said Pons. "You ought not to have responded to it at all. It was surely obvious that only the most pressing matter could have caused Lady Heltsham to pawn her valuables and then to take the extreme measure of borrowing money against His Lordship's genuine *Tamerlane*. Affandi must have taken a tidy sum from her. Men of his stamp never know an end to greed. I knew he could not resist the chance to make new demands upon her when he read the story of her inheritance, and I was certain his approach to her would be made very quickly, as it was."

"And the letters Affandi held?"

Pons shrugged. "I submit they were the customary letters of a woman in love unwise enough to put down in her own handwriting things which ought never to have been written at all. Affandi learned of their existence somehow, and probably bought them. Knowing that she could not afford to have her husband know of their existence, he proceeded with methodical coldbloodedness to blackmail her." He picked up the spurious *Tamerlane*, his eyes dancing. "I am delighted to add this curious memento to my little collection of items associated with what you call my adventures in deduction."

VI

THE ADVENTURE OF THE CHINA COTTAGE

"My esteemed brother," said Solar Pons as I walked into our quarters one autumn morning for breakfast, "has a mind several times more perceptive than my own, but he has little patience with the processes of ratiocination. Though there is nothing to indicate it, it was certainly he who sent this packet of papers by special messenger well before you were awake."

He had pushed the breakfast dishes back, having barely touched the food Mrs. Johnson had prepared, and sat studying several pages of manuscript, beside which lay an ordinary calling card bearing the name Randolph Curwen, through which someone had scrawled an imperative question mark in red ink.

Observing the direction of my gaze, Pons went on. "The card was clipped to the papers. Curwen is – or perhaps I had better say 'was' – an expert on Foreign affairs, and was known to be a consultant of the Foreign Office in cryptology. He was sixty-nine, a widower, and lived alone in Cadogan Place, Belgravia. A reclusive gentleman, little given to social affairs since the death of his wife nine years ago. There were no children, but he had the reputation for possessing a considerable estate."

"Is he dead, then?" I asked.

"I should not be surprised to learn that he is," said Pons. "I have had a look at the morning papers, but there is no word of him there. Some important discovery about Curwen has been made. These papers, you must have seen, are photographs of some confidential correspondence between members of the German Foreign Office and that of Russia. They would appear to be singularly innocuous, so much so that, I submit, they were sent to Curwen so that he might examine them for any code, since obviously they are not in the customary military codes of either Germany or Russia, which our people have broken long ago."

"I assumed," said an icy voice from the threshold behind me, "that you would have come to the proper conclusion about this data. I came as soon as I could."

Bancroft Pons had come noiselessly into the room, which was no mean feat in view of his weight. His keen eyes were fixed unswervingly upon Pons, his austere face frozen into an impassive mask, which added to the impressiveness of his appearance.

"Sir Randolph?" asked Pons.

"Dead," said Bancroft.

"How?"

"We do not yet know."

"The papers?"

"We have some reason to believe that a *rapprochement* between Germany and Russia is in the wind. Since it would be far more in the interests of Germany's containment that Russia be allied to us and the United States, we are naturally anxious to know what impends. We had recourse to Curwen, as one of the most skilled of our cryptologists. He was sent the papers by messenger at noon yesterday."

"I take it he was given the originals."

Bancroft nodded curtly. "There is always the possibility of invisible ink, though our own tests at the office could not turn up any evidence of it. Curwen always liked to work with the originals. You've had a chance to look them over."

"They do not seem to be in code," said Pons. "They appear to be only friendly correspondence between the foreign secretaries, though it is evident that some increase in trade is being contemplated."

"Curwen was to have telephoned me early this morning. When seven o'clock passed without a call from him, I put in a call. I could not get a reply. So we sent Danvers out. The house and the study were locked. Of course, Danvers had skeleton keys which enabled him to get in. He found Curwen dead in his chair at the table, the papers before him. The windows were all locked, though one was open to a locked screen. Danvers thought he detected a chemical odor of some kind; it suggested that someone might have photographed the papers – that kind of odor. But you shall see Curwen. Nothing has been touched. I have a car below. It isn't far to Cadogan Place."

The house in Cadogan Place was austere in its appointments. It was now under heavy police guard; a constable stood on the street before the house, another at the door, and yet another at the door of the study, which was situated at one corner of the front of the house, one pair of windows looking out toward the street, the other into shrubbery-grown grounds to a low stone wall which separated the building from the adjacent property. The house was Georgian in architecture, and likewise in its furniture.

When the study door was unlocked, it revealed a book-lined room, its shelving broken only by windows and a fireplace. The walls of books framed what we had come to see – the great table in the center of the room, the still-lit lamp, the motionless form of Sir Randolph Curwen, collapsed in his armchair, arms dangling floorward, his head thrown back, his face twisted into an expression of agony. Beside him stood, as if also on guard, a middle-aged bespectacled man whom Bancroft Pons introduced as Hilary Danvers.

"Nothing has been disturbed, sir," said Danvers to Pons' brother.

Bancroft nodded curtly and waved one arm toward the body.

"Sir Randolph, Parker," said Pons. "Your division."

I went around immediately to examine the body. Sir Randolph had been a thin, almost gangling man. A grey moustache decorated his upper lip, and thin grey hair barely concealed his scalp. Pince-nez – one eyeglass broken – dangled from a black silk cord around his neck. He appeared to have died in convulsive agony, but there was certainly no visible wound on his body.

"Heart?" asked Pons.

I shook my head.

He left me to my examination and walked cat-like around the immaculate room. He examined the windows, one after the other, tested the screen on the half-opened window to the grounds, and came to a pause at the fireplace, where he dropped to one knee.

"Something has been burned here," he said.

"Oh, elementary, my dear fellow," said Bancroft peevishly. "A cursory examination suggests that someone burned papers with figures on them – as you can see."

"Not part of the original material?"

"No. We'll collect the ashes and study them, never fear."

Pons rose and came around to the table. He stood to scrutinize it, touching nothing. Most of its top was spread with the papers from the Foreign Office; these were divided into two piles, with one sheet between these piles, this one being evidently the paper Curwen was reading when he was stricken. A pad of notepaper – free of any jottings – was at one side of this paper. The perimeter of the desk was covered by – in clockwise order – an inkwell and pens, a volume on cryptography, a row of books between bookends made of what appeared to be blocks of waxed mahogany, a carved box which contained pencils, erasers, a scissors, and the like, and finally a small white, rose-decorated cottage of china, with an open box of incense pastilles beside it. Curwen's chair had been pushed slightly back from the table, and around to one side, as if he were making an attempt to rise before death overtook him.

"Well, Parker?" asked Pons impatiently.

"A seizure of some kind," I replied. "But I fear that only an autopsy can determine the cause of death precisely."

"Can you guess?"

"If I had to guess, I'd say poison."

Pons flashed a glance at his brother. "You mentioned an odor on entrance."

"Mr. Danvers?" prompted Bancroft.

"We believe that the odor emanated from the incense burner."

"Ah, this," said Pons, his hand hovering over the china cottage. He gazed inquiringly at Danvers.

"We have tested for fingerprints, Mr. Pons," said Danvers. "Only Sir Randolph's were found."

Pons lifted the cottage from its base, where, in a little cup, lay the remains of burned pastilles. He bent his hawk-like face toward the cup and sniffed. He looked up with narrowed eyes, picked up the base of the china cottage, and thrust it at me. "What kind of scent might that be, Parker?"

I followed his example and sniffed. "Almond," I said. "They make these pastilles in all manner of scents."

Pons put the china cottage back together and picked up the box of pastilles. "Lilac," he said dryly.

"The room was locked, Mr. Pons," put in Danvers. "No one could possibly have got in, if you're suggesting that someone came and poisoned Sir Randolph."

"Child's play, child's play," muttered Bancroft impatiently.

"What did he find in the papers that someone should want to kill him?"

"And leave the papers?" asked Pons.

"Or burn his findings?" from Bancroft.

"You're irritable today," said Pons. "There's nothing here to show that Curwen found anything in the papers."

"On the contrary – there is everything to suggest that somehow someone managed entrance into this room, killed Sir Randolph, and burned his notes."

"Why not take them along? If he were clever enough to enter and leave a locked room without a sign to betray him, he must certainly have known that something could be determined from the ashes."

"You have solved it then, Solar?" asked Bancroft sardonically.

"No. But I submit that the papers in the grate were burned by Sir Randolph himself. He tore off what was on his pad and what had accumulated in his wastebasket under the table, emptied the wastebasket into the fireplace, and set fire to the contents. The ashes are substantial. There is among them at least a page or two from the *Times*, no reason for burning which I could adduce on the part of a foreign agent. Yours is the Foreign Office approach – all is intrigue and espionage."

"It is indeed," said Bancroft shortly.

"We shall see," said Pons.

He turned again to the china cottage. "If I may, I should like to take this back to Praed Street." He picked up also the box of pastilles. "And this."

Bancroft stared at him as if he were convinced that Pons had taken leave of his senses.

"This is bone china," Pons said, with a hint of a smile at his lips. "Of Staffordshire origin. It dates, I should say, to the early nineteenth century. Manufactured by Flight, Barr and Barr, of Worcester. This china, though translucent, will tolerate a surprising amount of heat."

"Pray spare me this lecture," said Bancroft icily. "Take it."

Pons thanked him dryly, slipped the box of pastilles into his pocket, and handed the china cottage to me. "Handle it with care, Parker. We shall examine it at our leisure at 7B." He turned again to his brother. "Now, then. Sir Randolph lived alone. Surely there were servants?"

"A Mrs. Claudia Melton came in to clean the house twice a week," said Bancroft. "And there was a manservant by day – Will Davinson. He prepared Sir Randolph's meals and tended to the door. He has come in, if you wish to question him. If so, let us get about it at once."

"Very well," assented Pons.

Bancroft signalled to the constable who stood at the threshold. The constable turned silently and led us out of the room to the rear quarters, where, in a combination kitchen and breakfast room, there sat waiting a middle-aged man, who, immediately on our entrance, sprang to his feet and all but clicked his heels together, standing like a ramrod.

"Mr. Davinson," said the constable, "Mr. Solar Pons would like to ask you some questions."

"At your service, sir," said Davinson to Pons.

"Pray sit down, Mr. Davinson."

Davinson regained his chair and sat waiting expectantly. For all the iron-grey hair, the thinning hands, and the deepening lines of his face, his eyes were alert and conveyed the impression of youth the rest of his body belied.

"You were Sir Randolph's batman in the war?" asked Pons abruptly.

"Yes, sir."

"You had reason then to know his habits very well?"

"Yes, sir."

"He seems to have been addicted to the burning of incense."

"He has burned it for as long as I've known him."

"Twenty years?" hazarded Pons.

"Twenty-one."

"You will have had occasion to ascertain how many pastilles a day he customarily burned."

"Sir, he released the fragrant smoke only when he retired to his study. This was usually in the evening. He seldom burned more than three in an evening, and commonly but two."

"His favorite scent?"

"Lilac. But he also had pastilles scented with rose, almond, thyme, and, I believe, lavender. He would buy boxes by the set – two dozen of each scent in a box – so that he always had a good supply."

Pons took a turn down the room and back. He stood for a few moments in silence, his eyes closed, his right hand pulling at his earlobe.

"Sir Randolph was a reclusive man?"

"He saw very few people."

"Whom did he see in the past fortnight?"

Davinson concentrated for a moment. "His niece, Miss Emily Curwen. She had come to London from her home in Edinburgh and came to call. That was perhaps a trifle over two weeks ago."

"No matter," said Pons. "Go on."

"Mr. Leonard Loveson of Loveson & Fitch in High Holborn. That was a business matter. Sir Randolph held a mortgage on their place of business."

"Sir Randolph held other such mortgages?"

"I was not in Sir Randolph's confidence, sir, but I believe he did."

"Go on, Mr. Davinson."

"Well, then there was a nephew – a great-nephew, properly speaking, Ronald Lindall, the son of Miss Emily's sister, also from Edinburgh; he was at the house six days ago, paying a courtesy visit, I took it." He paused.

"Anyone else?"

"Yes," said Davinson hesitantly. "There was a legal gentleman two days ago – all fuss and feathers. They had words, but briefly. Sir Randolph soothed him and sent him off."

"About what did they have words?"

"I believe the matter concerned another of Sir Randolph's mortgages."

"He was a hard man?"

"No, sir. Quite the contrary. More than once he remitted interest due him – even cancelled it. And on one occasion he forgave a small mortgage. No, sir, he was far too easy a man to deal with. Some of them took advantage of him."

"Go on."

"I do not remember any more, sir."

Pons took another turn around the room. "Of these people, which were familiar visitors?" he asked then.

"Mr. Loveson."

"You had not seen Miss Emily before?"

"No, sir. Sir Randolph had spoken of her, but she had not visited at any time that I was in this house."

"You admitted her?"

"Yes, sir. Sir Randolph never answered the door. If I had gone – unless he had an appointment – he did not answer the door at all."

"Will you cast your mind back to Miss Emily's visit? How did she seem to you?"

"I don't follow you, Mr. Pons."

"Was she composed – sad – gay – what?"

"She seemed to be a trifle agitated, if I may say so. But that was when she left, Mr. Pons. When she came in she was very much a lady."

"She and her uncle had words?"

"I could not say." Davinson was suddenly prim.

"Mr. Lindall, now."

"He was a somewhat truculent young man, but apologetic about disturbing Sir Randolph. They had a pleasant visit. Sir Randolph showed him about the house and garden, and he took his leave."

"Mr. Loveson. Do you know, is the mortgage a large one – presuming it has not been settled?"

"I don't know, but I had the impression that it is quite large." Davinson swallowed and cleared his throat. "I must emphasize again, Mr. Pons, that while Sir Randolph did not take me into his confidence, I was able to come to certain conclusions about his affairs."

"One could hardly expect otherwise of a companion of such long standing," said Pons.

Davinson inclined his head slightly as if modestly accepting faint praise.

"The gentlemen from the Foreign Office," Pons said then. "Did you admit them?"

"No, sir. They came after I had gone to my flat."

"You answered the telephone while you were here. Do you recall any appointments after your hours during the past two weeks?"

"The foreign gentleman."

"When?"

"Three nights ago."

"Did he leave his name?"

"No, sir. He asked to speak with Sir Randolph. He spoke in a German accent. Sir Randolph was in his study. I made the signal with the buzzer, and Sir Randolph took the call. I stayed on the wire just long enough to be sure the connection had been made."

"You heard their conversation?"

"Sir, only enough to know that Sir Randolph was very much surprised – I took it, agreeably. Afterward, he came out and instructed me to prepare some sandwiches and chill some wine. So I knew that he expected someone to come in during the evening. I assumed that it was the foreign gentleman."

Pons nodded. "Your leaving arrangements were by your choice, Mr. Davinson?"

"No, sir. That was the way Sir Randolph wished it. He never wanted to be valeted, didn't like it. But he needed someone to do the ordinary things in the house during the day."

"You have your own keys?"

"Yes, Mr. Pons."

"Sir Randolph was secretive?"

"Only about his work. He was a gentleman who, I should say, preferred his own company to that of anyone else. He treated me very well. Indeed, if I may say so, I should not be surprised to find myself mentioned in his will – he hinted as much to me on several occasions, and that ought to be proof enough that he was not unnecessarily secretive."

A smile touched Pons' lips.

Bancroft loomed on the threshold. "Have you learned anything?" he demanded impatiently.

"Gently, brother," said Pons, his eyes twinkling. "These matters take time. But we are done here. Thank you, Mr. Davinson. I may call on you again."

"I want to do anything I can to help, sir. I was very fond of Sir Randolph. We were – if I may say so – almost like step-brothers."

"Was that not an odd way of putting it?" asked Bancroft, when we were walking away from the kitchen. "One says, 'we were like brothers'. Step-brothers, indeed!"

"Probably not, for Davinson," said Pons. "I fancy it was his way of saying that they were like brothers one step removed on the social scale – Sir Randolph being a step up, and he a step down."

Bancroft grunted explosively. "You've frittered away half an hour. To what conclusions have you come?"

"Ah, I daresay it's a trifle early to be certain of very much. I submit, however, that Sir Randolph was murdered by someone he had no reason to fear. Sir Randolph appears to have been a cautious man, one not given to carelessness in the matter of his relationship with the public."

"You have some ingenious theory about the murderer's entrance into and exit from the locked room, no doubt," said Bancroft testily.

"I should hardly call it that. Sir Randolph admitted him, and Sir Randolph saw him out, locking the doors after him. Until we have the autopsy report, we cannot know precisely how Sir Randolph was done to death."

"We are having the papers gone over once again."

"A waste of time. We have both been through them and found nothing. No more is necessary."

"Nevertheless..."

"Ah, you Foreign Office people think in painfully conventional patterns. I submit the papers have nothing to do with it."

"I have heard you on more than one occasion decry outrageous coincidence, Solar," protested Bancroft. "Surely it is too much to believe that Sir Randolph's possession of these papers at the time of his death amounts only to coincidence?"

"It is indeed an outrageous coincidence, and of a kind I detest," said Pons. "But I am forced to believe it no less."

"Is there anything more here?" asked Bancroft.

"If possible, I should like to have a copy of Sir Randolph's will sent to 7B without delay."

"It will be done."

Back at our quarters, Pons retired at once with the china cottage and the box of pastilles to the corner where he kept his chemicals, while I prepared to go out on my round. When I left 7B, he was in the process of breaking apart one of the scented pastilles; when I returned two hours later, he had broken them all apart and was just rising from his examination, his eyes dancing with the light of discovery.

"You have learned something," I cried.

"Should I not, after two hours?" he asked. "Sir Randolph came to his death by his own hand."

"Suicide!"

"I have not said so. No, one of the pastilles contained cyanide. It was prepared and placed among the pastilles in the box on the desk unknown to him. Since he used not less than two pastilles a day and not more than three, and the box contains normally two dozen pastilles, we can assume that the poisoned pastille was placed there not more than twelve days ago. From the ashes in the china cottage it is possible to determine that the cyanide was enclosed in inflammable wax, and this in turn enclosed in the customary formula – charcoal powder, essence of lilac, gum benzoin, olibanum, storax and gum tragacanth. Sir Randolph fell victim to a death trap which had been laid for him by someone who both knew his habits and had access to his study."

"I thought it poison. What was the motive?"

"Ah, that's the question. It was certainly not the papers, as was evident the moment I concluded that the incense burner was the source of Sir Randolph's death. That faint odor of almond, you will remember, was indicative."

"His estate then?"

"Ah, we shall just see. Only a few minutes before your return a copy of Sir Randolph's will arrived. I was about to examine it."

He crossed to the table, took up the sealed envelope lying there, and opened it. He stood for a few moments studying the paper he unfolded. "An admirably clear document," he murmured. "To his faithful servant, Will Davinson, twenty-five hundred pounds. To Miss Emily 'who is otherwise provided for,' the sum of five hundred pounds. To Mrs. Claudia Melton, two hundred pounds. The bulk of his estate distributed equally among five charitable institutions. All mortgages forgiven!"

"There is certainly not much in the way of motive there," I said.

"Murder has been committed for as much as ten pounds," said Pons. "And less. But hardly with such care and premeditation. I fancy that the stake was considerably more than two or five hundred pounds."

"Davinson had motive and opportunity."

"He could hardly deny it," observed Pons with a crooked smile.

"He knew he was mentioned in the will. He told us as much."

"Rack up one point against his having planned Sir Randolph's death."

"Surely it's not impossible."

"No, only improbable."

"I recall your saying often that when all the impossible solutions have been eliminated, then whatever remains, however improbable, must be the truth."

"We have not yet reached that point, Parker."

"Perhaps, after all, your brother is right."

"He may be," said Pons with that air of knowing very well he was not.

"Davinson spoke of a foreigner, a German, who visited Sir Randolph only a few days before his death."

"We have only Davinson's word for it," said Pons.

"If not, after all the papers from the Foreign Office, we seem to be left with only Sir Randolph's estate for motive," I pointed out, with some asperity.

"His estate seems to be well accounted for."

"The mortgage holders!" I cried.

"I have thought of them. Even before I saw this document, I suggested that some inquiry be set afoot about them. But

I venture to predict it will be disclosed that Sir Randolph did not hold many unpaid mortgages, and that the total sum involved is not as large as Davinson, for one, believed."

"The man Loveson?"

"I have not forgotten him. His will very probably turn out to be the largest outstanding mortgage. I am well aware therefore that he may have had motive in addition to having opportunity. The probability, again, is remote, for it must surely have occurred to him, should any thought of killing Sir Randolph have crossed his mind, that his motive would be instantly perceived. Moreover, we have Davinson's word for Sir Randolph's lenience with his debtors – and this is given adequate support by the terms of Sir Randolph's will, forgiving his mortgages. No, there is something other here of which we have as yet no inkling – something that induced his murderer to go to great pains to prepare a deadly pastille, secrete it among those on the table during the time of his visit with Sir Randolph – or his secret entry into the house, if it were that – and then be safely away when by chance his victim selected the poisoned pastille for use. It was all very carefully premeditated; there was nothing impulsive about it. That is why, patently, the papers have nothing to do with the matter, for whoever put the pastille into the box did so well before even Sir Randolph knew that he would be sent the papers for examination. By the same process of deduction, the foreign visitor lacked motive – if there were such a visitor."

"And if not?"

"Then, I fear, we should have to put Davinson through it. But there is little reason to doubt Davinson's story. A foreign visitor to Sir Randolph is not unlikely. And Davinson does not seem to me to be capable of so elaborate a plan."

"Who then?"

"We must consider that Davinson was gone by night. Sir Randolph was alone. He could have given entry to anyone he pleased, regardless of what Davinson believes."

"Well, then, we get back to motive."

"Do we not!" said Pons.

So saying, he sank into a reverie, from which he stirred only once – to eat, with a preoccupied air, a lunch Mrs. Johnson sent up – and so he still sat, smoking pipe after pipe of his abominable shag, when at last I went to bed.

Pons' hand at my shoulder woke me while it was yet dark.

"Can you spare the day, Parker?" he asked, when I sat up. "We have just time to catch the four o'clock from King's Cross for Edinburgh."

"Edinburgh!" I cried, getting out of bed.

"I have an unyielding fancy to learn what the late Sir Randolph and his niece had words about."

"At this hour!"

"Time waits upon no one. We lose a day by traveling later. The four o'clock brings us into Edinburgh by one-thirty this afternoon. We shall have ample opportunity to make our enquiries of Miss Emily Curwen. You will have hours to sleep on the train."

"Miss Emily!" I cried. "For five hundred pounds! Preposterous."

"Unlikely, perhaps, but hardly preposterous," retorted Pons. "Poison, after all, is primarily a woman's weapon."

Pons had already summoned a cab, which waited below. As soon as I had dressed and made arrangements for my locum tenens to call on my patients for the next two days, we were off for King's Cross station, which we reached only just in time to catch the train for Scotland.

Once in our compartment and northward bound out of London, Pons sank again into cogitation, and I settled myself to resume the sleep Pons had interrupted.

When I woke in the late morning hours, Pons sat watching the lovely countryside flow by. We had crossed the Scottish border, and soon the familiar heights of Arthur's Seat, the Salisbury Crags, the Braid Hills and Corstorphine Hill would come into view. Here and there little pockets of ground mist still held to the hollows, but the sun shone, and the day promised to be fine.

The tranquil expression of Pons' face told me nothing.

"You cannot have been serious in suggesting that Miss Curwen poisoned her uncle," I said.

"I am not yet in a position to make that suggestion," replied Pons, turning away from the pane. "I submit, however, that a curious chain of events offers itself for our consideration. There is nothing to show that Miss Emily visited her uncle at any time previous to her recent visit. Then she comes, they have words, she hurries off, distraught. Does not this suggest anything to you?"

"Obviously they quarrelled."

"But what about? Two people who have not seen each other for many years – as far as we know – can hardly, on such short notice, have much to quarrel about."

"Unless there is a matter of long standing between them."

"Capital! Capital, Parker," said Pons, his eyes twinkling. "But what ancient disagreement could exist between uncle and niece?"

"A family estrangement?"

"There is always that possibility," conceded Pons. "I submit, however, that Miss Emily would hardly have come, in that case, unannounced and without an invitation to do so."

"Perhaps, unknown to Davinson, she had been invited to come," I said.

"Perhaps. I am inclined to doubt it. Miss Emily yielded to the impulse to confront her uncle to ask some favor of him. His failure to grant it angered her and she rushed off."

"That is hardly consistent with the premeditation so evident in the careful preparation of a poisoned pastille," I could not help pointing out.

"Granted, Parker. But there's nothing to prevent such premeditation in the event that the favor she asked her uncle were not granted."

"What could it have been that, failing its granting, only his death would serve her?" I protested. "If a matter of long standing, then, why not longer? No, Pons, it won't wash, it won't at all. I fear you have allowed your latent distrust of the sex to darken your view of Miss Emily Curwen."

Pons burst into hearty laughter.

"Where are we bound for then? Do you know?"

"Miss Emily lives in her father's house in Northumberland Street, in the New Town. I took time yesterday to ascertain this and other facts. She and her sister were the only children of Sir Randolph's brother Andrew. Her sister married unwisely, a man who squandered her considerable inheritance; both the elder Lindalls are now dead, survived by an only son, Ronald, who is employed in a bookshop in Torphichen Street which is only a few blocks from Princes Street Station. But here we are, drawing into Edinburgh."

Within the hour we stood on the stoop of the house in Northumberland Street, waiting upon the doorbell. Pons rang it three times before the door was opened, only a little, and an inquiring face looked out at us.

"Yes?"

"Miss Emily Curwen?"

"Yes?"

"Mr. Solar Pons, of London, at your service. Dr. Parker and I have come about the matter of your uncle's death."

There was a moment of pungent silence. Then the door was flung wide, and Miss Curwen stood there unmistakably shocked and surprised. "Uncle Randolph dead? I saw him within the month. The picture of health!" she cried. "But forgive me! Come in, gentlemen, do."

Miss Emily led the way to the drawing room of the old-fashioned mid-nineteenth century house, which was certainly at one time the abode of wealth. She was a woman approaching fifty, with a good figure still, and betraying some evidence in the care she had taken with her chestnut hair and her cosmetics of trying to retain as much of a youthful aspect as possible.

"Pray sit down," she said, and suited her own actions to her invitation to us. "And do tell me of uncle's death. What happened? Was it an accident?"

"Perhaps, in a manner of speaking, it was," said Pons. "He was found dead in his study."

"Poor uncle!" she cried, unaffectedly.

She seemed unable to fix her eyes on either Pons or myself, but was constantly wandering in her glance, while at the same time her hands were ever busy, plucking at her dress, or lacing her fingers together, or carrying her fingers to her lips.

"Perhaps you did not know he left you five hundred pounds?"

"No, I did not." Then her eyes brightened quite suddenly. "Poor, dear uncle! He needn't have done that. Now that he's gone, I shall have it all! All!"

"Somewhat over a fortnight ago you called on your uncle, Miss Curwen."

"Yes, I did." She grimaced.

"You found him well at that time?"

"I believe I have said as much, sir."

"You left him, upset. Was he unkind to you?"

"Sir, it was the old matter. Now it is resolved."

"Would you care to tell us about it?"

"Oh, there's no secret in it, I assure you. All the world knows of it here in Edinburgh. I suppose in London it is different. Who, in London, knows if I am alive?" She tossed her head and shrugged, pitying herself briefly. "Uncle Randolph was as hard a man as my father. My older sister Cicely made a very bad marriage in our father's eyes. He had settled her inheritance on her, and when he saw how Arthur wasted it, he made certain I could never do the same. So he put my inheritance – sir, fifty thousand pounds! – in trust, and made Uncle Randolph guardian of the trust. I could have only so much a year to live on – and you see me, sir, without even a regular maid. A pittance. My father lived frugally; my uncle did likewise. They expected me to do the same. But the world has changed, and everyone knows that it is not so easy to live on a restricted income as it was twenty-five years ago when my father died. But now all that's over and done with – now Uncle Randolph's dead, what's mine comes to me free of his control or anyone else's."

"You must have had assistance, Miss Curwen," said Pons sympathetically.

"Oh yes. My nephew, my dear boy! He's all I have, gentlemen. He has cared for his old aunt quite as if I were his own mother. I've been very much alone here. What could I do, what society could I have, on so limited an income? Now all that is changed. I am sorry Uncle Randolph is dead, but I'm not sorry the restrictions on my inheritance are removed."

Pons' glance flickered about the room, which looked as if it had not quite emerged into the twentieth century. "A lovely room, Miss Curwen," he observed.

"My grandfather planned it. I hate it," she said simply. "I shall lose no time selling the house. Think of having fifty thousand pounds I might have had when I was in my twenties! Oh, Mr. Pons, how cruel it was! My father thought I'd do the same thing my sister did, even after I saw how it went with them."

"I see you too are given to the use of incense, Miss Curwen," said Pons, his gaze fastened on a china castle.

"Any scent will serve to diminish the mould and mildew, gentlemen."

"May I look at that incense burner?" persisted Pons.

"Please do."

Pons crossed to the mantel where the china castle rested, picked it up, and brought it back to his chair. It was an elaborate creation in bone china, featuring three lichen-covered turrets, and evidently three burners. Carnations adorned it, and a vine of green leaves, and morning glories. Its windows were outlined in soft brown.

"A Colebrook Dale marking on this Coalport castle identifies it as prior to 1850 in origin," said Pons.

Miss Curwen's eyebrows went up. "You're a collector, sir?"

"Only of life's oddities," said Pons. "But I have some interest in antiquities as well. The Coalport burners were produced by John Rose. The leadless glaze is typical of these carefully modelled burners. So too the carnations." He looked up. "And what scent do you favor, Miss Curwen?"

"Rose."

"One could have guessed that you would select so complimentary a fragrance, Miss Curwen," said Pons.

Miss Curwen blushed prettily as Pons got up to return the china castle to the mantel, where he stood for a few moments with the opened box of pastilles in his hand, inhaling deeply the scent that emanated from it. He appeared to have some difficulty closing the box before he turned once more and came back to where he had been sitting. He did not sit down again.

"I fear we have imposed upon you long enough, Miss Curwen," said Pons.

Miss Emily came to her feet. "I suppose you will take care of such legalities as there are, gentlemen?"

"I fancy Sir Randolph's legal representatives will do that in good time, Miss Curwen," said Pons.

"Oh! I thought..."

"I am sorry to have given you the wrong impression. I am a private enquiry agent, Miss Curwen. There is some question about the manner of your uncle's death; I am endeavoring to answer it."

She was obviously perplexed. "Well, there's nothing I can tell you about that. I know he was in what looked like perfect health when I last saw him."

She did not seem to have the slightest suspicion of Pons' objective, and walked us to the door, where she let us out. From the stoop, we could hear the chain being slid back in place.

"I must hand it to you, Pons," I said. "There's motive for you."

"Poor woman! I'll wager she's dancing around by herself in celebration now," he said as we walked back down to the street. "There are pathetic people in this world to whom the possession of money is everything. All else pales before it. They know little of life and nothing of how to live. Presumably Andrew Curwen was such a one; I fear Miss Emily may be another. One could live well on the income of fifty thousand pounds if one had a mind to, but Miss Emily preferred to pine and grieve and feel sorry for herself. A lonely, deluded woman; I shall be sorry to add to her loneliness, but perhaps her wealth will assuage her. – But come, Parker, we have little time to lose. We must be off to the police. With luck, we shall be able to catch one of the night trains back to London."

Inspector Brian McGavick, a dark-faced young man with coal-black hair and sea-blue eyes, joined us when Pons explained his need. He was in plain-clothes, and looked considerably more like an actor than a member of the constabulary. "I've heard about you, Mr. Pons," said McGavick. "This morning – on instructions from the Foreign Office. I am at your service."

"Inspector, you're in charge here. I have no authority. I shall expect you to take whatever action the events of the next hour or two call for." He outlined briefly the circumstances surrounding the murder of Sir Randolph Curwen.

By the time he had finished we had arrived in Torphichen Street.

"Let us just park the car over here," said Pons, "and walk the rest of the way."

We got out of the police car and walked leisurely down the street to a little shop that bore the sign: *Laidlaw's Books*.

There Pons turned in.

A stout little man clad almost formally, save for his plaid weskit, came hurrying up to wait on us.

"Just browsing, sir," said Pons.

The little man bowed and returned to resume his place on a stool at a high, old-fashioned desk in a far corner of the shop. The three of us began to examine the books in the stalls and on the shelves, following Pons' lead. Pons soon settled down to a stall containing novels of Sir Walter Scott and Dickens, studying one volume after another with that annoying air of having the entire afternoon in which to do it.

In a quarter of an hour, the door of the shop opened to admit a handsome young man who walked directly back to the rear of the shop, removed his hat and ulster, and came briskly back to attend to us. Since Pons was nearest him, he walked directly up to Pons and engaged him in conversation I could not overhear until I drifted closer.

"There is merit in each," Pons was saying. "Scott for his unparalleled reconstruction of Scotland's past, Dickens for the remarkable range of his characters, however much some of them may seem caricatures. I think of establishing special shelves for each when I open my own shop."

"Ah, you're a bookman, sir? Where?"

"In London. I lack only a partner."

"I would like to be in London myself. What are your qualifications?"

"I need a young man, acquainted with books and authors, capable of putting a little capital into the business. Are you interested?"

"I might be."

Pons thrust forth his hand. "Name's Holmes," he said.

"Lindall," said the young man, taking his hand.

"Capital?" asked Pons.

"I expect to come into some."

"When?"

"Within the next few months."

"Ample time! Now tell me, Mr. Lindall, since I am in need of some other little service, do you know any chemistry?"

"None, sir."

"I asked because I saw a chemist's shop next door. Perhaps you have a friend there who might make up a special prescription for me?"

"As a matter of fact, I do have. A young man named Ardley. Ask for him and say I gave you his name."

"Thank you, thank you. I am grateful. In delicate little matters like these, one cannot be too careful."

Lindall's interest quickened. He ran the tip of his tongue over his lips and asked, "What is the nature of the prescription, sir?"

Pons dipped his hand into his coat pocket, thrust it out before Lindall, and unfolded his fingers. "I need a little pastille like this – with cyanide at the center, to dispose of old men and middle-aged ladies."

Lindall's reaction was extraordinary. He threw up his hands as if to thrust Pons away, stumbled backward, and upset a stall of books. Books and Lindall together went crashing to the floor.

"Oh, I say! I say now!" called out the proprietor, getting off his stool.

"Inspector McGavick, arrest this man for the murder of Sir Randolph Curwen, and the planned murder of his aunt, Miss Emily Curwen," said Pons.

McGavick had already moved in on Lindall, and was pulling him to his feet.

"You will need this poisoned pastille, Inspector. I found it in a box of rose pastilles in Miss Emily's home. You should have no difficulty proving that this and the one that killed Sir Randolph were manufactured for Lindall at his direction." To Lindall, Pons added, "A pity you didn't ask after my Christian name, Mr. Lindall. *Sherlock*. A name I assume on those special occasions when I feel inordinately immodest."

In our compartment on the 10:15 express for London Pons answered the questions with which I pelted him.

"It was an elementary matter, Parker," he said, "confused by the coincidence of Sir Randolph's possession of the Foreign Office papers, which could not have been the motivating factor in his death since the death trap had been laid for him well before anyone at all knew that he would see the papers in question. This motive eliminated, it became necessary to disclose another. Nobody appeared to dislike Sir Randolph, whose existence was uncomplicated and relatively reclusive, and it did not seem that any adequate motivation lay in the provisions of his will, for charitable institutions have no need to turn to murder for their funds.

"We were left, then, with Miss Emily's curious visit, angrily terminated, about which, as you saw, she made no mystery. Had she wished earnestly to break her father's trust provision, she could have resorted to litigation. There is no record that she did so. She went to London to appeal to her uncle for an end to the trust – as she had appealed by letter previously. She came back and complained to her nephew – her 'dear boy' who is 'all' she has – and clearly her designated heir, as an examination of her will will certainly show. In a fortnight, familiarized with Sir Randolph's habits by Miss Emily, he paid him a visit on his own, managed to slip the poisoned pastille into his box, and was off to bide his time. He had had two made, one for his aunt, and felt safe in slipping the other into her box of pastilles. He might better have waited a sensible time, even though he allowed for his aunt's less frequent use of incense to delay her death to what he, in his avarice, considered a reasonable time after her uncle's death. He had not counted on the death of

Sir Randolph being taken for anything but a seizure of some kind. He underestimated the police, I fear, and greed pushed him too fast. 'The love of money,' Parker, is indeed 'the root of all evil.'"

VII

THE ADVENTURE OF THE ASCOT SCANDAL

My friend, Solar Pons, raised his head suddenly from the cryptogram he was studying. "If I do not mistake the tenor of our good Mrs. Johnson's footsteps, she is coming up the stairs in a state of excitement."

"A car drove up a few moments ago," I said.

"I heard it," replied Pons, pushing back from the table to wait.

Our long-suffering landlady reached the threshold, knocked at first timidly, then more boldly and anxiously.

"Come in, come in, Mrs. Johnson," called Pons.

Mrs. Johnson opened the door and looked around it, her face flushed. "Oh, Mr. Pons, forgive me – they have no appointment – but it's Lord and Lady Gresham – dear me, it quite flusters me. They're waiting below."

"Show them up, by all means, Mrs. Johnson. The day thus far has been singularly devoid of challenge."

Mrs. Johnson backed out, closing the door after her.

"Lord and Lady Gresham," murmured Pons, reaching for the newspapers. "There was something in yesterday's papers about them." He paged quickly through the paper he had picked up, and came to a pause. "Ah, here we are. '*Scandal at Ascot. Thief in Lord Gresham's Box.* A daring thief at Ascot yesterday entered Lord Gresham's box by means of a forged card and created a diversion in the course of which he escaped with Lady Gresham's valuable diamond brooch..."

"And they are expecting you to catch him!" I cried. "Surely that is a matter for the police."

"Nothing is too trivial to lend it an ear at least," said Pons tranquilly. "But here they are."

Mrs. Johnson once again opened the door to our quarters and announced in a tremulous voice, "Lord and Lady Gresham."

It was rather Lady and Lord Gresham, however, for Lady Gresham made an aggressive entrance and His Lordship followed along behind with the same air of meekness that a curate might wear in the wake of his Bishop.

Her Ladyship was a sharp-featured, milk-skinned young woman with strawberry-colored hair worn in a modified Gibson coiffure. Her black eyes fixed upon Pons at once, and without preamble, she declared, "Mr. Pons, I want my brooch back."

"Pray be seated," said Pons, moving a chair forward.

She immediately sat down on the very edge of the chair, perched and thrusting forward into the room as it were, as if in disdain or eagerness or perhaps both, while Lord Gresham came to stand immediately behind her – a thin, almost scrawny young man with straw-colored hair and worried blue eyes. He wore a moustache on his upper lip, and a monocle in one eye, though this, it was evident within the first few minutes of his presence in our quarters, had an unfortunate habit of falling out, so that His Lordship was constantly engaged, whether speaking or not, in alternately dabbing at his forehead with a silk handkerchief or replacing his monocle.

"I don't care what it costs," Her Ladyship went on, "but I want it back. Daddy gave it to me before I came across to marry Archer, and I'm sweet on it because it's a keepsake from Daddy."

"Ah, Lady Gresham was an American," said Pons.

"Yes, but that has nothing to do with what happened at Ascot," she said.

"Let us begin at the beginning," said Pons patiently.

"Oh, fiddlededee!" she cried. "It's been in all the papers already."

"We shall want no more of it," said Lord Gresham firmly.

"And we shall want the brooch returned, no questions asked," said Her Ladyship just as firmly. "Go on, Pet, tell him everything."

"Very well, Dolly," said Lord Gresham. "It happened, as you know, at Ascot day before yesterday – but, of course, Mr. Pons, you've read the accounts in the newspapers surely?"

"I take everything in the papers with a grain of salt, Your Lordship," said Pons with the utmost gravity.

"Oh, I say, that's good, that is," said His Lordship appreciatively. "That's good, isn't it, Dolly?"

"Yes, yes," she replied with mounting impatience. "But do tell him, Archie, everything just as it happened."

Lord Gresham began once more. "Her Ladyship was in our box with some friends – Jack Luton and his wife, Alise, and Miss Grace Levinson, when this bounder came in, presenting a card giving him entry purportedly signed by me – a bounder, sir..."

"Oh, I don't know, Pet," interrupted Lady Gresham. "He was at first very charming, very agreeable. And rather handsome, too. I did think that he wore rouge or something of that sort. But when he was so attentive to Grace, and then to Alise Luton, and then, naturally to me" – she simpered briefly – "why, of course, we felt that he was hardly the sort of gentleman you could have given entry to our box. It did occur to me," she added, with a dark glance for her husband, "that you might be paying off some gaming debt or other – but you tell the story, Pet."

His Lordship sighed and made ready to begin again.

This time Pons interrupted him. "Your Lordship was not present?"

"Not then, no, Mr. Pons. I was delayed and I didn't reach our box until after it had happened."

Pons turned to Her Ladyship. "Perhaps then you, who were there, could set forth a clearer picture of what actually took place."

"Well, of course," she said cheerfully. "I should have told it all along, I know. But it's really Pet's responsibility, he makes such a point of being head of the house and all. Well, this man came up to me and presented his card, and what else could I do but let him into our box? After all, I thought His Lordship would expect to see him there when he came."

"Did the gentleman give his name?"

"A bounder!" put in Lord Gresham.

"Oh, yes, his name. Well, I think it was something like Evelyn Parkinson written on his lapel ticket – yes, that's it. But he didn't offer any explanation of how he came to have His Lordship's card, and of course I couldn't very well ask, after all, he was a guest, and all that, and I thought, naturally, Archie would explain when he came. Well, to make a long story short, he had brought a flask of liquor with him, and he took a nip now and then, and I guess he got a little tight, and the first thing we knew he had insulted Alise and made some further remarks about Jack, and he and Jack got to scuffling. Naturally, we ladies tried to separate the two, and you know, as I said, that man had been drinking, and he was hard to handle, Jack got in one punch – nothing serious, but that man couldn't hit anything, he was just all over us, but at last we separated them and I said, 'I must ask you to leave this box!' and he went. It wasn't long after that I missed my brooch."

Having finished her story, she settled back a little in her chair more at ease.

"You did, of course, search your box?" asked Pons.

"Oh, yes, we did that," she answered, somewhat impatiently, as if Pons need not have asked. "But there was nothing there. We even looked around outside of it. The brooch was gone. Oh, you needn't doubt it, Mr. Pons – it went with that man. And I want it back because Daddy gave it to me, and Daddy paid twenty-five thousand dollars for it at Tiffany's just before I left New York."

"What happened to the card he presented?"

"The card? Why, he put it back into the pocket of his weskit."

"I see. Now, Lady Gresham, you had every opportunity to examine your visitor?"

"Oh, I surely did. I naturally want to know who my husband associates with. Of course, I couldn't ask, you know – that wouldn't have been nice. But I looked him up and down, as you might say."

"Ah, then, you can describe him?"

"Yes, Mr. Pons. He was a young man. He had a very good figure and he wore his clothes so well it came as a surprise to me to discover he wasn't a gentleman, after all. He did appear to have rouge and perhaps powder on his face and I wouldn't be surprised to learn his hair wasn't – well, wasn't *all* his – because it was much darker than his eyebrows. He had brown eyes with very long lashes – I suppose *some* ladies would call him very handsome, but of course I always like to look farther than skin-deep. His mouth was just a trifle petulant and he had what we call in America 'cupid's bow' lips. He had a straight nose, a little longer than most, but not too long to unbalance his face. His fingers were slender – just the sort you might think right for an artist – or a thief. And one more thing, I can't be positive, but once in a while I could have sworn he talked like an American."

"Would you call him experienced?"

"Oh, yes, he certainly was that. He knew just what he was doing. He did it very well. He had come to that box to steal and he managed it."

"Was anything else of value missing?"

"No, Mr. Pons. We took inventory right away. Alise had a brooch on, too, that cost somewhat less than mine. He took the most expensive piece."

"You have circulated its description through the police, of course?"

"Well, no. Archie didn't want any more publicity, and that's why we came here. I said, 'It's either the police or some private enquiry agent.' I wanted to go see Sherlock Holmes – we've read so much about him over there – but Archie told me he'd retired to some place in the country to keep bees – so we came to you. If we can't have the best, we'll have to do with second-best."

Behind her, Lord Gresham reddened. I suppressed a smile, but I saw that Pons' eyes were dancing at Her Ladyship's gaffe.

"But I have the description right here, Mr. Pons," she went on, producing a piece of paper which she unfolded as she spoke. "I even made a drawing of it for you, life size." She handed the paper to Pons. "There's a large, flawless diamond in the center of the design – ten carats – then a circle of emeralds – then a circle of smaller diamonds, and there's an emerald pendant from the center. It's all set in platinum, and Daddy had it made specially for me."

While Pons studied Lady Gresham's drawing, His Lordship began to speak apologetically.

"I did tell Dolly that a discreet inquiry would be better, but that it was hardly an important enough problem for your talents, Mr. Pons. I know it would mean a good bit of purely routine enquiry."

"Oh, fiddlededee!" cried Her Ladyship. "Mr. Pons will be paid."

"Nothing is too trivial for my talents," said Pons with unexpected modesty. "And it would be a pleasure to return Her Ladyship's brooch."

Her Ladyship almost squealed her delight. "Now, that's what I always mean when I tell Pet that the Englishmen have it over the Americans – they're such *gentlemen*!"

Pons bowed, his eyes twinkling.

Lady Gresham thereupon became very businesslike. She took her handbag from the floor where she had placed it, opened it, and removed her cheque-book. Without more ado, she wrote a cheque to Pons and handed it to him.

"I understand you will want something on account, Mr. Pons. I hope a hundred pounds will do."

"Amply, Your Ladyship," said Pons.

Lady Gresham bounced to her feet. "We can go now, Pet. Mr. Pons will take care of it. And you needn't worry. I can tell he'll be delicate and tactful enough."

They bade us good-morning and walked out the door I held open for them.

"I wonder," said Pons reflectively, when I turned to him, "if all young American ladies are like that."

"You can take it from me that she married herself a title and he married himself some money," I said.

"I submit it isn't quite like that, Parker," said Pons, smiling.

"But this is surely a prosaic problem for your talents," I said.

"Is it not!" he agreed almost with enthusiasm. "Yet I think it has one or two little points of interest."

"I should like to know what they are. It seems to me a very ordinary case of theft – oh, smoothly done, perhaps, yes, but on the whole ordinary."

"Gently, Parker. We have here a most uncommon thief – and a most selective one. Was Lady Gresham's brooch famous: Perhaps it ought to have been, but I have certainly not heard of it before the account of its theft in the newspapers. Yet the thief seems to have been aware of its existence and of its worth; indeed, he seems to have gone to some daring lengths to appropriate it; he could hardly have chosen a more public place than a box at the races. He seems not to have been daunted by this. Did you think it of any significance that Her Ladyship detected something American about him?"

"Of course," I cried. "The brooch was specially made in America. Someone there certainly knew of it. Perhaps an ex-employee of Tiffany's?"

"I should think it highly unlikely that so respectable and well-established a firm as Tiffany's would risk retaining an employee about whose references or character there could be even the shadow of a doubt."

"Then an ex-employee of her father's."

"Would she not have recognized him, in that case? I should think so."

"He was made up to conceal his identity from her. Her Ladyship remarked on his rouge and guessed that his hair was not his own. He wore a wig."

"A wig would hardly conceal the identity of an old employee," said Pons. "Furthermore, Lady Gresham described him as young. But it is idle to speculate. We have certain facts. He was a young man. He was probably of American origin. He was aware of the existence of the brooch. He was evidently also aware that Lady Gresham would be wearing it at Ascot – though he could quite possibly have been waiting on the opportunity of her doing so. He was prepared to present himself boldly at Lord Gresham's box and pose as a friend of His Lordship. Do these circumstances suggest anything to you?"

"We are dealing with a highly resourceful scoundrel."

"Elementary. Nothing more?"

"Nothing, except that you are certainly not going to have an easy time finding him."

"Oh, I am a little less discouraged than you seem to be, Parker," Pons said jovially. "In fact, I almost have my hand on him."

"You are joking!"

"Far from it. It is not so much the thief as the whereabouts of the brooch that puzzles me. I already know enough about the thief, thanks to Her Ladyship's excellent description, to apprehend him in but the time it will take me to make inquiries. The brooch offers considerably more of a problem."

"It will surely have been fenced by this time."

"Ah, do you think so? It does not seem to you that a brooch of such distinction might be difficult to market in any fashion, short of cutting it up and disposing of it piece-meal? Flawless ten-carat diamonds cannot be so plentiful that the appearance of one would not excite comment. A diamond of such size would surely command between thirty-five hundred and four thousand pounds. Presuming the lesser diamonds to be, let us say, but a tenth of a carat, we can estimate another ten pounds each for them. The possibility is distinct that Her Ladyship underestimates its actual value."

"Pawned, then."

"It would surely have occurred to even the most amateur among thieves that the pawn shops would be under police surveillance from the moment the theft was reported."

"But Lord Gresham has not called in the police," I protested.

"The thief could hardly hope for as much," Pons pointed out. "But the police need not be 'called in' to take a hand. Crime does not occur simply at the decision of the victims."

"Could it not then be smuggled into Holland for disposal?"

"There is always that possibility, but any thief might expect police on both sides to be watching for it."

"Very well then. What avenues remain open for your search?"

"I fancy we shall have to have a word with the thief himself. Just hand me that city directory, Parker."

"Oh, you expect to find his name and address!" I said, not without sarcasm.

Pons merely smiled. He went through the directory until he found the references he sought. "Ah, here we are. The Actors' Guild Agency in Great Queen Street. Since that is the best-known actors' agency in London, it is certainly there that we should make our initial application."

"An actors' agency!" I cried. "Pons, are you out of your mind?"

"Surely it must have occurred to you that anyone who could carry off so daring a theft as that at our client's box at Ascot must be a consummate actor – perhaps an actor in need."

"And a thief!" I added.

Pons chuckled.

"What I am looking for," said Pons to the gentleman at the agency, "is an American born actor with a reasonably wide range of talents in bit parts. He should not be too obviously American, but should not have entirely lost his American accent."

"We have two, sir, on the waiting list at present. One is George Riddell. The other is Harold Pollard."

"I should prefer a young man, not over thirty."

"That will be Mr. Pollard. He is just thirty, sir."

"Straight nose, on the long side?"

"Yes, sir."

"Valentine lips."

"I believe you would call them that."

"Brown eyes?"

"Yes, sir. That will certainly fit Mr. Pollard."

"Where can I find him?"

"We will send him where you like."

"No, that will not be necessary. If you will be so good as to give me his address, we will just go 'round to his quarters and interview him there."

He gave us a Drury Lane address, and Pons thanked him.

Since Drury Lane was just around the corner from the agency, it was within easy walking distance, and in a few minutes we were out in the street and on our way. I could not help expostulating a little.

"This is surely no more than coincidence," I said.

"But how precise in every detail!" replied Pons, smiling. "You do my poor powers no honor, Parker."

More than this he would not say. Instead, as we went along, he spoke of the history of Great Queen Street and its residences. "Boswell lived here, and Sheridan," he said, "and Sir Godfrey Kneller and Perdita Robinson. Perhaps Mr. Pollard seeks to bask in their reflected glory from a respectful distance."

I could do as well, and reminded him that Pollard's quarters in Drury Lane were, for any actor, of greater significance, for the association of that street with Nell Gwyn, Garrick, John Kemble, Mrs. Siddons, Edmund Kean and many others.

"*Touché*!" cried Pons imperturbably.

We arrived in silence at the address we sought.

"At this hour of the afternoon Mr. Pollard ought to be at home," said Pons, as he rang the bell.

The landlady who came to answer his ring might have been a pale, somewhat thinner copy of our Mrs. Johnson.

"Mr. Harold Pollard?" asked Pons. "Is he in?"

"Yes, sir. First floor, first door to the right."

Pons thanked her as she stood aside to permit our entry.

We climbed the stairs and Pons rapped smartly on the first door.

A pair of stockinged feet struck the floor beyond the door, as had our quarry been lounging on a bed or sitting with his feet raised; in a moment the door was pulled open and a not unhandsome young man stood there.

"What can I do for you?" he asked.

"Mr. Harold Pollard? Unemployed actor?"

"That's me."

"My name is Solar Pons, Mr. Pollard. I am acting for Lord Gresham in the matter of Her Ladyship's brooch. I have come for it."

Pollard's jaw dropped, but only for a moment. Then he grinned. "Well, you're a cool one, I must say, Come in."

He backed away from the door, leaving it open, vaulted over a chair and, as we closed the door behind us, spun around to a small dressing-table and pulled open a drawer. From it he took a glittering object and handed it carelessly to Pons. A glance was sufficient to assure me that it was indeed Lady Gresham's diamond brooch.

"He's a fancy one – hiring Mr. Solar Pons, the Great Detective," said Pollard with the utmost *savoir faire*.

"Actually, Her Ladyship retained me," said Pons. "The police simply wouldn't do. 'No questions asked.' The police like to ask questions."

"And you don't!" said Pollard, his grin widening. "So I won't ask you any."

"Gentleman's agreement," said Pons.

"Right-o!"

"Good day, Mr. Pollard. A pity one of your talents should have to resort to such ventures!"

"There are some people have it good, and some haven't," said Pollard, closing the door behind us.

"You don't mean to let him escape scot-free?" I asked hotly.

"'No questions asked', our client said – and so it shall be. I am not the agent of justice," replied Pons.

"It is unlike you," I said.

"Ah, Parker, you are quicker to judge than I," said Pons. "Now I fancy we shall have a word or two with the Noble Lord. I shall just send him a wire asking him to step around to 7B this evening."

Pons spent an hour after our evening meal studying the workmanship of Lady Gresham's diamond brooch before he laid it away under the deerstalker on the mantel and returned to the cryptographic study which the arrival of our clients had interrupted that morning.

I could not keep from saying, "You have not done any more than any constable could have done. I'm surprised you accepted the problem."

"And disappointed?"

"I admit it."

"Ah, I was just in the mood for a less sanguinary diversion," replied Pons. "What with that little matter of the Bishop's Companion only last week, I have had enough of gore. Tomorrow, who can say, perhaps we shall once again have murder on our hands. Today's theft is an interim engagement."

I took refuge in silence.

Promptly at eight o'clock, the hour appointed, Lord Gresham presented himself.

"I hope you have news for me, Mr. Pons," he said, as he took the chair Pons proferred.

"I may say that I have. I must however, be certain of one or two little points."

"By all means, sir."

"Her Ladyship's brooch was insured?"

"Heavily."

"Have you made any attempt to collect that insurance, Your Lordship?"

"Not yet. I hope we may not find it necessary."

"And I. I have some scruples about conniving, even indirectly, in an insurance swindle."

"What do you mean, Mr. Pons?"

Pons crossed to the mantel and raised the deerstalker. He picked up the brooch, carried it over, and laid it on the table before our client. His Lordship goggled at it as if he could not believe his eyes.

He found his voice before Pons' silence. "Where – where in God's name did you find it, Mr. Pons?"

"I got it from Mr. Harold Pollard."

"Mr. Pollard?" His Lordship echoed faintly.

"Mr. Pollard is the gentleman who invaded your box at Ascot and took the brooch from Her Ladyship."

"Mr. Pons, I hardly know what to say."

"Perhaps, in the circumstances, you ought to say nothing, Your Lordship. You have my sympathy. How much, in fact, did you raise on Her Ladyship's brooch before you found it necessary to substitute this creation in paste and glass?"

Lord Gresham gulped and his monocle fell from his eye. He pulled the inevitable silk handkerchief from his pocket and mopped his brow.

"How much?" asked Pons inexorably.

"Two thousand pounds."

"Can you redeem it?"

His Lordship shook his head. He looked the picture of abject misery.

"Can Her Ladyship?"

"Easily. But she holds her wealth tight, Mr. Pons, very tight."

Pons' lips trembled, but he did not give way to laughter.

"Her Ladyship specified 'no questions asked'. Pray give her my compliments and tell her that her brooch is at – " He paused inquiringly.

"Chaim Kundrat's. He's a private money-lender. He's helped me before when I was short."

"And that she can reclaim it there, no questions asked, for the sum of two thousand pounds. As for Your Lordship – I can only suggest that you take more care in your gaming ventures in the future. Inform Her Ladyship that the retainer already paid covers my entire fee."

A wildly hopeful light came into being in His Lordship's pale eyes. "It might just work, Mr. Pons."

"It will have to do. Her Ladyship will stop at nothing to regain possession of her brooch. You will have to make that two thousand up to her in another way."

"Mr. Pons, I cannot thank you enough!" cried Lord Gresham, bounding to his feet.

"Pray do not try. These little domestic difficulties are bound to occur in even the best regulated households. You see, I am content to remain a bachelor."

Lord Gresham shook Pons' hand vigorously and would have taken his leave, had not Pons stopped him.

"You have forgotten your imitation brooch, Your Lordship," he said, handing it to him. "You may need it again."

"True, true," said His Lordship, pocketing the brooch.

"But do not make the mistake of going home with it in your pocket. Her Ladyship strikes me as likely to find it without effort."

Lord Gresham favored us with a wan smile and departed.

Pons fell into his favorite chair, shaking with laughter.

"Ah, Parker, the joys of wedded bliss!" he cried, when his laughter had subsided.

"You are being unfair to the state of matrimony," I cried.

"Of course. I should have narrowed my reference to those who marry for other reasons than love."

"Pons, you guessed from the beginning."

"Say, rather, I knew. Lady Gresham as much as told us. She identified the thief as an actor, however unwittingly. Actors are for hire for a great variety of occasions, and when she said to her husband that it had occurred to her that he might 'be paying off some gaming debt or other' the solution immediately suggested itself. Lord Gresham, unable to get his hands on some of the money for which he had married that redheaded charmer, had in desperation taken her valuable brooch and borrowed money against it. He had prepared an imitation but he had not counted on Her Ladyship's wearing the brooch, since presumably she set such store by it that she seldom wore it. When she began to wear it again, he had no alternative but to prevent her discovery that she was wearing an imitation, since he could not raise the money to redeem it; so he arranged for Pollard to steal it, giving him his ticket and card to gain him entry to his box at Ascot – a card Pollard naturally pocketed again, after having shown it, for any comparison with Lord Gresham's signature would have proven that they were identical and that no forgery was in fact involved. Lord Gresham might conceivably avoid having to redeem the brooch at all, or might redeem it only to sell it, if the gambit succeeded. But, alas! he had not counted on Her Ladyship's devotion to that keepsake from her father. He was able to put her off the police – it would never do to have them institute a search for it in view of the circumstances – but was unable to prevent her coming here." He sighed contentedly. "Ah, Parker, the single state favors my constitution."

"Say, rather, few women could bear to share it," I said.

"Your powers of deduction are truly remarkable, my dear fellow," replied Pons with a little chuckle of self-congratulation.

VIII

THE ADVENTURE OF THE CROUCHING DOG

The train had stopped at Chudleigh, and Solar Pons, chafing at every delay in our return to London from Cornwall and the puzzling matter of the Innkeeper's Clerk, had lowered the window and stuck his head out. He stood so for a few moments, looking up and down the station platform, his hands clasped behind his back; then he drew back into our compartment.

"You may think London is England, Parker," he said. "But it is not so. Out there is England – in a thousand villages and hamlets scattered across the face of the loveliest countryside in the world." He waited upon no comment from me to add, "At this point we are approximately two hundred miles and five hours from Paddington."

The guard's whistle sounded, and the train moved on.

Pons sat down after raising the window once more, for, though the October sunlight was warm, the wind that came in through the open window was chill.

We had hardly settled back for the remainder of our journey when there was a sharp rap on the door of our compartment, and a voice asked, "Mr. Solar Pons?"

Pons leaped to his feet and threw open the door.

A guard stood there with an envelope in his hands. He thrust it at Pons. "For you, sir."

Pons thanked him.

Standing with his back to the door, he tore open the envelope and drew out a wire.

"So," he said, having read it, "it was premature to count on Paddington today." He threw the wire to me. "I can hardly refuse Ramsey."

I read the wire. "STANDING BY AT EXETER. PLEASE JOIN ME. HORRIBLE CRIME AT JOWETT CLOSE. Ramsey." I looked up. "Who's Ramsey?"

"Sir Roderick Ramsey, Chief Constable of Devon. An old friend," replied Pons. "He must have telephoned Mrs. Johnson at 7B, and tracked us away from St. Mawes in the same fashion." He looked at his watch. "It can't be more than an hour to Exeter. Presumably he'll be at St. David's. We can only wait on our arrival there."

At the Great Western station in Exeter a tall, imposing man, whose most distinguishing feature was a fierce moustache, strode toward us as we descended from our compartment. He wore a rumpled tweed suit beneath a car coat, and on his head a checkered cap; he carried a swagger stick under one arm. His grizzled face, with his moustache and the bristling eyebrows, lent him the appearance of the popular screen-star, C. Aubrey Smith.

"My dear Pons!" his voice boomed across a hundred feet of the station platform. "Sorry, and all that – interrupt your journey – know how anxious you must be to get back to London." But with this he was upon us. He caught hold of Pons' hand and shook it vigorously, acknowledged Pons' introduction to me with equal vigor, and went on, lowering his voice only a trifle, "It's poor Larry Jowett – been done in – found him with his head bashed in – all torn – some animal – horrible thing." By the time we had passed through the crowd at St.

David's and got into Sir Roderick's Rolls-Royce, Pons managed to stay our host's ebullience, and the account came with more coherence.

"You may or may not know it, Pons," began Sir Roderick, as the car drew away from St. David's and began to thread its way through the historic city of Exeter, across the Exe toward West Devon, "but Jowett'd been out of England for two years. With Lord Carnarvon's expedition in Egypt. He was with the party when they opened the tomb of Tutankhamen, and all that. It sounds like balderdash, but wait until you've had a look into it. By my count, Jowett's the fourth man of that party to die, and I say it's enough to put the wind up a more rational man than I am.

"He came home in September. Jowett Close is an old manor house on the northeastern edge of Dartmoor, not far from Throwleigh – about an hour's distance from here. It's a big place – once a moor farm – but you may know that country, remote as it is; it's high moorland country – and Jowett's wife lived there with the servants, his two younger brothers, and one of hers. Jowett was a wealthy man; he had to be, to support such an entourage." He shook his head brusquely. "But that's neither here nor there – the fact is, he's dead. Shocking sight, too. I knew him well. It shook me, Pons. He went out some time in the night and the evidence shows that he went for a walk on the moor and something tracked him, he began to run, it went after, caught up, struck him down, and killed him. I've ordered nothing touched until you reached the spot. I lost no time tracking you down."

"So I see," said Pons dryly.

"I'm no amateur in these things, Pons," Sir Roderick went on. "What puzzles me is the complete absence of motive. And then Larry's going on – they tell me – about some sort of dog – a crouching dog, that's it – and the tomb curse and all that – and the look of his having been killed by some great dog! It's a bit unnerving. It needs a clearer mind. So I sent for you. What d'you think?"

"Let us just wait upon events," said Pons. "I'll want to look about at the scene of the crime."

"Naturally. A man can't do everything from an armchair!"

"Not everything," conceded Pons. "But I submit a man doesn't need to rise from an armchair to conclude that no dog, large or small, has as much motive for killing a man as one of his fellowmen."

"*Touché!*" boomed Sir Roderick.

"One question, however," said Pons. "You said Jowett was wealthy. Now he's dead, who inherits?"

"I gather his widow does. There were no children. And his brothers come in for something, I have no doubt."

"And her brother?"

"Nothing. She'll have the best of his estate, and the living at Jowett Close if she wants it."

"His brothers, now. Why have they been content to stay there? I assume, since Jowett can hardly still have been a very young man, to be with Carnarvon's expedition, his brothers must have reached their majority."

"Well, one was studying for the ministry. That's Harold. He gave it up and came back to Jowett Close about six months ago. Hasn't shown any sign of wanting to leave so far. John's a bookish type – reading, writing poetry, that sort of thing. Just the kind of fellow who'd be glad of any niche to settle in."

"Independent income?"

"Yes, but small."

"Education?"

"Oxford, I believe. Both of them. Her brother's an older man, retired barrister. I've had a game of darts with him, but I don't know much about him. One of those taciturn, pipe-smoking individuals."

Pons nodded, and gazed thoughtfully out at the fleeting landscape. He asked no further questions.

In less than an hour we drove into the grounds at Jowett Close. Sir Roderick leaped from his car, beckoning us to follow; with instructions to his chauffeur to stay with the car, he strode away toward the moor. The manor house, from what it was possible to see of it in our passage, was in large part very old – a low building of one storey and one and a half storeys, variously, and square towers of two and three storeys at some of its corners, bespeaking a conglomeration of architectural influences. It was winged on both ends with several small outbuildings, and there were signs that other such buildings had been removed long since.

Beyond the house loomed the moor. The hour was now high noon, but even so, the great expanse of desolate land, with its tors, its shadow-swept slopes and barrens, a lone grove of woods to our right, was impressively formidable, and yet not without a certain wild beauty inherent in its solitudes. Clouds had risen, and, driven by a high wind which could not be felt where we walked, crossed the sun from time to time, so that we walked alternately in sunlight and in shade, and the moor ahead of us was a patch-work of sunlight and swiftly-moving cloud-shadows.

Sir Roderick walked with singular purpose, sawing the air at his side with his swagger stick, his car coat flowing outward at no more than the impetus of his swift strides. He did not once turn to discover whether Pons and I followed, which was fortunate, for Pons had gone off to one side, and was now loping along almost like an animal, hunched over, dropping to his knees from time to time, paying no heed to the comments Sir Roderick flung over his shoulders.

The manor house receded behind us; the moor closed in, diminishing us in a world of sky, clouds, stone outcroppings and desolate moorland. We had gone perhaps a mile in this fashion when, rounding a granite tor-formation that crowned a little rise in the tableland, we came suddenly upon a party of people, grouped together at one side of a covered form lying still in death.

Sir Roderick plunged at once into introductions – two constables named Warburton and Jones, a pair of photographers, Dr. Horace Annesley, and a harassed-looking man of approximately forty, whose name Sir Roderick brashly mispronounced – Anthony Heyle, who had been, said Sir Roderick, lowering his voice, "Larry Jowett's old friend and legal counsel. And this," he went on, "is Mr. Solar Pons," at which he turned and for the first time noticed that Pons was only now coming up. He hastily amended his speech. "This is Dr. Lyndon Parker, and that fellow coming up is Pons – you see, he's already on the trail." He turned to the constables, gestured with his swagger stick, and commanded, "Uncover him – but take care how you step there – we'll want those marks untouched!"

Pons came up, his eyes blazing with keenness, his lips grimly pursed, just as the cover was removed from the body of Lawrence Jowett. Jowett was almost spread-eagled on the ground, lying on his face; his outflung arms ended in clawed fingers partly dug into the ground in his death agony, which could not have lasted long, for a great wound gaped in his skull where flesh and bone had been torn away, and below it, smoking-jacket, shirt, and undershirt, exposing his back and bloody, clawlike scratches deep in his flesh.

Pons walked delicately around the body, looking now at it, now away, at the ground around it. He bent to study the torn clothing as well as the horrible wound. Plainly Jowett had been felled by a single blow, seemingly made by a gigantic paw. Pons straightened and looked toward the physician who had been called to the scene.

"Dr. Annesley, would you say he lingered?" he asked.

"No, Mr. Pons. He may not have died instantly, but it certainly did not take him long to die with such a wound."

"You've examined him. When would you estimate death took place?"

"Some time after midnight and before two o'clock, possibly one o'clock. Rigor mortis is well advanced, but the night was chill."

"Hm! The marks of his running are clear. He began to run a quarter of a mile back."

"You saw the animal tracks?" interrupted Sir Roderick. Pons merely nodded. "But what kind of dog – or other animal – would strike him so? I submit that this may be the primary question. I commend it to your attention, gentlemen," he said to the constables.

Sir Roderick struck his leg with his swagger stick. "If you've finished, let's cover him, and get on with it."

"One moment, Sir Roderick," said Pons, as he bent and drew something carefully from beneath the clawed fingers of the dead man's right hand. "What have we here?"

He walked toward us, holding forth a stone, one face of which was engraved with a dog crouching above nine kneeling men.

For a moment no one spoke.

Then Heyle shuddered and said, "Mr. Pons, that is the seal of the crouching dog, the seal of the necropolis of the Pharaoh Tutankhamen."

"You are an Egyptologist, Mr. Heyle?"

"No, sir. Mr. Jowett explained it to me. This stone is only a copy. It had no value save as a curio. But Mr. Jowett had grown somewhat upset by the deaths which had taken place as a result of what he called the curse of Tutankhamen."

"Whose deaths, Mr. Heyle?"

"Lord Carnarvon's of a spider bite – Georges Bénédite's of a stroke – Arthur Mace's in New York."

"And now Larry Jowett's," said Sir Roderick, with a heavy sigh.

The constables had now lifted Jowett's body and placed it upon a stretcher which had been awaiting Pons' arrival, preparatory to bearing it away, and Pons turned once more to the spot where Jowett had lain, bending to scrutinize it with the utmost care. He lingered longest at the place where the dead man's hands had clawed into the earth, kneeling there for a few moments, while Sir Roderick watched him with narrowed eyes. Only when he had satisfied himself that nothing had escaped his notice did Pons rise and rejoin us.

The constables, followed by the photographers, were already leading the melancholy way back to the house. Sir Roderick, Anthony Heyle, Pons and I fell into step behind them. Pons walked for some distance in silence, his high brow furrowed in thought, his eyes fixed upon the ground. He carried his hands clasped behind him, and his lips, as before, were grimly tight until he looked up suddenly.

"You said, I believe, Mr. Heyle, that the late Mr. Jowett spoke with some concern about the curse of Tutankhamen. Can you repeat his words?"

"Well, no, sir," answered Heyle hestitatingly. "I can give you their substance, but, frankly, I didn't think them important enough to commit them to memory."

"Their substance, then," said Pons shortly.

"He recounted the deaths of the three men I mentioned. He seemed disturbed. Yet he joked about it, saying if any strange dogs were seen about the place – especially large dogs – he'd want to know in time to clean his guns. That sort of thing. Still he more than half believed in the curse."

"Damned queer business!" cried Sir Roderick.

"But you did not?" asked Pons.

"I fear, Mr. Pons, that the profession of the law demands more concrete evidence."

"He spoke of this matter frequently?" pressed Pons.

"What is 'frequently', Mr. Pons?"

"How many times did he mention this?"

"Since he came home five or six weeks ago, he mentioned it. I suppose, once a week. It seemed to be on his mind, but he did not seem to be worried about it. It was something that interested rather than worried him."

"When was the last time, Mr. Heyle?"

"Only last night."

"Ah, you spoke to him last night?"

"I may have been the last person to speak with him, Mr. Pons. We were up late – close to midnight. We had been going over some legal matters. Mr. Jowett had many investments I had been seeing to in his absence. Then there was his will, in which he planned to make some alterations."

"Specifically?"

"He wanted to increase his brother Harold's share of the estate. Since Harold had gone into the ministry prior to Jowett's joining the Carnarvon expedition, it had not then seeemed to Jowett that he would need as much of a stipend as John. Now that he had deserted this calling, it seemed to Jowett that he would need equally as much as John."

"So you spoke of this, and the curse of Tutankhamen cropped up again?"

"Yes, rather violently. I had tired of hearing about it. I don't have that kind of mind, Mr. Pons. I suppose mine was a professional reaction. In the end we had words about it, with Mr. Jowett becoming rather insistent in his belief that there was some pattern in the events which had taken place. Which was nonsense, of course."

"And you said as much."

"I did."

"As his counsel, what is your estimate of Jowett's net worth?"

"Something over a quarter of a million pounds. Of this sum, his wife will receive two-thirds, including Jowett Close, his brothers will share unevenly, since he had not had time to change his will – John will receive two thousand pounds a year, Harold five hundred, and the rest goes to some of the servants and certain charities. He left a very clear and unambiguous will, Mr. Pons."

"If Mr. Jowett had lived to alter his will, would Harold's increased stipend have come from the sum allotted to John?"

"Possibly," said Heyle. "But I really couldn't say, Mr. Pons."

"Were the brothers aware that a change was being contemplated in the will?"

Heyle answered cautiously. "I should think they may well have been."

Pons retreated into silence.

The head of the melancholy little caravan was now entering the garden area of the grounds around Jowett Close. The scene had gone grey and sombre; clouds had closed over the sky, the sunlight was gone. Behind us the moor brooded darkly, almost menacing, like a great sentient being lying in wait, the tors like sinister sentinels wrapped in stony silence. Even Sir Roderick said nothing as we moved upon the house, until, at the threshold, he turned to Pons and spoke.

"Mrs. Jowett has asked to see you."

He led the way to the drawing-room where Sybil Jowett sat looking emotionlessly out upon the moor. She rose as we entered, and revealed herself to be a handsome, full-breasted woman, of more than average height. With that intuition so common to women, she fixed her lustrous blue eyes upon Pons and advanced to meet us.

"Mr. Solar Pons. I'm pleased you could come."

"Thank you. A sad occasion, Mrs. Jowett."

With one clenched hand she briefly touched her lips, then flung her arm wide. "Sit down, Mr. Pons. Sir Roderick." She turned on me.

"Dr. Lyndon Parker," said Sir Roderick.

She bowed.

"Pray excuse me," said Heyle. "I have so much to see to."

"Certainly, Anthony," she said, and, reseating herself, turned to give Pons her undivided attention. "If there is any way I can help you learn who killed my husband, Mr. Pons, please ask me."

Pons thanked her, but for a long few moments he sat in absolute silence, contemplating her and allowing his glance to flicker about the room, as if to note its appointments, and out the broad window opening toward the moor.

"Your late husband is reported to have spoken to Mr. Heyle about the curse of Tutankhamen," said Pons abruptly. "Did he speak of it to you?"

"I believe he mentioned it, Mr. Pons."

"Frequently?"

"I would not say so."

"It troubled him?"

She shrugged. "Mr. Pons, I no longer knew what troubled my husband and what did not. He'd been gone two years. He came back virtually a stranger to me. After his first week at home, he seemed to withdraw into himself, he was very much preoccupied. He gave me to understand that he was returning to Egypt some time in the future. But he did speak about the curse to Mr. Heyle."

"Ah. Mr. Heyle mentioned it?"

"No, Mr. Pons. Mr. Heyle did not discuss my husband's business with me. I happened, quite by accident, to overhear them arguing about it last night. They were in my husband's study, which is next to this room. I had gone to my room but came back here for a book I had been reading. So I overheard them."

"What precisely did you hear, Mrs. Jowett?" asked Pons.

"Oh, just a phrase or two. I heard my husband shouting something about a 'dog crouching at the door,' and Mr. Heyle trying to calm him down, saying, 'Come, come Larry – you can't mean that.' And, of course, the crouching dog is on that guarding seal of that tomb they found and entered in Egypt."

"You saw the seal?"

"My husband showed it to me."

"Was he accustomed to carrying it about, Mrs. Jowett?"

She looked at Pons with uncomplimentary amazement. "Of course not, Mr. Pons. My husband was a very methodical man." She paused and added reflectively, "I still cannot believe he is dead."

At this moment the door from the adjoining study was flung open, and a tousle-haired young man burst unceremoniously into the room, his dark eyes flashing.

"Sybil!" he cried. "Don't tell him anything. Say nothing at all. Do you know who he is?"

"This is Mr. Solar Pons," said Mrs. Jowett tranquilly. "Mr. Pons, my brother-in-law, John Jowett."

"I warn you, Sybil," cried Jowett.

"My brother-in-law has a flair for the dramatic," she said, almost contemptuously. "He has a writer's temperament. Do go on, Mr. Pons."

Pons continued. "Your husband was in the habit of walking the moor by night?"

"By day and night. Alone. As everyone knew."

John Jowett stood for a moment uncertainly, looking wildly from one to the other of them; then he turned and flung himself out of the room as impetuously as he had rushed in.

"I hope you will forgive him, Mr. Pons," said Mrs. Jowett quietly. "He's a creature of impulse. Now, I fear, he'll send my brother in." She smiled ruefully. "I am supposed to be helpless, you see."

The ghost of a smile touched Pons' lips, reflecting her own. "My husband knew the moor very well," she went on. "And if, as they say, something pursued him out there, he could not have known what it was or he would never have run. He was running, wasn't he?"

"So the evidence indicates," put in Sir Roderick.

"My husband was not a timid man. He would not easily have run – even from – if I must put it into words – the ghost of a dog."

"Fact," said Sir Roderick. "I knew him well. Not a streak of cowardice in him. A brave man."

"Thank you, Sir Roderick."

There was a discreet tap on the door.

Mrs. Jowett shrugged her shoulders and called, "Come in, Hugh."

A man of perhaps fifty, bearing a marked resemblance to Mrs. Jowett, came apologetically into the room. "Are you all right, Sybil?" he asked.

Mrs. Jowett introduced him as her brother, Hugh Burnham.

"I don't want to intrude," he said earnestly.

"Stay," said Mrs. Jowett with an air of resignation.

Pons looked searchingly at Burnham. "Perhaps Mr. Burnham may have heard something in the night?" he suggested.

"I was in my quarters," Burnham said defensively. "I heard nothing. Nothing, that is, except the usual sounds – the dogs barking – and that hound somewhere, baying."

"When?"

"Some time after midnight, I think. It woke me, to tell the truth. A sudden baying, the like of which I never heard before."

Mrs. Jowett gazed at her brother, a faint line on her brow.

Pon's eyes flickered from one to the other of them. "A hound, you said?" he put in.

"I thought it one, yes."

Pons stood for a moment with half-closed eyes. Then he said, "There remains another brother of your late husband."

"Harold," said Mrs. Jowett. "He's in his rooms in the southwest tower."

"I'll take you there," said Burnham.

"No need, sir," said Sir Roderick. "I know the way."

We excused ourselves and followed Sir Roderick, who strode from the room and led us to a corridor, which in turn took us to the tower, in the second storey of which Jowett's older brother Harold had his quarters.

Sir Roderick's authoritative knock was answered by the door's being pulled open from inside. A heavily bearded man in his late thirties stood on the threshold, looking at us for a moment with resentment.

"Sir Roderick," he said then. "Come in." He stepped aside, still talking. "I suppose this is a continuation of the official inquiry into Larry's death. I've already told the constable all I can say."

Sir Roderick introduced us.

"And what, Mr. Jowett, is 'all' you can say?" asked Pons.

Harold Jowett favored Pons with a long, unwavering stare. "Mr. Pons, my brother was punished for what he did. He desecrated a tomb."

"I submit, Mr. Jowett, this is a matter of prejudice stemming from your early religious training," said Pons flatly. "Not of fact."

"Ah, you know about that. I wasn't worthy. Some day I may be."

The books lying on his lounge included, I saw, the *Confessions of St. Augustine* and Thomas a Kempis's *Of the Imitation of Christ.* He had been reading in them, clearly. A glance around his shelves indicated that most of his books were of a similar nature.

"In regard to matters of fact," pressed Pons. "Did you hear anything in the night?"

"I went to bed at eleven o'clock. At that hour, to the best of my knowledge, Larry and Tony Heyle were just getting ready to go to the study to discuss Larry's affairs. Larry intended to return to Egypt, and Tony meant to try to dissuade him. I'm a sound sleeper, sir. I heard nothing until John woke me to tell me Larry had been killed."

"Mr. Heyle was frequently in residence here?"

"I wouldn't call it 'in residence'. He often came down weekends. He was Larry's counselor and handled his affairs. Jowett Close is a rather costly place and it was up to him to see to it that Sybil had her accounts in order."

Pons turned to Sir Roderick. "Who found the body?"

"Why, I understood that John found him."

"Yes, John found him," corroborated Harold Jowett. "John customarily took early morning walks on the moor. He writes poems, you know. He prefers solitary walks, and always carries a pocket notebook for writing. John came back to the house and telephoned the police without saying anything to anyone – not even Sybil – until the police came. Then he told us."

"Let us just have a word with John," said Pons.

"He's – thorny," said Jowett bluntly.

"Temperamental – that's the word," said Sir Roderick, once we were out of Harold Jowett's quarters.

We found John Jowett on the edge of the moor, sitting on a tor-formation, and evidently writing, for a notebook lay open on his knee, and he held a pencil in his hand. He saw us approaching with marked displeasure on his handsome features, and waited with a kind of arrogant defiance for us to come up.

"So now you've come to ask me questions," he said as we came within his range. "I know no more than the others."

"But you have definite suspicions, Mr. Jowett," said Pons. "Some of which you feared your sister-in-law shared. What was it you didn't want her to say to us?"

"I've nothing to say about that."

"I see. You found your brother's body?"

"Yes. I made sure he was dead, no more. I disturbed nothing. I gave no one else a chance to disturb anything. I called the authorities, then told the rest of them."

Plainly he meant to tell us no more than he needed to.

A flush of irritation showed on Sir Roderick's face, but Pons was not disturbed. He stood for a few moments looking out over the moor. A wind had now risen in the east, and the clouds had lowered, presaging rain. He turned to Sir Roderick.

"Before it rains, some attempt ought to be made to take casts of such prints as are to be found leading to the scene."

"Even the dog prints?" put in Jowett sarcastically.

"Particularly the dog's," said Pons soberly.

"I'll have it done," said Sir Roderick, and hurried away.

Jowett grew more tense, as if he believed that Pons had deliberately sent Sir Roderick away. He waited, inwardly fencing with Pons.

"You write poetry, Mr. Jowett," said Pons.

"Yes."

"And, as a poet, you're likely to be more than ordinarily sensitive to your surroundings," Pons went on. "Your brother came home last month, and the atmosphere of Jowett Close underwent a change."

"My brother was a man of action. Harold is a contemplative man. And I suppose you might say I'm introspective. A dreamer, as my sister-in-law puts it. Would you expect that the invasion of a man of action wouldn't disturb the household?"

"His household."

"His household," repeated Jowett. He seemed disinclined to say more.

"May I see what you've written?" asked Pons. He held out his hand.

Jowett covered the page with one outspread hand. For a moment his eyes met Pons's. Then he reluctantly handed his notebook to Pons.

I looked over Pons's shoulder. "'Dark are the clouds that shadow moorland, tor,'" I read. "'And dark the deed that went before, In the night beneath the stars, Where hate and fury broke the bars Of reason...'" He had gone no farther.

"Mr. Jowett," said Pons, handing his notebook back to him, "did you, too, hear the hound baying in the night?"

"I heard what sounded like a hound, yes," said Jowett cautiously.

"And what was it that your brother did to disturb the household when he came back?" pressed Pons.

Jowett's eyes clouded. He slid from his perch, his notebook dosed in his hand. "What you want to know you can find out without my holding it back, I suppose," he said. "He put out the son of our housekeeper because he thought he'd been paying attention to Sybil."

"Had he?"

"I've always been too busy writing to know, Mr. Pons," said Jowett, and walked away.

Pons made no effort to halt him. His eyes followed him briefly. Then he turned to me, his eyes dancing.

"What do you make of it, Parker?"

"Well, for one thing," I answered without hesitation, "somebody here has read that book by Conan Doyle."

"Capital! Capital! Your growing powers delight me, Parker. I submit there is not a shred of doubt about that."

"And the dog?"

"There was no dog."

"The prints?"

"Come along and take a look at them."

We walked a short distance out to where stakes had been driven down to set off the paw-prints.

"If you'll examine any two of them, you'll find variations between the toe prints."

"Wouldn't such variations be entirely consistent?" I protested.

Pons chuckled. "Certain variations would – but not invariably precise variations between the second and fourth, and the third and fifth toe prints. The variation, I venture to say, is precise. I submit that the prints were hastily improvised with some sort of garden tool that had but three prongs, so that the prints had to be made in two impressions."

"By night?" I said incredulously.

"We have nothing to show that the prints were manufactured by night."

"The dog was heard."

"John Jowett put it very well when he said he heard 'what sounded like a hound'. I suppose even you, Parker, could give a passable imitation of a hound baying. I suggest it is significant that the dog portrayed as crouching on the seal of the Tutankhamen necropolis, presumably the guardian of the crypt and the avenger of its desecration, is not a hound such as was 'heard' baying – a little detail this devotee of the Baskerville tale seems to have overlooked."

"On the other hand, if you'll permit me to play Devil's Advocate, it can hardly be denied that three members of the Tutankhamen expedition have died before their time."

Pons smiled. "Who is to say what anyone's 'time' is, Parker? It can also not be denied that the overwhelming majority of those associated with the Egyptian expedition and discovery are very much alive, in good health, and not to the best of our knowledge haunted by anything, dog or otherwise. More than a year has passed since the opening of the tomb. Surely a phantom dog could get around faster than that! No, this has all the earmarks of an impetuous crime."

"And, of course, you know who committed it?"

"Say, rather, I have certain suspicions pointing to the identity of the murderer. The suspects are obvious."

"Oh, that is certainly elementary," I could not help saying. "Let me list them for you. The young man who was discharged for paying attention to Mrs. Jowett – or conceivably, his father bent on avenging him. John Jowett, who might have lost money if his brother changed his will..."

"Let us not forget the crouching dog," interrupted Pons dryly.

"But there was no dog."

"Yet someone desperately wanted us to believe there was," said Pons.

"One little detail you seem to forget," I said, "is that Jowett was unquestionably running from someone or something."

"Not proven," said Pons curtly. "The evidence shows only that he was running. Moreover, if you follow the footprints back far enough, you will find substantial evidence that two men set out upon the moor and only one came back. There is also evidence to show that one of them walked with exceeding care, avoiding any area of ground which might reveal his footprints. Further, there is good reason to believe that he also ran, but came back in the dawn to obliterate those prints at the same time that he made the pawprints of the dog. This murder was carefully planned, if on the spur of the moment, by a resourceful man whom it will not be easy to get into the dock. But come, let us get back to the house. Sir Roderick is on his way out."

We met Sir Roderick at the edge of the moor.

"Have you finished here, Pons?" he asked as we came up.

"For the time being, yes. I would suggest that your men make a careful search of the gardener's quarters for a three-tined hand-tool used for grubbing, and have the grounds searched for a claw hammer or rock. Both, when found, should be examined for traces of blood."

"So that's how it was done, eh?" said Sir Roderick.

Pons nodded.

"Can you say now who did it?"

"No, Sir Roderick. I'll need a trifle more information which, I think, you in your official capacity can arrange to obtain."

"Name it, sir."

"I want to know in as much detail as possible the extent of Mrs. Jowett's expenses over the past two years. And equally as much detail about the income from Jowett's investments."

Sir Roderick looked narrowly at Pons. "I'll probably have to apply to London for that," he said: "Is it necessary?"

"I am convinced that it is."

"Very well. That will take a while as you know. We can't have that before tomorrow." He took out his watch and looked at it. "It's almost four o'clock now. I'll telephone the Yard from home. And, of course, I've planned for you and Dr. Parker to spend the night at my place."

Pons thanked him and lapsed into thoughtful silence.

At Jowett Close house, we parted briefly – Sir Roderick to pass along Pons' instructions to the constables on guard there, ourselves to go around to the car. As we passed the large sitting-room window opening on to the moor, we could see Mrs. Jowett standing there, watching us inscrutably, no emotion of any kind on her attractive face. Her right hand was clenched at her side, her left holding to the drape at the window. She made no sign of recognition.

It was not until just after noon next day that a trunk call came for Sir Roderick from Scotland Yard. Sir Roderick took the call in his study and came out to where Pons and I waited, looking puzzled.

"Something is wrong in Sybil Jowett's accounts, Pons," he said. "Though how you got on to it, I don't know. There's just short of forty thousand pounds unaccounted for. What could she have done with so much money?"

"Let us just go on over to Jowett Close once again. I want to have another look at the scene of Jowett's death," said Pons. "You might send word ahead I'd like Jowett's brothers and Anthony Heyle standing by."

"Right!" said Sir Roderick.

In the car on the way to Jowett Close, Sir Roderick gave way to speculation.

"I've always thought Sybil Jowett a pretty level-headed woman," he said. "D'you suppose she made bad investments? Or worse, could someone be blackmailing her? Damme! she should have come to me!"

"At this point it is idle to speculate," said Pons cryptically. "I suspect that the explanation is not one that Mrs. Jowett thought might require your advice, Sir Roderick."

"Everyone here holds a good opinion of her," said Sir Roderick a little stiffly. "Does a good job of running her household. A popular woman, at home and outside."

Pons made no comment. His keen eyes were upon the landscape fleeting by, but he did not seem to see it, for he was looking inward and elsewhere, pondering Jowett's strange death. But there was in his expression a hint of suppressed excitement, as if the solution to Jowett's murder were within his grasp.

Once at Jowett Close, Pons lost no time in finding the two Jowett brothers and the late Lawrence Jowett's counsel, who were waiting in the study.

"Mr. Pons wishes to return to the moor, gentlemen," boomed Sir Roderick. "Will you all be good enough to come along?"

The Jowett brothers seemed almost surly in their assent, while Heyle only looked at his watch and said, "I'm due in court tomorrow, and I want to take the night train out of Exeter. Can that be managed?"

"It should not take us long, Mr. Heyle," said Pons.

He led the way out of the house to the edge of the moor, which was once again in sunlight and shadow, alternately bright and sinister in appearance, with an east wind blowing still, and occasional thin droplets of rain riding it.

"Now, if you'll all keep to my right," he said, "I will make an attempt to consider what must have happened here two nights ago." He came to a stop. "At this point two men came walking into the moor at an hour near midnight. It was a moonlit night, you will recall, and the sky was clear."

"Right," said Sir Roderick. "Clouded at sunset, clear by mid-evening."

"As it was in Cornwall," said Pons. "One of the men who walked here was undoubtedly Jowett. His companion and he walked a little way out into the moor. See here – and there – the remains of footprints, though some attempt has been made to conceal them, and who walked here with Jowett deliberately stepped wherever there was little chance of leaving prints whenever he could do so. Jowett walked along without thought of where he walked for three-quarters of a mile."

He fell silent, while a constable came up from behind us and whispered to Sir Roderick.

Pons went on for a quarter of a mile without speaking, then paused.

"Now at this point – as you can see by the staked prints, something happened to start Jowett running briskly toward the tor-formation ahead."

"The dog," said Sir Roderick.

"Ah, I think not," said Pons imperturbably. "Mrs. Jowett said of her husband – and you corroborated it, Sir Roderick – that he was not a man to run out of fear. Let us assume that he ran for some other reason. His companion was no stranger to him. They were walking here as companions of some standing. Let us suppose that Jowett's companion said something like this to him – 'Larry, have you lost any of your hardness these past two years? Do you think you can race me to that tor?' So Larry ran, and the other after, taking from his pocket the claw hammer concealed there, with which he struck him down."

Pons was now moving rapidly ahead. He came to the site of Jowett's death. "Now, then, let me call your attention to the imprint of fingers left by Jowett's right hand. Here, in the middle of the imprint, under the palm, the soil is disturbed – broken and pushed a little to the left. How came it to be so?"

"The reproduction of that seal he carried," said Sir Roderick. "When he fell..."

"I submit that Jowett carried no seal," said Pons crisply. "Even if he had carried it in his hand for some obscure reason, it would not have made such a mark as this. No, this mark was made by Jowett's murderer who pushed the reproduction of the crouching dog seal under the dead man's hand, and then stood back and bayed like a hound, after which he completed his preparation of the scene by returning to obliterate his own running footprints, and manufacture the paw prints we all see, by means of a three-tined garden tool with which he also tore the dead man's clothing and mutilated his body."

"We have both it and the hammer," announced Sir Roderick.

"But in God's name, why?" burst out Harold Jowett.

"Because he hoped to prevent your brother from discovering his peculation with his money, and to hide it forever by marrying your sister-in-law, Mr. Jowett," said Pons. So saying, he wheeled upon Anthony Heyle, and asked, "How did you lose it, Mr. Heyle?"

For a long, silent moment Heyle met Pons' grim eyes, while a fine line of perspiration began to gleam upon his brow; then he broke and began to run back toward the house. With a few running steps and a great leap, John Jowett brought him down. Harold Jowett was close behind him.

"Tony Heyle!" cried Sir Roderick Ramsey for the twentieth time as we rode through the late afternoon toward London in his car. "I'd never have guessed it. What happens to a man to bring him to such a pass?"

"The unlimited control of Jowett's money was too much for him," said Pons. "But I suspect that there was another factor. Sybil Jowett is, as you pointed out, Sir Roderick, an unusually attractive woman – and in a sense a dominating one, a mover. I should not be surprised to learn that Heyle's passion for her turned his head."

"You had your eye on him from the beginning," said Sir Roderick. "Why?"

"An elementary matter," replied Pons. "Heyle said that Jowett spoke of the curse of Tutankhamen 'frequently'. He said it 'seemed to be on his mind'. But he was the only one in Jowett Close who said so. Mrs. Jowett said just the contrary; yet if this superstition had prayed upon Jowett's mind, surely she would have been the very first person to whom he would speak of it at length, rather than Heyle, whose coldly analytical mind he must have known. They were, in your own words, old friends. So Heyle built up Jowett's superstitions fear carefully – deprecating it himself. But, of course, there was something more.

"When Jowett came home, he was like a stranger to his wife. He had treated her in rather a cavalier manner, had he not? But he could not have been home long when he learned that someone had been paying court to her. His first suspicion fixed upon the housekeeper's son; he ordered him from the house, however unjustly. He must have discovered how unjust he had been, and he must finally have learned that the culprit was not the housekeeper's son, but his old friend, Tony Heyle. There was an argument in the study, and it was doubtless there that the plan to murder Jowett was formed in Heyle's mind. What Mrs. Jowett heard was not a reference to the necropolis seal of Tutankhamen, though this was the context suggested to her. What she heard her husband shouting at Heyle was an accusation – that Heyle was the 'dog couching' – not crouching at the door – which is to say, courting his wife while he was in Egypt. Heyle's, alas! was a fine mind destroyed by passion and greed. A pity his literary interests were not on a somewhat higher plane! That Baskerville tale was his undoing.

"An interesting problem, Sir Roderick. You may stop my train any time for another like it."

IX

THE ADVENTURE OF THE MISSING HUNTSMAN

My friend Solar Pons laid a persuasive hand on my arm and slowed our progress along Praed Street not far from our quarters at Number 7. "Gently, Parker," he said. "What do you make of that lady across the street?"

I followed the direction of his gaze and saw an attractive young lady, contemptuous of the wild March wind, striding up the street and turning to go back. She was well-figured, with golden blonde hair worn long in the face of the growing trend toward shorter hair. As she walked, she struck at the calf of her right leg absently with a stick, and from time to time glanced up toward the windows of our quarters.

"She appears to be contemplating a visit to you," I said, "but cannot quite make up her mind."

"Ah," said Pons. "I thought her a young lady of singular determination."

"From the country," I said. "See how she walks."

"An equestrian," added Pons. "Observe how she strikes at her leg; that is a horse-woman's gesture."

"I put her age at thirty-five or so," I went on.

"And moneyed," said Pons. "Her clothing appears to be conservative in cut but even from here it is evident that it is of excellent quality. And I should not be surprised to find that that little sports car up the street is hers. She has driven down, on impulse and is now reconsidering that impulse."

"Or she has been to call and, not finding us in, was reluctant to wait."

"No, I think not," said Pons with annoying self-assurance. "She might have come down to sit in her car, but not to pace the street. She appears to be a young lady who cares nothing for the opinions of others or the attention she has already attracted. See there – and there," added Pons, pointing to pedestrians whose eyes had been caught by the lady and who had halted their own progress to fix their gaze upon her.

"But here we are," said Pons, as we reached Number 7, "and our would-be client is still so engrossed in her problem that she is not aware of our arrival."

We mounted to our quarters, where Pons crossed directly to the windows facing the street and gazed down. I came up behind him and saw that the lady had now come to a pause and stood looking directly across at us. And then, as if she had caught sight of us, she strode into the street with the intention of crossing to Number 7.

"Ah," said Pons, falling back and rubbing his hands, his eyes alight. "We shall soon learn what troubles her."

The lady Mrs. Johnson ushered into our quarters within a few minutes proved to be uncommonly attractive, with a sensitivity of features which the stubborn set of her chin did not diminish. Her violet eyes met Pons' gaze boldly.

"Mr. Pons, I am Diana Pomfroy," she said at once. "My husband is Colonel Ashton Pomfroy."

"Master of the Wycherly," replied Pons, and then turned to introduce me.

Our client acknowledged me with a courteous inclination of her head and turned again to Pons. "Then you will have read of the tragedy?"

"A man trampled to death by one of your horses – and the loss of your Huntsman, Captain Dion Price. Pray sit down, Mrs. Pomfroy."

She took Pons' favorite chair at the fireplace, and Pons leaned up against the mantel facing her.

"I may have come on a fool's errand, Mr. Pons," she began, sitting well forward in her chair, as if eager to impress upon us the importance of her words, "but I could not hold off any longer. There is something very much wrong at Pomfroy Chase. It is almost a month now that they found that man – and Mr. Pons, I should say at once that I saw the body – a horrible sight, and while I know that the inquest was conducted correctly, I cannot believe that everything was allowed to come out. Perhaps I feel some guilt myself because I did not say what I knew and what I suspected."

"And what was it that you knew, Mrs. Pomfroy?"

"Mr. Pons, the dead man – whom no one could identify – was wearing a weskit that belonged to Captain Price. I know because I happened to see it when Mrs. Parks was repairing a small tear for him, and I saw the repair on the weskit the dead man wore."

"And suspected?"

"I hardly know how to say it," said our client, lacing her fingers together, "but I couldn't escape the impression that the dead man had been *beaten* before he blundered into the stallion's stall. I could not understand how certain welts he bore could have been made by hooves. But then, I was unable to understand too how he could have blundered into that stall – the stallion's a brute, Mr. Pons, a fine horse, but a brute. Was it chance? Or was he guided there? Or worse – pushed into it? The day we found the body, Captain Price disappeared – or rather, he was gone – he was last seen the previous afternoon – and ever since then there has been such tension at Pomfroy

Chase – as if everyone were holding his breath for fear of something to come."

Our client reflected something of that tension herself, noticeably. She was now more agitated than she had been on her entrance, though only clenched fingers and pursed lips betrayed her.

"I recall that some effort was made to identify the dead man," said Pons.

"Oh, yes. Though his head was badly mutilated, a police artist drew a likeness and it was circulated in the newspapers, together with a full description of his clothing, though that was really very little, what he wore was so ordinary. Yet he was carrying a revolver, one chamber of which was empty and evidently recently discharged. He must have been an itinerant – a tramp or a laborer of some kind looking for work."

"Did he apply for it?"

"Not to our knowledge."

"Did anyone hear a gun discharged during the night?"

"No one reported it, Mr. Pons."

"A gunshot could hardly have been so commonplace as to have gone unheard, if the weapon were discharged near the house. What of yourself – or Colonel Pomfroy?"

"Mr. Pons, we were away from home until shortly after midnight."

"Was any search made for a bullet, Mrs. Pomfroy?"

"I cannot say, but I doubt it. Since no one heard a shot fired, I believe it was assumed that the shot was fired away from the house."

"Did anyone report having seen this man prior to the discovery of his body?"

"No, Mr. Pons." She sighed. "But, of course, someone must have seen him. How else could he have got hold of Captain Price's weskit?"

"He might have stolen it," suggested Pons.

"I suppose that is true," she said doubtfully.

"Captain Price," said Pons. "How old is he?"

"Thirty-nine. He came to us well recommended by Lady Cleve seven years ago."

"And the age of the dead man?"

"They put it at about forty. Not over forty-five, Mr. Pons."

"The staff outside the house itself," pressed Pons. "What of them?"

"Well, of course, Captain Price. John Ryan is our First Whip, Reggie Bannan our Second, and O'Rourke our Third. Then, of course, there are the servants in the stables. The Hunt servants and our four horsemen were all hired by Captain Price. We established the Hunt seven years ago and we've had Captain Price ever since. We dislike to believe that he may not return – that something may have happened to him."

"And what is it you ask of me, Mrs. Pomfroy?"

"Oh, if I could say precisely! To learn who the dead man was – to lift the tension at Pomfroy Chase – and, yes, to find Captain Price." She hesitated, caught her lower lip between her white teeth, and added, "If he is alive."

"I see. I take it you have some reason to feel that he may be dead."

She shook her head. "It is only unreasoning fear, Mr. Pons. That man – the dead man – had the same kind of figure Captain Price had; he wore his weskit well, as if it had been made for him – but of course, he had a beard, and Captain Price was clean-shaven."

"When you last saw him."

"Yes."

"And that was?"

"Ten days ago. I spent a week in London recently, Mr. Pons. But now we are about to start hunting..."

"But you don't yourself know whether Captain Price was clean-shaven at the time of his disappearance?"

"No, Mr. Pons. I must rely on the Whips, who make no mention of any change in Captain Price. They saw him as late as six o'clock that afternoon – of the night during which the man was killed in the stall. I have spoken with them."

"I shall speak with them," said Pons.

"Oh, I don't know that it would be wise," demurred our client. "They seemed reluctant to speak. Would it not be best if you and Dr. Parker were to come for the Meet next Thursday and remain at Pomfroy Chase as our guests? I should like your inquiry to be discreet."

Pons smiled wryly. "Murder – if murder is involved – can hardly be discreet, Mrs. Pomfroy. And it may be tantamount to murder to expect Dr. Parker to ride to hounds."

I protested indignantly. "I believe I can acquit myself as well as you."

"We shall see."

"Then you will come, Mr. Pons?"

"We will present ourselves at Pomfroy Chase in time for the Meet, Mrs. Pomfroy."

"Oh, thank you!" cried our client, as she came to her feet in a swift, supple movement.

"Do be good enough to show Mrs. Pomfroy to her car, Parker," said Pons.

When I returned, I found Pons deep in one of his carefully compiled files on interesting people and criminous events in Great Britain.

Without looking up, he explained, "Our client mentioned Lady Cleve, and I seem to recall making an entry on the lady some years ago. Ah, here we are. Lord Cleve, His Majesty's personal representative in Ireland. Eight years back. 'Daring Attempt to Kidnap Lady Cleve Frustrated.' Let me see," he went on, reading in a low voice as if to himself, "A daring daylight attempt to kidnap Ethel, Lady Cleve, by members of the Irish Republican Army was frustrated by a rebel, Sean O'Leary, widely known by his sobriquet, "The Black Prince", and a handful of his followers, who interrupted the attempt even as Lady Cleve was being taken from her carriage in a Dublin street by terrorists. No effort was made to harm Lady Cleve. The attempt was evidently planned to force a compromise in the attitude of Lord Cleve in negotiations with representatives of the Irish Republican Army.'" He paused, then resumed. "'Born Ethel Stewart, second daughter of Mr. and Mrs. Francis Stewart, Chelmsford, Essex.' That would make her Scottish in ancestry."

"I'm afraid I cannot see the relevance of Lady Cleve's ancestry," I said.

He laughed. "Nor I."

"But what happened to the kidnappers and the other men who thwarted them?"

"Oh, they got into a battle among themselves and the Black Prince escorted Lady Cleve to safety. Once she was free, the rebels vanished from the street."

"They probably repaired to the nearest pub and spent the night in tall talk," I said. "But, seriously, Pons – do you intend to go to the Meet?"

"It ought to be a welcome diversion," said Pons.

"What is to be gained by such violent exercise? Will it help you solve the mystery at Pomfroy Chase?"

"Perhaps," said Pons enigmatically. "It will at least give me the acquaintance of the Whips who show every sign, if our client is to be believed, of not having told all they know."

"Mrs. Pomfroy herself seems to be unsure about your role," I pointed out.

"Does she not!" cried Pons, delightedly. "Her little problem intrigues me. I do not recall anything similar in my experience. The victim is dead and buried almost a month – the Huntsman has vanished." He paused suddenly, reflectively. "I did not recall our client's giving us the verdict of the inquest," he said. "Let us just look it up."

He turned to the back of his most recent file, and took from it a packet of clippings he had not yet had opportunity to enter. He riffled rapidly through them, reading titles aloud as he went. "The Framblehurst Arms murder. The Swansea mystery. Manchester double murder. Ah – 'Death by Misadventure Verdict at Pomfroy Chase'. – I fancy it might not be amiss to reread the published accounts of the matter."

He settled himself to read again the trio of clippings which pertained to the Pomfroy mystery, but if he saw anything of interest in them, his expressionless face told me nothing. When at last he discarded the clippings and looked up, his face was reflective.

"Dr. Michael Paradine," he said, "is apparently the man we should talk to first."

"Who is he?"

"The examining physician. There is nothing in the published accounts our client has not already imparted."

"Pons, have you considered that this may indeed be a wild goose chase? That the matter may be exactly what the inquest determined?"

"Oh, I have considered it, but also discarded the thought," said Pons. "I submit our client's concern is well grounded. Even if we grant death by misadventure, we still have the problem of the missing Huntsman. But I am unwilling to grant even so much. The situation presents some interesting aspects. Consider that our client made no mention of anything untoward taking place at Pomfroy Chase prior to the night of the – let us just say, 'accident'. She held everything to be normal, I take it, or she would have said so. She would appear to be a young lady who is keenly sensitive to impressions. She related none. Then a man is found dead in the stallion's stall. The stallion was known to be a brute. The fellow might have been a vagrant, but Mrs. Pomfroy does not think so, because he was wearing Captain Price's weskit. And Captain Price is missing. Since then there seems to be a continuing tension at Pomfroy Chase. Now, does not this chain of events suggest anything to you?"

"For one thing," I said bluntly, "I would like to make a more careful examination of the dead man. I would like to know if his fingerprints and teeth were compared to Price's."

"Ah, that thought had occurred to me," admitted Pons. "It had also occurred to Mrs. Pomfroy, but she cannot believe that the dead man is Captain Price."

"Perhaps because she does not want to believe it."

"Perhaps," conceded Pons. "But I rather think that it would be elementary to rule out Price by the simplest of tests. So let us assume that the dead man was not Price. On that premise hinges another – what had he to do with Price? He wore his weskit – a repaired weskit, true – so we are left with the conclusion that he either visited Price and was given the weskit, or he stole the weskit in Price's absence."

"That seems beyond cavil," I agreed. "But who would steal a worn weskit? – one worn to the extent of being repaired?"

"Capital!" cried Pons. "And what do you make of the prevailing tension at Pomfroy Chase?"

"They are fearful that something will be discovered."

"The verdict is in and the case is closed," Pons pointed out. "What have they to fear?"

"Well, then, they are fearful of something to come."

"I submit that is far more likely," said Pons. "But perhaps at this point speculation is idle. We know too little of elementary matters. If Captain Price was abducted, why? If he chose to leave of his own accord, for what reason? The newspaper accounts speak of a 'sum of money' found on the dead man. Surely that is ambiguous! Why not a stated sum? The Meet is two days hence. I think we will just run down to Cranborne tomorrow and have a word with Dr. Paradine before going on to Pomfroy Chase. Let us wire Mrs. Pomfroy to expect us for dinner tomorrow evening."

The following afternoon found us at Cranborne, waiting upon Dr. Michael Paradine at his office. Dr. Paradine was a gruff, burly man, with cold, piercing dark eyes and a thick moustache worn almost truculently on his upper lip. He had kept us cooling our heels in the waiting room until Pons had sent in a note – "About the Pomfroy Chase Affair." – whereupon he had seen us at once.

"I am at a loss to understand this, Mr. Pons," he said curtly.

"I have read the published accounts of the matter with great interest," said Pons, choosing his words carefully. "I have had the privilege of speaking with Mrs. Pomfroy. We seem to be alike in the dark."

"Well, sir, you have no advantage over me and I none over you," said Dr. Paradine, smiling frostily.

"You examined the body, Doctor. You have that advantage."

"That is true."

"Did you, in fact, find on the dead man's head welts which suggested that he might have been beaten?" asked Pons.

Dr. Paradine looked at us for a few moments in silence. "I found certain welts," he answered at last. "I cannot say that they were the marks of a beating."

"You did not think it likely that they were made by the horse?"

"I cannot say, Mr. Pons."

"Come, come, Doctor," pressed Pons. "You must certainly have formed an opinion on the question?"

A fine dew of perspiration had come to show on the doctor's temples. "In my opinion, it was unlikely that the horse made them. They were not fatal. They were made before death, as their color indicated. The fellow was fearfully mutilated."

"Thank you, Doctor. Did any suspicion cross your mind that the dead man might be the missing Captain Price?"

Dr. Paradine smiled. "While they were of somewhat similar proportions, sir, no such suspicion entered my mind."

"One more thing. Newspaper accounts mention that a sum of money was found on the dead man. None mentions how much. You were at the inquest and you may remember the sum, which was certainly brought out at that time."

"One hundred fifty-seven pounds, Mr. Pons, and some shillings. He was hardly, as some people have suggested, a vagrant."

"It would certainly not seem so. Are you, by any chance, a member of the Wycherly Hunt, Doctor?"

"I have that privilege," answered Dr. Paradine somewhat stiffly.

"See you again at the Meet," said Pons. "Good day, Doctor."

Dr. Paradine's eyebrows went up. "You are guests of the Master?" he hazarded. Without waiting for Pons' reply, he asked, "Perhaps I could drive you to Pomfroy Chase – unless you have a car of your own?"

"We came by train," said Pons.

"Well, then, if you have no objection, I would consider it a privilege, sir."

Dr. Paradine's frostiness had evaporated; he was now all civility. He left the office in the care of his associate, and within a quarter hour we were on the road to Pomfroy Chase, which lay out of Cranborne in the direction of Salisbury.

It was soon apparent, however, that the doctor had an ulterior motive, for he plied us with questions, primarily designed to discover Pons's motives at inquiring into the affair at Pomfroy Chase – however delicately, secondarily to learn how much we knew of fox-hunting. Pons acquitted himself satisfactorily enough, without betraying the fact that he was acting for Mrs. Pomfroy, and Dr. Paradine left us at Pomfroy Chase a baffled and disgruntled man, though he was too much the gentleman to show it.

Pomfroy Chase was obviously the home of a wealthy man. It was evidently an old manor house which had been restored, a long, L-shaped building of stone, two storeys in height, of which the second was a gable storey, broken by dormer windows. The building faced lawns and flower beds and a handsome, circular driveway, while at the rear stood the kennels, and beyond these, well away from the immediate grounds, a septet of cottages, all of stone, which were clearly part of the estate, and very probably housed some of the Hunt servants.

The butler's reaction to Pons's name indicated that we were expected. We were shown without delay into Mrs. Pomfroy's presence.

"I'm glad you're here, Mr. Pons," she said at once. "I know something is wrong here, I feel it too strongly to ignore. The Hunt servants are so tense I fear for the day's hunting tomorrow."

"Surely it cannot be as bad as that," said Pons reassuringly.

"I know you must think it my fancy, but I assure you it is not," she said fervently. Then, sighing, she said, "But I impose on you. Let me show you to your room – I hope you will not mind sharing it."

"We have been sharing quarters for some years, Mrs. Pomfroy," said Pons dryly.

"Thank you. Please follow me. John will bring your bags."

Our hostess led us up the stairs to a comfortable room, the gable windows of which opened toward the stables and the cottages beyond. Pons crossed to the near window at once and stood looking out.

"I take it those cottages across the meadow are occupied by some of the Hunt servants?"

"Yes, Mr. Pons. The largest is – was Captain Price's. Bannan, Ryan, and O'Rourke each has one."

Without turning, Pons asked, "The Meet starts here?"

"Yes, Mr. Pons. We try to start at eleven o'clock."

"Thank you, Mrs. Pomfroy."

"Dinner at seven, Gentlemen," said our hostess and withdrew.

"I submit there was design in Mrs. Pomfroy's choice of this room for us, Parker," said Pons, chuckling. "We have a fine view of the stage upon which the Hunt servants must perform."

He came back to one of the two beds in the room and flung himself full-length upon it.

"What did you think of Dr. Paradine?" he asked.

"A cautious and ethical man," I replied.

"Pray do not be so defensive. I admire caution and ethics in a medical man, as you well know."

"I daresay he was fearful that there might be some disclosure reflecting upon his judgment," I said.

"I thought as much. In sum, however, his attitude reflects and bolsters our client's. He is certain that the stallion killed the intruder in his stall – but he is not certain the fellow came there by accident. 'Death by misadventure' is ambiguous enough to satisfy no one."

"You postulate the man was murdered. But who would murder a stranger except for money? – which was not taken."

"Ah, Parker, you make progress. I submit that to someone the fellow was not a stranger."

"You are thinking of Captain Price. Do you suggest that Price then killed him?"

"My mind is open on the matter. But I cannot deny that certain suggestive indications offer fascinating solutions to the riddle," said Pons. "For one – it can scarcely be doubted that the two events are in some way connected, though it does not follow that Price murdered the visitor."

"But who then?"

"Ah, I fancy that time and patience will tell us that, Parker.

With that he had finished; he would say nothing further.

He composed himself for rest – which, for Pons, meant the consideration of the particular problem which occupied his attention – and so he lay, almost inert, upon the bed until it was time to make ready for dinner.

Our host presided at the dinner table. Colonel Ashton Pomfroy was at least ten years his wife's senior. He was a ruddy-faced man with quiet blue eyes and a self-assured manner. If our client had told him why Pons and I had been invited to join the Hunt, he gave no indication that it was so; he was courteous almost to being deferential.

There were three other guests at dinner – General Hugh Pomfroy, our host's uncle – a great, shaggy-browed fellow, very hearty of manner – and the Chairman of the Hunt Committee, Richard Codrington – who, with singular punctiliousness invariably addressed our host as "Master", which Colonel Pomfroy's uncle did not always do – and the chairman's wife, who was seated next to me, and thus but one place removed from our hostess, so that conversation at dinner – which was, understandably, primarily of the morrow's Hunt, fell naturally into three divisions – among the two ladies and myself, which was somewhat disconcerting since they seemed to enjoy discovering how much I did not know about fox-hunting – between the Master and the Hunt chairman – and between Pons and General Pomfroy, who held forth pontifically about "some fellow named Pons" he had known "somewhere in France during the war" and was finally convinced that it was Pons' brother Bancroft, though he found it difficult to imagine that "that fellow could be in the Foreign Office," for he had evidently a military man's dubeity about any devotee of ratiocination.

Pons listened, but spoke no more than the proprieties of the occasion demanded, and when dinner was done, excused himself. I followed suit.

But, though Pons had spoken of retiring to his room, he made his way outside the house and around to the stables where the hounds were quartered.

"Do you know anything about fox hounds, Parker?" asked Pons.

"About as much as I know of fox-hunting," I answered. "What is the size of the pack?"

"Twenty couple, I believe our host put it."

"I gathered that it is to be a large Meet."

"I believe some seventy people will take part."

We stood looking at the hounds, I was certain, with some design on Pons's part, and presently we were discovered by a slender, greying man of perhaps forty, who came casually toward us, his narrowed eyes suggesting that we might not be entirely welcome.

"Is there anything I can do for you, gentlemen?" he asked.

"You must be Ryan," ventured Pons.

"Right, sir."

"Dr. Parker and I were wondering whether one of your Hunt servants is not young Jock Britney?"

"I hardly think so, sir," said Ryan. "We have O'Rourke, Callahan, Malone, O'Connor, and Keenan. Not a Britney among them. And none under thirty. You'd hardly call that 'young', would you, sir?"

Pons laughed. "Ah, well, then, we were misinformed," he said. He turned from contemplation of the hounds, and gestured toward the cottages well off beyond the stables. "Can you tell me, Ryan, who occupies those houses?"

"Sir," answered Ryan with a querulousness rising in his voice, as if he meant to say that this was none of our business, "we live there."

"'We'?" persisted Pons.

"The near one is Captain Price's – and next to it my wife and I live, and then Bannan and his family, and then O'Rourke and his, and so on."

"Ah, no family, Ryan?"

"No, sir," said Ryan stiffly.

"I thought, a moment ago, I saw an old man there," persisted Pons.

"My father's come to visit us for a while." His words were now so short as to be crystal clear. He resented Pons' asking questions, but he did not want to risk offending a guest.

"Ah, yes, Captain Price," murmured Pons. "That was the fellow who disappeared. Did you know him?"

"Sir, we all know Captain Price," said Ryan coldly.

"A good man?"

"None better."

It was now almost painfully clear that Ryan not only disapproved Pons' questions, but had tautened with suspicion of both of us.

"What weather will we have for the Hunt?" asked Pons then.

Ryan visibly relaxed. "A fine day. Some clouds, and a spot of misting rain. Ideal hunting weather, sir."

"This will be your first day's hunting without Captain Price, eh?"

Ryan froze once more. He nodded curtly, but did not trust himself to speak.

"Thank you, Ryan," said Pons.

"You're welcome, sir."

Ryan stood motionless while we walked back toward the house, for the March air had grown increasingly crisp with the dying day. I thought the First Whip's attitude proof of his cold suspicion.

"Surely you gained little by making that fellow suspicious," I said.

"Were not my questions innocuous enough?" asked Pons.

"They were pointless," I cried.

"On the contrary," replied Pons, with a tight smile. "Ryan's replies yielded a wealth of information."

"You cannot mean it!"

"I was never more serious," said Pons. "For one thing – it is now evident that Ryan, at least – and perhaps the others – have good reason to believe Captain Price to be alive – you will have observed Ryan's insistence on speaking of him in the present tense. It is quite possible that they are in touch with him. That is but one of the valuable facets of our little conversation. I am sure that you will, on reflection, think of others. I commend our dialogue to your study, Parker. You know my methods. You have only to apply them."

Questions crowded to my tongue, but I knew it would be useless to ask them. Pons had said all he meant to say.

Looking back, I saw that Ryan was no longer alone. Two other men had joined him, though at a little distance behind him; all three were gazing after us with motionless coldness, as if they meant to see that we did not turn back toward the stables.

Pons anticipated my saying so. "I saw them, Parker," he said. "I fancy we would have had a difficult time nosing about. Nevertheless, I intend to do so if you'll bear with me."

He made his way completely around the front of the house, and this time came to the stables where the horses were kept. We had not gone more than half way along the stalls when Ryan appeared once more.

"Oh," he said, "it's you again." His voice was like ice.

"Forgive me, Ryan," said Pons persuasively. "I had a fancy to see the stall in which that fellow was killed. Even in London, you see, we read about it."

"I don't wonder," said Ryan, and added, pointing, "That one."

Pons walked over to it under Ryan's watchful eye, looked in, and turned.

"The stallion's out at grass, if you'd like to see him," said Ryan sarcastically.

"It would be interesting to hear what he has to say," said Pons, "if I could only talk his language."

Ryan said nothing.

Pons walked past him, thanking him once more.

This time he had finished. We walked into the house and up to our room, where Pons made himself comfortable with every sign of meaning to stay where he was until morning. "Was there anything about the stall worth seeing?" I asked.

"You saw where it lies," said Pons. "I submit it would have been considerably easier to blunder into several other stalls before reaching the stallion's. It gives one food for thought, does it not?"

I agreed that it did. "It suggests that he was led or brought there. But again, if not robbery, what was the motive?"

"Ah, Parker, that grows with every hour the most intriguing question of this little puzzle. Indeed, unless I am very much mistaken, the solution to the events at Pomfroy Chase rests in it."

With this I had to be content, for he retreated into a copy of *Insurrections Against His Majesty's Government*, which he had brought along from our quarters in Praed Street.

The Hunt breakfast, for all its informality, was a gala affair, and a colorful one, with the field in pink and their ladies in dark garb. Our hostess had seen to us that we, too, had garb appropriate to the occasion. The members and guests stood about, inside and out, drinking coffee and eating the food set out on the sideboard and the table, and the hum of conversation filled the air.

After a few words with our hostess, Pons made his way outside, where he stood watching the scene. The Master was busy with Ryan and Bannan, who were also in pink, but at sight of Pons and me, he detached himself briefly and came over.

"Gentlemen, Ryan will bring around your mounts in good time."

"Thank you, Master," said Pons – quite as if he had been riding to hounds all his life.

Some members of the Meet had already finished and were mounted. The hounds had been brought out – twenty couple, as Pons had said. They sat or milled about, keeping close together, in an open space among the horses. The Whips were not far away. An air of expectation hung over the scene, and everyone waited on the edge of awareness of the event about to take place.

"How many horsemen do you count, Parker?" asked Pons.

I looked among the crowd. "Two," I said.

"Were there not four?"

"So Ryan said."

At this moment General Pomfroy caught sight of us and came bustling over. "Ah, Mr. Pons," he boomed, "I forgot to ask you last night in what capacity you served the Foreign Office." He had clearly, in the course of the night, convinced himself that Pons and his old military acquaintance were one and the same.

"Cryptography," said Pons without hesitation.

"Ah, fascinating, fascinating!" said the General, and launched into an account of an adventure of his own in military intelligence in France, an interminable tale which was interrupted by nothing and no one until the Master walked past to say, "Hounds, Gentlemen, please!"

One of the horsemen had come up with our mounts. Pons lifted himself to his horse with considerably more agility than I, but I fancied I sat my mount more securely than he, for he seemed to crane this way and that as if determined to take in everything at once – the hounds forward, the three Whips – the Master on his mount – our client in a little group leading the way after the hounds, leisurely – Ryan riding forward to join

Bannan near the Master – Bannan carrying two poles, one of which he thrust forward at Ryan as Ryan came up – General Pomfroy mounting as if he were engaged in storming the battlements of a fortress – the Chairman of the Hunt off to one side, looking a little anxiously at the weather, which was now dark and louring with a northeast wind and the smell of rain in it, though no rain had fallen.

The hounds moved in silence; here and there a stern whipped two and fro; the voices of the Whips cajoled and commanded. The field made a straggling party in the van of the hounds, with the distance widening between hounds and field; a babble of talk rose among the field in one place, subsiding in another. The field moved across the dark landscape in the grey morning like a great flower unfolding, going steadily away from Pomfroy Chase in the general direction of Salisbury, across a dale, between a knoll and a rambling copse, out upon the moor.

The wind felt raw, but Pons did not seem to mind it. He rode now more easily, having settled in to it, and having established for himself where the Hunt servants were and where the Master was; but he rode alert, I saw, as if he waited upon the first music of the hounds.

It came with startling suddenness when the hounds gave tongue. An instant later the cry "Gone away!" rang forth, and the field plunged forward. The hounds boiled out over the moor, their music ringing wild on the wind. From Huntsman to field and back among the other members the cry was passed that a dog-fox had been viewed, the hounds were hot on his scent.

What had been leisurely was now charged with urgent action. The hounds streamed across the moor; the field strove to close the distance between; and the music of the hounds filled the morning, beating back the dark clouds, the threat of rain, and the chill that had seemed so omnipresent an hour before. Countryside, hounds, pink-clad huntsmen and, somewhere ahead, a dog-fox running for his life were all the morning – all else belonged to another world, and the excitement of the chase filled me, as it filled Pons, too, for he urged his mount forward, passing several of the field in his insistence.

But the moor was difficult country. The flat of it had quickly given way to knolls, coppices, and an occasional rock, and the fox in his cunning led hounds and field through the most rugged parts of it. The field spread out and came together again. Ryan and Bannan were hard on the heels of the pack; the Master, as far as I could see, rode at the head of the field, with the Chairman of the Hunt Committee not far behind, and our hostess with six other women were close by. Pons was now well ahead of me; I caught sight of him from time to time, riding hard, just in advance of the ladies. General Pomfroy had fallen back – a lone figure bringing up the rear. Ahead, I could see the Whips and the horsemen – four of them, though I could have sworn we had started with but two.

The hounds came to a sudden stop, boiling around in confusion, and two of the Whips rode forward to help start them again. Whining, yelping, baying, the hounds set off in one direction, returned, set off in another. The Whips turned them again, back to the old line, and the pack streamed forward once more, the confusion gone from their voices, their bugling once again riding the wind and falling to ear in this place like a melody of Schubert risen to intoxicate one's senses in the concert hall.

The moments of hesitation and confusion, brief as they were, had enabled the field in the lead to close much of the gap between them and the pack, though the hounds were widening it once more. The cry of the hounds, the shouts of the Whips, Ryan blowing the Huntsman's horn, the renewed "Hollaing" ringing down the moor charged the morning again with excitement.

Pons had fallen back; now he was urging his mount forward again, using his crop. General Pomfroy had almost caught up. The Hunt Chairman wheeled from time to time to gaze, troubled, at the heavens. And now and then a drizzle of mist or rain whipped into my face. The clouds threatened to end the hunt before the hounds could find.

Up ahead, the hounds swept up the slope of a bush-crowned knoll which fell away sharply on the far side in a tangle of undergrowth – up and over, the music giving way briefly to a tangle of confused yelping, and then they swept into view again. The Whips and the leaders of the field followed – and then suddenly the Huntsman's horn called hounds off, a babble of voices rose, and the Hunt came to a stop. The field slowed to a halt on top of the knoll, though Pons had gone over.

The Master had dismounted and stood pale-faced and silent, almost encircled by the Whips and the horsemen. Something had happened. Perhaps one of the field had taken a bad spill. The Master found his voice. "Dr. Paradine," he called, and Dr. Paradine pressed forward on his mount just as I came to the edge of the knoll and saw what lay below.

It was the body of a man, certainly not one of the field, for he was roughly clad. Only a cursory glance was necessary to suggest that he had been resting or sleeping there, and that one of the horses had delivered a fatal blow to his head, for it was broken in, and blood was spilled from it. The road across the moor was not far away, and the fellow had very probably wandered in during the night, for the place of his concealment was well protected from the weather, though the plunging horses had torn away some of the vegetation there. Dr. Paradine, who had bent over the body, now straightened up, shaking his head.

"Dead, Master," I heard him say.

I saw Pons press unobtrusively forward and in turn make a rapid examination of the body, while Ryan looked over his shoulder at him in hostile amazement.

The tableau held but for a moment. The restless hounds crowded about offside, whining uneasily; voices rose querulously from the rear of the field. But the Hunt had lost its excitement in the tragedy before us, and the Master, remounting, announced, "We will return to the house, Ladies and Gentlemen," and turned his mount to lead the way.

I fell back from the main body of the field and waited upon Pons to ride up. His face, when he came abreast of me, was impassive, but his eyes glinted oddly.

"A shocking thing!" I said. "Was that fellow killed by one of the riders?"

"The wound in his head would indicate that he was certainly killed by something in the shape of a horse's hoof," said Pons cryptically.

"Who was first over the knoll?"

"I was unable to see."

"He must have wandered in off the road. Strange that the hounds did not wake him."

"Unless he were sodden with liquor," said Pons.

"True."

We rode for a few moments in silence. We were now well separated from the rest of the field, and Pons, I saw, rode with deliberate leisureliness because he was deep in thought. He turned to me presently, guiding his mount nearer.

"Would you not say, Parker, that anyone spending last night out-of-doors would have been rather wet with frost?"

"I would indeed."

"His clothes were not damp."

"Well, of course, he lay under bushes which would give him some protection."

"The scent presumably carried straight over him," continued Pons. "Would you say that is consistent with ferine behavior."

"No. It would seem to me that the fox could be aware of a man's presence in time to avoid stepping upon him,"

I conceded. "Yet, coming up the knoll and dropping over – it is just possible..."

"But unlikely," continued Pons. "The hounds divided and went around him. They were therefore aware of his presence. The fox could hardly have been less aware. I submit that no fox was ever near him."

"I'm afraid the evidence of the hounds must be set against that," I said. "They were clearly on the scent."

"You will recall that at one point the hounds were confused. There were two lines, one crossing the other. The hounds were bound for the fresher; they were whipped off and put on the other."

"I suppose it isn't unusual to put up a second fox."

"There was no second fox. The only fox was the dog-fox we were hunting. I submit he was never near the sleeping man."

"The hounds would never have left the scent!"

"Unless they were misled by a false scent made by a fresh fox, a bagged fox or even a recently taken dead fox."

"Pons!" I cried. "You can't mean murder!"

"It is something like that fellow found in the stallion's stall. Here, too, no one seemed to know him. He was, once again, therefore a stranger, but whether to everyone remains to be seen. His clothing, as I said, was rough, of decent quality, but of a kind worn only by someone not accustomed to expensive clothing. His hands were rough, also, and the calouses on them suggest that he was habitually engaged in some menial labor; there are certain indications that he was accustomed to using a trowel, and I should conclude that he was a mason by trade when there was work for him, though his hands are also accustomed to the use of a shovel. It was evident when one came only close to him that he reeked of whisky. Unless I am mistaken, he carried inside his clothing a long, thin weapon in the shape of a poniard. I rather fancy no startling amount of money will be found on him, but the presence of the weapon will disconcert the authorities."

"It disconcerts me," I admitted.

"Ah, Parker, if you have correctly assessed the facts in the matter, it ought to fall into place with little difficulty."

I might have replied, but held my tongue, for General Pomfroy had caught sight of us lagging behind, and waited for us to come up to him.

"Rum go, what!" he boomed as we came up. "The Master's in a black rage – can't say I blame him. First it was that fellow who blundered into Prince's stall, and now this drunken vagrant wandering into the field. Ought to have laws against that sort of thing."

In this vein General Pomfroy continued until we reached Pomfroy Chase and separated to go to our quarters.

Pons lost no time in getting out of his hunting clothes and into his own clothes once more. He seemed deep in thought and paced up and down our room for a few moments. He crossed to the windows and looked down. From where I stood, I could see the hounds being brought in, and our mounts being returned to the stable. An air of sobriety prevailed, with the Whips and the kennel staff going about their business in intent silence.

"I must go out and about," said Pons abruptly. "Are you coming?"

"I'm sorry, Pons. I must beg off," I said. "An hour afield has given me aches I haven't had for a long time."

Pons chuckled and left the room.

In a few minutes I saw him walking between the stables in the general direction of the cottages. I saw, too, that both Ryan and Bannan observed him, and their attitude, even from the distance where I stood at the window, was manifestly unfriendly.

They, like me, stood watching until Pons had passed the row of cottages and begun to walk through the open country beyond. Only then did they visibly relax.

I was awakened from a light doze an hour later when Pons came in. His eyes were twinkling, and he stood, once again, at the windows looking down, rubbing his hands together zestfully.

"There is nothing like a walk in the rain to stimulate logical thinking," he said.

"I never knew you to need it," I said.

"Ah, that is well put, Parker," responded Pons. "It is true, it is facts I went after. For instance – would it surprise you to learn that there is a pet fox kept outside Ryan's cottage?"

"Nothing ever much surprises me when you are on the scent," I said.

"I must say, a little nap sharpens you," said Pons, agreeably. "Are you ready for London?"

"What!" I cried. "You are giving up?"

"Tut, tut! One ought never to jump to conclusions. There is nothing for us to do here for the nonce. The solution of the puzzle is perfectly apparent. I shall be interested to learn what the authorities make of it. I am not disposed to intervene. Let us just get our things together and make our excuses to our host and hostess."

We found Colonel Pomfroy and our client in the drawing-room.

"Ah, Mr. Pons!" cried Colonel Pomfroy. "I had hoped for a word with you! I am half convinced I am the victim of some dastardly plot to ruin the Wycherly!"

"I should not be inclined to think so, Colonel," said Pons gently. "I fancy the solution to the matter lies farther afield."

"Mr. Pons!" cried our client. "You know it then?"

"I hope to resolve the problem directly after the inquest," said Pons with smooth confidence.

"You may need to come back for the inquest, sir," said Colonel Pomfroy.

"I am aware of that. But since no representations have been made to me, I shall feel free to go. You have our address, and we are on the telephone. We expect to return for the proceedings."

"I will have one of the cars brought around to take you to London," said the Colonel.

Our client came to her feet. "And Captain Price?"

"Do not be too sanguine, Mrs. Pomfroy," said Pons. "We may find him only to lose him."

With this enigmatic statement, Pons bade our host and hostess good day.

For a week Pons watched the newspapers for accounts of the events at Pomfroy Chase. Reasonably good likenesses of the man who had died on the moor were published, but no one came forward to identify him, though descriptions of him were detailed and precise – "Age about 48. Height, 5 feet 9 inches. No identification. Contents of pockets: one pound, six-pence." There was a description of the poniard Pons had felt – "A thin, stiletto-like knife, evidently manufactured by hand. The blade is seven inches in length."

"Lethal enough," commented Pons. He read further, aloud: "'The police regret that the presence of the field eliminated any ground clues, but it is presumed that the unknown man wandered in from the road nearby in an intoxicated condition and sought shelter in the lee of the knoll." The autopsy had disclosed that the dead man had imbibed freely of whisky some hours before his death.

The eighth day found us once again in Cranborne, present at the inquest on the unidentified victim of the Pomfroy Hunt. Pons sat with eyes closed during the preliminary evidence, but he grew alert as soon as Dr. Paradine took the stand and listened intently to the interrogation.

The coroner opened with, "Testimony has been advanced to show that you were the first medical man on the scene, Dr. Paradine. Will you recount your findings?"

"The dead man was lying on his right side in a foetal position. He had evidently been sleeping. A horse's hoof crushed his left temple. The bone was broken in for a distance of two inches."

"Was it, in your opinion, an accident?"

"It could hardly have been anything else, sir."

"Was death instantaneous?"

"Practically. He was dead when I examined him."

There followed a rather technical discussion which served only to allow Dr. Paradine the stage long enough to establish his authority. In the course of it, Pons took out the little notebook he carried, jotted something down, and passed it up to the coroner, who read it with a frown on his face. He turned then again to Dr. Paradine.

"Doctor, you say the man was dead when you examined him. How long, in your opinion, had he been dead?"

"It could only have been a matter of moments."

"Then blood was still gushing from the wound?"

Dr. Paradine opened his mouth to speak, then closed it again, before he finally answered, "No, sir."

"Would it not have been?"

"Technically, no, if he were dead."

"Only just dead?"

Dr. Paradine looked uncomfortable. "Considerable blood had been spilled. There may still have been seepage from the wound."

"Do you testify that there was?"

"I cannot so testify," said the doctor stiffly.

Dr. Paradine was excused and John Ryan was called.

He came forward warily and was sworn. At the coroner's request he set forth the details of the tragedy on the moor. The coroner listened without interruption. Once more Pons' notebook came into action. The coroner looked inquiringly into the audience to detect, if possible, the source of the note Pons sent up before he crumpled it and threw it into a wastebasket nearby.

When Ryan had finished, the coroner asked, "Will you tell us what the hounds did, Mr. Ryan?"

"When?" fenced Ryan.

"At the moment they came over the knoll upon the body."

"Why, they divided and swung around on either side of the body."

"But the fox evidently did not?"

Ryan sat for a few moments without answering. Then he said, "Sir, I have no knowledge of that."

"The hounds came together again beyond the body?"

"Yes, sir."

"So that we are to believe the line went straight over the body?"

"Sir, I cannot answer that."

"A pity the hounds could not be called," commented the coroner acidly.

Ryan's color deepened.

The coroner bent forward again. "Now, Mr. Ryan, in the case of the other unfortunate who was found in the stall at Pomfroy Chase, you testified that you had seen him on the grounds during the evening previous to his death. Had you also seen the man found dead on the moor before?"

"I do not believc so," said Ryan smoothly.

"Let me put it this way," pressed the coroner; "Had you ever known him before?"

Ryan was equal to the question which had certainly been prompted by Pons. "Sir, in my capacity as a hunt servant, I have occasion to meet many people. I could hardly be expected to remember them all."

Ryan was excused.

A few more perfunctory witnesses were called, and the inquest was closed.

The verdict, not surprisingly, was "Death by misadventure." Pons shot a glance at Ryan and Bannan, who sat with solemn faces. But the ghost of a smile shone through on each. Then Pons pressed through the crowd to the street, where he sought and found Colonel and Mrs. Pomfroy.

"If you will be so good as to drive us to Pomfroy Chase, I may be able to throw a little light on the mystery," he said.

"Oh, Mr. Pons, if only you could!" cried our client.

"Let us just see," answered Pons.

"Come along then," urged Colonel Pomfroy. "The sooner we get to the bottom of this, the better. I've had my fill of 'death by misadventure'."

Riding out of Cranborne, Pons said, "I submit that despite the verdict of the inquest both the visitors to Pomfroy Chase were done to death." He stopped Colonel Pomfroy's protest with an upraised hand and continued. "Quite possibly, it may be looked upon, in the circumstances, as committed in self defense, but I rather think the courts would take a different view of the matter. It seems quite unlikely that any stranger could have blundered into the stallion's stall, and it is wholly incredible that a fox's line should have naturally led across a sleeping man. Both these men were bearing lethal weapons, and one had actually been used; I think it a mistake not to have searched for a bullet somewhere about the stables. But no matter. The verdict is in. If the first visitor was led to the stall and pushed in, it was done in all likelihood by more than one person; and no one person, it follows, could have arranged the death of that fellow on the moor. In the circumstances, it would be next to impossible to bring a conclusive action against anyone for either of those deaths. I am not sure that it would be desirable."

Colonel Pomfroy found his voice. "But the motive, Mr. Pons! What could the motive be?"

Our client intervened. "What Mr. Pons is saying is that the Hunt servants expected something more to happen. Something has happened. And they are still tense, still expectant..."

"Good God!" cried Colonel Pomfroy. "You don't mean to suggest that there may be still others?"

"Not, I trust, at Pomfroy Chase," said Pons enigmatically. We rode the rest of the way in silence.

Once at Pomfroy Chase, Pons descended from the car with alacrity. "Now, then, if you please, let us settle the matter."

He led the way around the house, past the stables, across the greensward and directly to Ryan's cottage, where he knocked peremptorily on the door.

It was opened by a woman in her middle thirties, blue-eyed and dark of hair.

"Mrs. Ryan?" asked Pons.

"Yes." Seeing Colonel and Mrs. Pomfroy, she nodded a little shyly at them.

"Mrs. Ryan, I would like a word with Mr. Ryan's father."

She gaped at Pons, but recovered her composure in a moment. "If you'll excuse me, I will see if he's awake."

She would have backed in, closing the door to us, but a voice from inside said, "Come!"

"He heard," she said. "Please come in."

She stood aside, and we walked into the tidy living-room of the cottage.

There sat a slouch-hatted old man in an arm-chair. A shawl lay across his shoulders; he held it about him as if he were cold. His thick beard was streaked with grey, but, being relatively short, it gave him an appearance of grizzled roughness rather than of age. His narrowed eyes looked at us over spectacles.

"Mr. Ryan?" asked Pons again.

The old man nodded curtly.

Pons made as if to shake hands; instead, with a rapid movement, he tore the hat from the old man's head, revealing touseled black, ringletted hair beneath.

"Mrs. Pomfroy – Colonel Pomfroy," said Pons, "let me introduce you to Sean O'Leary, once known as the Black Prince of the Irish Republican Army, and, more recently, as Captain Dion Price, in your service, and at least co-author of the death by misadventure of the two agents of that army sent to execute him for his treachery in saving Lady Cleve, after he had been found at last."

"Oh, no!" cried Mrs. Pomfroy.

Behind us Ryan and Bannan, followed by the Whips, crowded into the cottage and pressed around the Black Prince, sullenly defiant, to resist whatever might be threatening him. "And those gentlemen, if I am not mistaken, are all that remain of the valiant little band that rescued Lady Cleve and caused them to be proscribed by the Irish rebels," continued Pons. "The Black Prince was under sentence of death – when he could be found. Here he and his band were as one and acted as one."

Captain Price found his voice. "I am sorry, Mrs. Pomfroy – Colonel Pomfroy – what this gentleman says is true." Then he looked squarely at Pons. "I am not sure what he proposes to do about it."

Pons smiled. "Gentlemen, the verdict is in. 'Death by misadventure.' I am not disposed to question what amounts to poetic justice. But you must know that your position here is untenable, that the men who came to kill you will eventually be followed by others, that you cannot go on dealing death even to would-be murderers. You have no alternative but to lose yourselves again."

Captain Price sighed. "Thank you, sir." And once again, to Colonel Pomfroy and our client, he said simply, "I am sorry."

"It was evident that our client did not believe in the verdict of the inquest," explained Pons, as we rode toward London in one of Colonel Pomfroy's cars. "Accepting that disbelief,

I found it intriguing to speculate on the motive anyone might have for beating someone into near-insensibility, and thrusting him into the stall of a horse that might be counted upon to kill him. Robbery was clearly not the motive. But the size of the sum of money the dead man carried immediately suggested blackmail, and the presence of the weapon suggested that he had come to commit a crime. Captain Price's weskit linked the two men. I immediately concluded that the dead man had had some design upon Captain Price, that the Huntsman had attempted to buy him off, then had reason to think better of it, and, with the aid of his fellow Hunt servants, arranged his death. That he did accept Price's money and then attempted to kill him, we now know. But the dead man's design had been large enough to make it seem advisable for Captain Price to disappear, which in turn suggested knowledge that the failure of the first man might bring a second, which accounted for the tension so patent to Mrs. Pomfroy.

"It was my brief and seemingly innocuous conversation with Ryan that brought to our notice two remarkable coincidences. The first was the fact that all the Hunt servants retained by Captain Price were Irish; this in itself was most singular, but most important, it suggested a motive out of the past. The second was the visit of Ryan's father, occurring almost simultaneously with Captain Price's disappearance. I was then virtually certain of Price's whereabouts, but before I could act, the second executioner sent from Ireland arrived and was dealt with by the Hunt servants, who managed to fill him with whisky – either by force or with his consent – and spirit him away to the moor – you will recall the absence of two of the Whips – where they placed him, well hidden, and either alive or dead – for he may well have been killed there by a weapon resembling a horse's hoof only a few minutes before the hunters arrived – led Ryan's tame fox to the place and away from it again, and made certain that the hounds followed the planted line so that another 'death by misadventure' could be staged.

"At that point, the fact that Lady Cleve had recommended Captain Price for the position immediately suggested that Price might be the Black Prince, and this in turn made it certain that Price might be sought out by the Irish Republican Army for his treachery to their cause, and punished. Instead, the executioners were slain. I did what I could to put the coroner on the right track," he finished, "but I have no wish to interfere with the curious workings of justice."

X

THE ADVENTURE OF THE AMATEUR PHILOLOGIST

My friend, Solar Pons, and I were discussing the trial of the French mass murderer, Landru, one May evening, when the outer door to our quarters opened, and a ponderous step fell upon the stairs.

"Surely that can be no one but Inspector Jamison!" said Pons. "Perhaps he's bringing us some little problem too unimportant to engage the gentlemen at Scotland Yard."

"Elementary," I said. "It would be difficult to mistake Jamison's heavy tread."

"Would it not!" agreed my companion affably. "Or his knock."

The knock that fell upon the door was of such authority that one expected it to be followed by a demand that the door be opened in the name of the law.

"Come in, Inspector," called Pons.

Jamison thrust his portly figure into the room, his eyes quizzical, his round face touched by a light smile. "Good evening," he said amiably. "I'm surprised to find you at home."

"Ah, we are sometimes here, Parker and I," said Pons. "No young lady is demanding Parker's services, and nothing of a criminous nature has engaged my interest in the past day or two. Come, sit down, Inspector."

Jamison removed his bowler and topcoat, put them down on a chair, and came over to stand next to the mantel, near to which Pons and I were sitting.

"I take it this isn't a social call, Jamison," said Pons.

Jamison smiled. "Well, you might say it is and you might say it isn't. We're not exactly befuddled at the Yard, and we'll have the fellow who killed Max Markheim within twenty-four hours. But you're right, Pons, there's a bit of puzzle troubling me. Ever hear of a man named Abraham Aubrey?"

"The name isn't entirely unfamiliar," said Pons thoughtfully. "He is the author of some trifling pieces on philological matters."

"That's the fellow. Has a place in Stepney – private house. Sells antiques and such. Dabbles in linguistics and philology.

About fifty-five. One of our men reported that a thief he was watching went into his place of business. After reading his report, we decided to go around and pay Aubrey a visit. We got there just as he was having a heart attack. We took him to a hospital. He's bad. Couldn't answer questions. One curious thing. He'd evidently just opened his mail, and he still had a letter clutched in his hand. We can't make head or tail out of it.

"You've brought it?"

Jamison took a plain envelope from his pocket and handed it to Pons. "I don't know that it had anything to do with his heart attack. Very likely not. We thought it might be in code and our code men have had a go at it. Made nothing out of it. Doesn't seem to be any code we know, or any sort of cipher. Since I had to be in the vicinity this evening, I thought I'd just bring it along and show it to you. I know your interest in oddments of this sort."

Pons had taken from the envelope a folded piece of lined paper which still bore the creases of having been crushed in

Aubrey's hand. His eyes lit, flickering over the message scrawled there; he looked up.

"It seems clearly an adjuration to Aubrey," he said, his lips trembling with withheld laughter.

"Aha, but what?" cried Jamison.

Pons handed the message to me. "Read it slowly aloud, Parker."

"'Aubrey, thou fribbling dotard, get thee to thy pinquid pightle to dabble and stolch about next rodomel tosy in dark. And 'ware the horrid hent!' – There's no signature."

"Aubrey must have known who wrote it," said Jamison. "And he must have known what it meant."

"I daresay he did – but it's hardly enough of a message to bring on a heart attack," said Pons dryly. "I have no doubt you already noticed that the paper is of the most common kind..."

"Of course."

"And precisely, too, that kind of paper issued to those unfortunates detained at His Majesty's pleasure."

Jamison nodded curtly. "The question is – what's it mean?"

"I daresay I'll have the answer to that in a few days," said Pons crisply. "If you want it. Parker, be a good fellow, and copy this message."

I took the letter to the table and set to work copying it. "There's no date on the letter; nothing to show when it was written," Jamison grumbled.

"But you found its envelope – which was not that in which you brought it. When and where was it posted?"

"Three days ago at Princetown, Devonshire."

Pons smiled enigmatically. "Now, then – Aubrey owns some property in the country. Do you know where it is?"

Jamison flashed a glance of momentary annoyance at Pons. "I don't know how you do these things, Pons. Hardly a minute ago you knew only that Aubrey wrote some philological papers – now you know he owns property in the country."

"Ah, I submit that is, as Parker would say, elementary. You know where it is. Come, Jamison, don't waste time."

"He has about fifty acres near Stow – that's the Stow in Lincolnshire, near Stow Park, not far out of Lincoln." He grimaced. "I know that country well. We were all through it with a fine-toothed comb looking for Lady Canevin's jewels – ten thousand pounds gone!"

"Ah, the cat burglaries. Let me see – that would be seven years ago. You took in Archie Prior for that series of burglaries."

Jamison nodded. "And we're reasonably certain he took Lady Canevin's jewels, too – we were hot at his heels that night, but he slipped away from us – took to the fields when we had the roads watched. We caught him in the Colby house in Lincoln next day – we had his prints on a little job he'd done a week before. He got eight years. We never recovered more of his swag than he had on him or on his premises in London. And precious little that was."

Pons nodded thoughtfully. He sat for a few moments with eyes closed, his long lean fingers tented before him.

I finished copying the letter sent to Aubrey and gave the original back to Jamison.

Pons opened his eyes. "Tell me about Aubrey. Is he tall, fat, short?"

Jamison shrugged. "Average. About your height. A bit heavier. Lean-faced, too, though he wears a full beard."

"Capital!" cried Pons, his austere face becoming suddenly animated. "He lived alone?"

The Inspector nodded. "I suspect we saved his life, coming when we did."

"Then you have access to his premises?"

"We locked the house after him."

"Pray send around the key, Jamison. And a likeness of Aubrey. I expect to take possession during the night. I fancy there is little time to lose. Give me three days. At the end of that time, I submit it may be well worth your while to conduct a careful search of the premises."

Jamison stared at him for a few moments. Then, choking back the questions in his throat, he nodded. "I'll have the key here in an hour – and a photograph of Aubrey. Though I may regret it!"

He clapped his bowler to his head, shrugged into his coat, and bade us good-evening.

"I must confess," I said, "I made little sense out of that letter."

"Tut, tut! The message was plain as a pikestaff to anyone but those who looked for riddles in it," said Pons. "Its author stirs my admiration and fires my interest. And so, too, does Mr. Abraham Aubrey. I trust he will recover, though his heart attack would seem to be fortuitous for our little inquiry."

"It is certainly too much of a coincidence that he should have a heart attack on reading that message," I said.

"Ah, not on reading it so much as its receipt at all. There is no signature, as you've seen. Yet I submit that Aubrey knew at once who had sent it to him. He had not expected to hear from that source, I'll wager. Let me call to your attention the fact that the letter was sent from Princetown, which is the site of Dartmoor."

"It came from someone in prison?"

"I should think that a sound deduction," said Pons.

"But its meaning – if it has any – escapes me."

"I daresay. It is one that a philologist might especially appreciate." He smiled. "But quite apart from its meaning, I submit it conveys certain facts. The writer, if not interested in linguistics or philology himself, has at least been intimately enough associated with Aubrey to have assimilated a ready familiarity with the subject. Presumably that association was broken. By what else if not the jailing of the writer? Quite possibly also there had developed a rift between the two, which might account for Aubrey's shock at receiving this directive in the mail. These facts, slender as they are, arouse some interesting speculations about the precise nature of the association between Abraham Aubrey, antique dealer and amateur philologist, and an unknown lag who is almost certainly being detained at His Majesty's pleasure." He shrugged. "But let us speculate no more. We shall explore the problem all in good time."

True to his word, Inspector Jamison sent around the key to the Stepney house of Abraham Aubrey, and a photograph of the man himself – evidently one newly taken by someone at Scotland Yard, for it revealed Aubrey lying in his hospital bed. At once upon their arrival, Pons sprang into action. He retired to his chamber, and in less than half an hour emerged, wearing a beard, bushy eyebrows, and sideboards making him to resemble Aubrey.

"Come along, Parker. The game's afoot. Mr. Abraham Aubrey is going home."

"Pons! You can't mean simply to walk into the man's home and take possession!" I protested.

"Ah, Parker, you have an uncanny faculty for reading my intentions," said Pons. "Perhaps you'd rather keep the peace at Number 7B?"

"Where is the place?" I asked, ignoring his thrust.

"In Alderney Road," he replied, consulting the tag affixed to the key.

"Stepney seems an unlikely setting for an antique shop."

"It may have certain advantages. It's frequented by seamen, and the sea is the source of many curios which could be profitably turned over by a dealer. If Aubrey is served there by a host of acquisitive seamen, it is not beyond the bounds of possibility that he found the means to turn a handsome profit on items about which no one was likely to ask embarrassing questions. But, come – we'll go there openly. I hope – nay, I expect to be seen."

We took the underground at Paddington, and went by the Inner Circle to Aldgate, where we changed on to the District Line for Stepney Green. The Alderney Road address was within easy walking distance of the station, and we set out for it on foot, through dubious streets, frequently ill-lighted, and haunted by as diverse a variety of human beings as are to be found anywhere in London.

The house, when at last we came to it, was ordinary, neither as shabby as some of the neighboring dwellings, nor as prepossessing as it might have been. In the feebly lit darkness, an air of secrecy shrouded it, given emphasis by shuttered windows. Pons went briskly up the little entrance porch, took out the key Jamison had sent to our quarters, and let himself in. He found a light switch and turned it.

The soft lamplight illumined another world – one of artifacts and curios, vintage furniture, glassware, carvings – all set about on shelves, tables, on the floor among the ordinary furniture of Aubrey's daily use – a fantastically apportioned room which lay beyond a small vestibule, from which a narrow stairs led up to another storey under the gables. Books, art treasures, handicraft – all wearing an aura of rarity – took on separate life in the dimly-lit room.

"Aubrey must be a wealthy man," I said.

"If wealth can be counted in possessions, yes," said Pons. "But for the moment I don't propose to make an inventory. We shall need to find a place to spend the night."

"Surely not here!" I cried.

"Where else? The role demands it," retorted Pons, chuckling.

A cursory exploration of the house revealed a bedroom upstairs, and a small alcove on the ground floor which had obviously served as Aubrey's bedroom; it contained a lounge with bedding piled at the foot and was as orderly as the rest of the house was disorderly.

"This ought to make a comfortable bed for you, Parker. We've slept in our clothes before this," said Pons.

"What about you?"

"I'll take that easy chair in the central room"

"Pons, you're expecting visitors?"

"I doubt it, at this point. Let us just see what tomorrow's adventure will bring."

So saying, he left me to the alcove. Lying on the lounge there, trying to relax, I heard Pons moving about for some time, upstairs and down; he was still at it, pulling open drawers, opening and closing cabinet doors, when at last I drifted off into an uncertain sleep.

Daylight made a kind of iridescence in the shuttered house when Pons woke me. "We have just time to find a trifle of food for breakfast, and get over to King's Cross for the train to Lincoln," he said.

I swung my feet to the floor and saw that he carried a stout sack, which hung from his hand laden with some heavy objects, but I forebore to ask what he carried, knowing his habit of putting me off, but the shape of the objects suggested metal of some kind.

We made a conspicuous exit from the house by the way we had entered it. Pons seemed to be in no haste to leave the porch, and when at last he sauntered out into the street, he stood for a few moments looking up and down, as if proud of his disguise, confirming my previous opinion that my companion took a singular if somewhat juvenile pleasure in disguising himself, which evidently fed upon a flair for the dramatic integral to his nature.

"I could sound a whistle to draw attention to us," I said dryly.

"Let us be seen, by all means, but not, thank you, by means of whistle or klaxon," said Pons.

So saying, we set off down the street.

Mid-morning found us on the train for the three-hour journey to Lincoln by way of Grantham.

"I heard you hunting about last night," I said, once we were moving through the countryside west of London. "What were you searching for?"

"Certain articles I thought I might need on today's journey," he answered. "In the course of my looking around, however, I learned that Aubrey was born in Stow, and came to London from there. Presumably the farm he owns out of Stow was his birthplace, and came down to him from his parents." His eyes twinkled. "If one can judge by the variety of his pieces, Aubrey is a man of parts."

He was not disposed to tell me more.

At Lincoln, three hours later, we changed to the Doncaster line for the brief ride to Stow Park, and there left the train for a walk of almost two miles to the hamlet of Stow.

The countryside was at its peak of green, and many blossoms shone in hedges and gardens. Chaffinches and larks sang, and the morning's mists had risen before the sun bright in heaven. In shadowed places, dew still gleamed on blade and leaf, and over the entire landscape lay a kind of shimmering pale green glow. Pons, I observed, walked without haste; the hour was now high noon, for the journey from Doncaster had taken only twenty minutes; he said little, save for making a momentary reference to the old Norman church at Stow; which lay just ahead. "A pity we hardly dare take the time to examine it," he said. "We can hardly be back in Lincoln for the 2:10, but we might make it in time for the 4:40. The last train leaves after six."

Not far past the church, Pons turned down a lane and came to a stop before a one-storey farm-house, set before a small group of outbuildings. He stood for a few moments surveying the scene.

"I fancy the area we want is well beyond those buildings, which will screen us from view," he said presently. "Aubrey evidently has a tenant on his farm. Come, we'll make a little circuit."

He walked on past the farm buildings.

"What are we looking for?" I asked finally.

"For a small pond or brook near to which we're likely to find a bower of roses and some bee-hives – all set in the middle of a pasture or small field. Pasture, I think we'll find it." He gestured to our left. "And there, I daresay, is our pond."

He turned from the lane as he spoke.

Before us now lay a little pasture, not quite in the middle of which stood a grove of four trees, a bower of bushes, and the round tops of what must be bee-hives. Since the ground there fell away into a little swale, it was not unlikely that a pond lay in that spot, particularly since a slender brook could be seen meandering away in the distance ahead.

We were not long in reaching the place, and there, just as Pons had foreseen, we saw that the bushes were indeed rosebushes, crowding upon a quintet of bee-hives. Pons put down the sack he carried and stood for a moment, briskly rubbing his hands together, his eyes twinkling.

"This, Parker, is a 'pightle' of land – or a 'pickel' or 'piddle' if you will have it so, of pasture land, moreover, or 'pinguid' land – a 'pinguid pightle,'" he said. "English is a noble, expressive language. A pity so many of its fine words have been relegated to oblivion."

"Capital!" I said, not without an edge to my voice. "And what, pray tell, led you to hives and rose bushes?"

"Another of those fine old words, my dear fellow – 'rodomel.' This means, if I recall correctly, a mixture of honey and the juice of rose-leaves – a poet's word. Or a philologist's. I have no doubt Aubrey apprehended instantly what it might mean." He bent to the sack. "Now let us just dabble and stolch about a little. That would be, I fear, in that muddy area between the water's edge and the grass."

He took from the bag first a pair of calf-height boots. Taking off his shoes, he put them on. Then he removed from the bag the joints of a rod, which he proceeded to fit together.

"I take it," I said, watching him, "that 'stolch' means to walk about in mud or quagmire."

"Excellent, Parker. But we shall do a bit more than that." He strode forward into the muck and began to probe it with the rod, which went down in some places for two feet. He kept at this for perhaps ten minutes before the rod struck something. He left it standing in the mud, and returned to the sack for a jointed shovel, with which he began to dig at the spot.

"Keep an eye open for strangers," said Pons.

"There's a farmer in the field across the lane back there."

"A native. We were observed both coming to Aubrey's house last night and leaving it this morning. We were also followed to King's Cross."

"I saw no one."

"Because you weren't looking for someone. I was. He gave up at King's Cross. I rather fancy he's back in Alderney Road with an eye on Aubrey's house."

He was digging as he spoke. Now he gave a curt exclamation of satisfaction, and with great care shoveled around the object in the muck before he dug under it and brought it up on the shovel. It appeared to be a bundle of leather, which had suffered some deterioration because of its immersion in the damp ground.

Pons carried it around to where the sack lay and deposited it carefully beside it, a broad smile on his face. Then he went around the muck to where the pond abutted upon a little bank; there he washed the shovel, the rod, and, after removing them, the boots. Only after he had finished with this task, and returned all the articles to the sack, did he carefully unfold the leather.

There lay revealed a sadly tarnished silver casket.

"Let me introduce you to Lady Canevin's jewel box, Parker," said Pons. "Somewhat the worse for circumstances, but with its contents, I am certain, untouched, just where Archie Prior hid it before he was taken."

He wrapped it carefully once more and thrust it, dirty as it was, into the sack on top of the paraphernalia he had brought with him.

"Now to get back to Aubrey's premises," he said. "We'll stop only long enough in Lincoln to send Jamison a wire."

We reached the house in Alderney Road in mid-evening. On the porch Pons paused and said, without turning his head, "A little man is walking down the other side of the street, Parker. I daresay we'll see more of him before very long."

Pons let us into the house.

"About time you came." Inspector Jamison's voice came to meet us out of the dusk inside.

"I trust you got in without being observed," said Pons.

"Came in from the rear, as you suggested," said Jamison. "Now, what's this?"

Pons dropped the sack he carried, opened it, and reached in for the leather-wound casket. He handed it to Jamison. Jamison reached for it, then drew his hand back. "It's dirty!"

"What else could you expect, being buried for seven years?" asked Pons. He put it down on a sideboard against one wall and unwrapped it carefully. "Handle it with care, Jamison. There may still be prints on it. Unless I am very much mistaken, this is Lady Canevin's jewel casket."

An exclamation escaped Jamison.

"Buried where Archie Prior told Aubrey he'd put it," Pons went on. He took out his watch. "Nine forty-five," he murmured, looking up. "Are the police standing by?"

Jamison nodded curtly.

"Good. We may expect that an attempt will be made to collect the jewel case tonight. The house has been under observation ever since we first reached it yesterday. 'Ware the horrid hent' means nothing less than that the jewel box, once recovered and brought here by someone not likely to be under police surveillance, will be lifted – 'hent' – by dark or night – 'horrid'."

"You broke the code!" cried Jamison.

"There was no code, but more of that later. For the nonce, let us just put out the light and wait upon events, without talking. We ought to be somewhat concealed. There's a spot under the shelving over there, and one of us can be concealed on the far side of the sideboard, and yet another behind the couch in the alcove."

Pons put out the lamp and we took our positions.

There began an interminable wait, which, to judge by his frequent movements, was most trying for Jamison, whose bulk made the crouching stance difficult to maintain for any length of time. The room gradually came back to life – objects took on a shadowy existence in the wan light that filtered in from outside. Clocks ticked, at least half a dozen of them from Aubrey's collection of antique timepieces, and an overpowering occasionally musky atmosphere of very old things became manifest. Not a sound escaped Pons, and I held myself far quieter than I had thought I might.

It was after midnight when the sound of glass being cut fell to ear. Evidently our nocturnal visitor cut out a piece only large enough to enable him to slip his hand in and unlatch a window, for presently there came the sound of a window being cautiously raised. Then, after a few moments of silence, a thin beam of light invaded the room, flickering rapidly from one place to another, and coming to rest at last on the silver casket.

The beam converged upon the casket as our visitor closed in upon it. Just as he put forth a hand to seize it, Pons' hand closed like a vise on his wrist. At the same moment I turned up the light.

"Goldie Evers," said Pons. "Not long out of Dartmoor."

"And aching to go back," said Jamison, coming out of his hiding place.

Goldie Evers, a slight, short man, with very blonde hair, was literally paralyzed with surprise. "I ain't done nothing," he said at last.

"Breaking and entering," said Jamison. "That's enough to begin on."

He went into the adjoining room to the open window and blew his police whistle.

"We'll need that key, Pons," he said, "so the window can be repaired and the house locked up again – until we have time to make an inventory here."

"You'll find, I think, that Aubrey has been serving as a fence for stolen goods for a long time," said Pons.

Jamison's constables came in by way of the front door, which had not been locked.

"Here he is, boys," said the Inspector. "Take him to the Yard, and take that silver casket along. Wrap it carefully, and take care not to touch it. Come along, Pons, – we'll take a police car back to Number 7B."

"There was very little mystery to the problem," Pons said, on the way back to our quarters, "though Archie Prior's note delighted me for its use of so many long forgotten English words. Your code men were looking far deeper than they need have looked, for the message was plain. Can you repeat it, Parker?"

"'Aubrey, thou fribbling dotard, get thee to thy pinquid pightle to dabble and stolch about next rodomel tosy in dark. And 'ware the horrid hent,'" I repeated.

"Capital!" cried Pons. "Well, now, let us look at it in the light Aubrey was expected to read it, with his knowledge of the language. The adjuration is perfectly plain to anyone versed in philological matters. 'Thou fribbling dotard' is of no consequence – it means only 'you trifling old man' – and is not related to the direct message, which instructs Aubrey to go to his plot of pastureland – 'pinguid pightle' and look around in the mud next to bees and wild roses – the 'rodomel' of the message, where he might expect to find something 'tosy in dark' – or snugly hidden in a safe, dark place – obviously in the ground before the bee-hives, which was just where we found it. Finally, of course, Aubrey is told that the casket, once retrieved, would be taken in the night. Presumably Aubrey would in some way be repaid for his services, though Prior makes no assurance of it.

"Now, then, obviously Prior, if released, will be kept under observation for some time. He cannot go to Lincolnshire, without immediately tipping his hand. Nor can someone who, like Goldie Evers, had been confided in, for he might also be watched."

"He wasn't being watched," growled Jamison.

"No matter. When you were hot on Archie's heels, he had to hide the Canevin jewels. Since he was near Aubrey's land, of which he knew, he managed to bury them there. He very likely did not know the extent of your evidence against him when you took him at the Colby house, for he certainly contemplated retrieving Lady Canevin's jewel casket long before this. He finally hit upon the ingeniously worded message we have seen, and probably smuggled it out of Dartmoor with Goldie Evers."

He chuckled. "He'll be a long time enjoying the fruits of his ingenious labors – and I daresay, Aubrey, if he recovers, will have ample time to perfect his knowledge of philology."

XI

THE ADVENTURE OF THE WHISPERING KNIGHTS

"The science of deduction," observed my friend, Solar Pons, "may at one and the same time be the most skillful kind of rationalization, and the most arrant guesswork. Would it surprise you very much, Parker, if I were to tell you that despite all our preparations, we are not likely after all to be partaking of Mrs. Johnson's admirable fare this noon?"

We were standing on the station platform in Chipping Norton, waiting upon the eight o'clock train for Paddington. Pons had completed work on the curious case of the Cottys Fleece too late the preceding night for the last train to London, and we were now off with the morning's first train.

"Nothing you said or did would surprise me very much," I said. "But since that's our train bearing down upon us, I fear, for once, you're over-reaching yourself."

"One ought not to draw conclusions until one is in possession of all the available facts," said Pons, his eyes dancing. "Look there!" He gestured behind me.

I turned. There, bearing down upon the station as furiously as he could pedal his bicycle, was a police constable.

"I fancy my presence in Chipping Norton was not a well kept secret," said Pons dryly.

The village glowed in the morning sun, which lay mellowly on its old stone buildings. Sunlight gleamed from the mullioned windows of the guildhall and the dormers of the almshouses as well as the glass and stone of the fifteenth-century clerestory of the church that dominates the center of Chipping Norton.

"It's hardly a morning for crime," I said.

"Ah, crime knows no season. You see, he has seen us."

The constable arrived at the same time from one direction as the train came from the other. Dismounting, he started toward us on the run.

"Sir!" he cried when he came within speaking distance. "I believe you are Mr. Solar Pons?"

"What can I do for you, Constable?" asked Pons.

"I would appreciate your advice on a matter that has come up.

He had now come abreast of us, and stood, a little breathless, trying to compose himself – a young fellow of not more than thirty, with firm clear blue eyes, and a very high flush in his thin cheeks. He had a long face, faintly equine in appearance, and wore a sparse moustache that complemented his equally sparse eyebrows and the sandy hair that could be seen below his helmet.

"Ruskin, sir," he said. "That's my name."

"And what is the problem, Constable?"

"I'm afraid it's murder."

Pons looked speculatively at me. "Parker, you have the choice between the train or another of those little adventures you seem to dote upon. Which shall it be?"

"Your choice is mine," I said.

"Capital!"

"Could we step off to the side, sir?" asked Ruskin anxiously. "We ought not to attract too much attention."

Passengers were leaving and entering their compartments.

We moved away from the train to the wall of the station. Constable Ruskin had now recovered his breath and his composure, but none of his anxiety had drained out of his face. He lowered his voice and spoke urgently.

"Sir, do you know the cromlech along the Birmingham road?" he asked.

"Called variously the Rollright or Rollrich Stones," said Pons. "Presumed Druidic in origin, but not one of the more important cromlechs in England."

"Yes, sir, that's right," said Ruskin, nodding. "Not many people visit the stones, that's true. But it is under the care of His Majesty's Office of Works, sir, and there's a caretaker. Well, Mr. Pons, about a hundred yards to the east of the circle is a rather large megalithic burial chamber. We know it hereabouts as the Whispering Knights. This morning two young American gentlemen, studying at Oxford on some sort of scholarship, I understand, were examining the area and came upon what they took to be a mound of feathers and strips of cloth in the chamber. It proved to be the body of an elderly gentleman wearing a mummer's costume. They reported it to the caretaker, who called me. Certain features of the crime impelled me to ask your assistance."

"For instance?" asked Pons.

"Well, sir – it's summer," said the constable earnestly. "The Mummers' Play is put on at Christmas. Not now."

"Ah, mummers still perform hereabouts, Constable?"

"Yes, sir. In many places here in Oxfordshire – Waterstock, near Thame – Cuddlesdon, Leafield, Heyford, Shipton under Wychwood."

"A dying folk drama," murmured Pons. "But perhaps we ought to proceed to the scene."

"If you'll wait here, I'll get a motor from headquarters."

He ran off at once, mounted his bicycle, and pedalled rapidly down the street.

"Forgive me," I said to Pons, "but what are 'mummers'?"

"Another proof of the persistence of folklore, Parker," he replied. "Living in London, we tend to be in our own urban way quite as insular as, say, the inhabitants of Chipping Norton. We are unaware of the way in which many of our fellow Englishmen live. Folk customs persist throughout the country – Bonfire Day at Lewes – wassailing the apple trees at Carhampton – the Furry Dance in Cornwall – the Morris Dancers in this shire – market festivals in various places – the Knutfsord Festival in Cheshire – harvest celebrations of many kinds. The Christmas mummers date back at least eight centuries, and were once to be found in every English village. They have declined in our time."

"But what do they do?"

"Essentially they re-enact some form of the fight between St. George and the Dragon. It may be King George and some other enemy, but this is the central theme of the performance, which is always done in grotesque costumes concealing their bodies and sometimes masks to hide the faces of the participants. Variations include some symbolic representation of the death of the old year and its resurrection as the new. And sometimes the performances represent sacrificial acts of sowing-time – a survival from pagan times to insure a good crop of grain. Though the mummers are reputed to take origin at the time of the Crusades and to be primarily performers in a Christian ritual, there would appear to be a good deal of paganism associated with the custom. The Mummers' Play is interesting particularly to literary scholars; it seems to be the only survival of pre-Reformation folk drama."

"Are these plays performed by professional actors?"

"No, Parker, the roles are all taken by amateurs. Sometimes, I believe, the roles are handed down from father to son. The plays are always performed by men – six or eight of them – and their characters are standard – Father Christmas, King George,

Quack Doctor, Lawyer, Bold Slasher, Valiant Soldier, Rumour, and Twing Twang, sometimes called Little Johnnie Jack. The characters' names are evidence of the essential medievalism of the mummers."

The train drew out of the station just as Constable Ruskin returned in his car.

Pons and I got into it and we started away through the village and into the country, once the pastureland of thousands of sheep, when, in previous centuries, the western shires supplied most of the wool used by the weavers in the low countries. It was an upland of gentle slopes and green valleys divided by streams, and dotted with stone cottages and little villages.

The cromlech stood on high ground almost at the border of Warwickshire. A grove of larch trees towered above the stones, which appeared to be all of local oolite, badly weathered; they were widely scattered, deeply pitted, and manifestly Bronze Age remnants. None was very high; a few of the stones seemed to be almost as high as a short man, but their average height otherwise was three feet. There seemed to be over fifty of the stones, standing upright under the trees, and making a rough circle of about a hundred feet in diameter. Off to the north side of it stood a single tall stone of over eight feet in height.

The caretaker stood alone near the road, waiting for us. He was a stocky man of middle age, with greying side whiskers framing his square-jawed, dogged-looking features; his dark eyes peered out at us from beneath shaggy brows.

"Mr. Pickering," said the constable, "Mr. Solar Pons of London has come to help us in the inquiry."

"Scotland Yard?" asked Pickering.

"We'll call in the Yard only as a last resort," said the constable hastily, at which Pickering nodded with a quaintly satisfied air, as if for some reason he disapproved of Scotland Yard.

"Right this way, gentlemen," said the caretaker, proceeding across the circle of stones in an easterly direction. Over his shoulder, he asked the constable suspiciously, "Where be the Americans?"

"I have their depositions," said Ruskin with reproving asperity.

Pickering fell into a glowering silence.

"Do the natives visit the stones frequently, Mr. Pickering?" asked Pons.

"Not much, they don't," answered the caretaker. "Some's afeard. Some don't care. There's old talk about the place. They do say come midnight All Saints' Day, the stones come to life and go down the hill to drink at the spring. There's some believe the old wives' tale that these stones came about when some witchcraft turned a king and his army into stone."

He tittered, but almost at once subsided into an uneasy bravado. "But there's witchcraft about! There's some of us hereabouts who know."

He said nothing more, perhaps because he caught sight of Constable Ruskin's tolerant smile.

We came presently upon the ancient burial chamber, a stone-walled recess which framed a grotesque and terrible scene. In the middle of it lay a huddle of cloth strips and feathers held to the ground by a pitchfork.

"Won't go no farther," said the caretaker abruptly, halting well back from the entrance. He pointed an unsteady finger at the strangely attired corpse. "It's Fletcher Dewson – that's who 'e is – and I say'e's been served right. There's others about who ought to be served the same."

Pons walked over to the body, taking care to step apart from such fragmentary prints as could be seen. I did not need to be told to do likewise as I made my way toward the dead man's side.

The costume that confronted us was indeed curious. The dead man wore a sort of imitation flower crown, from which long cloth streamers came down to cover his face. The body was that of a man of seventy or so, a wizened old fellow with a scrawny neck and hands, and a pinched face which, in life, appeared to be no stranger to a fixed expression of displeasure. His body was clothed in a coat and trousers to which had been sewn shorter cloth strips of various colors, mingled with feathers which I took to be those of hawks and owls. To the front along the right side of the coat three dolls were attached in such a way as to be an integral part of the costume. The pitchfork which had been stuck into the dead man's left side – either into or dangerously close to his heart – just missed the near doll with one of its tines.

But the fork was not the only weapon. When I parted the long cloth strips that concealed the old man's face, I saw to my horror that his throat had been torn away by the sickle blade of a trouncing hook, still embedded in the flesh.

Pons, however, experienced none of the horror I felt. His eyes were positively bright with interest. "That is the Little Johnnie Jack costume," he said. "Unless I am very much mistaken, the dolls are associated only with that costume." He turned toward the caretaker, still standing well away behind us. "Mr. Pickering! Was Mr. Dewson a mummer?"

"No mummers hereabouts now," said Pickering.

"Was he at one time a mummer?"

"They do say he was."

"I take it, Parker – judging by the amount of blood – this was the scene of his death?"

"Not a doubt of it," I agreed. "His jugular was severed."

"How long dead?" asked Pons.

"Sometime in the night. Probably about seven hours. That would put the time of his death at around one o'clock this morning."

I got up and stepped back, leaving the field to Pons.

He dropped to his knees beside the body with alacrity, first to examine the costume, then to scrutinize the fork and the sickle blade, after which he gave a remarkably close examination to the ground around the body. In two places he carefully gathered up what seemed to me specimens of the soil and put them into the little envelopes he frequently carried. Then he crawled about along the side of the chamber and out toward the entrance, peering intently at the surface of the earth, both where it was exposed and where it was overgrown with short grass.

He reared back on his haunches suddenly. "Mr. Pickering. How many visitors were there yesterday?"

The caretaker appeared to think. "Don't rightly think we had any," he said finally. "Nobody applied to see the stones."

"And the day before?"

Pickering shook his head. "No visitors for three days. The Americans this morning were the first in the four days."

"Capital!" cried Pons. He pointed to the ground. "We had rain two days ago, and all the footprints are no more recent than last night or this morning. Here we have your prints, Constable. And here are Mr. Pickering's. And these, I submit, are those of the two American students. All have walked in the morning's dew. But this indentation – and this – and this – all by the same foot – were made prior to the formation of the dew; there is dew on them."

Pons was measuring them appraisingly as he spoke. At the edge of one of the prints, where a half buried stick jutted forth, he bent and picked up another pinch of soil for depositing in an envelope. "Constable, look for a man who favors his left leg."

"With a limp?"

"I have not said so."

The caretaker muttered under his breath. "Jock Howells!"

"What was that, Mr. Pickering?" asked Ruskin.

"I say Jock Howells. Walks with a limp, 'e does. Not much to notice. He was another of *them*."

"A friend of the dead man's?" asked Ruskin.

"In a manner of speaking. They were in it together."

"I don't follow that, Mr. Pickering," said the constable, showing some exasperation.

"Mr. Pickering," said Pons abruptly, coming to his feet. "I take it you had no love for Fletcher Dewson."

"You take it right!"

"Nor Jock Howells?"

"Two of a kind. Always meddling with things better left alone."

"What, Mr Pickering?" put in Ruskin.

"Nothing city blokes would know about," said Pickering. "They do laugh at us. Warlocks! That's what they were. They did all sorts of dark things – black magic and heathenish rites. Twan't only the wind that talked here in the nights when there was no wind about!"

Ruskin turned to Pons. "The chamber gets its name from the belief that the wind-like sounds here are the whisperings of the knights turned to stone," he said with an apologetic manner.

"Aye! I've heard 'em," said Pickering.

Pons was not listening. He stood now with his hands clasped behind him, his head bowed, his eyes half closed, in an attitude of deep thought. Something significant had either occurred to him, or he had noticed some small detail which had certainly escaped me. The silence was broken by the song of a skylark flying ecstatically overhead. Pons' eyes opened suddenly.

"Where did Dewson live, Mr. Pickering?" he asked.

"You can see the place from the high ground," said Pickering. "A stone cottage."

"Within walking distance?"

"Easy," said Pickering. "It was one time part of the old estate. The old Dewson estate, that is."

"Ah! Dewson was wealthy?"

Pickering gave a short, barking laugh. "Not 'e! 'E's on the dole." He went on to explain that Dewson's grandfather had been a wealthy man, engaged in the wool trade; he had owned all the land on "this side" of Chipping Norton, including the cromlech. He had had two sons, the one preceding him in death, the other – Dewson's father – his sole heir. Dewson had never married, but he had a sister who had, and a brother. Dewson was the only member of his generation left, but he had a nephew – Arthur Keenan – in Africa, and a niece, Miss Rose Dewson, in Banbury. Dewson, his brother and sister had all inherited substantial sums, even after death duties, but the two men had been improvident, both given to making "wild" investments in foreign lands and worthless stocks, and his sister had had the bad luck to marry a ne'er-do-well, who had gone through her money before taking his own life in Rhodesia.

"Did he see his niece at all?"

"Aye. She came to visit him. Maybe once a quarter. And his nephew wrote him now and then."

"His friends?"

"Not many."

"His enemies, then, Mr. Pickering?"

"Plenty people had no use for Dewson." He seemed reluctant to say more.

"Why?" Pons prodded him.

"I said it before. Jock Howells and him and a few others – they belonged together – they met and had 'rites'. Mr. Welton – Henry Welton – said Dewson put a curse on his house and his old mother died."

"How long ago?"

"Ten years. Welton never spoke to Dewson since. Hated him."

"Dewson and Howells and their friends were still at meeting together?"

"They say not. Two of 'em's dead since."

"I take it this is common knowledge, Mr. Pickering?"

Pickering nodded. "Even the children got out of Dewson's way when 'e came near."

Pons thanked him and turned to Ruskin. "Come along, Constable, and take us over to Dewson's cottage, if you will."

"Certainly, Mr. Pons." He turned to the caretaker. "You stand guard here, Pickering."

Pickering nodded.

Walking across the high ground among the Rollright Stones, the constable asked diffidently, "Was there anything significant that caught your eye, Mr. Pons?"

"Let me direct your attention to the costume, Constable. And to the line of footprints."

"There was but one line of footprints before the dew came."

"That is the significant factor."

"Made by a man who favored his left leg when he walked. And, if I read them rightly, a heavy man."

"I doubt you have read them rightly, Constable."

We got into the car once more, and went on for a short distance to stop before a tidy stone cottage, along the front of which blossomed purple loosestrife and stonecrop.

"This was once a sheep-tender's cottage, I believe, sir," said Ruskin. "It probably kept him and his family."

"Close quarters," said Pons.

"They were all small houses, Mr. Pons."

The constable tried the door. It gave, opening upon a compact sitting-room, off which, in turn, doors standing ajar gave upon a cubbyhole of a bedroom and an equally small kitchen. Pons' attention was immediately drawn to fragments of cloth which lay on the floor of the sitting-room.

"Are those not pieces of a mummer's costume?" he asked.

Ruskin picked up one of them and handed it to Pons. "This is evidently where he dressed."

"Or was dressed," said Pons. "I submit, Mr. Ruskin, that Dewson was dressed here by his murderer, while Dewson was unconscious. You must have noticed how badly the costume was put on."

"I did that, Mr. Pons."

"The costume is an old one, and the material none too sturdy. See here." He took the ragged strip of cloth and tore it easily in two.

"I see," said the constable. "Then if Dewson was knocked out here, he was carried to the cromlech. That implies not a heavy man, but a strong one. The imprints were deeper than the others because he was carrying Dewson. And there must then be some connection between the scene of Dewson's actual death and the practises of which he was alleged to be guilty."

"Capital! Capital!" cried Pons. "You scarcely have need of my assistance, Constable. I commend you. But let us not proceed too hastily. I think it certain that Dewson was knocked out here, costumed, and then taken to the Whispering Knights to be slain. Beyond that point we ought not yet to go. Let us just look about a bit."

He dropped to his knees to examine the worn floor, while the constable examined the top of a small bureau which stood against one wall, in lieu of its proper spot in the bedroom, which was too small to accommodate it, and, finding nothing of significance there, began to pull open drawers, from one of which he took a packet of letters. He took out one of them, removed it from its envelope, and read it. Then another.

"Well, his niece wrote to him," Ruskin said presently. "And so did his nephew. They evidently cared for him, even if his neighbors had some reservations about him. Listen to this from Keenan: 'Dear Uncle Fletcher, I am just in from the bush and find yours of the seventh. I don't have much money right now, but I am sending you a note. You can buy yourself a little 'baccy with it' – The old man must have been hitting him for money! 'I hope you are keeping well and are in good health!' – Miss Rose wrote along similar lines, but didn't send any money. Here she is – If I could be sure you would not spend the money on vile tobacco or liquor, I would send you some. Why do you not permit me to come for you and bring you to stay a while with me here?' – A Puritan, Mr. Pons."

Pons came to his feet again. Ruskin handed him the packet of letters and Pons went rapidly through them. "Yes, he must have been asking often for money," he agreed. "And both niece and nephew were concerned about his health. They asked repeatedly after it – Miss Rose with moral observations, Keenan with none."

Ruskin, who had rummaged further in the drawers, came out with a long envelope across the face of which had been scrawled "Papers". "Now this looks like something, Mr. Pons," he said, and exchanged it for the letters.

The envelope was not sealed. Pons drew out first a list of debts Dewson had drawn up; some were marked "Pd." and some were not. The old man was still in debt by approximately a hundred pounds. The next paper was a melancholy one indeed; it was a list of his bad investments – stock in long bankrupt corporations, mythical "oil lands" in Canada, deeds for parcels of worthless land in Kenya, India, and Rhodesia. The list revealed only too well what Fletcher Dewson had done with his inheritance – he had squandered in this fashion between five and ten thousand pounds.

"A man without judgment, seemingly," observed Pons. He drew out the last of the papers. This proved to be a simple will, dated ten years before, in which he left "all my mortal goods, property, and whatever I die possessed of" to his niece and nephew with the pathetic adjuration that "they not squander it as I have done."

The constable chuckled. "Precious little he left them to squander."

Pons handed the envelope back to Ruskin. "I suppose you will have to notify these people, Constable."

"Yes. Miss Rose will be no problem. But if Keenan's in the bush, there's no telling when he can be reached. Miss Rose will probably take charge of the arrangements. Keenan couldn't get here, anyway, in time for the funeral, and he's hardly likely to come at all."

"I think we've finished here," said Pons then. "Tell me, Constable, where can we find Jock Howells?"

"He's the proprietor of the Black Fleece at the edge of town. On the Charlbury road."

Pons consulted his watch. "I think, Mr. Ruskin, our best course would be to re-engage our rooms at the White Hart. We can catch the noon train to London and be back in Chipping Norton late tomorrow. I have had one or two little things I must attend to in London."

"Do you think Howells had a hand in it, Mr. Pons?"

"In time, with our combined efforts, we shall manage to determine that, Mr. Ruskin," said Pons affably.

Pons remained uncommunicative throughout the balance of the morning and the brief lunch we took before we caught the 12:48 train for London. Once in our compartment, however, he broke his self-imposed silence.

"What do you make of it, Parker?"

It was the kind of leading question designed solely to persuade from me my own frequently wide-of-the-mark opinions. He knew very well I could not resist the challenge. "It seems to me plainly a case of murder for vengeance."

"Does it not!" he cried. "It recalls to memory the death of Ann Tennant in Long Compton, in 1875. She was an old woman of eighty, stabbed to death with a pitchfork by one James Heywood, who declared her a witch. The fork and the sickle are held to be peculiarly effective in the disposal of witches and warlocks."

"And Dewson was reputed to be a warlock," I put in.

"So we've been told. It does not seem strange to you that he should have been clad in his mummers' costume?"

"All this superstitious rigmarole is mummery."

"I beg to disagree," said Pons. "The Mummers' Play is a Christian ceremony. Wizardry is its direct opposite. That is diabolic work, Parker."

"Oh, come, Pons!" I cried. "Surely you don't believe in such claptrap!"

"It is not what I believe, but what the late Fletcher Dewson's neighbors may have believed. I, for one, find it difficult to credit one's confusing the Mummers' Play with the black arts."

"I have just done so," I said.

"Ah, but you are not a provincial, Parker."

"And why the cromlech as the site for the murder?" I asked.

Pons chuckled. "That poses yet another perplexing question. The cromlech is presumably of Druidic origin. Whether Druidism was the survival of an ancient form of oak-tree-worship or whether it was the cult of the wise seeker after truth – the authorities are divided on this point – is immaterial. What is significant here is the indisputable fact that Druidism was a form of pagan religion. Dewson's murder in the Whispering Knights therefore draws together three conflicting mythologies, each one opposed to the others. Either this was done out of ignorance or with design."

"Could it not have been simple coincidence?"

Pons brushed this contemptuously aside. "No, no, Parker. It is elementary that this crime was committed in this fashion to impress upon us Dewson's past affiliation with some bucolic cult of diabolism."

"Perhaps they once performed their play at the cromlech?"

"The Mummers' Play is customarily performed in the villages at Christmas or in the fields at the sowing – and before an audience. There could be no conceivable reason for the performance at the cromlech, where the very stones would be in their way. The Christmas mummers frequently visit the principal residences during the day, perform before them, and then repair to the inns after dark. The Mummers' Play demands an audience of people – not of stones, Parker."

"Well, it's certainly a puzzle."

"If intended to be so, it is meaningless. But the confusion may not have been intentional," said Pons enigmatically.

Thereafter he said no more, but sat with his head bowed and his eyes closed to the lovely English countryside flashing past the windows of our compartment – through that country Hopkins had so memorably described as "Cuckoo-echoing, bell-swarmed, lark-charmed, rock-racked, river-rounded," a land of drowsy rivers lined with willows. And so he sat until the train drew into Paddington in late afternoon.

Once back in our quarters at 7B Praed Street, with our patient landlady, Mrs. Johnson, getting dinner for us, I went around to arrange for my locum to continue in my office for a few more days – anticipating our return to Chipping Norton, while Pons repaired without delay to his chemical apparatus.

On my return, I found Pons just sitting down to our dinner. As I joined him. I saw that his eyes were dancing.

"Aha!" I cried, "you've discovered something in your envelopes."

"I have indeed," he replied. "Evidently the late Fletcher Dewson was wealthier than his neighbors suspected."

He pushed over to me a piece of black paper on which lay three tiny particles of what appeared to be glass – one as large as a grain of sand, the others hardly more than dust motes.

"Crystals of some sort," I said.

"These little pieces are technically known as diamond dust, Parker," said Pons.

"Yet he begged tobacco money!" I cried. "You found them in the house?"

"No. In the burial chamber."

"But how came they there?"

"Ah, that is indeed an intriguing problem, Parker. They were in one envelope only – the last I filled. The other envelopes yielded nothing but the expected soil, some fragments of old peregrine falcon feathers, evidently crumpled from the mummer's costume, which appeared to have been quite old and long in disuse, and some particles of cloth either from the costume also, or from Dewson's clothing – or both. I have sent off a wire to Constable Ruskin suggesting a more intensive search of Dewson's house and grounds, particularly the latter, since the soil also revealed grains of a kind of blue-green serpentinous rock. I observed nothing of this sort at the cromlech or in its immediate vicinity. It suggests kimberlite."

"That puts a different complexion on the murder," I said.

"Does it not!" agreed Pons.

"If he had valuables hidden at his place – and his companions in diabolism somehow learned it!"

"Gently, Parker. I fancy we may stray too far afield. Can you get away for a few more days?"

"I've arranged for another week."

"I fancy we'll not need that long. We'll take the 2:10 from Paddington tomorrow afternoon."

A short, buxom woman, clad in a severe black ensemble and wearing a pince-nez from behind which sharp eyes looked out, waited for us at the White Hart late the following afternoon. The clerk at the desk made a sign to her at our entrance, and she rose at once to face us, her mouth prim and her mien stern.

"Mr. Solar Pons?" she asked as Pons strode up. At his nod, she introduced herself. "I am Miss Rose Dewson, Mr. Pons. I came to ask that you spare no effort to discover the murderer of my uncle. He was not a man of strong moral character, but he scarcely merited such a death as this."

"Will you come up to our room, Miss Dewson?" asked Pons.

A flicker of disapproval crossed her face. "That would hardly be proper, Mr. Pons," she said. "Thank you, no. What I have to say can be said here. I have saved enough money for your fee, and I know my cousin will join me in this."

"Ah, you have heard from him?"

"I cabled him at once. I had his reply only an hour ago. He expects to leave Somabula within twelve hours. While he cannot be in time for the services, he will be here to help settle my poor uncle's estate. Now, Mr. Pons, is there any help I can give you?"

"You saw your uncle from time to time?"

"Yes. Mr. Pons, Uncle Fletcher was a most improvident man. He did not know how to take care of money. It isn't given to some people. He was one such. I came sometimes to bring him a hamper of food or to take him out to dinner."

"Your uncle was in straitened circumstances?"

"Mr. Pons, he had been on the dole for a long time."

"Did he ever, at any time, suggest that he had hidden resources?"

She smiled fleetingly. "Mr. Pons, the very idea is totally ridiculous. If he had such resources, he would have spent them on liquor, tobacco or on his cronies in the pubs. Mr. Pons, I assure you, my uncle was a poor man. My cousin and I have been contributing what we could to him from time to time."

"Ah, you have been in touch with Mr. Keenan right along?"

"Hardly," she said. "A card at Christmas, no more, up until about two years ago when he wrote to inquire about Uncle Fletcher's health. It surprised me a little, because I had always understood my cousin to be in the family image – inimical to real work, and more or less indifferent to the rest of the family. But many people change with age. Since that time Arthur has written perhaps once a quarter. He seems to be now engaged in mission work among the natives in Rhodesia and surrounding areas, and his kindness toward Uncle Fletcher shows that some Christianity has taken root in him."

"Miss Dewson," said Pons then, dismissing her cousin, "I am not clear in mind as to your uncle's habits."

"Mr. Pons, he lived as a sort of recluse. Oh, he used to go about, but now he seldom went anywhere but to the pubs, especially Jock Howells' Black Fleece."

"We hear tales of his interest in diabolism."

Miss Dewson immediately seemed to withdraw into herself. "I know nothing of that, Mr. Pons."

"He was found, you know, dressed in his mummer's costume and put to death precisely as warlocks and witches were done away with in centuries past," said Pons.

"My uncle did take part in the Mummers' Play at Christmas, Mr. Pons," said Miss Dewson. "I believe he took the role of Little Johnnie Jack – he was not a big man, you know, but short and slight, and he fit that part. Of course, it may be uncharitable to suggest it – but you do realize that much of the Mummers' Play was performed in the inns and pubs, and I suppose my uncle, who was much given to the consumption of alcohol in various forms, was hardly averse to performing in such places and reaping the customary liquid reward." Of Fletcher Dewson's reputed diabolism she said not a word.

"Very well, Miss Dewson," said Pons. "I will undertake the inquiry."

"Thank you, sir. You will find me at 147 Cherwell Street, Banbury – along the river – if I can be of further help to you." She smiled tightly, turned, and walked out.

"A tartar," I said.

Pons' eyes twinkled. "She is a lady who knows precisely what she wants, and whose world is clearly divided into what is good and what is bad – and liquor and tobacco are bad, no mistake about it."

We mounted to our room.

"Well, Parker," said Pons, "what ought our next move to be? We shall see how well you've studied my methods."

"Why, that's elementary," I said. "We'll look up Jock Howells."

"Precisely! It delights me to observe your progress. We shall do just that, after a bite of supper."

Before we could leave our room, however, Constable Ruskin presented himself at the door.

"Come in, Constable!" invited Pons. "I see by the look on your face you're more perplexed than ever."

"I am, Mr. Pons," said Ruskin, taking the chair Pons propelled forward. "I am that. Your wire now..."

"Ah! You searched the house?"

"Thoroughly."

"And found nothing?" hazarded Pons.

"Nothing. Not even a copper. I doubt the lot of his stuff would fetch ten pounds."

"Curious! Curious!" murmured Pons. "As to the grounds, Constable..."

"No evidence of digging there for a long time. But we didn't dig much. We used one of those metal detecting devices. There's nothing in the soil there, Mr. Pons."

"No metal," said Pons dryly. "Tell me, Constable, is there any blue clay or rock on the property?"

"None, sir."

"Do you know of any in or about Chipping Norton?"

Constable Ruskin looked dubious. "I do think there's a bit of blue clay on the Welton land."

"Henry Welton?"

"Yes. He has a farm out of Chipping Norton. Raises some corn, and has a few pigs and sheep."

"Pons, is not that the same man who disliked Dewson?" I put in.

Ruskin replied. "He was only one of many, Dr. Parker. Pickering didn't exaggerate at all; I may even say he understated the case. Dewson led a reclusive life. He stayed at home during the past ten years. Now and then he showed himself in Chipping Norton to shop, or he went to the Black Fleece. People normally begin wondering about those who keep to themselves too much, and from the wondering the talking begins."

"There is, however, no doubt but that Dewson was a member of a group that dabbled in diabolism?" asked Pons.

"None. We've had a go at Howells. He won't admit it, he won't deny it. We're official, you see. I thought, now, if you could go out there, Mr. Pons... ?"

"We expect to, Constable, directly after supper."

"He's an irritable man, sir, and no stranger to violence."

"Nor am I," said Pons, chuckling.

Howells did indeed offer a formidable appearance where he stood behind the bar of his pub when we entered it an hour later. He was a stocky, broad-shouldered man of sixty or thereabouts; his face was grizzled with a short, black stubble, but even a thick moustache did not conceal a sensuous, full-lipped mouth. His eyes were as black as his hair.

We went directly to sit at the bar, where Pons ordered a bitter, and I a draught of ale. Howells served us in silence. I observed, as he moved back and forth, that he distinctly favored one leg, and saw that he was manifestly strong enough to have tossed a small man like Dewson on to his back and carried him easily.

"Retired seaman?" said Pons casually.

Howells gave him a sharp glance.

"Late of the *Cathay Prince*," Pons went on.

"Near thirty years ago," Howells growled, suspiciously.

"Retired because of injury to your left knee," continued Pons.

Behind Howells on the wall, I saw the framed photograph of the *Cathay Prince* Pons had seen.

Howells now came over to stand facing Pons. He gave him a hard look. "What's your game, Mister?"

"I want a word with you, Jock."

"You've had it."

"Ever hear of a man named Crowley? Aleister Crowley?"

"What's it to you?"

"The sooner they find out who killed Fletcher Dewson, the sooner they'll let you alone."

Howells flung himself away with an angry snarl. "What's all this about Dewson? They were bothering me before he got killed. First it was that reporter from London. I was fool enough to talk. Then the police. They were here half the day. What's your business?"

"I've been asked by Dewson's family to look into his death," said Pons.

"What's done's done," said Howells. "Sure, we played with Crowley's cult. Devil worship and all that. No harm in it. We never did any harm. But the word got out and talk blew it up to far more than it was. Spells – curses – suchlike – all just words. Never came to a thing. Only *they* thought it did. Welton and Forham and that lot. Dewson family or police – I'll give you one question and that's it."

"Tell me about the reporter who bothered you," said Pons.

For a moment Howells stood agape. Then he shrugged. "Came in maybe eight, nine days ago," he said. "Name of Brown – Ted Brown. Short, slow-moving fellow, about forty-five, for all his thick beard. Wanted to write some kind of story about queer country customs and lore. That sort of thing. I told him about our mummers – we've not done that for years, either – and I talked to him about the little coven we had for the cult, for all it was over and done with long ago. Old Fletch was in here that day, and when he went out I told Brown he'd been one of us. I gave him a few other names. He came in once or twice after that. Asked about Old Fletch and the others. Seemed to think it funny – laughed a bit at us. I saw him nosing about yet this afternoon. He had a room at the White Hart."

"Thank you, Mr. Howells," said Pons.

"What about Dewson, now?" asked Howells, surprised.

"One question, I think, you allowed me," said Pons. "You answered it. I know enough about Fletcher Dewson. If you don't mind, I'll use the telephone and we'll be off."

I waited while Pons put in a call. Then we set out from the Black Fleece to walk back to the White Hart.

"I've asked Constable Ruskin to meet us," said Pons. "Unless I am very much mistaken, we will be on our way back to London by the late train, thanks to Old Fletch's friend."

"Howells!" I cried. "Why, he told us nothing."

"On the contrary. He gave us the only possible corroborative information." And, having said so much, Pons would say no more, but strode along with an enigmatic smile on his lean, hawk-like face.

Constable Ruskin waited for us at the White Hart. "Constable," began Pons without preamble, "we'll want Mr. Ted Brown registered here."

Ruskin did not question Pons, but went immediately to the clerk at the desk and asked for Brown.

"I'm sorry, Mr. Ruskin," said the clerk, "but Mr. Brown checked out a few moments before you came. He expected to take the 9:28 for London."

Pons looked at his watch. "A quarter past nine. We have enough time. Brown very probably walked to the station. Parker, arrange to pay our bill and check out. We'll take the same train." And to Ruskin, as he came back from the desk, he said only, "I submit it is of the utmost importance that we talk to Brown before he leaves Chipping Norton. His information will be decisive."

"The car's outside," said the constable. "We can be there in a minute."

We reached the station platform at Chipping Norton almost on the heels of the man we sought, for he was the only bearded passenger awaiting there – a short man, jaunty in appearance, though he walked with singular dignity.

"Look at his shoes, Parker," murmured Pons.

I saw that one shoe was creased with use; that on the left foot was smooth.

Pons went directly up to him and stood, towering over him, to ask, "Mr. Brown? Ted Brown, representing – ?"

"*The Daily Express*," said Brown.

"My name is Solar Pons. You may have heard of me."

"I don't know the name," said Brown coolly, making his indifference to us plain.

"Mr. Brown, let me introduce Constable Ruskin," said Pons. "Constable, let me introduce Ted Brown – a reporter who has been busy exploring country lore in Chipping Norton. Mr. Brown is more correctly known as Arthur Keenan, late of Somabula, Rhodesia; he has been busy murdering his uncle so that he can come into control of some diamond-bearing property Fletcher Dewson didn't know he owned."

For a moment Pons' extraordinary announcement seemed to freeze the four of us into a tableau. Then, with an oath, Keenan flung his bag full in Pons' face – the constable dove for his legs just as he turned to run – and I fell upon him. After but a brief scuffle, Keenan was subdued.

"Ah, there comes our train," said Pons, brushing dust from his coat. "I'll send you a *précis* of the evidence, Constable, and if you need us, we'll come back in time for the assizes."

"As I saw it," explained Pons once we were comfortably settled in our compartment and on the way to London, "the solution of the puzzle turned upon the manner of Dewson's death, specifically, on the curious confusion of mummery, Druidism, and diabolism. We were meant to believe that Dewson had been slain by someone who believed him a warlock – hence the pitchfork and sickle as instruments of death. But for this, neither the mummer's costume nor the setting in the Whispering Knights was pertinent. It followed, therefore, that if the primary assumption were correct – that we were intended to associate Dewson's death with his diabolism – the murderer was ignorant of the fact that there was essentially no connection with the mummer's costume or Druidism.

"I submit that no one native to Chipping Norton would be unaware of this. This suggested, of course, that the real motive for Dewson's death was unrelated to his diabolism. My findings in the Whispering Knights, however, implied a stronger motive than mere vengeance. You will recall that the third pinch of soil – that containing the diamond dust – which I took from the burial chamber came from the embedded footprint beside a twig which had undoubtedly caught in the cuff of the murderer's trousers, for Dewson, we know, did not walk to the cromlech. Now, anyone, working with diamonds, could have collected such dust, but only someone close to their source in kimberlite pipes – as the blue-green serpentinous diamantiferous rock is known in Africa – could have also carried with him the grains of that rock.

"Diamonds, you may not know, are found in Europe only in Siberia and the Urals. In Africa and India, yes. In Brazil, British and Dutch Guiana, in Borneo and Australia, among the alluvial deposits and the moraines of several of the United States, notably the Carolinas, Wisconsin, Michigan, California, and some others. But certainly not anywhere in England. Furthermore, the kimberlite pipes are to be found only in Africa. They give

Kimberly its name – one long associated with diamonds in the popular imagination. So we are left with an obvious conclusion – that Dewson unwittingly owned diamond-bearing property among all the 'worthless' land he had bought, and the bankrupt investments he had made. But Keenan – who was on the spot – discovered it, and what was mistaken for his solicitude and concern about his uncle's health was instead the expression of a hope that he might hear that his uncle's health was failing. Fear that the old man might somehow learn about his potential wealth overcame his judgment.

"He grew impatient and came back to England, bent upon killing his uncle and assuring his claim as one of his uncle's heirs. Very probably he planned to let his cousin keep the cottage in exchange for the 'worthless' land in Rhodesia. He had not been in England for a long time; he may not even have been born here, though I should think it probable that he was and left with his parents for Africa as a child. He came to Chipping Norton posing as a reporter and under a false name – surely there must be almost as many Ted Browns as John Smiths in the English-speaking world! – and, nosing about, hit upon the gossip of Dewson's diabolism. It seemed to him that local hatred and superstitious fear of Fletcher Dewson offered a perfectly credible motive for his murder, one far removed from the real motive. No one would have believed that someone had broken into Dewson's cottage and murdered a man on the dole for his money!

"Keenan was reasonably secure. He was unknown. Moreover, his beard was a natural disguise. He was on his way to London or some way station between Chipping Norton and London to remove his beard and, after an interval long enough to allow him 'time' to reach England from Rhodesia, where he undoubtedly had a confederate waiting to answer the cablegram he knew would be sent, he meant to appear in Chipping Norton and play the role of the grieving nephew.

As you saw, he has a wooden foot, which was betrayed in the footprints found at the Whispering Knights.

"In his greed, he over-reached himself."

"And any doubt you might have entertained was surely dissipated when Keenan confessed he had never heard of Solar Pons," I said.

"*Touché*!" replied Pons, settling back with a chuckle for the slow journey home.

XII

THE ADVENTURE OF THE INNKEEPER'S CLERK

We were just coming in off the estuary after a morning of sailing that day at St. Mawes, when Pons' keen eyes picked out a grave pair standing motionless on the wharf.

"Is that not our landlord?" he asked. "And with a police constable at his side."

It was difficult to mistake that pear-shaped figure. "That is certainly Mr. Penworthy," I said.

Pons' eyes lit up. "I should not be surprised if our little holiday is about to be enhanced. A taxing problem after three and a half days of sailing will certainly not come amiss. Let us make haste."

As we came closer, Pons added, "Something serious has certainly taken place. I have seldom seen so grim a pair!"

The two men hurried toward us as we reached our mooring.

"Mr. Pons," cried our landlord before he had quite come up to us, "we've been waiting this half hour. This is Constable Liskeard. A terrible thing has happened. My night clerk, Saul Krayle – " He caught himself, short of breath, and started again. "He's dead, Mr. Pons."

"Strangled," added the Constable.

"We found him an hour ago."

"Nine and a half by the clock," said the Constable.

"Strangled in his bed. A maid saw his door ajar, and that was so unusual she looked in. Oh, he was afraid of something ever since the ring came," Mr. Penworthy went on.

We had now begun to walk back to the *Seaman's Berth*, the quiet inn at which we had chosen to take quarters during the brief holiday I had persuaded Pons to enjoy after closing the extraordinary matter of the Solitary Walker. The morning was gay with color; the estuary was filled with boats, and across, on the Falmouth side, visitors to that part of Cornwall were already making their way aboard the *Cutty Sark* and the *Implacable*, to examine those two famous training ships upon payment of a small fee. Yachts had put out from shore, flags flying, and the scene was framed, as always, by the two castles of Henry VIII, one on each side of the estuary. The thought of death was alien to the setting. But Mr. Penworthy, hustling along with some effort, red of face and breathing heavily, and the taciturn Constable at his side, bespoke crime.

"He was a quiet fellow," said the landlord jerkily. "Never said much. Kept to himself. Never told us much about himself. He drifted in one day and asked for the job – wasn't concerned about the wages – and they're not high, you know how small the place is. Said, 'Anything'll do!' And he got along on it, better'n most. I hardly knew he was there. He stayed in his room quite a lot. And then one day, when he came in to work – he was out that afternoon on the water – he had a little package waiting for him. I was there when he opened it. It was just a plain gold ring with some initials on it, that's all – but he stared at it and went all white."

Mr. Penworthy took a few rapid steps in a burst of speed and turned to look anxiously up into Pons' face, as if to seek there some clue to the solution of his puzzle. Pons' features were inscrutable, and he fell back again, resuming his narrative.

"Next morning he gave notice. 'Is it the wage, Mr. Krayle?' I asked. He said it wasn't. 'If it is, I'll raise it,' I said. He just shook his head. 'Don't 'e feel well?' I asked. He said he was all right. But I could tell he was scared. Scared stiff, he was. 'Is it anything I can help about?' I asked then. 'Nothing,' he said. 'It's nothing. Don't trouble yourself, Mr. Penworthy,' he said. Well, sir, next evening I took to watching him a bit, and he that was accustomed to sitting there reading and waiting on the trade was all eyes and ears."

"Ears, Mr. Penworthy?" asked Pons.

"Aye. He *listened*."

"For what?"

"I had no chance to ask. But I stood next to him, and I saw how he listened, and once he grabbed my arm and asked, 'Was that a dragging sound?' I said I hadn't heard it. 'What sort?' I asked. 'Like a man dragging his foot,' he said, and I saw how the beads of sweat had come on to his temples. And it's cool these October nights."

Here Mr. Penworthy pushed himself forward once more and looked hopefully into Pons' face, scanning it. Disappointed, he fell back again, and resumed his narrative.

"And that's how he was from that day to this. Two weeks' notice he gave, and his time would've been up day after tomorrow. Now all his time's up. He's dead."

"Strangled," put in the Constable as if he had not said it before.

"He had a fever in his mind," Mr. Penworthy went on. "That dragging sound, now. Came out it was Mrs. Ruthven he hears. A widow lady on the second floor. Poor lady has a club foot. She's been in my place for six, seven months now, and Saul heard her walk all that time and never turned a hair. But after he got that ring, everything that sounded like a man dragging his foot or walking with a bad limp shook him up – bad, bad, Mr. Pons. What do you make of that, sir?"

He hastened forward again and looked up into Pons' eyes, his forehead wrinkled anxiously.

"The ring was very probably Krayle's black spot," said Pons.

The allusion was lost on Mr. Penworthy. He grimaced and fell into step once more.

"You have the ring, Mr. Penworthy?" asked Pons.

"We have it," said the Constable.

"How long has Krayle been with you?" asked Pons.

"Short of four years. He came in 1920, summer of 1920, I make it. The war was done better than half a year."

"You said, I think, he was out that afternoon on the water," said Pons. "Sailing?"

"Yes, Mr. Pons."

Mr. Penworthy stopped suddenly and gripped Pons' arm. He pointed off toward the estuary. "You see that craft over there? That belonged to Saul. There's not a handsomer craft on these waters."

"A costly boat for the night clerk at the *Seaman's Berth*, is it not, Mr. Penworthy?" mused Pons. "Small wonder he made no complaint about his wage."

"Oh, he never bought that from what he earned, Mr. Pons," said our landlord hastily. "He had independent means. He'd saved a nest-egg, I took it."

"So young a man must have been in service," observed Pons.

"He was thirty, thirty-one – something like that. He was in the war, in France. He let that drop one night when one of the boarders came out point blank and asked him. A wonder it was he said as much, as tightlipped as he always was. But here we are, Mr. Pons. You shall see for yourself."

We had now reached the *Seaman's Berth*, a quaintly weathered inn kept picturesque to attract holiday visitors to St. Mawes. A police officer stood at the desk only the previous night presided over by the dead man. All was silence when we passed through the lobby and made our way up the stairs to the top floor, Mr. Penworthy in the lead, the Constable bringing up the rear. Another Constable standing at the threshold opened the door of Saul Krayle's gable room.

The scene before us was one of wild disorder. Central to it was the bed and Saul Krayle on it, lying with arms outstretched, his face mottled and blue, his mouth wide, as if he were still gasping for the air that powerful hands had shut off. The morning light entering the one dormer window cast a pale glow over the scene. It was obvious that someone – presumably the murderer – had searched the room in haste, for the contents of the bureau drawers had been emptied, the one chair had been slashed, and the mattress on the bed had been cut in various places.

"Saul got off at four this morning," said Mr. Penworthy in a hushed voice. "He was tired then, and most likely went straight to bed. He always kept his door locked. It wasn't locked when we found him. Maybe he forgot to lock it. Maybe he opened it to somebody."

He continued to watch Pons' every move, as if he expected a miracle to be performed.

Pons stood for a long minute taking in every aspect of the room. I tried, as usual, to follow his eyes about, to guess at what he saw and what conclusions he came to. Krayle's body lay not in the center of the bed, but athwart it; he might have been on his feet and been thrown to the bed. He was still clad in pajamas; so he had prepared for or gone to bed. The condition of the bed suggested that he had been in bed, thrown back the covers and got out again. The appearance of the body suggested that he had not been attacked while asleep. The dead face wore an expression of shocked surprise, as closely as I could read it for the agony in it. If he had admitted someone to the room, he must have been attacked almost at once.

Pons' minute of observation ended and now, ignoring the body on the bed, he began to carry on an intensive examination of the contents of the bureau thrown about on the floor, of the bureau itself, and of the clothing hanging from several hooks in a curtained alcove. Then he dropped to his knees and carefully examined the rag rug on the floor just before the bed on the side where one of Krayle's legs hung down. He picked something up between thumb and forefinger and dropped it into one of the little envelopes he always carried, and he found something more on the body itself to put into a second envelope.

"Eh, now, what might that be, Mr. Pons?" asked Constable Liskeard.

"If I had known, I would not have troubled to take it up," said Pons. "When I know, you will also know."

The Constable grunted and nodded in satisfaction.

Then, from among the things scattered on the floor, Pons picked up a yellowing envelope, into which he but glanced briefly. Yet he kept hold of it.

"I should like to examine this at my leisure, Constable," he said.

Mr. Penworthy looked anxiously at Liskeard's sober visage.

"Mr. Pons is a famous detective, Liskeard," he said hastily.

"We'll want it by evening," said the Constable.

"You shall have it," promised Pons.

"We took note that Krayle was killed by a powerful man wearing gloves," said the Constable challengingly. "Did you find anything to the contrary, sir?"

"Nothing," said Pons. "I submit he was given entry by Krayle, who then walked back toward the bed – not to get into it, but to take up and put on his dressing-gown. Observe how it hangs, one sleeve still over the top, the rest crumpled on the seat of the cane chair where he had thrown it – as if he had picked it up and dropped it suddenly, surprised by his visitor, and, turning, was attacked and slain. He would appear to have been so shocked and frightened by his attacker that he offered little resistance. But let me call your attention to his hands."

I craned forward. The dead man's hands seemed to be covered with an oily substance. Constable Liskeard also gazed at it.

"Smell it, Constable," directed Pons.

Liskeard bent and sniffed the nearer of Krayle's hands.

"It is not unpleasant," said Liskeard cautiously. "He must have put on some of that cream to keep the hands soft so much used now."

"I submit he would have been likely to rub it in a little more, if so," said Pons. "Let me commend it to your earnest study, Constable."

"Yes sir," said Liskeard, his brow wrinkled in perplexity.

"What does it mean, Mr. Pons? What does it mean?" asked our landlord, literally dancing about in his impatient excitement.

"We shall have to wait upon events to tell us that, Mr. Penworthy," said Pons. "I fancy we shall know in a day or two. Can you tell me now how many new clients have come to the *Seaman's Berth* in the past fortnight?"

"Yourselves, Mr. Pons – Major Andrew Grimesby – and but two days ago, a Frenchman named Noel Fromard. You shall see them all at luncheon, sir."

Pons turned to Constable Liskeard. "You said you are in possession of the ring Krayle received by post."

"Yes, sir." The Constable fished in his pocket and brought out a simple gold band which he handed to Pons. "This is it. Mr. Penworthy made the identification."

"Yes, that's it, Mr. Pons. A plain gold ring. A man's ring, as you see."

Pons was now examining the ring, studying the initials on the inside of the band. "S. K." There was nothing more to be seen on the ring.

"Not too long worn," observed Pons. "Perhaps five or six years." He handed the ring back to Constable Liskeard and asked our landlord, "Did you happen to see the package, Mr. Penworthy?"

"A glance is all I had of it, Mr. Pons."

"A pity. You cannot say where it was posted?"

"No, except that it came from France. I recognized the stamps. I've a hobby of stamp-collecting, Mr. Pons. But as to the place why no, I'm sorry, I couldn't see that, had no reason to want to. The box was in Krayle's slot until he took it out, and I only glanced at it, nothing more. The post's not my affair, Mr. Pons. I like to think our guests have as much privacy here as in their homes."

"If you've finished here, Mr. Pons," said the Constable then, "we'll need to move the body. And you can tidy up the room, Mr. Penworthy."

"Certainly, Constable," said Pons. "I want to ask Mr. Penworthy a few more questions, but perhaps he will accompany us to our quarters."

"By all means, Mr. Pons," said our landlord.

We bade Constable Liskeard good-morning and made our way back down the stairs to our quarters on the floor below, where we had a duo of connected rooms which opened upon a splendid view of the estuary and Falmouth on the fair side.

"I need hardly tell you, sir," said our landlord the moment the door of our quarters closed behind us, "I am most anxious to have this affair over and done with in as short a time as possible, and anything you can do will be most earnestly appreciated."

"I rather think Constable Liskeard is a very capable young man," said Pons, "but I shall be happy to lend him any assistance within my power. To that end we should know all we can about Saul Krayle."

Mr. Penworthy's honest face betrayed his unhappiness. He clasped his hands together and cried, "Perhaps it might have been better if I had been more curious! Now I think of it, we know nothing but the most superficial facts about him. A young man, who evidently came from London..."

"Who had seen military service, had independent means, owned a sailboat, and led an existence far more reclusive than is customary for young men of his years," added Pons. "Did he have references, Mr. Penworthy?"

"None."

"Did he receive much mail?"

"Very little, Mr. Pons. Now and then he sent off for something in response to an advertisement. Hardly more than that."

"Was Krayle in the habit of fraternizing with the guests, Mr. Penworthy?"

"No-o," said our landlord with some hesitation. "I wouldn't put it that way. He was always courteous and sometimes friendly."

"Did he have any special friends?"

"I wouldn't say so. Mrs. Ruthven seemed to hit it off with him well enough, but they seldom exchanged more than a few sentences at a time. He seemed to take to Major Grimesby, but I gathered that it was more or less a matter of mutual reminiscences of the war. And he seemed very friendly with M. Fromard."

"We shall want to speak to them," said Pons.

"That can be arranged."

"One thing more. Was any stranger seen entering the inn since the day clerk came on duty?"

"Certainly not by the day clerk, Mr. Pons. I asked. But, of course, the clerks don't always stay at the desk. They leave it from time to time; so someone could have slipped in."

"You were present when Krayle opened the little package from France and discovered the ring?" asked Pons then.

"Yes. I was at the desk. He came in from the water late that afternoon. He always had the desk from four in the afternoon to four in the morning. He saw the box in his post slot, took it out, and opened it."

"Did he seem apprehensive?"

"No, sir. Just curious. When he saw the ring, he sort of tightened up. When he saw the initials on it, he went white. I told you how it was on the way from the shore."

"Indeed you did, Mr. Penworthy. I recall it," said Pons. "Did you not think it strange that Krayle was so much to himself?"

Mr. Penworthy shrugged. "Every man to his taste, I always say. Besides, what chance had he to mix? He might leave the desk for a few moments to look in on the bar or watch a game of darts, but he could hardly take part and still discharge his obligations to the house, Mr. Pons."

"You have seen this man for almost four years, at least in the closing hours of the day, if at no other time," pursued Pons, "and you must have observed his habits."

"Oh, Mr. Pons. He was a painstakingly clean man. He smoked a pipe on occasion. He never drank – though, truth to tell, I thought he looked longingly at the glass now and then." Mr. Penworthy chuckled. "But perhaps it was an old man's fancy. He read the *Times* every day and the *Observer* every week. When we talked together it was of sailing, political matters, the weather, the trade. I could say I thought him a Conservative but would that help you? I'll wager not. There must be some other way I can help you, Mr. Pons."

Pons smiled. "There is, Mr. Penworthy. When the police are finished up there, I would like the key to the room."

"What will the police say?" asked Mr. Penworthy anxiously.

"My compliments to Constable Liskeard. Ask him not to seal the room – if he means to do so – until tomorrow. Ask him to stand by until I send word to him."

"Yes, Mr. Pons," said Mr. Penworthy, backing to the door, ducking and bowing, and letting himself out.

"Now, then," said Pons briskly, suiting his actions to his words, "let us just see what this evidently treasured envelope contains."

He opened the envelope he had taken from Saul Krayle's room as he spoke, and began to remove its contents, piece by piece.

"Hm! A photograph of Krayle as a boy – in a Lord Fauntleroy suit," he murmured. "Discharge papers. Ah, he had reached corporal rank! – Two death notices, clipped together. Henry and Perdita Kraven. Evidently relatives, married – died a year apart. Country folk in Northumberland." He pored over the notices for a little while before he put them aside with, "Nothing here to suggest anything but modest means."

Next he brought forth a small packet of newspaper clippings. Taking up the first, he read, "'Escape of Two Burglars – A pair of agile burglars escaped capture after looting a flat in South Norwood last night. The two made their way to freedom over the rooftops after P. C. Leonard Worden slipped and fell while in pursuit...'" He took another clipping from the packet. "A listing of burglaries committed by the soldiers of various nations in the course of the war." He turned to a third. "'Daring Burglary in Kent.'" The fourth was in French, which Pons translated – "'Part of Famechon Loot Recovered. – Some of the jewelry stolen from Count Gilbert de Famechon's chateau at Bordelais two years ago was recovered near the scene of an avalanche near the Swiss border yesterday....'" He took up another paper, shaking his head. "Yet another clipping about criminal activities, this time in England. Krayle seems to have had a fondness for the criminous." He riffled through three or four clippings which were patently of a similar nature, pausing only to read another concerning the disappearance of a soldier, Charles Fenn, from the Swiss border. He went on to a briefer clipping. "An advertisement. 'Anyone knowing the whereabouts of Simon Kraven or James Fenn, late in His

Majesty's military service, please communicate with Scotland Yard.' – The description appended would fit a quarter of all the young men in England, except for a shrapnel wound in Fenn's leg," he added, chuckling. Pressing his examination, he went on. "The photograph of a young lady. No identification. Very possibly a sweetheart. – Another photograph, this time of Krayle in uniform."

At the end of half an hour Pons had taken from the envelope all it contained. The material testified to some degree of sentimentality on the part of its former owner, as well as to his interest in the criminous. There was an almost total lack of anything that might help an inquiry into the life of Saul Krayle.

Pons restored the papers and photographs to the envelope and put it aside. Then he sat for a few minutes with his eyes closed and his fingers fondling his unlit pipe, a meditative attitude I knew well enough not to interrupt. Presently, however, he opened his eyes and fixed his gaze on me.

"What do you make of it, Parker?"

I chose my words with care. "It would seem to me that if Krayle wished to lose himself, he might have chosen a rural village rather than a watering place."

"Would not a stranger in a little village stand out far more? I submit he would. You are then of the opinion that Krayle wished to leave behind him his former haunts and companions?"

"It would seem so."

"It does not seem to you strange that a young man, with much of his life still before him, should choose to lead a reclusive existence as a night clerk at an obscure inn?"

"Far stranger events are commonplace, Pons," I said, ticking off a few of them rapidly for his benefit.

"True, true," agreed Pons. "Go on."

"He may have suffered a disappointment in love. Or he may have been the victim of traumatic shock as a result of his experiences in the war," I went on. "It took me many months to recover from seeing one of my friends blown to pieces virtually at my side."

"You and I both spoke to Krayle on more than one occasion while he was on duty," said Pons. "Did he strike you as anything but cool and collected?"

"No," I said reluctantly.

"As someone easily upset by a broken romance or subject to trauma?" pressed Pons.

I had to concede that he did not. "But these things do not always show on the surface, Pons," I objected.

"Very well. Let it pass. What did you make of his reaction to the ring?"

"It was obviously something he had once seen and never expected to see again."

"Capital!" cried Pons. "That is well put."

Thus encouraged, I went on. "Specifically, it was apparently not so much the ring as the identifying initials."

"'S.K.'" mused Pons. "They were his own initials. Perhaps his own ring?"

"A wedding ring – abandoned and now sent back to him with meaning he understood very well," I added.

Pons chuckled. "You insist on romance, Parker!"

"Why not? Though you are somewhat singular in this respect, I assure you it plays a major part in life."

Pons bowed in mock humility. But in a moment his smile faded. "The room was searched for something," he pointed out.

"Why is it that the obvious is always avoided?" I protested. "Robbery could have been the motive for Krayle's death."

Pons shook his head in disappointment. "Oh, come, come, Parker!" he cried. "It was evident that Krayle opened his door to his visitor. Moreover, the initialed ring was not taken. Nor was some fifty pounds in his wallet on the bureau. His watch was undisturbed. In view of these facts, robbery does not seem to warrant being considered as motive. No, the murderer was someone Krayle had no reason to distrust. He opened the door to him without hesitation very probably not long after he had turned in. His visitor knocked at his door between four and five o'clock this morning, murdered him, and searched his room – in such obvious haste that there was no time to restore the contents of the drawers before the coming of dawn might catch him abroad. What he sought was not, evidently, the valuables so ready to hand. No, what he wanted is not immediately apparent. It might have been a document – a packet of letters – incriminating evidence – or something of similar nature. It was certainly not Krayle's modest valuables."

"What was it you put into your envelopes?" I asked then.

"Ah, from the floor what appeared to be lint foreign to the room – of relatively little importance. On Krayle's body, however, if I do not err – I have not had time to analyze it, and I don't know that it is necessary – a drop of heavy face cream mixed with talcum powder."

"Wherever from!" I cried.

"Ah, that is a question to which I would like to know the answer. I suspect I may have it, but the circumstances at the moment elude me. But it is now time for lunch, and I suggest that we ought to go down and have a word with those guests whose company the late Saul Krayle did not find too offensive."

Accordingly we descended to the dining-room of the *Seaman's Berth.*

Mr. Penworthy awaited us there, and came to meet us, anxious to be of service.

"Mrs. Ruthven has come in for lunch," he said. "She's waiting to be served. Perhaps it might be possible for you to speak with her now."

"Very well," said Pons.

"But, I beg you, Mr. Pons, do not betray unpleasant surprise at the sound of her voice. The poor lady has not long since had an operation for throat cancer, and her voice is harsh."

Pons nodded his understanding, whereupon Mr. Penworthy led the way to a little table beside a window, where the lady sat. I saw, as we approached, that Mrs. Ruthven appeared to be a lady of middle age, still hopeful of presenting the impression of youth, for she was not sparing of cosmetics, and her hair, I felt sure, had been tinted to conceal the grey coming into it. About her neck she wore a velvet band with a brooch on it, evidently to conceal the scar of her surgery.

Mr. Penworthy introduced us. Mrs. Ruthven, who inclined her head but did not offer her hand, gave no sign that she had ever heard of Solar Pons.

"If I may take but a few moments," said Pons. "We understood that you occasionally spoke to Mr. Krayle."

"Poor Mr. Krayle!" she murmured, pressing a handkerchief to her lips.

"Did he ever speak of his background?"

"No, sir. We spoke of little things like the weather or political matters we had both read about in the London papers. Mr. Krayle was such a thoughtful young man – very much like my late husband." She sighed. "I suppose it was that made me feel a certain bond to him."

If Pons was disappointed, he did not show it. He excused himself and we retired. Mr. Penworthy, however, now steered us across the room to a portly man in early middle age, a florid-faced, fat-cheeked, moustached man whose military bearing identified him as Major Andrew Grimesby.

"Heard of you, sir," he said, shaking Pons's hand vigorously. "Don't they call you 'the Sherlock Holmes of Praed Street'? Of course they do. Harumph! And not without reason. What can I do for you? Harumph!"

Major Grimesby harumphed after almost every sentence he spoke. He seemed to be happy in a sense of self-importance. Pons explained.

"Oh, the night clerk," said the Major, "Jolly good fella! Harumph! Damned shame he had to die! Oh, I've been through it on the Western front, Mr. Pons – saw a good many of my boys die – but this isn't war, you know. Harumph! But I don't know anything about the fella. Fact. Never talked about himself. Just listened to me talk about myself. Ha! And we talked about the war. He was in it. So was I. Ypres, Mons and all that! Jolly good show, what? Harumph!"

Major Grimesby was a complete extrovert, but of no more help to us than Mrs. Ruthven had been.

M. Joel Fromard was just entering the dining-room when we turned from Major Grimesby's table, and Mr. Penworthy's signal caused him to stand where he was. He seemed a little wary, but wariness was inherent in his figure – tall, muscular, broad shoulders surmounted by a rather thin, gaunt head, which seemed out of place on him. Moreover, he was young – certainly not over thirty-five.

He, too, had evidently never heard of Pons, but he listened politely to him and when he answered, chose his words with great care.

"I did not know the man Krayle," he said precisely in rather good English. "I chose this inn because it was recommended to me by M. Andre Fouyoird."

"He was a guest here," Mr. Penworthy hastened to assure Pons.

"Mr. Krayle spoke to me about France. He had fought there in the war. So had I. That was all. I know nothing more of him."

Pons thanked him and withdrew to a table of our own. Mr. Penworthy came along.

"I was sure it would be so," he lamented. "It is as I told you, Mr. Pons. Krayle communicated with no one, though he talked to many. But he spoke only of trivial things. 'A fine day, Mr. Penworthy,' he would say. Or, 'Raw morning,' and such matters. He said little more than the almanac!"

He saw us seated, volunteered to order for us, and then, leaning forward, pressed something into Pons' hand.

"The key to his room," he said conspirationally. "Liskeard understands."

Pons thanked him, and at last Mr. Penworthy left us to our own devices.

We ate lunch in silence, since it was obvious that Pons wished to contemplate the problem of Saul Krayle's death. While we sat at table, Mrs. Ruthven finished and made her slow and rather awkward way out of the room. Major Grimesby, too, finished presently and strode away. M. Fromard, however, brooded over his coffee and a liqueur I took to be chartreuse; more than once his black eyes flickered toward us. There he sat still when we finished and in our turn left the dining-room.

Our landlord waited at the foot of the stairs. His eyes beseeched Pons to solve the mystery of Krayle's death without further delay.

"One of my guests has left," he said mournfully.

"I am sorry to hear it," said Pons, though his lips trembled a little with laughter he did not permit to escape. "Was he of long standing?"

"A month. Of course," said Mr. Penworthy, "he reserved only for a month. Still, one could hope, and I cannot help but feel that the thought of a strangler loose in the *Seaman's Berth* decided him against staying longer."

"Be of good heart, Mr. Penworthy. We shall do what we can."

We escaped our landlord and mounted the stairs.

But Pons did not pause at the door to our room. He went on up to the top floor and let himself into Saul Krayle's room, which had undergone a transformation since our earlier visit that day.

The bed had been made, the furniture had been put to rights as much as possible, short of repair, the contents of the bureau drawers had been replaced and the bureau set back against the wall.

"What can you hope to find here?" I asked.

"The murderer either found what he sought, or he did not find it. Let us assume for the nonce that he did not find it. Krayle had almost four years to conceal it, and the murderer scarcely an hour to discover it. I think it unlikely that he did so. We shall, then, begin – ignoring the bureau drawers, the bed and the chairs – with the alcove."

Thereupon, all the clothing hanging in the alcove was subjected to the most methodical search, rather more of the padding and lining than of the obvious pockets which Pons had searched previously. Pons took each article of clothing and subjected it to such careful scrutiny that I knew nothing could have escaped his notice. Having finished, he came back into the center of the room.

There he stood for some moments more, gazing at each item of furniture in turn, before he flung himself to his knees and began to crawl along the baseboard, tapping it as he went and listening for any hollow sound. Slowly, painstakingly, he crept around the room until he had returned to his starting point without reward for his efforts. Nothing daunted, he then gave his attention to the window frame, to the walls, even to the ceiling – all without result.

Baffled, he stood back from the walls, and once again his attention went to the room's spare furnishings. I could see that he discarded the two chairs from consideration, as he fixed upon the bureau and the bed.

"The drawers were emptied," he said of the one, "and the mattress slit," of the other. "But a resourceful man would not be likely to utilize such prosaic hiding places."

He now dismissed the bureau from consideration and began to study the bed, which was of stout manufacture, three-quarter in size. It was of wood, and evidently of some age, with carven posts of a considerable thickness.

"Lend me a hand, Parker," cried Pons.

We set about taking the bed apart. Pons' object was, clearly, to detach the foot from the rest of the bed. Once that had been accomplished, Pons raised the foot of the bed and, to my astonishment, shook it, listening.

His face fell.

He turned the piece bottom side up, and at once his face lit up.

"These posts have surely been tampered with," he said with some satisfaction.

I pressed forward. The posts, which I had thought of one piece, were evidently of two, with a central rounded section framed in the square of wood that made up the outer shell of each post.

Pons produced his jackknife, and began to pry away the central piece.

"Pons, that is vandalism on such an antique as this!" I protested.

"Tut, tut, this bed was never manufactured in this way. I submit these posts have been hollowed out and this piece is but the cork."

Even as he spoke, the "cork" came out. With it came a few strands of cotton batting.

Pons gave a cry of delight, turned the post bottom-side down and rapped it, all in one movement, sharply on the floor.

Out of the hollowed leg spilled jewels of every description, together with the cotton batting which had been used to pack them in lest they give out a rattling sound whenever the bed was moved.

"If I am not mistaken," said Pons, "this is part of the remainder of the loot from the Famechon robbery. I fancy we will find the rest of it in the other posts."

For a moment my astonishment held. "You knew!" I accused him.

"Nonsense!" he retorted. "It was a logical deduction, but not knowledge. Come now, let us repair this post and go on to the next."

In half an hour we had disclosed, gathered from each of the four bedposts, a veritable horde of jewels – some still intact as rings or small brooches, but most of them obviously pried from their original settings. The bed stood once again as we had found it.

Satisfied with the appearance of the room, Pons withdrew, locking the door behind him, his pockets filled with the treasure we had discovered. We repaired in silent haste to our own quarters, where Pons spread the loot out before him and contemplated it with some degree of self-satisfaction.

"The central problem remains unsolved," I could not resist reminding him.

"True, but that is now merely a trifling matter of a little more patience," replied Pons imperturbably.

"You don't know the murderer's identity?"

"I am reasonably certain of it."

"Then why not take him?"

"At the moment I lack the proof to convict him. We shall wait upon him to tip his hand. That he will almost certainly do, as long as he does not possess this treasure for which he did not hesitate to murder Krayle."

"If he knew, as you suggest, that the treasure was hidden in Krayle's room, why was it necessary to murder Krayle in order to get his hands on it? Krayle was at the desk all night, and his room was empty."

"Ah, I submit that the murder of Krayle was as important to the murderer as the discovery of the treasure," said Pons. "Now, let us send word to Constable Liskeard through Mr. Penworthy, and ask the Constable just to step around here as unobtrusively as possible before dark."

Mr. Penworthy brought Constable Liskeard to our quarters just as dusk came down on St. Mawes, though he himself could not remain, since he had taken over the night clerk's duties until a suitable applicant for that position presented himself.

"Ah, Liskeard," said Pons, "I trust you will be free long enough tonight to keep watch for the murderer of Saul Krayle?"

"If you know him, Mr. Pons, we should take him," said the Constable.

"I prefer that he deliver himself to us. Look here."

Pons had concealed the jewels in a stout leather pouch which he now emptied on to the bed.

"God's mercy!" cried the Constable in astonishment. "Where did you find them?"

"In Krayle's room," replied Pons.

He explained how we had come upon them.

"The murderer hunted this treasure," he went on. "He will be back again – before the room is reoccupied."

"In short, tonight," put in Liskeard.

"I fancy he will lose no time," agreed Pons. "I propose that we slip up to Krayle's room – one by one, if you please – and conceal ourselves there. You first, Constable. Here is the key."

Constable Liskeard took the key and slipped out of our quarters.

I followed soon after, and Pons came at last to join us in the gable room where Saul Krayle had met his death. Pons carried the jewels.

"Let us just surprise him," he said, and emptied the pouch on the counterpane of the bed. He glanced at Liskeard. "You are armed, Constable?"

"Only with my truncheon, sir."

"That will do. Take up your place behind the door. Parker and I will conceal ourselves in the alcove. The door may be kept unlocked, since, the room being unoccupied, the murderer may expect it to be. Now then, let us be silent."

We took up our posts, filled with anticipation.

As the evening wore on, however, and the night closed in, anticipation waned and the monotony of waiting took its place. The sounds from the inn below came more remotely than the ringing of bells and blowing of whistles from craft on the estuary. Through the partly open window the salty pungence of the sea invaded the room; it must have come in often before, for Krayle's clothes, which still hung in the alcove, were permeated with it to such an extent that all other odors were secondary to it. I was conscious there of small sounds which would have been lost in other circumstances – the clicking of a beetle in the wall and the patter of mice, which kept the stillness from becoming oppressive.

We had come to the gable room before nine o'clock; it was not yet midnight when Pons gripped my arm in warning to be particularly quiet. I strained to listen, and heard presently, as if it came from a great distance, the slightest of sounds – as of someone shuffling or scuffing his feet somewhere; but it was more than half unreal, so I was utterly unprepared for the sudden beam of torchlight that cut into the room from the door, and fell, naturally, since the bed was in line with the door, upon the jewels on the counterpane.

There was a muffled gasp, the light moved closer to pause directly above the jewels, and a gloved hand came down into the glow of the torch.

"The light, Constable," Pons called out.

Instantly the light in the ceiling was turned on.

I had expected to see the Frenchman, Fromard, but it was Mrs. Ruthven who stood there, the torch already held clublike in her hand as if for use as a weapon.

For only a moment the scene held. Then Pons bounded forward, even as Constable Liskeard closed in from the wall. With a quick movement Mrs. Ruthven could not fend off, Pons tore the wig from her head, exposing closely cropped hair beneath.

"Let me introduce you to James Fenn, former partner and recently murderer of Simon Kraven, alias Saul Krayle," said Pons.

Fenn burst for the door, but the Constable was on him like a cat and Pons closed in from the other side to subdue him in a matter of moments.

"He had it coming," said Fenn in his natural voice, giving up his pretense. "He left me for dead and got away with the stuff."

"In the avalanche?" hazarded Pons. "You fought over the loot?"

Fenn nodded sullenly. "He wanted it all. It was the fight started the avalanche. He knocked me into it, saw me covered, and thought I was done in. Then he was off. It was true, I was near dead under all that snow and the stones, but I got out – a pair of country folk found me and took care of me – I was sick a long time, and knocked about pretty bad. Simon went to hide somewhere – but I found him – I found him!"

"And the ring?"

"I had it in my hand. Just at the end, when he toppled me into the crevasse that started the avalanche, I wrenched it from his finger."

His eyes dancing, Pons turned to Liskeard. "I congratulate you, Constable. The rapidity of this capture ought to earn you a promotion!"

"The ring, of course," explained Pons when we sat later with Mr. Penworthy, "was sent from here to France – and back to Kraven by some obliging friend who very probably had no idea he was indulging Fenn's macabre urge to put the wind up his victim before he murdered him.

"The sequence of events seems eminently clear. Fenn and Kraven – very probably while still in military service – robbed the Famechon chateau, concealed the loot, and went back for it after the war. They fell out. Kraven attacked Fenn and left him for dead in the avalanches, but Fenn was not dead. Nursed back to health by Swiss peasants, he had only one desire – vengeance.

"Meanwhile, back in England, Kraven changed his name and turned up in St. Mawes, waiting upon the time when the Famechon robbery was forgotten, and feeling secure in Fenn's death – in the absence of any word concerning him in the newspaper accounts. He had another reason to hide here – Scotland Yard had begun to inquire for him, as well as for Fenn, though the Yard does not seem to have pressed its enquiry very thoroughly. I submit that the burglaries of which Kraven kept newspaper records were very probably the work of Kraven and Fenn before they went into military service.

"That Kraven came to St. Mawes with resources to draw upon was clear to you, Mr. Penworthy, since he had to have more than his wage to buy a sailboat. But perhaps it did not occur to you that he could hardly have saved money in military service, and no doubt you concluded that he had inherited a competence. It would not strike you that he might have come by it illegally. It is a curious fact that the overwhelming majority of us regard crime as something that takes place beyond our immediate ken.

"Fenn, finally recovered and back in England, set out to search for Kraven and ultimately found him here. He disguised himself elaborately, as you saw, and took residence here, settling in even to the extent of striking up a conversational acquaintance with his victim. His wound was concealed by a simulated club-foot, and his assumption of a feminine guise deceived even Kraven – though Kraven was certainly not on the alert for Fenn. Fenn had ample time in which to assure himself that Kraven had not deposited the jewels anywhere – how could he, knowing they were stolen and must certainly be listed with the police and the dealers who might be offered pieces from the loot? So they must be with him in his quarters. And so they were. Unhappily for Fenn, it had not occurred to him that Kraven might have hidden the jewels so skillfully that he could not readily find them in the hour he allotted himself."

"But who could have suspected 'Mrs. Ruthven'?" asked Mr. Penworthy.

"Kraven had time to reach toward Fenn's face before he died. His hands, you will remember, were covered with cream and talcum powder; this immediately suggested a heavy makeup, which left one with scarcely any choice but 'Mrs. Ruthven'," said Pons. "A further touch of it lay on the body – enough to indicate that it was being worn heavily enough to conceal evidence of a beard. And, of course, our brief meeting with 'Mrs. Ruthven' was quite sufficient to convince me of her real identity – the injured leg disguised as a club-foot, the supposed operation for throat cancer to explain 'her' husky, harsh voice, the clever artlessness of 'her' concealment of 'her' large hands in handkerchief or gloves. 'Mrs. Ruthven' was easy to take at face value – unless you happened to be looking for James Fenn. Since the data Kraven had kept was extremely suggestive, together with his fright at sight of a ring he had last seen in the possession of what he supposed was a dead man pointed to James Fenn, I was."

AFTERWORD

(From the 1965 Mycroft & Moran Edition)

More than a third of a century has gone by since Solar Pons and the first pastiche came into being. Certainly, at that time, no great body of work in this limited domain was ever contemplated. Having learned, from Sir Arthur Conan Doyle, that no further stories of Sherlock Holmes were to be written, I determined with the buoyant enthusiasm of nineteen that I would myself set down perhaps half a dozen tales imitating the characters and the manner of the stories in the Canon as closely as possible – even as, to a large extent, Sir Arthur had been influenced by Poe's C. Auguste Dupin. And thus, one day in my room at 823 West Johnson Street, in Madison, Wisconsin, where I had not long before matriculated at the University of Wisconsin, Solar Pons came into being in *The Adventure of the Black Narcissus*. The time was autumn, 1928.

Writing the pastiche is, of course, an elaborate game, not an art, and it is one that only someone who has time and energy at his disposal – to say nothing of a certain amount of brash self-confidence – can undertake. It was never my intention to do any considerable number of pastiches, but there are, as everyone will admit, forces beyond one's control, and when Harold Hersey, who, with his string of magazines in the late 1920's, was forever in search of material, promptly bought that initial pastiche and called for more, I was powerfully motivated – since I lived meagerly in those years at $8.00 a week, out of which rent took $3.25, and whatever supplementary income I could manage from the efforts of my pen, and I could not afford to reject any invitation. In one day, I recall, by dint of cutting classes, I turned out three pastiches. They came rapidly – *The Adventure of the Missing Tenants*, *The Adventure of the Broken Chessman*, *The Adventure of the Late Mr. Faversham*, *The Adventure of the Sotheby Salesman*, *The Adventure of the Limping Man*, *The Adventure of the Black Cardinal*, and others – and then came to a sudden halt, for that year was 1929, and the economic collapse of that autumn swept away Hersey's magazines and my market, and the burgeoning adventures of Solar Pons of Praed Street came to an abrupt end.

And at that point Solar Pons would have been suspended but for a further circumstance over a decade later, when the bibliographer of the detective story, Frederic Dannay, announced *The Misadventures of Sherlock Holmes*, and I was impelled to revise an unsold tale, *The Adventure of the Norcross Riddle*, and submit it to him. His enthusiastic acceptance of the story, and his eagerness to know whether there were any others – perhaps enough for a book of them – an interest that was seconded and furthered by Vincent Starrett – aroused a dormant affection for Solar Pons and set in motion a curious desire to see a book of the pastiches come into being, particularly since Vincent Starrett had offered to write the introduction for such a book. Moreover, the revision of *The Adventure of the Norcross Riddle* had put new life into Pons, and at the same time had whetted my ambition to write other pastiches.

There were not enough for a book of them – not enough acceptable tales, that is – there were, in fact, only five of the early tales I thought even possible for such a book. How many more need there be? – but an even dozen, of course, the same number Sir Arthur had had in *The Adventures of Sherlock Holmes*. So I wrote seven more, Vincent Starrett wrote the introduction to the book, which I titled "*In Re: Sherlock Homes*"

– *The Adventures of Solar Pons*, because I had indicated on my desk calender in Madison the date on which I would begin my first pastiche by writing "In Re: Sherlock Holmes" on a date chosen at random ahead of time, and I submitted the book to but one publisher before I determined to publish it myself in a small edition – not under my Arkham House imprint – but, of course, under the imprint of Mycroft & Moran, with the deerstalker as colophon, and Baskerville the typeface – all were inevitable and part, so to speak, of the game. The year was 1945.

The book was so well accepted by readers and reviewers, winning even a recommendation in the *Book-of-the-Month Club News*, that I found it easy to continue writing adventures of Solar Pons, and when, six years later, there were enough tales for another book, it seemed only natural that that book ought to be titled *The Memoirs of Solar Pons* and contain, as did the canonical *Memoirs*, eleven tales. With publication of the *Memoirs*, I suspect, the idea of pastiching the entire sequence of the Sherlock Holmes tales was born, and now, at this writing, with this book, that grandiose design in this elaborate game has come to pass. Indeed, it has been slightly exceeded, for there are now fifty-six published Pontine tales, and one uncollected, separately published novella, which have appeared in this order –

The Adventure of the Frightened Baronet
The Adventure of the Late Mr. Faversham
The Adventure of the Black Narcissus
The Adventure of the Norcross Riddle
The Adventure of the Retired Novelist
The Adventure of the Three Red Dwarfs
The Adventure of the Sotheby Salesman
The Adventure of the Purloined Periapt
The Adventure of the Limping Man

The Adventure of the Seven Passengers
The Adventure of the Lost Holiday
The Adventure of the Man with the Broken Face
– in "IN RE: SHERLOCK HOLMES" THE ADVENTURES OF SOLAR PONS (1945)

The Adventure of the Circular Room
The Adventure of the Perfect Husband
The Adventure of the Broken Chessman
The Adventure of the Dog in the Manger
The Adventure of the Proper Comma
The Adventure of Ricoletti of the Club Foot
The Adventure of the Six Silver Spiders
The Adventure of the Lost Locomotive
The Adventure of the Tottenham Werewolf
The Adventure of the Five Royal Coachmen
The Adventure of the Paralytic Mendicant
– in THE MEMOIRS OF SOLAR PONS (1951)

The Adventure of the Lost Dutchman
The Adventure of the Dorrington Inheritance
The Adventure of the "Triple Kent"
The Adventure of the Rydberg Numbers
The Adventure of the Grice-Paterson Curse
The Adventure of the Stone of Scone
The Adventure of the Remarkable Worm
The Adventure of the Penny Magenta
The Adventure of the Trained Cormorant
The Adventure of the Camberwell Beauty
The Adventure of the Little Hangman
The Adventure of the Swedenborg Signatures
– in THE RETURN OF SOLAR PONS (1958)

The Adventure of the Mazarine Blue
The Adventure of the Hats of M. Dulac
The Adventure of the Mosaic Cylinders
The Adventure of the Praed Street Irregulars
The Adventure of the Cloverdale Kennels
The Adventure of the Black Cardinal
The Adventure of the Troubled Magistrate
The Adventure of the Blind Clairaudient
– in THE REMINISCENCES OF SOLAR PONS (1961)

The Adventure of the Sussex Archers
The Adventure of the Haunted Library
The Adventure of the Fatal Glance
The Adventure of the Intarsia Box
The Adventure of the Spurious *Tamerlane*
The Adventure of the China Cottage
The Adventure of the Ascot Scandal
The Adventure of the Crouching Dog
The Adventure of the Missing Huntsman
The Adventure of the Amateur Philologist
The Adventure of the Whispering Knights
The Adventure of the Innkeeper's Clerk
– in THE CASEBOOK OF SOLAR PONS (1965)

I cannot promise to write no more of them.

– August Derleth

ENDPAPER MAP BY LUTHER NORRIS

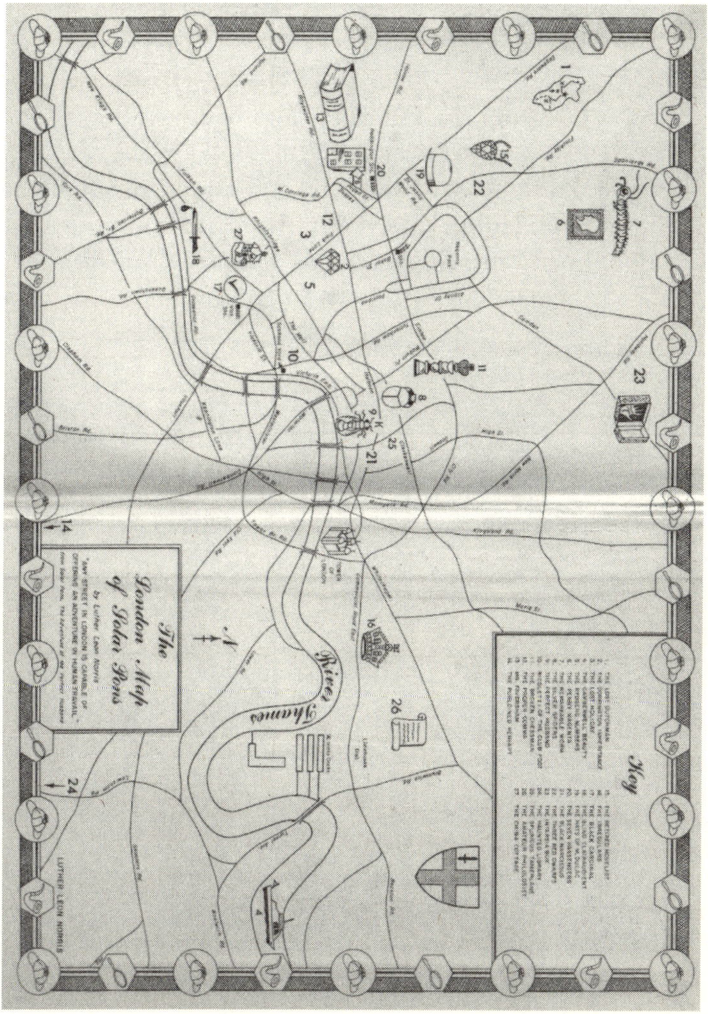

H. Rider Haggard
MR. MEESON'S WILL

Melville Davisson Post
MASTER OF MYSTERIES
THE COMPLETE UNCLE ABNER COLLECTION

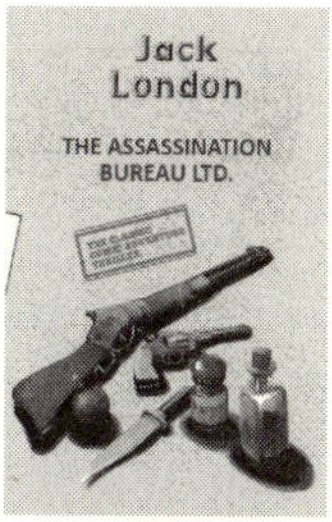
Jack London
THE ASSASSINATION BUREAU LTD.

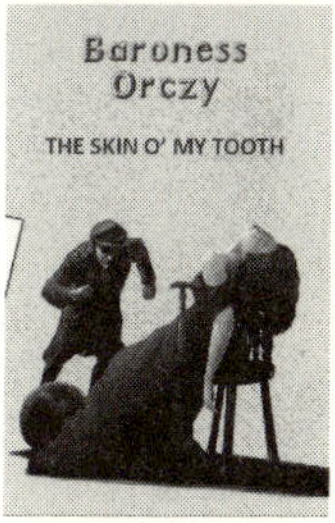
Baroness Orczy
THE SKIN O' MY TOOTH

Earl Derr Biggers
SEVEN KEYS TO BALDPATE

Horace Walpole
THE CASTLE OF OTRANTO

Sexton Blake
THE SEXTON BLAKE COLLECTION
VOLUME 1

Francis Beeding
THE HOUSE OF DR. EDWARDES

A. E. W. Mason
AT THE VILLA ROSE

Fergus Hume
THE MILLIONAIRE MYSTERY

Donald Henderson
A VOICE LIKE VELVET

Richard Hallas
YOU PLAY THE BLACK AND THE RED COMES UP